Praise for *A Watermelon*

'Potentially sentimental material is rendered moving thanks to the ability of Lefteri to recreate a difficult chapter in the island's past. Scenes of disturbing violence are overlaid with lyrical descriptions of life in the coastal village of Kyrenia. Much more than another romantic beach read, this is a powerful piece of writing underscored by Lefteri's understanding of her family's history and experiences' *Sunday Telegraph*

Praise for *The Beekeeper of Aleppo*

'This is a novel of international significance. Courageous, provocative, haunting, it will open our eyes' Heather Morris, author of *The Tattooist of Auschwitz*

'This book dips below the deafening headlines, and tells a true story with subtlety and power' Esther Freud

'This compelling tale had me gripped with its compassion, its sensual style and its onward and lively urge for resolution' Daljit Nagra

'Christy Lefteri has crafted a beautiful novel; intelligent, thoughtful and relevant. I'm recommending this book to everyone I care about. So I'm recommending this book to you' Benjamin Zephaniah

'A redemptive tale of hope in the midst of shocking adversity' *Irish Independent*

Brought up in London, Christy Lefteri is the child of Cypriot refugees who moved to the UK in 1974 during the Turkish invasion. She is a lecturer in creative writing at Brunel University. *A Watermelon, a Fish and a Bible* is her first novel; *The Beekeeper of Aleppo* is her second.

A WATERMELON, A FISH AND A BIBLE

Christy Lefteri

riverrun

First published in Great Britain in 2010 by Quercus
This paperback edition published in 2011 and reissued in 2019 by

riverrun

An imprint of
Quercus Editions Limited
Carmelite House
50 Victoria Embankment
London EC4Y 0DZ

An Hachette UK company

A CIP catalogue record for this book is available
from the British Library.

ISBN 978 1 52940 563 7

10 9 8 7 6

Printed and bound in Great Britain by Clays Ltd, Elcograf S.p.A.

Papers used by Quercus are from well-managed forests and other responsible sources.

Mum

When I don't know which path to take
I feel you by my side.

When a dream comes true
I feel you by my side.

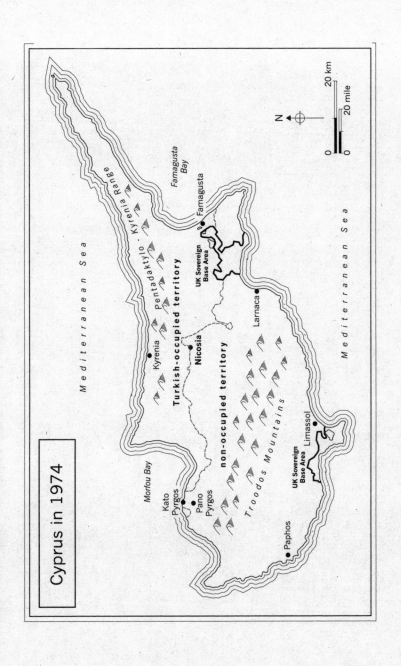

Cyprus in 1974

Day 1: 20 July 1974

First a rose. A scarlet rose. Only one. On a hill maybe, but nobody knows yet. That is not important. The rose sparkles with sugary dew, even in July when the sun is sharp and hot; iridescent red drops shimmering in that immense, oppressive light. Droplets a little like blood tears, if you've ever seen them; the last tears of a dying man. A man who's been put to death, like Christ. Internal bleeding. Eternal bleeding. But the little girl must not know this.

The stem of the rose is a hundred miles long. It is horizontal, as normal, for the first six or seven inches and then it bends and twists round and in, out and down, like a road with thorns and leaves. Whoever plucks the rose will hold Christ's heart in their hands and behold the secret of immortality. They will be free of this world once and for all. However, unless looking

I

from above, it is impossible to see where the rose is located. One must follow the stem and one must know that it will be a terrible journey.

So much for fairy tales that keep us from the bleak reality of life. So much for those stories that give us hope in a place where hope does not exist. And who, by the end of this tale, will be the one to tell the girl that the rose does not exist? And should anyone tell her at all?

This is a rose in a story told by a mother to her daughter on the day that she knows that she will die. The mother is lying on the floor and is reading the story from a little green book. The girl does not know that the pages are empty, each one as white and bare as the snow on the Troodos Mountains. The mother has just returned from the well and has been shot in the left shoulder, just above the heart. Struggling to breathe, she points at the dried bramble in the garden and tells her daughter that this is where the stem begins. The girl looks at it with wide eyes. 'Everyone is fighting for this rose, but nobody even knows how to begin looking for it. Only you,' the mother says, touching her daughter's chest. 'The closer you get the larger the thorns will become. You will see bad things, the darkness of the world, but you must not give up. People will come. They will be dressed in green. Do as they say, yes, do as they say and you will be safe, but never tell them about the trail of thorns. Just follow the stem and the red petals, like the ones around me.'

These are her last words. Her white skin is covered in blood that is also scattered around the floor. In the sunlight the young daughter strokes her mother's hair.

'Let's go together, Mama,' the little girl says, but her mother's eyes have closed and her face is still. She leans forward and shakes her mother's shoulders. 'Mama. Mama,' she says. 'Mama, Mama!' she screams, but there is no answer. All is quiet apart from the radio that has been incessantly playing in the background. 'Do not panic. They did not manage to invade. They did not.' She listens to the words. The voice marches around the room. 'Do not panic. We threw them into the water. We threw them into the sea.' The little girl takes her mother's hand and holds it to her face. 'I want to go together, Mama.' She rubs it on her cheek. She weeps over her mother's body until her tears dry and her hands can no longer hold up her mother's arm.

She tucks her legs into her dress and wraps her arms

round her knees. The morning sun floods through the window, making a perfect square of light on the floor. The girl stares at it. The square of light is still, golden, unspoilt. A mirror of an empty world.

She stands up and walks to the doorway. The adjacent houses bleed with smoke. Silence is rising from distant corners of the town, much like the chanting and chiming of bells that once ascended from various ends of the town.

There is no other sound now. No men at the roadside calling 'Watermelons, melons, cucumbers, tomatoes'. No boys shouting obscenities at one another while unloading fish from the little boats that rock in the port. Not even the snapping of beans where the girls sat with bowls on their laps preparing the evening meal, and the old grandmothers dressed in black with scarves around their heads complained about the heat. In the shade of the tallest building there is quiet where the women embroidered silk into roses and sang. Auntie Maria's nine children are not screaming and crying. Uncle Vasos and his wife are not arguing.

There is no movement now. No pins rolling over dough or bread removed from clay ovens in the sun. No hands reaching for lemons on the trees. There is no one chopping onions, or scrubbing clothes, or sprinkling sesame seeds onto cinnamon fingers.

Only smells remain: the whiff of sweet Greek coffee left in little cups. The zest of lemons discarded on the floor. The must of wheat still soaking in water. The sea on the scales of fish. The blackness of burnt bread.

The young girl kneels in the prayer position, and through the open doors of the back veranda she catches a glimpse of the speckled world beyond the vine leaves. She looks across the veranda at the dry brambles and imagines the red rose, sparkling with dew, blood pulsating in its veins. Glowing on a dark hillside. She stands up and straightens her dress and the apron that her mother tied round it. They were about to make olive bread when her mum had gone out to get some water from the central well. She looks at her mother. Red petals are flowing from her mouth and onto the little green book whose pages lie open. She stares at the rose on the white page. The petals are thick and the colour is deep. It is a beautiful rose, and where the petals open up it looks a little like a heart. Maybe a heart that is bleeding, the little girl thinks. In fact at that moment, in that town, most hearts are bleeding and hanging with silk thread from the trees, like decorations or prayers. The little girl must not know this, though.

The young girl closes the book and tucks it into the pocket of her apron. She thinks for a moment about what she will need for the journey. She finds some scissors in one of the drawers and wraps the sharp ends with some red ribbon. They will be useful when she finds the rose; the stem may be thick and coarse. Imagine travelling all that way and being unable to cut the rose. She puts the scissors in the pocket of her apron.

She stands by the doorway and straightens her feet to make a line. A donkey walks across the field ahead, its lead dragging on the floor. She looks over the flat roofs of whitewashed bungalows, over the lemon groves and olive trees, over the bumpy road, through the arches of the church tower and up towards the hilltops. The dried, thorned stem of the rose begins a metre from her feet. She takes a step towards it. From the trembling heat a man appears. He is dressed in green. The little girl smiles.

Adem Berker sees a girl standing in the doorway of a hut. He comes closer and notices her black hair, like coal, and her black eyes. The sun is strong and shines in shards. The young girl curtsies as he enters the house and then holds out her hand. 'Maroulla,' she says. The girl's hand is still outstretched. Adem does not move. He observes her like a man looking at an old photograph. He moves his eyes down to where her mother lies drenched in blood. He looks behind him suddenly, as if waiting for someone. He crouches down, checks the dead woman's pulse and stands again. He puffs his cheeks, exhaling deeply. Then, listening to the repetitive mantra on the radio, he stands up and switches it off. Now only the chorus of the cicadas fills the room. His eyes dart across the kitchen and pause for a moment on something on the counter. He moves past the girl and picks up a bottle. The liquid inside is clear like water, but moves more slowly when the bottle is tipped. He turns the cap and brings the bottle up to his nose. Aniseed. Ouzo. He opens a few cabinet doors, searching for glasses. 'The last door to the left,' the young girl says. She waits a moment and then walks over to where he is standing, heaves herself onto the counter and retrieves a large ceramic mug from the cupboard. Adem takes the mug and turns to the kitchen table, where there are two wooden chairs. He sits down and pours the ouzo into the mug, just over halfway. He's going to need it. Adem rubs his thumb over the stubble on his chin. He has not shaved for a few days. He takes a swig of the ouzo. Adem frowns and pushes his temples with his thumb and middle finger. He takes off his cap and puts it on the table.

The girl turns to face him. 'When will our journey begin?' she asks. He looks at her thick hair that leaks onto her face like oil and those lashes that cast slight shadows on the soft skin beneath her eyes. He does not understand what she means. He rubs his eyes and pours another glass of ouzo. He watches her. She must be just five, or perhaps six at the very most. Around her waist she wears an apron. He cannot bear to look at her. She stares at him expectantly; a look so warm and innocent that it stabs him through the heart. He looks again at her mother on the floor and back into those dark questioning eyes. Adem feels sick. He swallows some more ouzo. He wishes he could take her with him; somewhere safe. But where? The dangers are too great. They would capture her, rape her, kill her. Here she would be safer. They would not be back to check the house, this was part of his territory.

Adem pours another glass of ouzo. The young girl

is now sitting on the other chair, looking at him. Her legs are swinging beneath the table. She is drinking from a glass, milk with rosewater.

Adem rises abruptly, puts on his cap and straightens his jacket. The girl stands up. He rubs his eyes once more and looks through the door at the town ahead. He walks out of the house without saying a word as though walking out of a terrible film at the cinema in Istanbul. He leaves the girl standing in the doorway.

He does not know how desperately she wishes him to come back.

The heart of the town starts beating again, but differently this time. Now everything is different. A little way out of the town, Koki stands in the doorway of her house. She is still waiting for her son. She peers out through the branches of the lemon trees. He should have been back hours ago. He left with the other boys when, very early in the morning, they had heard the sound of planes and bombs. They wanted to find out what had happened, and she had begged him not to go. She had never managed to hold on to him, however hard she tried. He was always much older than his age and too much of a free spirit, like his father used to be. Being half Turkish and half Greek, he had been forced to live between two worlds. Two worlds so similar, yet so far apart. As a result he had lived in a neither, a place not on this side or that. He flowed like the river that separates the town from the village. He became like the rushing water. And Koki always loved him well, and he loved her back with hugs and kisses and a laugh that quenched the dryness of her world. But, somehow, she always knew that she could hold on to him only as long as it takes for water to slip through your fingers. It was in the look in his eyes and in the way he walked, as though he had places to go. And he grew so tall, too tall for this town, and he looked more like a man than a boy of eleven, and when he ran, oh, when he ran, he looked as though he could easily fly.

She paces up and down. The radio is on low and a faint voice repeats reassuring words. 'Do not panic. We have thrown them into the sea. They did not manage to invade. They did not.' But in the distance she had heard running and frantic words drifting across the town. 'They are coming! Run! The Turks are coming!' She could not believe them. She would never leave without her son. Why had he not returned?

She looks ahead, waiting for her son's familiar, mischievous smile. 'They have not managed to invade,' the voice on the radio repeats. Koki pushes her forehead with her fingers and shuts her eyes. Her mind is out of control, her imagination wild with fearful thoughts. She pulls her hair with both hands. There are stranger noises now from the town beyond. The rumbling of a truck. The sound of things breaking or falling. But she cannot be sure. It is too far away. She walks to the radio and shakes it. 'What's going on?' she shouts at it. 'What in the devil is going on?' Her hands shake and her eyes fill with tears. She quickly tunes it to the Turkish station. Just as before, there is only white noise. She shakes it again. Nothing. 'Please,' she says to it, 'please!' She shakes it harder and a fragmented voice comes through. 'Turkish troops . . . invaded the island of Cyprus . . . landed . . . Kyrenia. The invasion has been a success . . .' Koki's body feels cold despite the rising heat. She picks up the radio and throws it on the floor, it smashes hard onto the flagstones and the voice crunches to a halt. She runs to the door and calls her son's name, 'Agori, Agori, please, where are you?' but her words come back to her, faint and solitary. There is movement in the distance, and the sound of gunshots, and another, much nearer. Koki pulls her hair again. And then she runs. She just runs ahead. Not knowing where to go or where to look. The town flashes past her in a streak of colours. Her head spins. She runs and runs, past the houses, looking left and right, through the field and, suddenly, there on the ground in the shadow of the orchard, she sees two feet. She runs towards them and looks down. She freezes.

There lies her son. There lies *her* son.

There, with his eyes closed and a rose placed neatly on his chest. Koki falls to her knees. She nudges him and shakes his arm. She lifts the rose and sees that it hides a bloody hole. She puts her ear to his chest. Nothing. Empty. She wraps her arms round his torso and cries into his stomach. 'Agori,' she says, 'Agori, Agori, wake up.' She tries to lift him. His body rises only slightly from the ground. 'Agori,' she pleads, 'get up; we have to go, my love. We have to go.' She looks at him. Maybe he will speak. 'Please, speak.' But his face is still and peaceful. His lips are still red.

She kisses his face and strokes his hair and her tears flow tempestuous with the wrath of the sea. She cannot take him with her; she cannot even bury him. She takes a gold chain and crucifix from around her neck, kisses it and places it on his chest. She lies down beside him and stays there for a while holding on to his hand, with her head on his shoulder. Her body shakes with inner pain. She could just close her eyes and never wake up. She wishes this life were over. She stays there for ten minutes, fifteen, maybe more. She holds his hand tighter and prays, wishing his spirit to be free, to be safe, to be close to God. She stays there as the sounds of the war pass over them, as the spirits of the life they had known drift past them. The sound of distant laughter. In the sunlight memories move around them. There he is, under the lemon trees, just a year old, learning how to walk. And there he is at five now, on a bicycle. And over there, at seven, with a catapult in hand. And there, at eleven, just yesterday morning, beaming proudly, with a basket of cherries for her. He is running and laughing, he is calling her. She hears his voice. It rushes past like the sound of the river. It comes to her, then fades away, like the sound of the sea. But a feeling passes through her mind. Her heart thumps harder and suddenly she is struck with fear.

Koki looks around. She hears the sound of gunshots and sees a distant wisp of smoke. She holds her son's face and kisses his cheek. 'Goodbye,' she says, 'for now, only for now,' and stumbles back to their home.

Koki sits on the kitchen floor with a crucifix in her hand. She has sharpened the end with a knife, the part where Jesus' feet join. To make a knife. 'From this moment on, their land a desert, their lives deserted. Their children . . .'

How could she wish this on the children of her neighbours, the daughters of women who were present at the birth of her own son? Who was she now that she felt this hatred? She rocks over the crucifix and repeats Matthew 5.22 three times. 'If you are angry with a brother or sister, you will be liable to judgement.' It is no good. The animosity burns in her throat, behind her eyes, in the cracked fingertips of her right hand that presses into the gold-plated wooden halo.

She holds the crucifix like a knife, its toes buried in the folds of cloth about her breasts. She contemplates for a moment while the morning sun shines on the whittled features of Christ. Or is it the glow of fire that casts such an evil light? The air is filled with the smell of a burning church: the wood, the incense, the candles, the flesh of the icons. She can see him, again, as though he were still alive, running towards her. Coming home for dinner. If only the Turkish soldiers knew his real name.

Not all Turks are murderers, she hears herself say, but the voice is distant and comes from the mouth of a woman whom she had once been. Koki thinks of her son's body and shudders. What had she come back for? Why had she not stayed there until they killed her? The pressure with which she holds that sharpened cross is so immense that splinters now dig into her palm but she does not seem to notice.

The sounds are getting closer. Koki should leave before they reach her. 'It is not our friends that are murderers, it is some other barbaric race,' she says aloud and thinks of the Turkish–Cypriot children her son had once played with by the well, and the man she had loved. They had not killed her son. So why could she now see her son's blood on their hands? How could she hate them?

Agori! Agori! Agori! She cannot scream, or move, or cry. Her blood is frozen in her veins. The monster laid a rose on his body. A rose on his body! A rose on his body! He placed a rose on her son's body and walked away. She rocks over the cross. She presses the crucifix into her chest until her skin rips.

'The devil will take you. Black and darkened be your lives.' Koki rocks like the sea, as though it is an external force that is making her do so. She cannot feel the pain in her chest, so she presses harder. The wood crumbles from the pressure. Why does she not just use the knife?

Koki hears a noise. She slides behind the door frame and peeks out. Just ahead Koki sees old man Vasos scampering from his villa and grabbing his wife and his most prized watermelon. He secures one beneath his right arm, although it has grown to such immense proportions that it keeps sliding even from the tight grip of his farmer's hands and seizes the other, dear Old Maria, who is of equal diameter, round the waist. He is a man of a little world who still believes the earth is square and that a Greek coffee and a cigarette are the best remedies for everything. Until today Maria believed that heaven was reserved for people who fasted at Easter. She thought that the English spoke gibberish interspersed with Greek words. To her the world was this town.

At this moment Maria is spitting hysterically at the

sky. 'To hell!' she calls to God on his throne. 'Fall to hell! For that is where we're going!' She hugs her stomach and opens her mouth into an excruciating silent scream. Her face stretches to such proportions that the folds between the creases appear as white birds' claws. Her husband grabs her by the arm this time and tugs her with fresh fervour. Weakened by her emotions, she relents slightly and shuffles alongside him, but as she sees the glow of the sky and approaches the little gate which would lead her out of her home, she changes her mind. Holding her black dress above her knees she runs back into the house. Koki watches, and after a moment Maria emerges. In this turmoil, she has succeeding in swooping up a sea bass which she had probably laid on the counter about a quarter of an hour earlier to prepare for lunch, and a Bible. 'Jesus and Mary!' she shrieks, as she stands there, clinging like a famished seagull to the book and fish, 'bring down your hand and help us, do not let them take our house!'

'Shut up, woman!' gasps her husband, with a face as red as the heart of the fruit he holds beneath his arm. 'We will be back before we even finish eating this watermelon!'

But this makes her sobs louder, and the old farmer

struggles to sustain his pace. Maria stops again. Her mouth set into a line. These contours of hard work and antiquity and her sudden exhaustion make her appear, for a moment, as though she has grown from that earth-patch like one of the old lemon trees. Her ankles, just visible beneath the seam of her lace petti-coat, are the colour and texture of two tree trunks, dusted with the dry terracotta soil. Her face still, her body rigid, her arms slightly raised with the two objects she has managed to seize in each hand. Her eyes turn to him, and with a look of desperation she pleads, 'Get something, and get something else!'

'We'll be back soon,' is his reply, but she wants to root herself there. She looks at her husband's anxious feet and then at their pathetic possessions.

'From all the land my grandfather had, from all the cattle we've grown and slain, all I have to show for it is a watermelon, a fish and a Bible.'

Koki watches as the old man tugs harder at his wife and eventually they disappear behind the lemon grove.

Now Koki can hear something scrambling in the brambles, from the west, where the Loizou home tips over a hill. The little white house had always looked as though it would subside over the Kyrenia slopes and into the valley. Most of the time, what with the seven youngsters yelling in the fields and with their older sister, Yiola, singing unremittingly, the neighbours secretly hoped that it would.

Now only reticence imparts and echoes, like the desolate harmony of an unused church bell. Apart from two scuttling feet coming towards Koki the surrounding area is tranquil.

Koki quivers and rocks over the cross. A moment later, half crawling, half running, the eldest daughter Yiola appears. Her satin hair matted, her eyes red, her skirt ripped. Until today Yiola believed that God listened to music rather than prayers and musical notes drifted in the air like forlorn petals. She believed that she would be a seamstress who would marry a gardener who would have lots of children who would work in the fields.

Yiola stops when she reaches some bushes. Between gasping and sobbing she bends down and rubs her hands into the red soil on the ground. She repeats the motion about three or four times, and from a distance, if one had seen her from the back, it could have looked as though it were a normal day and that she was washing her widowed grandmother's black laundry in the copper basin.

It is peculiar that during this manic scrubbing her whole writhing body suddenly comes to an abrupt halt. Then, kneeling peacefully in the prayer position, she opens her palms to her face and looks at them yearningly as though they are two midnight flowers. Koki stares curiously at that young girl's face as she opens her mouth; it appears as though she is about to sing. 'Devils!' she says instead. 'Devils!' she repeats.

Her knees now buried in the soil, she proceeds to frantically smear it on her face. The problem is that her tears keep rinsing the soil away, which makes her claw the ground and her face with fury. 'Make me ugly!' she calls, and her mouth opens wide so that saliva trickles down her chin. Koki suddenly notices two men in green uniforms approaching Yiola. Koki finds the strength to move. Her breath quickens. She cannot stay, they will be here soon.

She tucks the crucifix into her dress so that it is flat against her stomach and stands. At just twenty-seven Koki is still young and her purple dress flows about her ankles and her unconventional red hair surges like fire around her. She is adamant to choose how she will die. But just as she is about to exit the house she remembers something and rushes back into her bedroom. She searches beneath her bed and retrieves a silver tin. A tin that has her savings and other sentimental things. She can hear the soldiers approaching, the crunch of their boots on the gravel. She stands up and runs out of the back of the house.

Moving briskly through the scattered shade of the lemon groves, Koki trips over a watermelon. A watermelon, cracked slightly in the middle, and a fish by its side. The dried thorns on the ground pierce the palms of her hands and her knees. She stands up, and wipes her hands on her dress. A lemon drops to the floor and there is a slight crunch when it meets with dead weeds. She freezes for the pause of a heartbeat. She looks down. Where's the Bible? she wonders. She gets back down on her hands and knees and searches the surrounding area. A watermelon, a fish, but no Bible. Koki takes the watermelon in her arms and continues to run to Maria's ovens that are tucked neatly at the back of the lemon groves.

The ovens stare at her open-mouthed. She lifts her dress and climbs into the one at the back. She puts the watermelon by her side and closes the door. The walls are still warm, like a sleeping body. She is engulfed in the soft, sweet smell of ashes and bread. It warms her like death when life is cold and for a moment the darkness seems eternal. She sleeps.

When Commander Serkan Demir enters Koki's house with another soldier, it is empty. Serkan walks with his back as straight and unyielding as iron. He instructs the accompanying soldier to search the kitchen, the bedroom, the bathroom and beneath the bed. He must tap each floorboard with his foot, in case there is a basement and check the ceiling with the barrel of his rifle, for loose wood and hiding places, then he must search the perimeter of the house. 'Being meticulous is important,' says Serkan with his chin held high, never looking at the soldier in the eyes. He wipes his finger over a shelf and looks at a photograph of a young boy.

This is the last house on the square, apart from the one at the bottom of the hill. That's where he sent Berker. This town has now been conquered. He looks outside and marvels at what now belongs to the Turks. The morning sun is hovering on the promontory of the church and the shadows are long. The other soldier moves through the house and proceeds to check outside.

Serkan smiles again. He looks around at what is now theirs. Look at what they have! They own it. Every bit of land, every handful of soil, every house, every ornament, every single thing, big or small, is theirs. Feeling elated, he walks to the kitchen and puts his hand in the cupboard, retrieving a plate laden with thick slices of cured pork. He slams the plate on the kitchen table and stares at the pig's flesh.

There is shouting outside. He lifts his head and looks out of the kitchen window. There is a man running. The soldier outside stands frozen, holding his rifle in trembling hands. Serkan kicks a chair out of the way, runs outside, takes aim and shoots the running man in the back. The man freezes and falls face down to the ground. Without lowering the rifle, Serkan turns it around and forces the butt into the soldier's chest, bringing him to the ground. The soldier gasps for air and looks fearfully up at his commander. 'Hesitate again and I'll rip your heart out! Get out of my sight.' The soldier heaves himself to his feet, bows his head and continues searching the perimeter of the house.

Serkan returns to the kitchen and resumes his

inspection of the cupboard. There is a large finger of sesame bread and a tub of green olives. Serkan examines the olives; they are coated in coriander, garlic, lemon and olive oil. He holds the tub up to his nose. He takes a deep breath. It smells like home. He arranges the bread and olives on the table and pushes the cured pork out of the way.

Sitting down on the chair of the kitchen table, as though this is his house, he rips a chunk of bread and dips it into the olive oil. His feet are propped up on the chair beside him. He savours the taste of the olive oil on the soft bread. He throws an olive into his mouth, noticing the crunch of the dried coriander and that pungent sting of fresh garlic in the sides of his jaw. He takes the pip from his mouth with his thumb and forefinger and places it on the table.

The other soldier returns and shakes his head. 'No one,' he says.

Serkan grunts, 'No one else, you mean.' The soldier looks at his feet and does not wait to be offered a chair. The commander leans deeper into the chair, and the soldier turns and stands by the doorway with the rifle by his side.

Serkan looks around and sees a radio on the floor.

He crouches down, looks at it closely, holds in the broken panel and tries to adjust the tuning. A Greek voice eventually can be heard. 'Do not panic, we threw them into the sea.' Serkan smiles. 'Brainless idiots. I am already here.' He then looks at the walls. The face of the Virgin Mary stares down at him from above. 'Not even she can help you now.'

Walking away from the house and the little girl, Adem looks around at the shattered town. He remembers the place as it once was, buzzing full of life. He cannot stand to look at the empty homes. What's he doing here? Has he made a mistake? Maybe he shouldn't have come back. But he had to. He had to try.

He remembers his journey into Cyprus. Abundant in those black waves. In that dark sea. Deep as light. The ship rose and fell. Rose up as heavy as heat and fell as light as rain so that his mind and his stomach could not help but do the same. It was in this turmoil, where his soul was lost, when he was a fool enough, or human enough, to think that it was in fact the waves that were rising and falling.

Departing from the port of Tasucu, standing by the rail, a younger man had stood beside him; his head down, then up, then down again. His fingers pulling at the collar of his jacket. His foot tapping on the floor, not rhythmically, but manically.

Adem reached into his pocket and retrieved a packet of cigarettes. He pulled one out slightly and offered it to the younger man. 'I don't smoke, sir,' said the younger man, but took one anyway and put it to his mouth. Adem struck a match. The man's eyes flicked down to Adem's badge.

'You are my sergeant,' the man said.

Adem nodded. 'My commanding officer is Serkan Demir, barrack number seventy-six,' he said.

The young man nodded. Adem noticed that the man was actually just a boy. Maybe fifteen or sixteen. His voice was just breaking. The boy threw the unfinished cigarette into the sea. A dark-blue breeze touched their faces. The boy had sweat on his brow. The Turkish port drew further away and gradually turned black, and soon the lights from the rocking warships hovered in darkness like fireflies. Four hours across the water and they would reach Kyrenia.

On the deck, a little further down, other soldiers sat on wooden boxes and talked. In that immense darkness only the faint flicker of cigarette ends looked out to sea, like eyes. 'The Greeks own pearls as many as sand grains and wine as much as the sea. They wear dresses of silk and diamond buckles on their shoes while the Turks wear goatskin robes,' one of the Turks said to the others.

'Their churches are lined with yellow gold that drips from the ceilings like wax and the priests wear red rubies in glistening chains round their necks, while our mosques are made of mud and stone,' said another.

'The Turks do not even have a mosque, they are forced to pray on their knees in the sun-starched fields and forced to eat the grapes that have already fallen from the vines.'

'Yes,' agreed the first, 'and cutting onions does not even make them cry; for how decayed they have become.'

'They cannot drink fresh mint tea as their mint is stolen by the Greeks to be dried in the sun for their salads.'

'And when they kill a cow, the Turks are left with the carcass.'

'And there is no nourishment for the Turkish children because the Greeks bathe in pools of milk and come out with skin as white as the moon,' said the only man who hadn't spoken yet. The other men laughed.

'That's ridiculous,' said one. 'Where would they ever find that much milk, there'd need to be cows as many as stars!' The other men held their stomachs and the laughter swept low over the sea like a hawk.

The boy and Adem shared a quick glance. Adem, leaning on the rails of the deck, looked at the silver light of the moon on the points of the waves. The young boy pulled at his collar again. Adem looked over at the men on the boxes. 'People will believe anything,' he whispered to the boy with a tone of discreet animosity coming up from the back of his throat. The young boy looked at him suddenly as though for the first time. 'Have you ever been to Cyprus? Do you have any family there?' Adem asked hurriedly, and when the boy opened his mouth to speak Adem intercepted him. 'It's beautiful,' he said definitely.

'No to enosis!' One man stood and stamped his feet.

'We will help our fellow Turks, our brothers, keep their land,' shouted another. 'They will not be discarded by the Greeks.'

'Cyprus belongs to the Ottomans!' called a younger man of about fifteen who was holding a rifle in his hand. 'Long live *taksim*! Long live *taksim*!' The men sang. '*Taksim*! *Taksim*! *Taksim*!' Their voices drifted out to sea.

The boy looked at Adem again. Adem thought for a moment. An air of sadness came over him. 'On the streets you can't even tell a Greek from a Turk. They drink from the same wells, milk the same cows, raise the same children.' His voice trailed off a little and he clenched his jaw. 'My life could have been much different.'

The boy looked at him and scrunched his eyes against a strong gush of wind. He leant in with interest, but Adem shuffled his feet uncomfortably and looked out to sea.

It seemed as if a very long time had passed before either of them spoke again. Even before the tip of the sun appeared, the sky and the sea changed colour many times: from black, to purple, to navy, to red, to a pink that now streaked across the horizon.

'What's your name?' Adem asked.

'Engin,' the young boy answered.

'Vast, boundless, open sea,' Adem said.

'It was my mum's choice; I'm afraid of the sea.'

In the distance planes seared through the sky, and

then there was the muffled sound of bombs exploding. Engin's face suddenly dropped and was consumed with fear. 'They're clearing the way for us,' whispered Adem and noticed Engin's shaking hands.

'You will tell this story one day,' he said to Engin. 'You will tell it with your own tones, just as those men will tell it with theirs.'

'If . . .' the young boy said.

'Only a story never told is true in entirety,' Adem replied and the boy scrunched his brow.

'My father owned the pawnbrokers,' the boy said and looked at his fingers. 'We exchanged memories for money. We sold things that people threw away to people that thought they needed it. The truth is nobody needs anything. That same thing would be back again a month, a week, a day later. A glass eye for a dollar. A broken watch for half. A diamond ring for fifteen. A shoe, a spleen, a teardrop. A china doll, a reel of thread, a crystal glass, a lamp, with and without the genie. A dream. A smile.'

Adem thought for a moment. 'What the hell would anyone do with somebody else's glass eye?' They both laughed as the ship fell and some seawater splashed on the deck, bringing with it the smell of fish and salt.

'My dad made me come here.' The boy said, and looked at the deck ashamedly. 'I wanted to make him proud.' Adem looked at the fear in the boy's eyes.

'I wouldn't have chosen to come either,' Adem said. His mind was full of memories. The boy looked intently at Adem, waiting for an explanation, but Adem remained silent.

'Your dad made you come too?' Engin said, and Adem laughed again.

The ship rose and fell. A general passed every ten minutes. Two of the men on the boxes were asleep with their heads rocking over their chests. The other three laughed occasionally or raised their voices to tell an anecdote. One of them still smoked, but the seam of the sky was almost the same colour as the cigarette tip so that now they could see his fingers and the cuff of his sleeve. The deck was now scattered with other soldiers standing upright with hands in their pockets or else crossed over their chests. A few were deep in conversation. Behind them another sixty black ships rose and fell. 'The air is different without the crickets,' said the boy. 'It's thinner and so is time.' He looked over at the stranger beside him with fear-stricken eyes.

Adem took a glance at the other warships that

followed them. They were like a flock of seabirds travelling south.

'We learnt in school that in Egypt they launch a ship with white sails full of flowers into the sea for the wind to take,' said the boy, looking at his feet. 'And here we load it with bombs.'

'I guess all bombs start off as flowers,' Adem said. 'The blossoming of a hope of prosperity and safety and protection.' He noticed the boy's distress and realised how different he was from the others. Some knowledge or intuition of the bigger picture, of the bitter picture, lived and breathed within him. It gripped him with sadness and fear. Something which cannot be acquired or taught; not compassion or wisdom but a blank, black knowledge of something that can only be felt as a foreboding when the reasoning of others seems crazy.

'We all have a devil,' Adem said. In the distance the light of another port shivered over the sea. The boy remained silent. Then, nodding his head, the boy moved closer to Adem. 'That's where I used to live,' Adem whispered. The boy leant forward slightly with interest. A white seagull swept low over their heads. The underside of its wings touched with gold light that flickered from the bottom of the world. Adem imagined the little boats in the port with nets falling over the deck and sun caps left on the benches by boys that would never return. He imagined the donkeys shuffling their feet by the carts, awaiting a journey to the mountains to collect olive oil or to the fields to collect wheat. And the smell of the bread fingers and the rosewater and the early-morning incense. That musty smell of burning olive leaves rising from the church.

'You are afraid to remember, aren't you, sir?' Engin said suddenly and Adem turned quickly and looked into the boy's eyes.

Adem hesitated and took something from his jacket pocket, slipping it into Engin's hand. The boy brought his fingers slightly forward and looked down. A photograph. A girl with unusual-looking hair and clear eyes stared back. 'She is not Turkish,' Engin said.

'No,' Adem replied.

'Your wife?' Engin asked.

'No.'

'Someone you think about then?'

There was no reply. Adem took the picture back and slipped it into his breast pocket. He opened his mouth to speak, but then stopped and moved closer to Engin and spoke in a whisper so that his voice and the sea merged together. 'I had to leave,' he said, and at this his eyes became larger and he moved even closer and grabbed hold of Engin's arm. His grip was tight. His eyes staring fixedly at Engin. 'They would have killed me,' he said and looked into Engin's face, searching for something, reassurance, perhaps, or the words he had longed to hear all these years – you did the right thing – yes, you did the right thing. Engin leant back slightly, and turned his head a little to the left, but his eyes were soft as he looked at Adem sideways with the face of someone who cannot bear to look directly at an open wound.

Adem continued, his breath quicker this time, his words sharper. 'Many years ago I came to Cyprus and while I was here I fell in love with a Greek girl. Times were hard. The Greeks and Turks were at each other's throats. The towns were already divided. People started sniffing around. They beat me and . . .' Adem suddenly stopped there and a new wave of rage filled his heart. He then took a deeper breath and looked down. He let go of Engin's arm, who immediately rubbed it. 'She never really knew how bad it was and one day I just got up and left. What else could I do?'

The boy looked out as the ship drew nearer to the port and the sky began to turn blue. Adem noticed sweat beads on the boy's forehead. 'I'm here to find her,' Adem said definitely. 'I will not leave until I have found her.' And his voice flew above the sea.

Further and further from the little girl, the memory of his journey into Cyprus fades away. Adem touches the photograph in his pocket. He walks towards the well where he had arranged to meet Engin. They had been separated at the commencement of the first attack and told to search different houses. Adem had promised to meet Engin at the well. As he approaches he sees the boy standing there pulling at his collar, eyes darting here and there.

Somewhere far from the Mediterranean coast a man dressed in grey sits in an armchair. The bedsit is completely still apart from the black and white flickering of the television. A cup of tea is cold on a cardboard box. A midsummer morning. A taxi rolls by on Queen Victoria Street, past the memorial. Its pillars cast shadows in the sunlight. A flock of seagulls sweeps across the Thames and dives left, towards Trafalgar Square, to pick up the first crumbs of the day. Laughter sounds faintly from the television and Big Ben chimes over the mighty chessboard of towers and forgotten kings.

Richard is half asleep still. His head tilts to the left, onto his shoulder. The lines on his face are deeper than they should be. The pathways of a long-ago journey etched onto his skin. His hair recedes slightly at each temple, making the shape of a grey bird flying in a young child's drawing. And his eyes, if they were open, would be a clear grey sky buried somewhere in deep clouded lids. A train rumbles far below him, but he does not feel it this time. A large green-bottomed fly buzzes around the cup of tea and finally sits on the handle.

A phone rings somewhere on another floor and Richard opens his eyes a little and focuses on the television set. He suddenly remembers the sound of the crickets. In fact, although he wouldn't admit it, he has never forgotten. Even after all these years he still wakes up each morning with a memory of Cyprus; with its sweet citrus smells and dusty fields and yellow-red flowers that lined the hills. It has been fourteen years since the international treaties of 1960 named the Republic of Cyprus and gave Cyprus its independence from Great Britain. It has been fourteen years since he had sat on that ship watching the Mediterranean Sea roll away. He remembers the lights of Kyrenia Port flickering in the distance like fireflies, and finally disappearing into the back of the world like the sun at dusk.

In this grey room, where he has lived ever since, he looks towards the wardrobe where his officer's uniform still hangs, uncreased, with its badges on the left breast.

He nods off again, and some time later the telephone rings and Richard looks towards the cabinet in the far corner of the room where it is located. Richard looks at his watch, 12.30 p.m. It rings again, but he does not stand up. It continues to ring like the phones in homes whose occupants have gone out, to work, or for a meal, or to catch a film. The telephone stops and after a minute starts again and continues to ring like a phone in a home where the elderly occupant has died. Like William at Number 27.

'Answer it, you old fool!' a woman calls from a window above and a pigeon flies low and lands on his windowsill. The floorboards tremble slightly from the train deep below. His bedsit is unfortunately located over the Circle and District Lines, in between Blackfriars and Mansion House stations. He imagines those faceless travellers with their newspapers open like blankets or rolled into cones and filled with steaming chips.

Richard picks up his mug of tea, takes a sip, realises it is cold and places it back on the cardboard box. It is highly annoying when, about half an hour later, there is a knock at the door. The voice that follows is familiar and has a heavy accent.

'Cam on Ndinckey, mboy, I've got lunch, chips and fish!'

There is a pause and another knock. 'Get that, how do you say? Mbonny? Mbony arse of yours off that stinking chair and cam and open the door. Food is getting cold.'

Richard heaves himself reluctantly out of the chair and opens the door. Paniko's weighty features seem grave and his hefty shoulders slump over his chest. He holds a brown paper bag in one hand and a box of cigarettes in another.

'You know I don't like to be called that.'

'OK, Rrriiichaarrrd,' says Paniko, rolling his rs and extending his vowels in an attempt to sound English. His face falls again. 'Why you no answer the bloody phone?' He does not wait to be invited in. He speaks soberly as he walks to the centre of the room. 'The damn kids, five of them! I feel like a damn goat-herder. My cousin Andro, the one in Luton, had heart attack last night. It'll be me tomorrow, what with the café and the wife. He live, though. Poor fool!'

Paniko puts the paper bag on the cardboard box. The television is now showing Laurel and Hardy and he laughs as Hardy bites his hat. Then he touches the controls on the left of the television set and changes the channel.

'Make yourself at home,' Richard grunts, 'take the only armchair as well.'

Paniko's Greek manners do not pick up on the hint of sarcasm and he obliges, sitting down on the edge of the cushion. He rubs his head. 'All morning, from six, I am at council for stupid alcohol licence, soon you need licence to piss in this bloody country!' Paniko changes the channel again; he looks agitated now. 'Something's going on in Cyprus, I'm not sure . . .'

'You just can't forget about that measly little spot of a country, can you? It's been twenty-four years since you left. You're one of us now,' Richard says, sounding quite convincing.

'When you in Cyprus did you forget about London?' Paniko flicks the channels again. Nothing.

The train rumbles and the floorboards and windows tremble slightly. 'I forget about this place even when I'm here.'

'Fourteen years and you no once visited my café. Fourteen years and all you done is sit on that ugly *kolo* of yours,' Paniko indicates, pointing to his backside. 'You no work. You no have children. You no visit me. You stuck in this hole like a ndamn mole since you came back. You stop your life completely. Why? God knows . . . maybe not even him.' Paniko shrugs his shoulders and sticks out his bottom lip. He stands and flicks the channels again.

Richard does not answer. The phone rings twice. Richard walks across to the cabinet and picks up the receiver. The faint resonance of a female voice is heard. Richard nods sharply at Paniko, whose back jolts slightly. 'Yes, Elli, don't worry, he's right here. Yes, I understand. Greek men, yes . . . well . . . a donkey might be more useful, yes, I understand, yes . . . yes . . . yes.' Richard holds up the receiver and Paniko stands up. He cups the receiver with his hand and talks in an inaudible whisper. The female voice on the other end is louder and lyrical. Richard stands by the window now, lost in his thoughts, staring at the window frame.

'At least you never married, you lucky sod!' says Paniko, putting down the receiver. 'I got an embroidered tablecloth as a dowry! An embroidered tablecloth? What the hell was I going to do with an embroidered tablecloth? And not forgetting the saucepan! I should have told them there and then that I'd rather eat from the floor!'

Richard does not reply. A cloud blocks the sun and darkness fills the room. Paniko drops his head and stares at the ground, but continues to talk in a lower tone as if he cannot bear the silence. 'I have to sit to piss because she says I no can handle my penis. She just about lets me shit alone. I tell you I'm going to eat her when I get home. The woman can break a camel's back!'

Richard reaches for the paper bag, takes out two newspaper parcels, places them onto the cardboard box and opens them neatly. The steam rises. 'When you told me to set up a place for you I no think for one minute that you be in this hole all these years. I would not help if I knew, there two Cokes in as well,' says Paniko, all in one breath with a full mouth.

And yet, Paniko finds comfort in visiting this

unchanging room, a place where he can come and discuss Cyprus with his friend and the life they used to have there. Paniko normally drinks and talks, usually through Elli's persistent attempts to get him home or to work, about the parties and festivals and glasses of ouzo of the past. He remembers the thick black hair of young Greek women and the thick black coffees in the café by the port. He never mentions the riots and the coup and the uncertainty, although they prey on his mind. He does not even refer to the Turkish or the British or the Greeks. He simply talks about the big feasts they used to have and trips to the beach and excursions to the mountains. He remembers eating snails with toothpicks and all being together, Paniko's whole family and Richard. How he loves to talk of Cyprus! And Richard always listens with his own pains and his own failed dreams. He has never been able to tell Paniko the truth about his life, the secrets that he has kept hidden all these years.

Paniko changes the channel again and stares intently at the TV. His eyes have widened and he leans forward. 'Something *is* going on,' he says suddenly and jumps to put the volume up. Paniko is standing now, listening anxiously. The voice of the news reporter resonates through the room. 'Thousands of Turkish troops have invaded northern Cyprus after last-minute talks in the Greek capital, Athens, failed to reach a solution. Tension has been running high in the Mediterranean island since a military coup five days ago, in which President Archbishop Makarios, a Greek Cypriot, was deposed. The coup led to fears among the Turkish–Cypriot community that the Greek-backed military rulers would ignore their rights and press for unification for Cyprus with Greece, or enosis. Archbishop Makarios became the republic's first elected president in 1959 only after agreeing to give up plans for a union with Greece. A Turkish armada of thirty-three ships, including troop transporters and at least thirty tanks and small landing craft, has landed on the northern coast.' Paniko slams a fist onto the top of the TV and brings his hands up to his face. 'Oh God, Oh God, Oh God,' he says. 'Oh God, Mary and God, Christ and Mary!'

Richard stands up: his face is pale, his hands shake. 'Jesus Christ,' he says and moves closer to the television set. The news bulletin finishes and Richard flicks between BBC1 and ITV frantically. 'They have to tell us more than that . . .'

Paniko raises his arms in the air and remembers his

other family members, "My cousin Maria! Bambo and Litsa! Elena and the kids! Grandmother Zoe! Mario! Andro . . .' And the list continues as Paniko shakes his head from side to side. 'What if they hurt them?' He looks up at Richard with a desperate look in his eyes. Richard is holding his head in his hands.

'You English!' cries Paniko, 'always pretending you care. Well, you have drunk the wine and tasted the lemons. What do you have to be upset about? This is our home now. Ours! The Greeks! Not you English. Or the Turkish. You all came and mixed everything up!' He moves his fingers around in a circle and then slumps his shoulders as though he suddenly feels ashamed of his words.

Richard does not reply. In his mind he has a flash of a woman standing by the river and shakes his head, dispelling a thought that would be too painful to remember, especially now.

'Oh God! I must get to the café, my wife. She will go mad if she finds out before I get there; she will have a fit and die . . .' Paniko's broken English cannot be sustained, due to his emotions, and he starts rambling in Greek as he rushes out of the bedsit in a panic.

As Richard stands there by the open door he

remembers the jasmine flowers, hanging like snow-drops in the white light of the summer sun, and he cannot stop himself this time, he remembers Marianna, with eyes and hair as dark as the night. He remembers her as though it were yesterday and all those years had never passed. And he remembers a little girl, red hair tumbling to her waist, passing by him, and a sense of fear fills his heart.

Koki wakes at the darkest hour. Her cheek is pressed against the base of the oven, covered in ash. A flash of light streaks through the crack of the oven door. The ground rumbles. Ash falls on her head. She sits up and pauses for the blink of an eye. When she pushes the door open the crickets' song explodes like light. There is another flash. The sky blazes with red and yellows. Night turns to day and back again. The ground shakes beneath her feet. She climbs out of the oven, takes the watermelon from beside her and feels her way along the bodies of lemon trees.

As she reaches the clearing, the bombs stop for a few moments and darkness settles, soft and thick around her. Just for this brief interlude, the moon drops on the town. And for that moment all is touched with the silvery-white of childhood dreams. The tips of the leaves, the wooden wheels of the vegetable cart, the trays and baskets scattered about the gardens, the piles of onions, the strings of garlic, the washing lines that criss-cross the air like a web. Another flash and the sky turns red and all these things before her glow with the orange-white of a fire poker.

Koki reaches the bottom of the hill. All is dark apart from a candle that flickers in the doorway of Daphne's cottage. She wonders if Daphne and her daughter Maroulla have left. She has to get past the house to get out of the town. Koki trembles as she nears; she places her feet carefully on each step, afraid that the crunching brambles may be heard, hoping and praying that it's not a soldier in there. She approaches slowly, holding her breath, keeping her eye on the doorway for any movement. She stops behind a fig tree and winces as another burst of light fills the sky. She takes a breath, then she peeks round the tree and looks properly at the house. She realises that the orange glow is shrouding the body of a little girl. Koki looks around, then she remains completely still, listening for any movement from inside the house.

Eventually she creeps towards the door and crouches

down, putting the watermelon on the floor. In that hush the girl's chest rises and falls. Like the waves. Koki scans the room quickly. She notices the mother's body and the blood seeping onto the little girl's green dress.

Maroulla opens her eyes. Colourless and open as mirrors. 'Is it time?' she asks. Outside, the crickets' pounding knocks like a clock. A never-ending reminder of the passing of time, even if there were no one to tell it. Koki leans over and touches Maroulla's arm. She cannot bear to look again at Daphne. She holds Maroulla's hand in between her palms.

'We have to go,' says Koki gently. 'It's not safe here,' and Maroulla stares at Koki's flamelike hair, rippling in the light like fire in a breeze. Maroulla shakes her head and removes her hand and rubs her eyes.

'I'm not meant to,' replies Maroulla, 'we're not supposed to talk to you.'

Koki leans forward and blows out the candle. A ribbon of smoke rises. 'Not a good idea,' she says, 'it is not safe, sweetie, we have to be in darkness.' Maroulla looks at Koki and creases her brow. She is confused; she shakes her head and looks over at her mother.

'I didn't want to go alone,' Maroulla says.

Koki leans closer to her, 'It's OK, you don't have to.'

She stands up, takes the watermelon and holds out her free hand. Maroulla looks at it. Her mother had always instructed her never to talk to the red-haired woman, or her Turkish son. Maroulla looks outside. There is a distant flash of light and the man in green has gone. Koki's hand trembles and Maroulla looks intently at it. 'Come on,' Koki says gently, 'it's OK.' Maroulla looks once more at her mother and finally takes Koki's hand and stands up.

Maroulla brushes her dress with her hands. She looks around. She checks the pocket of her apron for the green book and the scissors. She crosses the veranda and takes her first step. Maroulla walks a little behind Koki; she will not hold her hand. She follows like a moth pursuing a flame, her tiny feet shuffling behind, sometimes forced into a run. Maroulla looks down as she walks, and stares only at her feet and the dried thorns. She does not want to look ahead. The sky is full of black smoke. She had never before noticed how big darkness could be, how it stretched out across the world like a dreamless sleep, further than the furthest she had ever known. Further than the café where the men sat, further even than the hilltop where Christaki rode his donkey, further even than the church they had visited once at the very point of the world. Further than the rose.

Maroulla looks up at the sky and, still running, when another flash fills the sky, she trips and grazes her knees on those dry thorns. Her knees and palms burn, but she does not cry. She will not cry. Koki stops and looks back; she sighs, walks towards the girl, stands above her for a moment and then kneels down, putting the watermelon on the floor. She helps her up and takes her hands into hers, she rubs them soothingly between her palms, she licks her fingers and pads them gently on her knees and dusts her dress. As Koki looks down, brushing the girl's legs, Maroulla looks at Koki's forehead and eyelids fuzzy and unfamiliar, especially in the darkness. A breeze blows and Maroulla catches the smell of jasmine from Koki's hair. It reminds her of her mother, and Maroulla nestles her face into Koki's hair. She reaches up and holds the ringlets and just then a stream of tears flows. Koki puts her arms round Maroulla and holds her close as Maroulla cries on her shoulder. After a while the girl stands straight and looks at the woman kneeling before her. Koki reaches up and, with her hand, brushes the hair away from Maroulla's forehead. The sky flashes. 'We have to go,' she whispers. The little girl nods.

This time, as they walk, Maroulla holds onto the string of Koki's purple dress. They follow the trail of thorns, through the fields of wheat and the fields of cotton, accompanied always by the sound of the crickets. Maroulla feels as though they are climbing higher and higher. They are going to the hilltop.

They are far out of the town now, on a road that does not even have a name. They follow the trail of thorns until they reach a tiny house on a hill, hidden behind some sycamore trees. They approach the house from its side. Maroulla notices that the haste in Koki's walk has subsided, and now, for the first time, the little girl feels as if she is leading. Koki's arm draws across Maroulla's chest as she guides the girl so that she is tucked safely behind her. They make their way around the house to the front door. As they ascend the veranda steps, Koki peers inside the window, and Maroulla cannot help but mimic Koki's movements, reminding her of the game of hide-and-seek she had played with the other children yesterday.

Koki opens the door. The house is dark inside, highlighted only by the moonlight flooding through the window. It is empty apart from a cat that scuttles away at the sound of the footsteps. There is a candle on the table with a box of matches beside it, but Koki knows they must not light it. She sighs deeply, puts the watermelon down and sits on a wooden chair. In the moonlight her eyes are a transparent blue, like the bottom of a flame. The little girl is standing by the doorway. She puts her hand into the pocket of her apron and feels the cover of the green book, then the handle of the scissors. She closes the door, walks into the house and sits on a wooden chair next to Koki. She puts her elbows on the table and rests her face in her hands.

Koki stands up and opens the cupboard. Inside is a loaf of bread, olives and dried wheat. She finds a knife, slices the bread and puts it on the table next to Maroulla with some olives.

Koki takes a few bites of the bread, but it is hard to swallow. There is water in a jug on the table. She pours it into two glasses. Koki watches the girl pick at the inside of the bread and eat it, leaving the crust on the table. Then Maroulla drinks the water, wipes her mouth with the back of her hand and resumes her original position, with her chin in her hands. Koki stares at Maroulla: at her pale cheeks, at her sad eyes, at the way she sits so still, slumped into that chair, like an abandoned doll.

They sit like this for a while, unmoving; and though they sit together, they are both far away, lost in their own thoughts. Soon Maroulla's eyes begin to close and she leans on to the table, resting her head on her arm. Koki lifts Maroulla and carries her to a bed in the adjoining room. She puts her down and lies down beside her. Koki lies on her back and looks up into the darkness. Her son's face flashes into her mind, she imagines him beside her, smiling. His voice fills the room, he is saying words that she cannot understand, words that merge with the crickets and Maroulla's breathing and the distant waves, and soon she is asleep.

The girl dreams. There is a red rose on a hill and all around is black. A strong wind blows her dress. She tries to walk forward. The girl wakes up. The crickets pound the air. The night pulsates. Koki is sleeping by her side. Maroulla sits up, gently climbs over Koki and gets off the bed. The room is grey from moonlight; there are no shutters in this room, just a thin net curtain. Maroulla looks at the picture over the bed. A man with fairly long fingers sits on a chair, a woman stands behind him with her hand on his shoulder. Neither is smiling. On the bedside cabinet there is another picture, this time of a girl: she is standing next to a bus, looking at the camera. She is smiling as though she is going somewhere and her eyes are a little sad. Her hand rests on the door. Next to the photograph is a ceramic moneybox and a silver tin with a mixture of buttons and some pins. Maroulla remembers how her mother had kept buttons rolled up in a piece of cloth, always in the third drawer down, beneath her scarves. Maroulla looks down at the dress she is wearing and remembers the day the button had fallen off.

Searching with the tips of her white fingers, as though she were dipping them in water, her mother could not find a green button to replace the one that had fallen off, so she chose a black one instead and sewed it into the gap at the base of the spine. It was a bit smaller and smoother than the others. 'No one will ever know,' her mother had said as she pulled the needle through the buttonhole, into the air so that the black thread straightened into a line. The needle came down again and her mother licked her thumb to tie the knot. She cut the stray thread with the scissors and held the dress up.

Maroulla places her feet into her shoes next to the bed. She stands up and straightens her dress. With her fingers she feels the button at the back of the dress. She walks out of the bedroom, through the kitchen and out onto the veranda. The night is thick and the leaves of the grapevine and the trees are soft around the edges as if seen in the reflection of a lake. She breathes in: the air is black and heavy. A short breeze tiptoes across the veranda and brings with it the sickly-sweet perfume of jasmine. Then all is still again.

There is no road leading down the hill. She walks through the field. At the end of the flat field there is a wheatfield. The wheat stands tall like a platoon of soldiers. The little girl hesitates and decides to walk round the field and then down to the silver road of thorns.

The thorns lead her past the well and over a little stream that passes white and cold over stones and rocks. The moon is low and looks like an opening in the darkness. It shines on the dead flowers, sprinkling them with silver, so that the dead leaves glimmer slightly in the darkness. Maroulla follows them and on the way she stops at a tree. Something drips onto her face and she looks up. The tree has a large trunk with broad shoulders and thick branches that jolt out like arms. And on each on of these branches, hanging delicately, is a horde of flowers. Red as blood even in the moonlight. They drip with dew from the heat. The girl stands beneath and holds out her arms. The droplets fall onto her face, like the rain on the mountains, she remembers. She feels cool now and a red breeze blows. Maroulla looks up at the tree. Red shimmers all around. The crickets' song beats in the air. There was a fig tree in their garden, like most orchards in Cyprus, but she had never seen these flowers on it before. This is definitely not what she is looking for, but she will take one back for the woman anyway. She jumps and tugs one off the branch. It leaks onto her hands like ink. She is surprised that it is warm and soft, like her body. She holds it in her arms and looks down at it. She struggles to see it in the darkness. Then, feeling it soak her hands and her dress and smelling something rotten and rank rising from it, she chucks it fearfully to the floor. The sky flashes and the ground rumbles. She suppresses a cry and spins around suddenly. Her heart beats fast and, terrified, she runs back past the cornfield and wheatfield, trying hard to remember the way she had come. She runs frantically until she gets back to the house.

Adem and Engin walk through the town. Adem touches the photograph in his pocket. He tries to picture her face now, after all these years. There would be lines round her eyes and mouth. They walk across the dark land. Engin shuffles behind, always uncertain, always anxious. 'Now I know the pathways like the lines on my palm,' Adem says, as they walk round the bends and over the bumps, following the road as he had done so many times before. 'When I first came here the paths would appear to change; sometimes they looked deep, aged almost, and at other times they would be so smooth that I could hardly see them. I remember my first week in Cyprus, years ago, and those long walks, following yellow paths at dusk. One path would lead to the port, the other to Bella-pais or St Irakleon, another to the wheatfields or Pente Mile, another fell beneath the shadows of palm trees and large eucalyptus trees where birds flocked in hundreds. It was impossible, even after a month of living here, to remember where each one led.' If only he had known then that those paths would one day remain etched on him, deeper even than laughter lines or scars.

They continue round the well, through the field, past the chicken shed, underneath the lemon groves and down along the silver path that curves into the centre of the town. The white stone of the church is iridescent in the moonlight. Outside, beneath the arches, is the wooden chair with an empty bread tray that one of the nuns would have left after the service. The doors are open, and from inside drifts the thickness of ash and the stillness of dead flames.

They continue silently along the path. They pass the fishmonger's on the right. Adem looks in through the open shutters. Engin hangs behind; he bites his nails and looks around anxiously. The scales of the fish shimmer in the darkness. On the floor is the dark lump of a body. Adem closes the shutters.

They continue; the dried olives from the arched branches that were scattered in hundreds on the path crunch beneath their feet. Adem walks towards a small house. 'The gate to Nikos' house is still open,' Adem says, touching the gate with his fingers, feeling the grain of old wood, the small splinters piercing his skin. He closes it and it screeches on its hinges. 'I remember

Nikos standing in his garden, with his grey overalls and those eyebrows that obscured his eyes, leaning on the gate, saying that he would fix it that weekend. That was twelve years ago now.' There is a deep sadness in his voice.

Engin stumbles as he walks, trying desperately to keep as close to Adem as possible. The air is thick with the smell of flowers and rotting bodies. Vines lie over sleeping houses where orange courgettes hang like severed limbs. Adem remembers the women sitting in the speckled shade, sewing wedding dresses with silk. Silver needles and white cloth flashing in tiny pools of light.

He suddenly stumbles over a large mass on the ground. He looks down and sees Nikos' face staring back at him. His eyes and mouth are open. His arms spread out like a dead bird. His stomach, bigger than before, drooping to the left. Adem looks up at Engin, who is hovering awkwardly above the body. Adem leans over and closes Nikos' eyes. He touches his skin and notices the creases. He lights a match and looks at his white hair, that was black when he had last seen him, and the liver spots on his forehead, that were not there last time. He carries the match over his body. There is a hole in his chest. Open, like a flower. They have taken his heart.

Engin bends over and vomits to the right of the body. Adem puts his hand on the boy's shoulder. 'Are you all right?' he says, and a gasp of tears escapes Engin, and then he swallows hard and wipes his eyes with the back of his sleeve. He nods. 'We just have to keep going,' Adem says, and Engin nods again.

In the distance the faint whistling of falling bombs can be heard, continuous like the song of the cricket. A few metres down, a twisted fig tree bleeds onto the ground. A shimmer of red catches his eye. The arms hold the hearts that hang from silk. The tree bleeds as though it were the end of spring and the blossoms were falling. The thinner arms of the tree arch from the weight of the hearts, some bigger than others, and the tree looks, in that darkness, like an old man holding the weight of the world.

Adem notices something hard beneath his foot. He looks down into the darkness and scrunches his eyes. He bends down and feels it with his fingertips. The rough of leather, the slice of paper. A book. He lifts it up and lights another match. An orange glow illuminates a word inscribed in gold calligraphy. He recognises the ancient Greek script. Bible.

Standing by the tree of hearts, at the edge of the night, with his head bent down and a match flickering in his hand, Adem opens the book that is resting in his palm. The leather is red and the pages inside are translucent and as thin as a layer of skin. He looks up and wonders about the owner of this book. He sees them praying before their last breath. He sees their eyes staring at the hearts of their loved ones. He opens his jacket and tucks the book into his inside pocket.

Finally they reach the first place Adem was looking for. The shoemaker's hut. The door is locked, so he looks in through the small window on the side. It is too dark to tell, but he can smell the mustiness of leather and dried mud and that black aroma of the hot iron that always clung to the walls and his clothes. He can smell the residue of footsteps, of a thousand journeys, from here to the sea or from the sea to the mountains; in the cracks of leather he imagines a grain of sand, soil from the hills and on rare occasions even a thorn from a distant land. He stands on the step of the doorway, looks down at his boots, and a sinking feeling overtakes him.

He lifts the metal hook, opens the window, climbs in and signals for Engin to follow. Adem walks like a blind man in a familiar room; his memory has not faltered. With his hands he searches the worktop for a candle. Finally, feeling old wax on the wood, he finds a match, strikes it on the stone of the wall and lights the wick. A halo of gold expands in the darkness. Dust swirls in the orange light. All around, shelves line the walls and on these shelves, touched by a veil of light, are thousands of shoes, one piled on top of another. As unmoving as the night. 'No more journeys,' Adem says and a breeze blows through the window.

Engin stands quietly looking up at the shelves of shoes and their elongated shadows. 'What are we doing here?' he whispers, but Adem does not answer. Instead he picks up a shoe and inspects the sole; it is worn and grey from friction. He feels the side of the heel. The glue is fraying. He turns it around and inspects the top; the tongue is bent and it has no laces. He puts this shoe down and picks up another. It is the shoe of a young boy this time; rounded at the front. The sole has unglued and the top is scratched a hundred times. Adem imagines the boy running through fields, chasing lizards. He can hear his mother calling. He puts the shoe down. In a pile on the floor is a pyramid of farmers' boots with old mud and manure greying in the crevices.

He takes another shoe and walks round the counter and perches on a wooden stool. He turns the shoe over to look at the sole. 'A working man,' he says to Engin and lowers his eyes to the stool opposite. Engin sits down somewhat reluctantly, with a worried look in his eyes. He looks over his shoulder. 'Don't worry,' Adem says, 'we'd be able to hear anyone coming.' Adem rubs his palm across the sole. 'It is rough,' he says, 'you can tell a man's life from the lines on his shoes and the creases on his face.' Engin looks down at the shoe. Adem reaches to the left and picks up a brush, which he uses on the surface of the shoe; he works all the way round from toe to heel, covering the sides of the shoe as well. When he has done this he brings the shoe closer and inspects the scuffs and scratches. He picks up a thin brush, dips it into a tin and repairs a bit of leather that has lifted off. 'The difference is that shoes can be fixed a bit, smoothed over,' he says, looking up at Engin.

'You should work on my grandmother,' Engin says, laughing, and making a scrunched-up face with his jaw sticking out. Adem smiles and picks up a pencil, rolling it over the tear to smooth it over. Then he puts the shoe down and exhales heavily. Suddenly in that orange light Adem sees a glimmer of red hair. He shakes his head and composes himself, but in a misty replay of the past there is a woman sipping coffee on the stool, and the same woman standing, drenched in rain, by the doorway. He smells lemon blossoms and polish. His heart is heavy.

'She would sit right there and watch me while I worked. This room came to life when she was here. She filled it with warmth and laughter and colour. This room of browns and blacks and greys transformed whenever she walked in.' Adem pauses and looks around. He lifts the candle and walks to the centre of the room. 'I made shoes for her, beautiful ones, the best I've ever made: red, green, purple leathers embossed with various things. I made many. And she'd drift around the room, looking at the shoes on the shelves, or lie down with her head on her arms listening to my stories.' Adem lowers the candle and moves it around close to the floor as if looking for footprints. 'In this little room we climbed mountains together, threw rocks, swam oceans.' Adem laughs and passes the candle across the counter. 'Sometimes she sat right here. I remember one day she took a pencil and some paper, and she sketched the paths of the town for me, she even drew the well and the biggest fig tree and the boats in the port. I would often use it as a map, but even then I still couldn't define logically where each path began and ended. She was always so intent on making me learn the twists and dips of the town so that maybe I would feel at home and stay here; but I would always recite an old Greek proverb . . .' Adem looks up, trying to remember. 'Time has turns and a year has weeks – meaning: to have patience. And she did. She had all the patience in the world. She had learnt somehow, through the type of life she had had, to not expect things too quickly, to wait, to watch things unfold slowly. As a child, she had spent much time on her own, watching the others from the outskirts of the fields as they played and she had to learn to find happiness elsewhere, in the smallest of places. She would lead me round the town and show me every corner, every tiny cave beneath the hills where the bats slept, she could tell me the path the snails would take when it rained. She told me one day that it wasn't really the roads that she wanted me to know, but that she had always wanted someone to walk beside her and see what she saw, maybe even feel what she did.'

Adem looks around at the still walls and unmoving shoes. 'That was when there was still some hope, before I locked myself away in the utter darkness of the hut.' The candlelight illuminates a pair of shoes on a shelf of their own. 'The priest's shoes,' he says, in a heavier tone now, 'this is their shelf. In those days Pater Yiousif was the town priest. She went to church one day to confess about our relationship. I told her not to go, but a love between a Greek and a Turk was forbidden and her heart was burdened. She told me that she loved me and that, out of all people, a man of God would understand love above anything else. She said she needed to be forgiven for the lies she had told her father. I remember her very words; she stood right here and said that when Jesus first appeared to the apostles after his resurrection, he said, "Receive the Holy Spirit. For those whose sins you forgive, they are forgiven; for those whose sins you retain, they are retained – John 20:22–3."' Adem freezes with the candle held high and he looks ahead fixedly as though she were standing right there before him. 'She truly believed that she would be forgiven,' he continues in a quieter voice that falters and cracks slightly with retained emotion. 'But the priest told one, one told two, two told five and five told ten . . .' Adem looks down at the shoes. 'Eventually her father found out and then the nationalistic youths, and that's when it all went wrong and she said that maybe we were never meant to be forgiven, maybe our crime was too great . . .' Adem's voice trails off and there is a moment of silence where the crickets beat outside. Engin swallows hard.

Adem looks more closely at the shoes; they have already been fixed and polished. The fronts are smooth as boiled eggs. The black of the polish is watery and deep in the candlelight. There is a slight gleam. The tongue is straight and the sole is new and strong. Adem brings one of the shoes up to his nose and smells the leather. He then sits down on the stool and in those still shadows, unties the laces of his army boots, and, to his relief, removes them, wiggling his toes now freed from the constraint and slips on the priest's shoes. The leather is still tight. He moves his toes around, then bends over, pulling each segment of the laces through the holes gently and evenly. Finally, he ties them with a double knot and stands up. Jutting out of his army trousers, the tips of the shoes glimmer slightly in the light of the candle. He stands tall, like a man who believes in a cause. Adem smiles. 'Choose a pair,' he says to Engin. 'Take off your army boots. We're not here to fight. We have a different journey to make.' Adem's voice sounds different now, more definite, stronger, and Engin stands up from the stool and smiles too; he takes the candle and rushes to the shelf, quickly passing the light up and down. He takes a pair of dress shoes with slightly pointed toes. He sits on the stool, discards his army boots and puts the new ones on. In the distance feet crunch on dried brambles and a gunshot is heard.

They both climb out of the window and stand back on the path and begin walking, the leather squeaking with each step. Finally, they reach a fork in the road. Adem breathes in. The smell of the sea drifts from the port, where he imagines the white sails of fishing boats flapping gently in the breeze. He looks ahead at another path. 'This leads up the mountain to her father's taverna,' he whispers to Engin, but even as he says the words, he is not sure what he is expecting to find. Either a body or a clue. He braces himself and takes a step up the hill. 'Vasilaki, the farmer, used to ride his donkey down from the mountains with baskets of figs, or cucumbers or watermelons in the wicker baskets at his sides and his tiny son Christaki flapped his legs behind him.' Adem pauses and looks further up. 'The goats passed here too in a white line in the setting sun, and she would run down the path while I hid behind the tree here to meet her.' Adem hears her laugh. The sea rolls on.

As they climb the hill the sound of crackling music emerges. Incessant martial music, booming louder and louder in the immense darkness. The music silences the crickets and the bombs and the roaring of the flames on the Pentathaktylo Mountains.

They climb the steps at the top of the hill and enter the veranda of the taverna. In the distance the mountains glow red from the raging forest fires, and far below a dark abyss lingers where the dead town meets the sea. There are no tables on the veranda, no chairs or salt-shakers, no cups or glasses scattered about after the end of the night. There is no longer the intense smell of fly-killer and there are no baskets of lemons on the floor. 'It doesn't look as though this is still a taverna,' Adem says. The music continues, making the place seem more still, more deserted.

They enter the kitchen and follow the music, walking through to the house at the back. 'I've never been this far before.' They walk through a corridor that smells distinctly of men's cologne. Adem lights a match and follows the music into the bedroom, where he puts the flame to the wick of a candle on the bedside cabinet. The music comes from a radio on the dressing table. He walks towards it as it crackles slightly and turns it off. Silence buzzes in their ears.

Adem takes the candle and passes it over the pictures on the wall. The first is of an unfamiliar man in a three-piece suit, holding a pair of spectacles in his right hand and standing on what appears to be the veranda of this very house. Adem looks at the photograph more closely. Those are definitely the fields and hills that the house overlooks: he recognises the grey ghost of the Pentathaktylo Mountains behind. The second photograph is of a young boy on a bicycle looking at somebody outside the picture, and a dark-haired woman with a long dress holding a sun umbrella, who is not looking at the boy but smiling directly at the camera.

'The family was clearly wealthy,' he says. On an antique desk beneath the window is an old typewriter. Adem looks at the make: Hammond Multiplex. 'Probably imported from the States.' He stares at it for a moment and finds that he cannot walk away; it sets a precedent for a multitude of memories. He lifts his arm, hesitates and presses the space key. The typewriter clunks and clicks. The too-familiar sound makes his stomach churn. He thinks about his childhood home on the outskirts of Istanbul, and their living room with his mother's brown armchair, and that little desk with the typewriter where his father used to sit for hours typing the names of the dead. 'Reminds me of my father,' Adem says. 'He was a failed journalist, confined to writing obituaries for *Gece Posatasi* and later for the *Yeni Sabah*.' Adem is consumed for a few minutes by the past. He pulls his hand away, looks closely at his palm and then turns away from the typewriter without looking back. Engin grabs the candle.

'What did you want to find here?' Engin says, catching Adem up, but Adem doesn't answer immediately. He keeps walking straight out of the house.

'If her possessions were scattered around I would have known that she had fled with the townspeople that escaped. Or . . .' he says, but does not finish the sentence. 'Well, it's obvious that Kyriaki's father no longer owned the taverna. I have no idea now what happened to her,' Adem whispers, and Engin senses that same desperation in his voice again, the tone he had used on the ship when he grabbed Engin's arm. Adem blows out the candle in Engin's hand and they walk out of the house back onto the veranda, where the dark sky bleeds red from the rising sun and the rising fires. It is now possible to see the grey smoke rising like the souls of the dead. They stand on the edge of the veranda looking down at the devastation. Adem leans over the railing. 'Where now? Where do I search? What do I do? Where do I start?'

Day 2: 21 July 1974

The first cockerel sings and the sun slides in through the shutters. Koki wakes up. She opens her eyes. She has almost forgotten where she is. The room is drenched in a red light. The sun bleeds the slaughter of yesterday. She opens her eyes and looks at Maroulla beside her. Then something catches her eye. She sits up. The girl by her side is drenched in blood.

Koki does not breathe and her body has frozen. A breeze blows outside. The shadows of the leaves move overhead and her heart pulsates. The cicadas' beat fills the air. The sun throbs through patches of darkness and thumps on her temples. She cannot move. The cicadas march like soldiers in the silence. There is no other sound.

Koki holds her left hand over the young girl's body. Her hand trembles. A breeze blows again and the shadows move. Only slightly this time. Again all is still. Her hand shakes. She cries. She brings her hand down to the young girl's chest and realises that she is breathing. Her chest rises and falls. Like the waves. Like the sun. Koki sobs. She searches her for a wound. Nothing.

Maroulla's eyes open. Her pupils widen, then dilate almost immediately. 'What are you doing?' Maroulla asks.

All is still for the beat of a heart. Koki sits up and looks, bewildered, at the little girl.

'What did they do to you?' she says through sobs, and in an instant turns to look at the door.

'Who?' the little girl asks, but Koki is already up, checking the rooms of the house. The girl follows her. 'There is no one here,' the young girl says, but Koki does not hear her.

'Did they leave?' Koki screams. Terror in her voice. The girl is shocked and stands straight.

'There is no one here,' the young girl repeats. A tremor rises in her throat. Koki closes all the shutters, and pushes a chair up against the front door. The little house is drenched in a cool darkness and breathes quietly like the streets after a rare summer rain.

Darkness in the morning is different to that of the night; it has the quality of water.

The little girl stares up at Koki. 'I went for a walk last night,' the girl says, and the shadows of Koki's frown deepen. 'I wanted to pick a flower for you. It was the same colour as your hair.'

Koki looks, perplexed, at the girl's dress and apron. She walks towards her and touches the red stain, shaking her head from side to side. 'What is this?' Koki says, but Maroulla does not answer. Koki finds a cloth, pours a few drops of water onto it and gently wipes Maroulla's face and arms. There is not much more she can do until she can be sure that there is more water about. Koki then puts the cloth down and collapses into a chair. As she looks to her left she suddenly realises that all around are reels of silk of various sizes and colours. On the other table in the corner of the room something glimmers like snow. The table is laden with a thousand cocoons, transparent and marbly in the streaks of morning sun. Next to the table is a large cauldron resting over unlit wood. The girl tiptoes a little way and looks out of the window. Koki stops and looks up with wide eyes. 'What is it?' she asks. The little girl does not turn around and does not reply.

Koki stands up and walks towards the window. She peeks through the crack of the shutter. A white flake flutters across the window. And another. And another. All around pearly specks shimmer against the yellow sky. They coil and fall like ash. The little girl runs to the door. Koki opens her mouth to stop her, but the light has already flooded in and Maroulla is standing very still on the edge of the veranda.

All around, a thousand pure white butterflies swarm the cottage. They dip and turn as the sunlight trembles on their wings. And for that moment all is white. Koki and Maroulla stand on the doorstep of that abandoned cottage on the top of that abandoned hill sheltered within a ball of floating butterflies. A few stray into the valley far below and over the gold wheatfields and a few fly into the balmy darkness of the cottage while the two refugees stand smiling as if this were their home and as if they had known each other all this time. 'They were silkworms,' says the girl. 'My mother used to sew. They only live for a day, but that day for them is like eighty years for us.'

Every minute of this day does in fact feel like a part of a lifetime in another creature's life. Koki and Maroulla go outside and sit on the veranda, looking down from the top of the hill. The sun is strong and drenches their faces in white light. Koki's hair is like the flames on the hillside. Her eyes are just as wild. They are mirrors of the world. Her feet are bare and her toes touch the brambles at the edge of the field. Maroulla looks at the thorns. She imagines the trail, a hundred miles long, leading to the red rose. She remembers her mother's words. She misses her, but she does not cry. Maroulla turns to the last page of the green book and looks at the dewy rose. Red as blood on a white, snowy plain. She imagines it on the glistening slopes of the mountains and thinks that that is probably where she must aim to go.

Maroulla closes the book and puts it back into the pocket of her apron. She looks at Koki sitting on the floor.

In the distance a Turkish jet spins into the side of a mountain; its wing is missing. There is an explosion and a trail of smoke wisps into the sky. Overhead a flock of fighter jets sear across the sun, their bellies black as night. For a moment a cool shadow falls over the house.

Koki turns and looks at the red stains on the little girl's dress and wonders now whose blood that is. She stands with a fresh look of purposefulness and gazes around, eventually finding a copper basin resting on what seems to be half an old broken door. She places her hands on the basin's handles. They are scorching hot so she uses the bottom of her dress as a glove to slide the basin to the side. She lifts the door to reveal a deep hole. From within rises the smell of damp conifer bark. A freshwater well. Koki looks around her for the bucket that must be nearby. She walks towards a black bucket with a rope tied round the handle which has been discarded beneath an olive tree. Returning to the well, she holds the bucket over the centre of the hole and drops it in, wishing all the way down that it still has water. A smile creeps across her mouth as she hears a splash. She waits a few seconds and starts to pull. The first heave is always the worst.

As the bucket emerges, reflecting the clear blue of the sky, within it she sees the reflection of another time. Dipping her hand in, she drinks some water from her palm. It is clear and fresh; the town well she was accustomed to was further than the natural springs of these hills. She calls Maroulla over, who also drinks some of the water. Then Koki turns her attention to the copper basin. She pours into it the contents of the first bucket and notices the sound of a light sizzle as the cold water touches the hot basin. Koki repeats this ritual until the basin is full and walks into the house. She returns with a bar of white soap in one hand and a green one in the other. As Maroulla watches Koki, a delicate ribbon of water and red soil manoeuvres towards the girl's feet.

Koki puts both soaps down, unties Maroulla's apron, unbuttons her dress and pulls it up over the girl's head. The little girl does not complain. She likes the soft touch of the lady's fingers and the smell of fire in her hair. Maroulla stands bare in shards of light. Her skin is the colour of sun-soaked sand in the morning sun.

The water in the basin shimmers a nostalgic gold and blue as it reflects the sky. Koki remembers her son and feels sick. She shudders and looks at the bleeding hills, the edges still fuzzy with red-yellow poppies, the rest alight or burnt to char. Far below, fields as dark as the sea ripple with ash in the breeze.

Maroulla does not wait to be told. She climbs into the basin. The water is cold, but she does not shudder. She sits and stares at the five fingers of mountains in the distance that tremble grey-blue in the heat while Koki scrubs her body with the white soap and her hair with the green one. Koki makes sure she scrubs her clean, she rubs her elbows, knees, neck and even her fingers. She scrubs hard to remove all traces of blood from the young girl's body. And when all is done Maroulla notices a tear forming in those glassy eyes. Or is it a reflection?

When she has finished Maroulla climbs out and stands to dry naked in the sun. Koki removes the crucifix from her breast and the silver tin from her apron and hides them beneath a large leaf. She takes off her apron and purple dress, places them on a chair on the veranda and climbs into the basin herself. Maroulla notices her translucent skin with blue rivers of veins and sprinkles of golden moles on her back. She sees how her hair, drenched in water, turns the colour of red soil after a winter storm.

When both Koki and Maroulla are clean and dry Koki leans over the basin and scrubs the stain out of the dress and apron. Maroulla sits beneath the shade of the jasmine tree, wrapped in a silk-woven blanket, amongst the sweet-smelling petals, and holds the little green book and the scissors in her lap. The white butterflies flutter around her.

Once Maroulla's clothes are dry and she is dressed,

Koki fetches two wicker baskets that she has seen beneath a tree and hands one to Maroulla, telling her that they must go together to find some food. They walk just a little way down the hill, Koki constantly on the lookout and listening intently for the sound of another's footsteps. But when all is quiet and the sun is soft and low and the afternoon breeze touches their clean skin and freshly washed hair, it is, for a moment, tempting to believe that it is just a normal day. A few stray butterflies weave between them as they walk.

In a very short while they reach the small orchard that must have belonged to the owner of this house. There is a lemon tree, a fig tree and a pomegranate tree. In a vegetable patch in the middle are courgettes and artichokes. Koki tells Maroulla to pick some courgettes as she collects figs and grapes and pomegranates. Maroulla kneels down and feels the courgettes and inspects their colour. She knows exactly what to look for as she had done this so many times before with her mum. Soon, with baskets full, they make their way back to the house. Koki saves the courgettes and rinses the fruit with some water. They sit together on the veranda, peeling and eating figs and pomegranates.

Before they know it the sun has begun to set. The

white butterflies start falling like snowflakes over the cottage. Soon all is obscured beneath a sheen of white wings and carcasses.

That same morning, Richard sleeps on the armchair in his bedsit. Gently, and from the distance, a marching sound emerges, like an oncoming train. The air trembles, but he does not hear it yet. With each beat the marching gets louder and now voices are heard chanting inaudible words. A woman shouts some obscenity from the window and Richard wakes up in a pool of light. Slowly, the room comes into focus and as the unusual marching beats in his ears, he remembers again the sound of the crickets. The marching suddenly becomes apparent. He pushes himself out of the armchair and walks towards the window. A flickering of colours. A train of people. A protest. Thousands with banners, stamping and shouting along Queen Victoria Street. From shop windows and the edges of the pavement the locals stare bemused. 'Bloody foreigners!' a voice calls from far below, but from other corners people wave at friends in the crowd.

Distorted faces call words in a glottal tongue. The hour strikes. Big Ben cannot be heard. The chorus has drowned out the normal noises of the city. It has swept over the grey streets like a river from a faraway sea. The voices rise like smoke.

Richard backs away from the window and rushes to the television, where he switches impatiently to BBC1. He puts the volume up and sits on the arm of the chair.

'Thousands of Greek Cypriots in London have been protesting about the disputed government of Cyprus. More than ten thousand Greek Cypriots and British left-wing activists march through the centre of London in support of an independent Cyprus and the restoration of Archbishop Makarios as its elected president.'

Richard rubs his eyes, his mouth becomes dry and pins seem to prick the tips of his fingers. 'Britain has been airlifting troops and equipment into Cyprus whilst a ceasefire in Nicosia is protecting foreign civilians from the warring factions. The two thousand British holidaymakers stranded on the island have criticised the Labour government for failing to anticipate the onset of fighting.'

Richard feels sick and notices the empty bottle of ouzo by his side. There is a blanket that has dropped to the floor. He stands up, washes his face in the basin.

He walks to the wardrobe and removes a pair of black trousers and a grey shirt. He takes off the dirty trousers, folds them, places them into the empty laundry basket and steps into the clean ones. His legs look thinner, he notices how his knees appear larger, his skin is grey like the walls of this damned place, like the wall of clouds outside. He hears the persistent marching of the protestors; distressed voices rise up to his window. He feels ill. His heart is ill. The grey walls around him are ill. Even the measly sunlight coming through the window is ill. A fly buzzes over the basin and settles on an empty glass. He fastens his trousers slowly, adjusts the belt carefully, and buttons the shirt purposefully, with the same precise movements as he would have once used to put on his uniform. He adjusts his collar in the mirror between its splatters of toothpaste, pads down the sides of his hair with his hands and exits the apartment.

Usually, he would only leave the bedsit to visit the grocer or the launderette down the road, but today he has something else in mind. He wants to tell Paniko the whole story, the true story, from beginning to end. Paniko is the only connection he has to Cyprus. Richard feels even more nauseated. Why did he not just tell him all these years? He might have been able to help him. Tears prick at the back of Richard's eyes. 'You idiot,' he says to himself, 'you idiot.' He shakes his head from side to side. He feels restless, troubled, full of nerves. It's time, he thinks. It's definitely time.

He walks out into the crowd of people. Faces full of rage and tears sweep past. Red words flash on white banners. Richard steps up onto the pavement. An old man standing beside him pulls a cigarette out of his shirt pocket. Richard looks over at him and touches his own blazer pocket. He has left his upstairs. The old man notices and offers one to Richard who accepts it and nods in appreciation. 'There are riots in Camden Town outside the All Saints Greek Orthodox Church,' shouts the old man, barely audible in all that noise as he lights Richard's cigarette. 'The Greek Cypriots are fighting about enosis with Greece, even the Greeks are against each other. The world has become a carnival.' The old man shakes his head. 'They say that Makarios is turning Cyprus into a, what was it? Mediterranean Cuba, whatever that means. I don't know. I don't know what I believe any more.' He lights the match, puts it to the end of his cigarette that is now hanging from his mouth, and breathes in deeply. 'They are preparing a force of volunteers to join the Greek army.' The old man puffs out smoke and then disappears into the crowd. Richard stands there for a few more minutes, looking at the fear on people's faces and feeling more and more sick.

Eventually, he walks across St James's Park, up through Piccadilly and right into Soho towards Old Compton Street. Richard looks up at the sky as a military taskforce plane flies overhead. He clutches his knuckles and shrinks into his collar as he ascends a slope. He is afraid of flying. Once, a Royal Air Force pilot, now living off the state and terrified of planes. A useless excuse for a human being. His chest tightens and he looks down at his feet. The pavement is damp from last night's rain. He continues past the post office, the bookshop, the off-licence, the cobbler, until he reaches a drab-looking window where a coffee shop bubbles behind steam and condensation. In blue letters, swinging above on a white sign, the words: Amohosto Café. The door swings open and a middle-aged man walks out, putting his arm through the sleeve of his coat, and the sounds of the café spill out onto the street: of cutlery and loose change and that loud sing-song lyrical talking. The café is packed for breakfast. Richard hesitates outside, moves closer to the window and looks inside at the men, mostly dressed in casuals, sipping their coffee, taking the last drag from their cigarettes before setting off for the factories again. There is only one man in a suit, who takes a note out of a money-clip as he stands and picks up his umbrella from the floor.

Richard enters the café and a few men look up from their coffees and conversations. There is a dark, sombre feeling in the room, shoulders are slumped and feet tap restlessly on the floor. The man in the suit drops the note in a saucer and leaves. Richard observes that the man has left far too much for what seems to be a coffee and the leftover crumbs of a cake. Richard walks towards the now-empty table by the window, but a large man, squeezing through from the right, beats him to it. There is another chair. The fat man adjusts himself on the seat, and then looks up at Richard. Richard sits on the empty chair. Paniko then approaches through the crowd with a white apron, without a pad, and grunts something in Greek, and the fat man asks for a coffee and some olives. Paniko then starts mechanically and blindly clearing the table, and suddenly pauses and looks over at Richard, who nods and says that he would like the same. There is a look of confusion on Paniko's face, and he hesitates with the cup still hovering over the table. He approaches the situation quietly, not wanting to scare him off, like a man luring a cat. 'My friend,' he says hesitantly, but contains a smile as if he is holding water in his mouth. He then walks off without another word and disappears into the kitchen at the back.

The man next to him is holding a tin of mints. He looks at his watch and then quickly at Richard, but does not speak. He seems to be several years younger than Richard. Richard looks around him at the yellow walls dotted with wicker trays, dried wheat stems, old photographs, maps and pictures of Cyprus. On the counter, at the back of the café, are myriad clay vases and jugs beneath a painting of whitewashed houses on a hill. He can just about bear it: the smells, the colours, reminding him of a time that only caused him pain and a feeling of hopelessness.

'You English!' The man beside him speaks suddenly, and Richard looks at him. The man narrows his eyes and is flushed with anger. 'What are you doing hanging around Greek man's place!' The man waves his hand around and looks at Richard contemptuously, with yellow teeth appearing slightly behind thick lips. Richard does not say a word. He shifts in his chair, moving a little away from the table, with his legs pointing safely in the other direction. The fat man reaches across the table and takes a fistful of peanuts throwing them into his mouth. Richard looks out of the window. A light flashes blue across the road. He can smell a unique combination of fresh mints and peanuts from the fat man's breath. Richard wishes he had chosen a different seat. He can feel the man's eyes fixed on him: a heavy gaze full of years of politics and conflict. Richard looks around at the other Greek men talking and a few glance over to where he sits. Perhaps he should leave? He doesn't belong here; he never has. Who is he kidding? Here he sits, Paniko's oldest friend, and he feels like an outcast.

Soon the fat man finishes the coffee and the olives, leaves some change in a saucer and exits the café. Most of the men have left already and there is a thick silence and old smoke still hangs in the air.

Paniko soon emerges from the kitchen with two coffees and places them on the table where Richard sits. He slumps hard into the chair opposite him and, finally, taking the weight off his feet, lights a cigarette.

Richard looks out of the window and his eyes follow the feet of a passer-by.

Paniko stares at his friend, wondering what has finally brought him here after so many years. 'You look tired,' he says, and Richard takes a deep breath and sits a little straighter. He fumbles with the cigarette box. The shadows on Richard's face are dark.

'Do you remember how we became friends?' Richard says, and Paniko shrugs, wondering if he had made enough *koubes*. 'Nineteen forty-six. Long time.'

'I guess I wouldn't be sitting here today if it wasn't for what happened,' Richard persists, leaning into the light, and this time Paniko's thoughts stray from his lunchtime menu as he notices life in Richard's eyes.

'Eh?' Paniko grunts and lifts his hand, indicating that he is confused.

'It was a curious incident and one that sparked off a succession of other incidents, which were all at once curious and pleasing and dangerous. That day I had been running flight exercises from the crack of dawn and I was enjoying my lunch break when a woman flapped towards me like a blackbird. "All of them mad!" she declared. "Come quick!" We ran through the streets and as we neared I could hear what sounded like a circus, and once the walls cleared and the road opened and faced the hills, I stopped for a single moment and stared at the mad scene which confronted me. Turkish and Greek women alike ran for cover with their dresses held above their knees. Some goats had gone bloody crazy! They darted around wild and mad and their sharp eyes flashed and their hind legs kicked the dry soil. They were completely out of control. And then, as if the scene needed more drama, your grandmother arrived and screamed as her livelihood ran rampant in a dirt field. Then, taking the stance of a goalkeeper, she stood waiting to catch one. Of course, when one of the goats spotted her it charged towards her like a bull! Yet the crazy woman did not move. It shot towards her with such accumulated speed that it knocked her down with a crash. An earthquake came straight after.'

Paniko smiles while stubbing out the cigarette.

'Then all was still at last. All the goats at once stopped running and stood calm and aloof while the men gathered them together. And there she lay, as still as a raft.'

'I was laughing for two days when I hear this story,' Paniko says, chuckling and tapping Richard's arm. 'You the hero! You save her.'

'Well . . . not quite, you see, that's what everybody thought . . . When I saw her lying there I realised I had not helped at all, so I, rather self-consciously, ran towards her, lifted her limp arm and felt her pulse. Everyone had gathered and held their breath. They stared expectantly with open mouths. I felt the pressure, all depended on me. I stepped back and opened my mouth ready to admit that I had no idea what to do next, but stopped when I saw the pleading eyes of the crowd. I decided to have a go at mouth-to-mouth resuscitation, even though I was sure it would be as useful as feeding her grapes. They wouldn't know the difference. So, I bent down reluctantly and proceeded to do the only other thing I knew how to do. I pinched her nose and held her chin, and brought my mouth to hers. Thank goodness, she moved! Her arms twitched, her eyes opened and she slapped her lips onto mine. Everyone remained silent for a moment and then broke out into a cheer. Your grandfather ran towards me and kissed me on both cheeks. Then the rest of the people cheered and your grandmother stood up.'

Paniko laughs, pointing at him with a cigarette between his fingers. 'You sneaky man . . . and all these years . . .'

'You bloody Greeks don't let anyone get a word in edgeways,' Richard smiles, 'and anyway . . . was I stupid enough to give up all that attention? When the commotion was over your grandmother slapped me on both cheeks and told me that she was going to hold a feast in my honour. My honour,' Richard says, tapping his chest. 'Come on, I was an Englishman in Cyprus. No one had done anything like that for me before.' Richard fumbles with the cigarette box again, takes one out and lights it.

'Do you remember that feast?' he continues. 'The whole town was invited. They all brought food with them. Greek and Turkish women carried trays of bread and plates of stuffed vine leaves, rabbit stew and lady's fingers, *kleftiko* and baked potatoes. The children carried the salads and yoghurt, *tsatsiki* and tahini in bowls and the men carried jugs of wine and bags of coffee and offerings of fruit and vegetables. I had never seen so much food in my life! There was enough to feed three towns! I was used to baked beans.

'I was offered the seat at the head of the table. At first I felt awkward and out of place. Some of the neighbours obviously did not approve and shot me inconspicuous looks of disgust and, sure enough, my presence sparked conversations in English about Cypriot politics. I remember one particular man going on about enosis, independence, the Second World War and how the Cypriots gave their lives for freedom and how the British now owed them the right to self-governance.

'Your grandmother told him to shut up. She stood behind the old man's chair and said, "You've been talking about the Cyprus problem for a hundred years. Tonight we are just people at a table." She then raised her glass and this was followed by a cheer. And for the first time I felt at home. Your grandmother accepted me; she opened up a whole new world for me.' Richard stops talking there and looks at Paniko, who is now leaning forward.

'Do you remember? That was the first time I met you. You came and sat beside me, and said, "What's it like to kiss a seventy-year-old woman?"'

Paniko guffaws and claps his hands.

'And all the men that were congregated around that end of the table burst into fits of laughter, and the man next to me said, "I think it like kissing a chicken's bottom!" and I chuckled, and stopped when I saw your grandfather looking at us, and he pointed a finger at me and said, "Don't mock, I have to kiss her every day!" and we all laughed till it hurt. My God, it was fun that night. We joked and drank far too much of your grandfather's over-fermented wine, and you and your cousins taught me how to dance the drunk man's dance. I remember you showing me the moves and then throwing me right in the middle of a big circle of people!'

Paniko stamps his feet and laughs as though he has truly been transferred back in time and for now he has completely forgotten about everything else. 'You looked like a drunk rooster trying to fly!'

'Everybody clapped and cheered, and as I spun clumsily around I remember clearly the feeling I had: this is what life's about – having people to laugh and dance with and honestly I wished that it would never end.'

Richard pauses and looks out of the window.

'That was when I saw her,' he whispers. His eyes are intense and Paniko notices that his fingers shake as he takes a cigarette from the box on the table and lights it. Paniko leans back in his chair now and folds his arms over his chest; he waits for Richard to continue.

'Do you remember Marianna?' Richard asks.

'Marianna?' Paniko replies looking more confused.

This was the most his friend had spoken about being in Cyprus since he had come to England.

'Marianna Leonidas from your town.'

'Yes, yes,' Paniko nods. 'Beautiful woman,' he says with a big smile. 'She lived next door to my grand-mother.'

'Well . . . I remember as she clapped from the edge of the circle. I couldn't take my eyes off her.'

'So, all the Greek men liked her.'

'But I wasn't a Greek man,' Richard interrupts Paniko abruptly. 'And yet I couldn't stop myself, all night, I tried to catch flickers of her through the other people: her fingers on the wine glass, her shoulders, her eyes! Jesus Christ, she was beautiful.'

Richard stops there and looks at his friend anxiously. Paniko rubs sweat off his brow and looks down. He sighs and nods, and then looks up at Richard, who starts to speak again.

'You see, after that night your dear grandmother invited me to every party in the street. They all wanted to see me dance and your uncle even tried to teach me Greek. Marianna was always there. And perhaps I would have called myself an idiot and brushed it off had she not peeked at me through the glasses and bottles and people and smiled as though she had singled me out, as though she had seen me amongst all those things and paused just for me. And even on the quieter nights, I remember, whenever I used to come to your grandmother's house and sit on the veranda, Marianna would stroll onto her own veranda and hang out washing or sweep the floor or pick grapes from the vine; whatever she was doing she would sneak looks at me and while I spoke to you or your grandfather I would catch an opportunity here and there to smile at her. There was something fiery in everything she did, from the way she brought out coffees, to the way she cleaned, to the way she hung out the washing. It was all done with a certain manner as though there was someplace else she ought to be.

'One day your grandmother sent you and your grandfather to the Co-op while I sat by the low wooden fence on the veranda eating watermelon and halloumi, which your grandmother had brought out for me before returning to her tasks indoors. Marianna strolled out barefoot and walked around her veranda. She did not say a word to me and leant over the fence at the far end and whistled as though I wasn't even there. You see, this was the way with

Marianna: I never really knew how she felt or what she was thinking. Then she meandered over, grabbed a chair and placed it against the fence where your garden met hers and where I was sitting. She had a way of crossing one leg over the other, placing her elbow on her knee and resting her chin in her hand. In this position, she swung her leg and looked across the field. But very gently and almost unnoticeably, her body inclined towards me, her shoulder slanting slightly in my direction. Young, unmarried girls were not meant to talk to men, especially English men, so she remained quiet. We stayed there for a while, and that whole time all she did was stare ahead and some-times up at the sky. While sitting there with her, time stretched out differently; it lacked that sense of rest-lessness. If I had not enjoyed the silence so much in her presence and felt a sense of relief that I cannot explain, just because she was there beside me, per-haps the rest of it wouldn't have happened and my whole life would have been different.'

Just then the door opens, bringing in the sounds and smells of Soho. Paniko looks anxiously at Richard and stands and puts on his apron.

★

Serkan lights a candle in the church. The light sputters callously over the faces of icons. On the wall behind is a row of men with white beards in a golden aureole of light holding open red-rimmed books. On the adjoining walls saints in robes of blue and green and pink look down from the backs of horses. The soldiers sit at the congregation as though at a Sunday service. Serkan stands on a platform at the altar. He stands as straight as a rifle. In the flickering light of the candle flame his face has the chiselled loom of carved stone. He stands like a statue. A memory of a hero. Half-remembered for his triumphs, as passers-by, in years to come, still salute him as they pass. Stones remain alive for ever. Unmoving even in the breeze. They have a silent voice of virtue. Splinters from heaven carrying messages to earth. Serkan fights a smile. The dome above is like the roof of a cave. Now the air is static. The rest of the soldiers face him. Serkan has a rock by his left foot that he has had his eye on for some time. At his feet there is also a soldier crouched down. His forehead is pressed upon the ground. His arms are flat by his face. His badge has been ripped out and is on the floor beside him.

'Your thoughts should be consumed with victory.'

Serkan's voice echoes through the church. 'After the coup against President Makarios and the declaration of the notorious EOKA terrorist Nikos Sampson as provisional president of the new government, it is our job to re-establish security and order and to protect the Turkish Cypriots. It is our job to give our brothers a new life, a better life. One in which they do not live in fear. Fear of hunger. Fear of death. Fear of insignificance in their own homes. Our brothers will be free. They will not pray in the mud. They will keep their homes. They will keep their lives. It is up to us.' He looks at the faces of the men in the crowd. He points at the man on the floor. 'This man, this failure of a man, could not protect his brothers and the future generations that rest in our hands. He could not kill a traitor. He could not throw a stone at the devil. He does not have the genes of an Ottoman!' The crowd remain still, but unbeknown to Serkan a few have shut their eyes. Serkan hands his rifle to an officer who has been standing near him. He bends down and picks up the rock from the ground. There is a shooting pain in the base of his spine, but he will not flinch or move his arm up to his waist to support himself. Standing up straight, he holds the rock in his right hand. The soldier on the floor looks up; tears are in his eyes. 'And so he cries,' says Serkan in a softer voice, 'like a child. You are not an Ottoman.' He says, '*We* are made of stone.' Serkan signals with his eyes for two of the officers to hold the soldier's arms. He lifts the rock above his head and brings it down onto the soldier's skull. Then he lifts the stone and brings it down again. Harder this time. The veins in his arms turn blue and he continues to bash the man's head, as though he were combating sin. He imagines the casting of stones onto the devil's landmark during the hajj. He pounds at the evil faster so that his rhythm matches the song of the cicadas.

Now that he has finished Serkan flicks the blood from his hand and asks for a towel. He wipes his hands thoroughly, gives the towel back, removes a flask from his belt and takes a long swig. None of the soldiers can see that a drop of water is hanging from his chin. He wipes it with his sleeve and puts the flask back into his belt. Nobody moves. 'Don't go pulling any bullshit like that,' he says.

Then Serkan straightens his jacket and looks at the men he is addressing. 'These hills will be burdened' – Serkan stops and coughs into a fist – 'I mean to say, laden, laden with domes and minarets, golden in the sun, just like they should have been. The children of Allah will toss emeralds into gutters instead of stones. Three hundred years ago the Ottomans wore robes of gold and rode on horses, now they walk with the goats.'

'Now they are treated like the goats!' calls a man from the crowd.

Serkan ignores this and continues. 'We ruled Greece for nearly four hundred years and Cyprus for three hundred. When the British took over in 1878 they described the Greek Cypriots as *non*-Muslims! Not as Greeks, or Christians, but as *non*-Muslims!

'We will rebuild the domes and look upon them glittering in the sunlight; we will weave silk rugs for pavements and line the streets with marble. And from across the sea we will see the golden domes of Istanbul and our brothers living like kings within them.' The soldiers clap and Serkan bends over the corpse on the floor. He takes off his jacket and unbuttons his cuff, rolling the white sleeves of his shirt, equally and carefully, to precisely above the elbows. He then straightens his arm and places his hand into the blood on the floor. He stands up and holds his bloody hand in the air like a rose. 'They are trying to kill *our* kings with *theirs*!'

His voice bellows and pounds on the high shimmering dome of the church.

Serkan walks over to the wall and smears the blood over the hand-painted icon. The crowd remains silent and the candle throws shadows over their eyes. 'Let not Shaytan deceive you!' His voice bellows through the church and he looks momentarily at the faces of the icons that look down at him. Serkan then dips his hands into a large silver basin. The clear water turns red. He asks for a towel. He wipes his hands and walks over the corpse and onto the carpeted aisle, wiping his feet. He walks towards the white light spilling in through the large oak doors of the church.

Outside the church, on the hillside, Serkan stands up straight, with another shorter man beside him. With his hand shading his eyes, Serkan looks down proudly at Pente Mile Beach and then at the little sun-baked houses on the hillside. Most are empty now. Some people would have fled, others been killed and the remaining would be prisoners at Bella-pais. He stands beneath the shade of the church. The fields around him are speckled with yellow flowers. The soldiers have all exited the church and are resuming their designated tasks. The church is now empty and dark inside and is scattered with rifles and grenades.

After a while a soldier drags in the first Turkish casualty and puts him on the floor, leaning against the stand of an icon, his leg bleeding through his trousers onto the ground. Serkan takes no notice. He looks down from the top of the hill at the tiny flakes of soldiers and prisoners moving lugubriously along unseen paths to Bella-pais. High above, the engines of British jets blast through the air. Somewhere, from the centre of one of the surrounding towns, a church bell tolls. The bells reverberate without reply like the song of a captive bird. Serkan clenches his fists, digging his nails into the palms of his hands. He purses his lips and juts out his jaw. His eyes narrow. The operation is moving too slowly. He decides to send out another group.

'Berker,' he calls, and Adem, who is unpacking medical supplies from a large wooden trunk, turns reluctantly to face him.

'You are in charge! Gather another ten and head down the hill, there are probably some still clinging to the walls or hiding in the cracks – they are like cockroaches. I want you to do the centre of the town.

I've already got some of those useless donkeys checking the hills. Take the women and children to Bella-pais. Kill the rest.' Adem nods.

Adem is about to walk away, but hesitates. 'There was a soldier,' he says, 'surname Bulut, I have not seen him since last night – you sent him to Bella-pais and said he would return in the morning.'

'He doesn't know,' replies the man beside Serkan. 'And address him properly in future, he is your commander . . . it's not his job to count flies.' Serkan narrows his eyes again and looks at the little man, irritated that he has spoken for him. Adem looks up at the church, shading his eyes from the sun. The little man follows his gaze.

'This is the church of Saint Evlavios. Isn't it beautiful?' the peculiar man continues suddenly and unexpectedly, with a gleam in his eye. Serkan has had enough, he takes a step closer and raises the back of his hand to the little man's face. Another flock of British jets soars through the air. Serkan looks up.

'If only our father could see us now,' the little man says.

'Bloody hypocrite!' says Serkan, and lowers his hand.

★

In the mellifluous midday heat a lizard scuttles across the wall. Koki and Maroulla sit in the kitchen. Far below a church bell tolls unceremoniously. The crickets beat the air and the sunlight pounds around the edges of the door frame.

The sound of footsteps becomes apparent. Koki looks up. The footsteps approach and Maroulla sees the movement of light in the glassy reflection of Koki's eyes. The door has opened. 'This is it,' Koki whispers.

In a pillar of sunshine stand two soldiers. Koki notices first their army boots, encrusted with mud. Then she looks up to where they stand, like pillars. They wear unbuttoned white shirts and green trousers. The little girl stands up. She does not curtsey this time or hold out her hand. The soldiers' dark eyes emerge through the light and a rifle twinkles, suddenly silver. Koki stands up and raises her arms. She looks quickly at the watermelon on the floor. The soldiers point their rifles to the door, indicating for them to exit without a struggle. Koki walks in front, with Maroulla behind, and as she passes she bends down to take the watermelon.

The soldier nearest to her pulls her hair with the same force as the sailors once pulled the full nets from sea on a good day. The skin around Koki's eyes stretches.

She succumbs and allows her body to be lifted upright and her scalp throbs with the beat of waves. She remembers how the waves pounded the hours, far far away at the bottom of the hill, and how the world moved to a different time. A slower time. A moment later the soldier is holding a gun to her head. 'This is it,' she whispers to Maroulla. The soldier takes no notice. He taps his finger on the trigger. Koki looks into the dark barrel of death, black until the end, and remembers her son's face. She trembles and shuts her eyes and at that moment sees her dad's face so many years ago and her own hand touching his and how the colour of their skin was so different especially in the clear November light on the morning he died. Would this be her last thought?

A gunshot is heard, and a bird flutters away outside. For a moment the crickets stop singing and the report echoes in the silence. Maroulla's fingers touch Koki's hand. Koki breathes out. The sunlight is red and hot on her eyelids. She dares to open them. The light is bright and envelopes her like the first light after sleep. As her eyes adjust slowly she sees that the white walls are stained with red. The watermelon has shattered into pieces. The red juice dripping on the walls. The soldier bends down; Koki notices the black flash and the crease of his boots as he crouches over the fruit. He picks up a piece, puts it into his mouth and closes his eyes, savouring the cool sweetness in that midday heat. He stands up and his trouser legs drop religiously over his boots. He picks up his rifle and signals again to the door.

Koki and Maroulla are led down the hill. There is a hot breeze and the white cottonfield sways to and fro and the carcasses of dead butterflies flutter wild and white as though they were alive. The cicadas beat another minute. And another. And another. It is a long time, even in our life, that it takes to walk down that hill when you do not know what awaits. Ahead black smoke rises. The sun is strong and sits heavy on their shoulders. A pearl of sweat runs down Koki's forehead.

When they reach the bottom of the hill there is a soldier propped up on the trunk of an olive tree, basking in the cool shade. His rifle safely in his hands. About a metre away, standing upright in the sun, is Olympia, the schoolmistress, and Elenitsa, a young woman, holding her baby in one arm and a small bag in the other.

The soldier nods at the ones approaching and pushes the new prisoners towards them using his rifle; he mumbles something in Turkish and walks away in the opposite direction.

The two remaining soldiers stand upright and signal to the prisoners to keep walking. Now there is a silhouette of travellers walking along the dusty road. In front is Koki, with a purple dress that flaps about her ankles and hair that is like a flower in the sun-baked fields. Maroulla holds onto the string of Koki's apron. Then Olympia, head down, shoulders jolting like a wingless angel. Behind is Elenitsa, holding her baby close to her chest. Then, on either side, are two men with rifles, so that the group walks across the land in the shape of a cross. Maroulla looks at the gold-coloured brambles on the floor. Her shoes crunch over tiny thorns.

Ahead is a stray cat licking its paws, and in the distance the frowning shadows of boats rest on white. They pass a field of blooming vegetables and trees. 'My husband planted those,' says Elenitsa, 'look how red they have become . . . and the olives are ready for picking.'

'My son Yiakovos killed his first snake beneath that

fig tree over there,' says Olympia, 'with the help of a cat.' She stops talking and nods at the ground, then looks at Koki. 'Your boy doesn't even have a name,' she says to her. 'He's one of them.' Koki keeps her eyes on her feet. 'He always stood at the edge of the port staring out at the domes of Turkey.'

'He just wanted to be a fisherman,' replies Koki.

Unexpectedly, an old song shimmers in the heat. They all look up and listen: a ghostly sound, not quite real, like the voice of the wind. 'It's the song of the dead,' says Olympia. 'An echo of the past.' The song glides in and out of nets and sails and leaves and vines and hills and flames.

'It's the song of the dying,' says the mother with the baby. They can all see the distant twinkle of a white sea and a glow of orange flames.

'It's the song of the ones still living,' says Koki. 'Maybe of the sailors calling us to port. Or of the wind calling us to sea . . .'

'Or of God calling us to death,' the mother interrupts, holding her baby tighter. They all continue through the town and the song blows past them softly with the breeze. The song gets louder as they draw nearer. It becomes apparent that it is sung with the weighty and grave tones of men's voices. Slowly the words are audible:

> I shall always recognise you
> By the dreadful sword you hold,
> As the earth, with searching vision,
> You survey with spirit bold.

The soldiers pause and hold their rifles tighter. The women look up as the words stroke their faces with the warmth of the sun.

'Maybe they are coming to find us,' says Elenitsa, 'perhaps we have won. They are coming to us. I know it. They are coming!'

The soldier on the left turns towards Elenitsa and bashes the back of her legs with the rifle. She stumbles, clutching onto her baby, but she manages to recover. Her face is now full of fear. The song continues to drift across the land, it flies overhead, fluttering with the wings of ancient stories.

> From the Greeks of old whose dying
> Brought to birth our spirit free,
> Now, with ancient valour rising,

Let us hail you, O Liberty!'
Now, with ancient valour rising,
Let us hail you, O liberty!

Suddenly the song is replaced with a wave of gun fire and there is silence. The women all look at each other, waiting, hoping that the song might continue, but instead there is a dull thumping like the falling of bodies. Elenitsa cries and brings her baby close to her cheek, and just then the baby starts crying.

The priest's shoes creak as Adem continues to walk, as though they have not made many journeys. His feet feel light as he enters the town. He is constantly on the lookout for Engin, wondering if perhaps he has been kept at Bella-pais to mind the prisoners.

As instructed, he sends the other soldiers off around the town to search the houses. He remains alone, just as he was hoping. He stands in the square of the town and looks around. Flies swarm around dead bodies and leftover food. A cockroach scuttles at his feet. The leaves whisper over blossoming gardens. He stares at the house that used to be Vasos' and sees the door open wide. He longs to find him there, sleeping in the deckchair amongst the browsing chickens. Feathers rise as a warm wind blows. Dust swirls around him and the salt of the sea touches his nose. He looks over at the Miltiades' house, shrouded beneath the olive trees. How they have grown. He has also planted a lemon tree, which drips with yellow in the sun. How he wishes to see him, pulling his moustache, staring with that beady eye at passers-by. He stares at the house at the top of the foothill and longs to hear little Yiola screeching like she did and hear the patter of her feet upon the sloping hill. The leaves of a banana tree clatter and a cockroach stops by his feet. Adem touches the photo in his breast pocket. He remembers Kyriaki collecting lemons from the old tree at the edge of the orchard beyond and sees the black soles of her shoes as she stood on tiptoe on a wooden stool, reaching for a branch. That is one of the pictures he always remembers. The ones from the beginning are far better. More powerful than a photograph, as it has the ability to move; sometimes it is just a leaf touched by a breeze, sometimes a lock of hair, sometimes the tips of her fingers, white against the yellow of a lemon. She never takes the lemon. She never turns around.

He decides to search the houses. He enters the first

and sees eight bowls of egg-lemon soup laid out on the kitchen table. The pictures on the walls are familiar; the children have glimmers of other faces, long forgotten. He picks up a spoon and tastes the soup; the rice is sour now and the soup is warm from the heat, but somewhere, striking the back of his tongue, is that distinct, homely taste. Egg-lemon soup for the one returning home or for the stranger visiting, egg-lemon soup for the Easter feast or a Sunday morning, egg-lemon soup for the sick or for the sick at heart. He shuts his eyes, takes a deep breath and walks out of the deserted house.

In the next house he stares at the frames on the wall: faces of nameless people stare down at him and the silence is thick. He looks around at the stillness of the furniture; at the empty armchairs and the glass of water left on the side table. The room smells of rosewater and mothballs and is dusty in the corners with old cobwebs. As he turns around to leave he notices that an old man has been sitting, unmoving, on a kitchen chair. He is as still as a picture and looks at Adem as if he is a long-awaited visitor. The old man smiles and allows his worry beads to clatter to his lap; he then scratches his ear, takes off his spectacles and brings his hand down over his eyes. He puts his spectacles back on and focuses on Adem's face. 'I might as well see the devil clearly before I die; that way I'll know what to avoid when I cross over.' The old man's voice trails off and he smiles again, this time revealing a row of crumbling teeth. He clears his throat and stares unblinkingly at Adem. 'Maybe you would like some help with your gun,' the old man says gruffly.

'Why are you still here?' Adem asks.

'You speak Greek?' the old man replies, and Adem nods. The old man contemplates for a moment, nods his head, and takes the worry beads into his hand.

'So, you like to get to know your enemy before you shoot their brains out?' Adem does not reply, but glances quickly out of the window. 'Under any other circumstances I would have offered you an ouzo, or maybe some sweet comandaria,' the old man says.

Adem continues to stare out of the window, then, without warning, he pulls his gun out, runs across to the old man and pushes him to the floor. The old man rattles like a heap of bones and holds his arms up to his face. 'Put your head down and don't say another word!' Adem demands, and the old man obeys. Adem points his gun just above the old man's head. Footsteps are heard approaching and Adem shoots. Four soldiers enter the house. 'Another one down,' says one, glancing quickly at the old man on the floor. 'It's hard to know if there are still some hiding,' says the other. Adem does not reply. The soldiers look around, sniff the air like dogs and stride out of the house.

On the floor the old man exhales. He opens his eyes and looks up at Adem. Just above him is a hole in the barrel of wine; it leaks upon him like blood. He looks up at Adem. 'Thank God it was red,' the old man says, 'and to think, I almost bought the white.' Adem offers him his hand and helps him back into the chair. Soaked in red, the old man sits for a moment in silence, nodding his head as if he has acquired some new knowledge. He looks at Adem and nods his head once more. It is a slow nod, slow and uncertain, like the nod of someone that has just accepted something long repressed.

'You can't stay here,' Adem says.

'This is my home,' the old man replies.

'They will kill you,' Adem insists.

'In my home,' the old man replies. He flicks the rosary beads in his hand and mutters beneath his breath. The old man's gaze is impatient and full of fire. His skin, withered and rusty, as if he has been knocked about the world a lot; his face furrowed, weatherbeaten. He tosses the rosary beads up so that the top end flicks onto his thumb. He then looks down and takes each bead individually, rolling it between forefinger and thumb, then separating it and pushing it onto the other side. He does this until there are more beads on the left than on the right. 'You cannot separate the waves or the years,' he says suddenly. 'They all roll into one.' He looks down at the beads; without the blazing of his eyes, his face suddenly appears still, like old, eroded wood. Adem remembers his father beating at the keys of the typewriter, his face as smooth as stone until the day he died.

'What's your name?' Adem asks.

'Georgios Kyriakou,' the old man says, 'but most people know me as Psaroboulis.'

Adem looks at the old man more closely. 'You were a fisherman,' he says definitely.

'I am more than a fisherman, I live with the sea. I've ridden its fury. The sea never forgets.' The old man looks up and belatedly bashes a fist onto the table, as if there are still more unspoken thoughts rocking inside him. The rosary beads rattle. His eyes alight, he looks around quickly, as though searching his surroundings, like a lighthouse. 'My life and the waves and this house are tied together. I built that boat with my own hands many years ago and she could sail the Aegean a hundred times. I'm sure she is safe. Thank God and the saints that I never keep her at the main port.'

'Forget your boat. They will find you,' Adem says.

'And why are you not *they*?' The old man looks hard into Adem's eyes as though he were looking out to sea. He searches them fiercely.

'Don't you remember me?' Adem says, and the old man narrows his eyes further. 'I once made your shoes.'

'Ha!' the old man says. 'You are that bastard who left the redhead. You played and then you left!' The old man chuckles and then coughs into his fist.

'It wasn't a game. I loved her. If only they would have let us be, we could ha—'

'You could have what? Married and lived happily ever after. Ppaa! A Turk with a Greek! Don't get me wrong, my boy, I have Turkish friends but . . .' The old man looks down, flicks his rosary beads and thinks for a moment. 'Her life was awful without you. They treated that girl so badly.'

At these words fury rises from Adem's chest; these

people's antagonism seemed to know no end. They got rid of him and yet they still could not just let her be. The resentment he feels mounts up and he is suddenly maddened by pictures of the past flashing through his mind. He takes a step closer to the old man. His stance has changed: his features sharper, his eyes, somehow, darker. 'I had to leave. Don't you see, I had to! They put me through hell!' Adem's face is red now, with the rage that was stirring up inside him now rising to the surface. 'How dare you judge me!'

Adem's eyes burn now, with torment, with hatred, with rage. The past crashes against his mind and the words he has wanted to say for so long come gushing out. 'Look at me!' he says, thumping his fist on his chest, 'I'm just a man.' He pulls at his collar, ripping the first two buttons off, revealing a gold pendant. 'Just because I wear this moon and star did they have to engrave their hatred onto me?' His voice is so tempestuous and at the same time so full of sorrow that the old man is taken aback. 'Look at what they did to me and you tell me if you would have stayed!' His voice trembles and so do his hands as he unbuttons his shirt and pulls it down with his jacket.

Adem turns around. Etched deep into the skin of

his back, reaching from shoulder to shoulder and running the length of his spine, is the branded scald of the Christian cross. The remnants of scorched flesh callously embroidered on his body in leathery crevices. The raw pain set for ever into the disfigured engravement of this symbol of sacrifice. 'Am I such a devil that I have to have Allah watching me from the front and Christ watching me from the back? I'm imprisoned between these two bars.' With his back still to the old man, his face drops. His body shakes and he hunches with the weight of these two worlds: his shoulderblades jut out, defacing the shape of the cross even more. Adem pulls up his shirt and jacket, covering the scar, but stares at the ground. 'They came in one night as I was working, five or six of them, they took the poker from the furnace.' Adem turns around and the old man looks into his red eyes.

Adem's shoulders are still hunched. The old man stands up and walks to the cupboard, opening it and grabbing a small bottle of ouzo. He holds it up, opens it and hands it to Adem. Adem looks at the old man timidly and takes the bottle. He drinks some. The aniseed burns his throat. The old man touches his arm. 'Take it with you,' he says, searching Adem's face again.

Adem closes the cap and slips the bottle into his inside jacket pocket.

'You saved my life,' the old man says. 'Just as my old friend Mustafa once did. We were nine, playing cowboys and Indians. He was an Indian. I was a cowboy. Yet he threw me to the floor as a stone, about the size of a starfish, catapulted towards me. Could have broken my nose. Friends ever since. Lived down the road until three days ago.' The old man's eyes fill with water, but the fire still blazes within them like the reflection of the sun in the sea. He swallows hard. 'If there is anything . . . What can there be? But if there is anything. I'll be here until they kill me.' The old man's voice is obstinate, his tone adamant. He flicks the beads. Adem nods and leaves the old man sitting in that chair, flicking the beads and inhaling that distant salt of the sea. Adem can smell it seeping from his own pores as he exits the house. The smell of salt and fish. So familiar. The mist of every memory. The vapour that followed him through life. Mediterraneans don't have a shadow; they have a haze from the sea, one of the few phrases his father loved to say, words that, as a boy, Adem found intriguing. He thought his father didn't have a shadow because he never stepped out of the darkness.

Adem turns back and looks at the old man's house, then down at his own shadow, grey and defined in that afternoon light. With effort, he straightens his back, his shirt and his jacket, watching his shadow change shape, and walks like a man with chains on his ankles.

He thinks about her again and continues strenuously into the next house; it is just as hopeless, there is no sign of her anywhere. On every wall faces of nameless people stare down at him and the silence is thick.

Until he reaches a particular house, set aside as though it has been discarded. He remembers that an old lady had lived here whose name he cannot recall. As he walks through the door he steps on a knife on the floor. He bends down and picks it up. It is a normal kitchen knife with a plastic handle, sharp at the tip. A photograph on the mantelpiece suddenly catches his eye. He is sure of what he has seen, but he is not prepared for it. He looks away for a moment and catches his breath. He looks back, and those grey eyes are wide and stare back at him. He walks towards it and picks it up. There is a boy of seven or eight standing beside her; he is holding her hand. He is darker than she is, he does not have her hair or her eyes, but he has the same smile and the same point at the end of his nose and that slightly square jaw. Her face seems longer than it was and more gaunt. There are grey shadows beneath her eyes and lines on her neck, but her hair is still the orange of flames. He holds the photograph still between the fingertips of both hands. The shadows move in the breeze. The walls of the house pulsate and so does the blood in his ears. He turns the photograph round: 1971. Did she get married? He looks again at the boy, at the curve of his hairline and those dark eyes . . .

'Empty?' says a deep voice behind him. Adem turns around. A soldier from his group stands at the doorway, his rifle tucked beneath his arm. A short, round man with sloped shoulders and arms that curve slightly outwards like a skirt when he stands straight. He lifts his arm and wipes the sweat off his forehead. 'I've done all the houses here,' he says, and squints his eyes against the sunlight that floods in through the window opposite. 'Apparently they found loads of them nearly scorched to death in those fields, and some on the outskirts.' Adem nods and tucks the photograph into his pocket as the other man looks behind him into the kitchen. 'Water?' he asks, and Adem answers, 'No.'

★

Richard sips the coffee. It is cold now and tastes thinner. He places the cup back into the saucer and looks out of the window at Old Compton Street. There, in the City of Westminster, parcelled between the red phoneboxes and buses and cigarette butts of Oxford Street and Piccadilly Circus, he feels a sudden sense of security. This familiar road in Soho, knotted with its craftsmen and tailors and silversmiths, red lights, stilettos and prostitutes, shimmers slightly beyond the window amongst a grey drizzle. Except he has never looked upon it through this window before. He has never been able to accumulate the courage to enter a Greek café and taste again that bitter coffee. Shop shutters creak in the wind, horns bellow, cars and buses rumble past, but all somewhat idiosyncratically, with undertones of foreign tongues. Just outside the window a Mediterranean lady drags a small screaming boy by the wrist, shouting foreign words, and a man calls something from a window above the tailor's. Richard can hardly believe, amongst all the bustle, that Soho was once a hunting ground, an area of farmlands and fields and tiny cottages. In the seventeenth century, the Greek Cypriots fleeing from the Ottoman Empire were of the first wave of settlers. And here they still are, he thinks. Bloody Greeks!

He lifts the coffee cup again, brings it to his mouth, remembers it is cold and places it down indignantly. The café is starting to fill up more. He taps his fingers, irritated, wishing they would go so he could talk to Paniko. But the anger inside him, despite his attempt to ignite it, fades, and is replaced by a sadness which starts in the pit of his stomach. He is immersed in the smell of olives and *koubes*, garlic and lemons, sweet *shamishi* and *lokoumades*, and that rusty whiff of money and cards and rolled-up tobacco, all encompassed in this tiny shop. This café is like a little porthole, like many others along these streets, into Cyprus; it was as if the Greeks had planted lemon trees into the landscape. And once again, there he sits, just as he had done so many times before, so long ago, there he sits beneath the grapevines, by the white arch, overlooking the magenta flowers and clay pots and green shrubs at the bottom of the hill, longing always for Marianna. She occupied his every thought in those lonely days at the barracks; she was all he thought about, even before he had touched her.

He suddenly remembers the night back in 1947, the night of the Easter feast. As the bouzouki strings resonated through the night and wine glimmered a ruby red in the candlelight, he had sat there trying not to look at her as she dipped in and out of the crowd, smiling and laughing and dancing. He remembers her carrying a tray of whiskies, and kneeling down to offer him one, and then again, she was gone, just like she always was, lost somewhere amongst the dancers and the music and rings of smoke.

It was late when he decided to leave. Most people were sitting down with empty glasses and ashtrays full of cigarette butts. Even Paniko had disappeared somewhere, and the musician played sombre songs as an old man sang to himself. Richard stood up quietly amongst the shadows and made his way to the back of the olive trees towards the gate to leave. But at that point he had felt a hand pulling him into the bushes, and there, shrouded in the trees, in the thickness of the night and the echoes of the songs and the crickets, somebody pressed their lips onto his. Stunned at first, he jerked backwards, but her body rose and she kissed him again. She held his face with her hands. He felt the brush of her hair on his cheek. She smelt of oranges and baked bread and the lingering of old perfume. He pulled away, and 'Marianna' was all he said as he looked into her round black eyes in the moonlight. Then she leant over and kissed him again, pressing her stomach onto his. For those few moments he was lost in a balmy, blue fantasy, and he allowed himself to enjoy the touch of her olive flesh, warmer than the night.

Then she stopped and pulled away so that he could see her standing in the speckled moonlight. Richard leant in to kiss her again, but she stepped back and lifted her arm so there was a quick flash of the marble-white of her underarm, then she leant forward, lifted his soldier's cap, touched his hair with her fingertips and laughed. 'Like oranges,' she said. Placing his cap back on his head, she turned her back to him so that he could see the curve of her spine beneath her linen dress. She paused for a moment, looked at her feet, said something to herself beneath her breath, tutted and sighed as though she were in some sort of struggle in her mind, and then started to walk away.

'I think of you all the time,' Richard called out to her, and just then she stopped, wavered for a moment and turned back to face him.

'I saw you smoking,' she said precisely, as though she had remembered it from English grammar classes.

'Yes,' Richard replied.

'I like one,' she continued and walked back towards

him. Richard fumbled in his jacket pocket, took one out, handed it to her and lit a match. In the light of the flame he looked at her face: at her eyes, at the soft curve of her nose, at the wisps of hair about her neck, at that red glow in her cheeks, at her chin and her lips and again at her eyes. The flame reached the tip of his fingers and he threw it to the ground. Marianna lowered her cigarette and he leant in and kissed her. It was a longer kiss this time, and he reached up and touched her hair and her shoulders, but she suddenly stepped back and looked at him hard in the eyes. There was a look on her face, one that Richard did not understand. Was it fear, regret? He wasn't sure and all she said was 'Thank you', and this time walked off and left him standing there alone with the sound of the crickets.

Someone grabs his shoulder and Richard comes to his senses with a start. Paniko stands above him, smiling. 'You were either being killed or fucked,' Paniko chuckles, but Richard does not reply and Paniko asks if he would like another coffee. Richard says no and then leans back onto the window again. His memory returns to that night, a little later, while walking home with his jacket in his hand and his cap wonky on his head.

Richard proceeded to walk back to the base, but decided to go the long way, along the harbour where the white boats were as still as the fingernail moon. Warehouses full of fruit awaiting export lined the harbour, and the smell of the carobs engulfed him. He untied his boots and sat down, swinging his tired feet round and allowing them to dip gently into the water. How soothing it felt. How he loved this place at night. God, how he loved the peace of the rippling waves and the silent little boats that circled the harbour like people at a table.

Something soft brushed against his fingers. A grey, emaciated cat with large cave-like ears and lemons for eyes. Its back arched into a 'Stroke me' position and then a purr as soft as the breeze. 'Shoo,' said Richard and flicked his hand, but the cat strolled round him and rubbed its head on his knee. 'Bloody vermin!' he exclaimed and tried again to push the cat away, and then laughed at the contrast with his aunt's pampered tabby in England.

'You know why they so ugly?' said a voice behind him. Richard spun round to see an old man sitting on

one of the chairs of the closed harbour café. He smoked
a pipe and wore the traditional black breeches that puffed
at the knees. He held the pipe in one hand and flicked
worry beads in the other. The flicking of the worry beads
was muted by the sound of the crickets. White noise in
that darkness. The old man rested his pipe on the table,
lifted his walking stick that was leaning on the chair and
tapped it a few times on the floor. The cat meowed and
strolled towards him with its tail in the air. 'About hundred years go, after long drought, the cats were shipped
from Egypt for kill-snakes.' The old man leant the walking
stick back against the table and dropped his hand so that
it dangled between the legs of the chair. The cat touched
his finger with its nose. Richard winced with disgust;
back in England it would be like stroking a rat. 'Vermin,
they say,' continued the old man, 'but without these cats
Cyprus would be full with snakes.' The wind purred
over the white sails of the boats.

The old man brought his hand back to the table,
picked up his pipe and relit it. A halo of smoke was
carried away by the wind, and the musty tobacco mixed
with the smell of lemons and jasmine.

Richard looked at his watch. 'What are you doing
here on your—'

'I like here at night better,' the old man interrupted. 'It no matter where I sit at night.'

Richard knew immediately what the old man was referring to. The three cafés along the port front each had a different clientele. There were no signs, but everybody knew. The Greek civil war had started and the people in Cyprus were equally divided between pro-royalists and pro-Communists. Richard knew that the British openly backed the royalists in order to restore the monarchy in Greece. The café on the left was mainly for the left-wing Communists, the one on the right for the right-wing royalists and the one in the middle for the Turks. 'This, how you say? Political crap. Their mind been taken by the wind and by ideas that not serve them. The stupid thing that these youngsters not know is together they make a bird.' The old man balanced the pipe between his lips, and with his hands joined at the thumbs mimicked the flight of a bird. Then he put the pipe onto the table and spat phlegm into a white handkerchief.

'I'll walk you home,' said Richard.

'Pah, I know these streets if I was dead,' said the old man, standing up, balancing himself onto his stick and walking off slowly along the harbour, past the fruit warehouses and towards the town. The cat stayed behind.

Richard stood up and allowed his feet to dry on the road, then, slipping his socks and shoes back on, followed the old man's footsteps back to the town. The cat followed too. As he walked he thought of Marianna and the old man's words. As much as the Greeks had accepted him and loved him, he was still an outsider, and beneath the dancing and the bubbling conversations, the people of this town were still divided. He wondered then what could ever become of him and Marianna. Could he ever really have her?

His bedsit at the British base in Kyrenia was small and old with just a cast-iron single bed and a bedside table with a basin and a terracotta jug, but it had a little balcony that overlooked the hills. At this time of night the hills were black and buzzed with crickets. Richard unbuttoned his shirt and hung it on the balcony. He slapped a mosquito from his arm and took off his boots, feeling the cool white of the flagstones beneath his feet. A breeze blew, carrying the smell of red soil and cattle. Richard leant over the balcony and thought about the kiss. Despite the fact that he knew the problems that could arise, he ached to see her again, and with the thought of her lips and the taste of red wine and the smell of red soil his eyes began to close and he walked over to his bed, let his body drop and drifted off immediately. The cat slept on the floor beside his bed.

In the present, a door slams, another customer comes into the café and Richard's head vibrates on the window. He looks around and realises that the café is now almost full. Paniko has replaced his old coffee with a new one, but he had not even noticed. He leans back on the window and remembers how the next morning he had woken up an hour too early with the cat sitting on his face. Irritated, he threw it off and washed himself in the basin. He decided to take a short walk to the harbour for a cup of coffee and a cold glass of water.

Women with trays, sitting on wicker chairs, lined the streets where the houses offered a respite from the sun. Some snapped beans, others rolled wheat into fingers, others chopped, others peeled, others folded mince into vine leaves. And the street smelt pleasantly of onions and coriander and aubergines. A few stopped and waved at Richard, who smiled and continued past the houses and along the path that overlooked the wheatfield. Here, amongst the gold of the wheat, women with colourful headscarves were dotted throughout the field like flowers. Each carried a tray and bent her head from the sun.

When Richard finally reached the harbour it was not surprising to see that the old man was not at any of the three cafés. Richard walked to the pro-royalist café, as this was where he was expected to sit, but spotting his friend Paniko at the pro-Communist café, he hesitated and walked towards him. Paniko was rolling a cigarette, with a steaming cup of Greek coffee on the table. Richard sat down and saw a few looks of disapproval from the neighbours. Paniko, then an apprentice farmer, was the same age as Richard; his skin was dark and black hair flopped haphazardly over one eye. He wore a white shirt that was creased and stained and rolled to his elbows.

'You need a wife,' said Richard, stopping to order a coffee from the waiter. Paniko looked down at his shirt.

'New shirt is what I need,' replied Paniko, 'they are paying me . . . *kounes.*' He picked a peanut out of the little bowl and held it up to indicate what he meant. Richard smiled and Paniko threw the peanut into his mouth.

'You coming to Pente Mile tonight, for the *banairi*?'

'Why not?' said Richard, drinking his coffee as soon as it arrived so that he burnt his tongue and accidentally drank some of the chalky residue at the bottom.

'You no learn how to drink coffee yet. Us Cypriots take time slowly. No rush. Where's the fire?'

Richard laughed, 'And that's why you earn *koubes*. I've got to get back to base.' He tapped his friend on the back and left a shilling on the table.

Paniko shook his head. 'You English will work yourselves into an expensive coffin.'

'See you tonight, my friend,' said Richard, and Paniko nodded his head and sipped his coffee.

'By the way,' Paniko called after him, 'the real word is *kounes*! *Koubes* is wheat stuffed with mince! Bloody *Englezo*!'

That night Richard arrived at the fair with two other soldiers who immediately disappeared into the crowd. Richard continued alone along the path between the stalls, weaving through people and cats and running boys with catapults. An old man with a bouzouki played music while men threw stones at Coca-Cola bottles and women looked at lace that draped and shimmered over tables and the younger girls stood in small groups drinking homemade lemonade and looking at the young men that passed. Scarves and skirts hung, as if from the sky, in a multitude of colours, creating the burlesque of a theatre-like lavishness, where below the curtains, dramas dripped only from the mouths of the women. Cypriot men always said that the women made a flea into the size of a camel. And although Richard agreed that there was plenty of truth in this, he also perceived that the men did the same and thought that the size of the island and a definite megalomania was accountable for this.

On the far left some English soldiers drank wine, but Richard ignored them and continued past the nut stall that was laden with trays full of almonds and pistachios and pecans; past the toy stall with rag dolls, china dolls, marbles, hand-made puppets, wooden cars and other wooden creations, and past the traditional clothes stall where burgundy Greek dresses with white lace hems and white petticoats hung on wire hangers in all sizes and varieties of red.

Hoping to see Paniko sitting in one of the food areas, Richard ordered a 'metrio', which he had learnt was a Greek coffee with one sugar, and wandered round the little plastic tables where families sat eating syrup-laden baklava with small forks. He sat at one of the tables and listened to a man who spoke with a loud voice and grandiose hand gestures. He could not understand the story that was told, but watched intently the dip of his hands and swoop of his fingers. He could not help but notice the fierce lift of his eyebrows, accompanied by a knocking back of his head when asked a question by a younger man at his table. Richard knew that this latter gesture was commonly used to affirm the negative. The man paused for a moment and then continued with his anecdote. Richard thought it was not surprising that these people needed a siesta, with all the energy they used to talk.

He then looked down at his coffee and resisted the desire to down it in one as he was so used to doing. Richard decided he would take his time for once and brought it up to his lips slowly and delicately, first inhaled the aroma and then savoured the chalky *kaimaki* on his lips. A soft breeze, that carried with it the smell of fried sweets and jasmine and lemon, touched his face. The night was soft and balmy and the coffee sharp and sweet on his tongue. His shoulders relaxed and he melted further into his chair. He could definitely get used to this.

Just then someone pushed his shoulder and then grabbed his arm. 'My friend!' announced Paniko. 'Come quick, now!' Richard, still holding the damned coffee, was forced to stand. 'But . . .' he resisted, looking into his undrunk coffee.

'It is time for the dance. We can look at girls.' Paniko sniggered like a schoolchild and Richard was forced once more to down his coffee in one go. So much for taking it easy, he thought, as he followed Paniko into a dense crowd. All stood gossiping and looking at the empty centre of the circle. Then a man in traditional breeches entered the ring, followed by three or four other men who stood around him. The man in the middle remained serious and raised his arms like a magician or religious leader or politician; it was hard to tell which in this day and age, thought Richard.

The man then raised his arm and clicked his fingers imperiously, and an old man with a bent moustache started playing the bouzouki and singing in a voice that the cats couldn't tolerate, scuttling away between people's feet. Then the dancer smacked his lips, clicked his heels and started kicking his legs and turning, almost in time with the music. The crowd cheered and clapped. Then two men that were now standing on either side of him repeated this leg-kicking fiasco, before standing together and bowing.

'This is the good bit,' said Paniko, nudging Richard. The man in the middle bowed again, swept back a strand of black hair from his face, clicked his fingers again and then flicked his hand, so that the crowd parted, making an aisle. The music resumed and five women, dressed in traditional Greek dresses and red headscarves, danced into the crowd. Holding hands, like schoolchildren singing 'A Ring o' Roses', they formed a circle and moved their feet simultaneously in little kicks and steps. Richard watched as the women turned slowly and purposefully and suddenly caught a glimpse of something that made his face turn involuntarily red; something the Greeks always seemed to find amusing. It was that thick hair that spilled out of the headscarf disobediently and touched her olive, apple-shaped cheeks, as she hopped and kicked and turned. Against all his best efforts Richard's heart beat faster as he watched her. Paniko continued staring at the other women; he had found this opportunity to stare at women longer than what was normally socially acceptable. Paniko bit his lip. And Richard, too. Sensible, controlled Richard was somehow now afraid that he was in love with this woman with the black hair, as she spun so beautifully before him. These damned Greeks are rubbing off on me, he thought, what with the coffee and now this.

It was later, yes, much later, when the night was almost white with stars and the waves far below powdered onto the shore and the people that remained sipped whisky and threw dice onto backgammon boards or packed unsold pashminas and headscarves and toys into boxes for next time. It was much later, while Richard walked the now empty and therefore much shorter length of the stalls with a cigarette in his hand, that he saw her again. She was talking to an older woman behind the nut stall. Her fingers danced about her as she spoke passionately and the woman nodded and bent down to retrieve a basket from the floor. She suddenly turned and winked at Richard as if she had already noticed him, and then without hesitation signalled to the trees. Richard looked behind him self-consciously; they would kill him if they saw. An English man with a Greek woman! They would take out his insides and put them in one of those disgusting lemon-gelatine mixtures they so seemed to enjoy. He suddenly had a grotesque image of his eyes floating with the pig's eyes within this mass of discarded bits of apparent delicacy, in a clear jar, encased in off-white jelly. When he came to his senses again he realised that she was no longer standing there and so proceeded towards the trees.

'Reading the future!' called an old woman suddenly from a table.

'No, thank you,' Richard said, and continued to walk.

'Sometimes when you look inside you find that there is a different gift to the one you were expecting to find.'

Richard turned around. She was dressed in black and held a steaming cup of Greek coffee over a white tablecloth. On the table there was a folded piece of card with the words 'Tasseomancy – Kafemandeia' on it. 'Drink,' she said, holding up the cup so that the steam slightly masked her face and her white crooked hand stretched out, knobbly and rumpled. Her eyes were small, buried amongst deep creases and her nose had a large pale mole on the side. She suddenly reminded him of the wicked witch holding the apple in *Snow White*, and he stepped back slightly at the realisation of this strange resemblance. 'I tell you tomorrow,' she said ambiguously, lowering the cup.

'My house by the church. Come.' Richard hesitated for a moment, propelled by the intense look in her eyes, but did not reply and looked over towards the trees as he saw Marianna disappear into the foliage. As he turned away from the old lady, passing beneath the arch of the first tree and entering the pounding darkness, he heard the whisper of her words, 'Many moons will pass before you get yours.'

He felt a touch on his shoulder. He spun around and could just make out Marianna's face in the darkness. She lifted his cap and touched his hair. This time she did not laugh, but smiled and kissed his forehead. He ran his hands down her arms and then through her hair. She stepped back and he was afraid that she would leave but instead she slowly unbuttoned her dress and allowed it to fall to her feet and they lay down together in the midst of the fig trees. They made love and then they lay on their backs, side by side, staring up through the trees at the stars. Where their hands met in the middle, she moved her fingers ever so slightly over his. Her touch was so gentle, almost non-existent, elusive, like wind passing. He turned his face towards her and stared at her profile. She did not turn to look at him; she continued to stare up at the sky. 'To others you are hero, a knight,' she said. 'To me you dragon. You breathe fire on everything. You capture people. You got me.' She turned now to look at him. Her eyes shimmered. Her words were just as obscure as her touch. Richard looked back at her, but did not reply. She turned completely onto her side to face him. 'I could put my head on your chest and drop sleep there,' she said and she closed her eyes. She did not put her head on his chest and she did not say another word, but Richard rolled on his side and stroked her hair for what seemed like hours. He did not want to move, he wanted to be close enough to feel her warm breath and smell the sandy orange of her skin.

Later that night he walked along the port, passing the old man, who was sitting in a different chair this time, at a café further down the strip of rocking boats. He flicked the worry beads incessantly. 'Eat good?' the old man asked. Richard stopped and nodded. 'Drink good?' Richard smiled. 'Life goes in our mouth and out our arse,' the old man continued and this time he smiled. 'The rat?' the old man asked, and Richard quickly shuffled his feet and looked down instinctively. The old man chuckled. 'You no remember even your own words. The vermin. The cat!' he finally exclaimed. Richard shook his head to indicate some kind of resignation. 'Cats are no loyal,' said the old man. 'They give promise of love only when they want, but still we need them.' Richard nodded, and the old man stared at him for a while. He seemed to look for longer at the jacket in his hand. 'Goodnight,' the old man said, stressing the word 'good' so that the meaning was obscure. He looked at Richard for a few more moments, as though waiting for a reply, and then continued to flick his beads and stare up at the milky sky. Richard hesitated briefly and then continued on his way along the port to where the road split finally into little branches of bumpy soil. He automatically took the one on the left that would lead down a hill, through the fields and towards the base.

A loud clatter brings Richard back to reality. He turns around and sees that Paniko has dropped a coffee cup on the floor and has a stain on the front of his apron. Paniko curses and angrily wipes his hands on a kitchen cloth, before rushing to the kitchen and returning with a mop.

★

Koki, Maroulla and the other two prisoners are led into a house at the bottom of a hill. The soldiers use their rifles to shove them in and then proceed to the back of the garden. Inside the living room are myriad women, all facing away from each other as though they are there alone. Sunlight sweeps in through the window, illuminating the beautiful colours and florals of their dresses and headscarves as they would have been on a normal day, dotted amongst corn in the golden fields. The back door is open so that a soft breeze drifts in, but nobody exits or attempts to leave. Soldiers stand amongst the trees that line the yard. The house has an orchard of lemon and olive trees and a trellised vine that spirals into a blanket of shade over the porch. There are marbles on the floor and a hunting bitch in a cage, who is whimpering now in her sleep, and some chickens roaming about and clucking gently. There is a window with green shutters that overlooks the garden of a church, where the remains of dead flowers from spring lie entangled like bones.

The new prisoners hesitate at the entrance. Bent at the spines, with arms dripping to the ground, they all stare down at the unmoving women, displayed in this dismal room like ceramic statuettes. Life is only evident from the slight slide of their eyes, which, red and raw, serve to reveal a story of fear and loss. Koki recognises Litsa Miltiades, the daughter of Dimitri; her father's old friend. The same age as Koki, with black oily hair and dark eyes and olive skin and a soft sprinkling of extra hair on her forehead and upper lip. She lies on the floor, in foetal position, knees tucked into her chest, with her eyes open.

Elenitsa walks across the room, sits down on a chair and rummages through her bag, retrieving a bottle. Amongst the chaos of stillness and fear, a gentle humming drifts soothingly around the room, soft and sweet as rosewater. She is feeding her baby while rocking him in her arms. There are other women and young girls scattered about. A middle-aged milkmaid, Costandina, sits cross-legged, staring at the stone wall, on a bed that is covered in a multicoloured handwoven blanket in the corner of the room. She still has a towel tucked into her skirt. Koki remembers her twin sons, who churned the milk to make cheese and yoghurt. Costandina would then take her donkey, fill up two baskets, tie them to the donkey's sides and go around the town to sell the produce, all the while keeping her eye out for prospective brides. Whose daughter was sweeping the veranda? Or busy making *koubebia* for lunch? Who was procrastinating beneath the shade? Koki's heart aches as she remembers her own son and a flush of tears clouds her vision.

In the other corner, Sophia, a young girl of fourteen, is looking at the ground. She had no siblings and lived with her very elderly grandfather. There are no more tears. Her eyes are dark and distant. The house is a prison now.

The forty-year-old schoolmistress, Olympia, also walks across the room without saying a word and sits upright and perfectly straight on a kitchen chair. Koki has an image of her standing with her students in church. Olympia starts praying, and a few words here and there leak from her thoughts. Her hands are clenched tightly round a gold cross that hangs from a chain, as though this is her only salvation, her only grip of hope.

Koki sees Old Maria sitting on the floor dressed in black, and remembers her running from her home with her husband and those three measly items in their hands. Maria had been scrutinising the women who entered with her beady, telescopic eyes. Maria had worn black since 1957, the year of the death of her brother,

Andreas, who was imprisoned and then killed during the anti-colonial liberation struggle, fought by EOKA fighters demanding independence and enosis with motherland Greece. He had died for his country. Maria was proud to talk of her brother's death. He was one of George Grivas' guerrillas and had fought a ten-hour battle in the Troodos Mountains near Machairas Monastery. He was forced to surrender and was captured by the British and held for months; when he died the British buried him in secure grounds so that his family could not visit his grave and he could not be worshipped as a martyr. 'What tactics! What a damned and evil ploy,' Maria had always said. 'They will do anything to wipe Cyprus clean of Greek heroes.' In 1960 she had even taken part in demonstrations protesting vigorously against British colonialism and was often the flag-bearer, holding in her large hands the Hellenic and Greek-Cypriot flags. It was true! She had become part male. She had taken her brother's patriotic nationalism after his death and nourished it with good Greek food, seasoning it with her bitter, sour Greek memory. 'Never forget' was her motto.

Maria thinks of her husband, also an EOKA fighter, a survivor, once young and fighting in those mountains.

She crosses herself and looks at the sky. 'My beloved deceased Vasos,' she says out loud. 'He said we'd go home soon!' she cries, looking around at the women in the room. 'He didn't listen to me! He said we'd be back soon!' This sorrowful howl causes the others to stare upon her with hopeless dread. Maria looks directly at Maroulla and Koki. 'This is hell!' she says, bashing her hand on the ground. Koki stares at the old lady's creased face and her liver spots and disappearing eyes. The black scarf hides her neck and rests over her shoulders on a black dress. Koki does not reply, but pulls Maroulla closer to her.

Koki leads Maroulla to an old porch chair in the living room; she sits and Maroulla kneels on the floor beside her. The others do not look up. The old lady, whose arthritic knees jolt through her dress, struggles and leans to one side. She winces from the pain, but she insists on sitting on the floor. Koki notices that her knuckles are also large and swollen.

'War is a chance for men to be both the Devil and God. To destroy and then create a new world from the chaos. Maybe the Devil was born first.' Maria looks at Koki more intently. She suddenly leans forward and spits on the ground towards her. 'Devil hair!'

she says to her and then clasps the crucifix round her neck.

Somehow, the other prisoners do not lose themselves completely either, for even in this room, close to hell, all of them, even Sophia, give Koki displeased looks as though the biggest sin still is the colour of her hair. Costandina especially throws evil looks in her direction. Her discomfort and irritation at Koki's presence is clear. Now, away from the confinement of her own home, she suddenly feels exposed. Eyes seem to dart to and fro, to and fro. There is a look of repulsion, and Olympia shakes her head. The old lady still stares at Koki, as though waiting for a reply. Koki lifts her arms, sweeps her hair away from her face and twists it self-consciously into a roll, tying it into a knot; she then rips a portion of her purple dress and uses it as a headscarf. The other women pretend not to notice. Maroulla looks up at Koki as she ties the scarf into a knot. Maria shifts uncomfortably to her side, looking away from Koki.

From the back of the garden, a soldier approaches. He is holding something else apart from his gun. As he nears it is clear that his eyes are distant and dark. He enters the living room; Koki looks only at his feet now and notices his army boots encrusted with mud. Without looking at any of the women, he places a small basket on the floor and leaves again. The women, except for the old lady, slowly unfold themselves from their positions and gather limp as linen over the basket. It contains half a loaf of bread. 'There must be more on its way,' says Costandina and reaches over to take a piece.

Litsa grabs her arm and pushes it away. 'No,' she says severely. 'What if this is all?' The other ladies look down at the measly pieces, dry and crusty.

'We've had no water or food for a day,' says Elenitsa, 'this can't be *all*.' They look into the basket. Litsa stands up and walks into the open kitchen area. She opens the fridge. Empty. And the cupboards. Empty. And puts her hand to her face in a state of desperation. Litsa then takes the basket and places it in her lap, then counts the women in the room, including herself, and divides the bread into so many pieces. The other women watch expectantly. Each waits patiently and takes a piece from the basket. Koki and Maroulla wait until the end, take their pieces and sit in the far corner. There is one piece left in the basket. Koki looks at Maria. She has not moved, and is now looking at the other women, who have eaten their pieces of bread and are still immensely unsatisfied. 'It is evil food,' says the old lady. 'It is the flesh of the Devil,' she continues, looking disgustedly at the women around her. Maroulla puts her hand on her stomach, feeling nauseous. Koki notices, and takes her hand away, winking at the little girl.

'She's mad,' Koki whispers, and Maroulla smiles doubtfully.

'*You* should eat it,' Maria says, looking in the direction of Koki, and the others turn to look at her. The old lady pushes the basket with her foot so that it slides closer to Koki. Koki does not look down, she continues to stare at Maria, who has her eyes fixed on her. 'I am offering you a gift; it would be rude not to take it.' Koki looks down at the portion of bread, secretly salivating, despite Maria's cruel intentions.

'That is your portion, not mine,' Koki says finally and pushes the basket into the middle again. Maria looks down angrily, her face red with disappointment; she cannot bear to be defeated.

'You belong with that dog,' Maria continues, as adamant as a child to have the last word. She points to the garden where the dog walks from corner to corner of the small cage, its paws scratching the ground.

One of the women sniggers, and Koki feels fury rising up within her.

Adem looks down at his shoes. He imagines the priest's footsteps in the silence of the church. A thousand-mile journey on the same stone floor. The pretence of the certainty in the click of his heels. The creak of the leather as he adjusts his posture; his collar, his hat. Adem moves his hand from his hat and tastes the sweet, bitter taste of ouzo. He looks across the falling hills as soldiers pass behind him with stretchers and guns. Adem watches their faces as they pass. He looks out beyond the houses and realises that he can just about see the jagged edges of the big Troodos Mountains, cool and grey against the blue sky. The Kyrenia range would be on the other side, bombarded with carob and orange trees, pomegranate and wild flowers, crumbling castles and mosques. Fire upon fire, destroying all. He thinks of the white Taurus Mountains, silent across the Levant, and suddenly remembers the view from his childhood window, overlooking the Golden Horn harbour that stretched from Europe to Asia. He remembers the mosques, castles, churches, palaces and towers and then that dark living room, so full of death and void of dreams, his father behind that typewriter, hiding from life in the safety of tragedy, typing those names and those eulogies. One after the other, one after the other: Akara Gokhun, Emin Haluk, Cemil Gun, Abud Ajlan, Halis Halit. His father had made their final print in their journey of life. For his father there were no journeys. He ventured only sometimes to the edge of the harbour and spoke of the palaces that dazzled in the sun as though they were imprinted on pages in an old book. He lived in the shadows, existed only in that unknown space between this world and the next. The space where one's name is crossed off the list. People feared him; believed him to be Azrael, the Angel of Death, the last to die, recording and erasing constantly in a large book the names of men at birth and death. The neighbours would whisper about him at the harbour, in the town stores, even outside the mosque, they would have conversations about whether he would rip their soul out or separate it like a drop of water dripping from a glass. His father, on some rare occasion, when he left that room and encountered such stupidity, would argue that the Angel of Death has four faces and four thousand wings, and his whole body consists of eyes and tongues of the number of people inhabiting the earth.

Adem, as a child, had itchy feet. He was so frightened of being sucked up by that dark room, lost in
those rows and rows of names and faces and eyes and
tongues that he became the errand boy, running from
house to house, along those smoky, gridlocked streets
of Istanbul, sewing mats, selling tobacco, polishing
shoes. He avoided telling people his name, he was
known as the son of Death, and after his father died
they called him nothing, out of respect; they usually
grunted at him, or whistled as though he were a dog.
Sometimes he would run to the harbour, toss his shoes
off and dip his feet into the water of the Golden Horn,
elated at the thought that he was somehow touching
two continents.

When his father's name, Halim Berker, was the first
on some other poor sod's list, his mother died shortly
after and Adem decided to leave. To put on his father's
shoes and take them across the Levant to that little
island his father had so admired from a distance. The
island that also bore mosques and churches side by side
on what seemed to be two mountain ranges, one
smaller than the other. Well, he did it, he came to
Cyprus. But, as fate would have it, he had somehow
turned into his father, living in that hut, afraid to go

out, terrified of making his own journeys, of finding his own paths. Adem looks down at his shoes. What has become of him, of his life, of his dreams? He thinks about the mistakes of his life and the person he could have been.

Adem looks around at the other soldiers and wonders about their families back in Turkey: their wives, their children, their parents waiting for them anxiously. It becomes increasingly apparent that Engin has not been among them. He fingers the photograph in his pocket. He longs to tell Engin, to have someone to talk to. He remembers Engin's nervous twitching. He grabs one of the soldier's arms as they pass. The soldier looks down at his arm and up into Adem's eyes.

'Engin Bulut?' he says, but the soldier shakes his head and continues. He tries a few more times but the response is the same. Until, finally, he reaches one soldier, the small man who had stood beside Serkan, who hesitates, looks at Adem's bottle of ouzo, looks over his shoulder and says, 'I will tell you for the ouzo.' Adem nods and follows.

They walk round the church and through the graveyard. The man in front limps slightly and does not look back. His shoulders are square and his left side slopes a little to the ground, making his left arm seem longer. The pace of his footsteps is steady, giving no indication to where they are going. There is no real urgency to his movements and no uncertainty.

They reach a wooden gate. The soldier in front lifts the latch and opens it. It creaks slightly. There is no one around. The cicadas buzz in nearby trees. A bird rustles above. The air is white with jasmine and yellow with citrus and the blue sky pokes through the leaves. They climb down five steps, deeper beneath the cool arch of the trees, and walk across a small sloping orchard until they reach a wooden basement door. The other soldier turns to him for the first time. 'It leads to the storage room beneath the church. It was built at the end of the orchard for convenience. The priest liked fruit. Grapes especially. Like the kings of the past.' The soldier smiles.

He opens the door, opens his palm and signals for Adem to descend first. The darkness is sharp and sudden, and from it emanates a peculiar smell. Soft and thick and sweet. As nauseating as rotten figs.

Adem enters the darkness, right foot first, lowering himself into a corridor. The sound of his shoes hitting the ground bounces off the walls. The song of the cricket stops here. Time is silent. The air is static; there is no marching or beating, just a soothing, soft silence. A drop of water suddenly drips from the curved roof. The other soldier enters. His boots echo differently as he jumps into the corridor. In the darkness he casually rummages on the floor, looking for something. Then the flick of a match is heard and a candle is lit. It is quite a short candle; it has been lit many times before.

The candle creates a ball of light in which they walk. Adem looks at the crevices in the walls and tries to ignore the smell. Stronger than rotting chickens. Decaying rats? Yes, that's it. Or maybe not, the smell is too immense to be rats. The smell swells in the thick air and he struggles not to put a hand to his stomach and lean forward and vomit onto the priest's shoes.

The corridor widens and becomes a room. The smell is thicker than smoke. It strangles the air. The soldier now in front lowers the candle. The shape of a small mount emerges in the darkness. Rubbish? A face. An arm. The gold glimmer of a button. The gleam of shoes. Discarded corpses of neighbours. But above and between, the murky green of Turkish uniforms. 'Soldiers,' Adem says, and his voice is thrown back to him in the form of an echo, as a question this time. He looks at the legs and army boots tangled in a web, the soft petal-white of open eyes, the nameless bodies discarded in a heap.

'Sour grapes,' the soldier says. Adem swallows hard. Acid rises to the back of his throat.

The soldier opens his hand again; the lines on his palm are like paths in the candlelight. Blood moves through a vein. It whispers as the river does. Adem hears it, swirling in his ears.

'Be my guest,' the soldier says. He smiles and hands him the candle. Adem takes it reluctantly. He hesitates and bends down. His trouser legs rise and the priest's shoes glimmer in the light. He shuffles closer to the bodies.

Adem moves the flame over still faces. Their features stony and unmoving; grotesque chimeras on a hidden wall. The light drifts across the figures, unreal and grey in the shadows. Eventually Adem sees Engin's face staring up at him. 'What have you done to him?' Adem calls and his voice bounces off the walls of the basement. He stands and walks closer to the other soldier. 'How did this happen?' he says, quieter now, but the soldier stares at him silently. Adem is enraged, he gnashes his teeth and clenches his jaw. His hands tighten into fists. He looks at the pathetic little man and stares at his stupid eyes. Bitter tears sting the back of Adem's eyes and he holds his breath. He looks back at the pile of bodies. 'Engin,' he whispers, shaking his head. Adem kneels down again and looks at his friend closely. His arms and legs free of anxiety now. He leans forward and closes Engin's eyes, then he looks again at the soldier, who is standing in darkness behind him. 'Serkan is killing his own people?' he asks.

'He is getting rid of the ones that don't belong here. If our army is to be strong we need to get rid of the weak ones,' the soldier says definitely. 'They were useless traitors. A hindrance, we could hardly even call them men.'

Adem stands up and moves right up to the soldier's face. His hand twitches. He could kill him, he could strangle him right here and now in this dark basement, to get rid of the real scum of this earth. Adem looks into his fear-stricken eyes in the candlelight and backs away. He straightens his jacket and his trouser legs so that they fall neatly over the shoes. He hands the candle to the soldier. It lights up his face. The soldier stares at Adem and then coughs and looks at his jacket pocket.

'You promised me something,' he says. Infuriated, Adem grabs the bottle and shoves it into the soldier's hand. The soldier smells it, smiles and gargles the whole lot down to the last drop, then he smacks his lips.

Serkan sits alone on a throne in the abandoned church. He has bolted the door. The icons on the wooden stands have been removed so that the step onto the aisle seems bare and lacks the warmth of the Virgin Mother and Child. There are no candles or shrines or books, he has taken them all away. On the floor is a bucket of blood and a wet cloth. The grandeur of the walls has been washed away with a coat of this blood, and now the church stands, merely a house, robbed of its memories. From the mere darkness of the blood, the sudden poverty of images and impoverishment of life and stories, the church stands as if without walls, and Serkan sits as if in some Protestant nightmare; but in fact with no religion at all, although he will still not drink the wine in the bottle beside him.

He cannot hear the outside world. Not the crickets or the marching or the bombs or the rolling sea. He can only hear the ticking of clocks. Thirteen, fourteen, fifteen small clocks and pocket watches; each from a different house, all in the church now, ticking manically, frantically, hastily. He had taken one with each victory, snatched it from the mantelpiece or from the pocket or wrist of a dead man and carried it back to the barracks as an emblem of his continuing life. Now tick-tocking, tock-ticking. Mockingly chattering constantly; filling the church with a stagnant sense of time. And motionless. Motionless. Motionless it spins. And these mechanical beings, with round faces that create a string of regularity across the town, now beating together, show the real chaos beneath. As if there is no time. Or that time does not exist. And these clocks beat the air as the crickets do, and thrash the silence, as the waves do, and in amongst all the noise, somehow create peace. As the war does. He cannot smile. He is immovable now. His arms and legs are heavy rocks. He looks at the hands of the clocks moving.

And copious are those black waves of time. In that dark space. Deep as light. Time rises and falls. Rises up as heavy as heat and falls as light as rain so that the mind and the stomach cannot help but do the same. In this turmoil, this is the place where the soul can get lost, where one is fool enough, or human enough to think that it is in fact time that is rising and falling.

He stands up. The clocks capture him and force him to be still. The tick-tocking calls at him and freezes time and life so that through the window the waves in the distance are still and sculpted from ice and the boats hang frozen above, like sparkling ornaments with unmoving crystal sails, and the sky is made of glass and around him the heat hardens into small shimmering droplets. And the outside world has been stained onto this window and frozen still to compensate for the walls inside. And if he moved, but just an inch, this world would break into clear blue shards of sky and sea and heat.

A drop of sweat forms on his forehead and slides down his cheek. He clenches his jaw and grinds his teeth. There is a knock at the door that resonates and echoes through the church. Hesitates for a moment and walks down the aisle. He stops in the middle of the aisle and twists his belt to make sure it is straight. He touches his collar and puts one hand in his pocket so that his jacket lifts slightly in a relaxed manner. He continues to walk and opens the door in that stance, but his shoulders drop when he sees who it is. A soldier enters and heads down the aisle; there is an air of overfamiliarity in the way he enters and a distinct lack of the fear that grips the other soldiers. 'We have another witness to the dead in the basement. If that doesn't knock them into shape, nothing will.' The soldier looks for a moment at the bloodstained walls, but does not mention it. He is not surprised by it. He lifts his longer arm up to his smooth face and holds his chin. He takes a breath and looks out of the window at the swaying sea. 'We'll run out of men if we continue this way,' he stammers very slightly, but covers it with a cough. 'Apparently, other groups have succeeded without taking such measures, maybe we—'

'Enough,' says Serkan, 'this is my herd and I have enough experience to know how to discipline my men. To steer them in the right direction. Didn't Aba teach you enough?'

'Dad was a shepherd, you are a commanding officer.'

'Yet somehow, Hasad, we followed the same path,' replies Serkan.

Hasad taps his foot on the stone floor, adding an extra rhythm to the beating of the clocks. From the top corner of his mind a flock of sheep descend like white birds and fill up the blackness with an immense white glow. He holds his temples and shakes his head to dispel the image. From the altar he picks up a pocket watch, holds it in the palm of his hand and looks at the time; the dial glimmers in the sunlight. He then turns it over, winds it, attaches the chain to his jacket and slides the watch into his pocket.

'Maybe you should have stayed home, your back is fragile, Mum was right.' Hasad looks at the bucket and nods.

'But even if we get rid of them all, they won't disappear,' he persists. 'They will live on here, even without these walls.'

'The Turks deserve—' begins Serkan.

'Look,' Hasad intercepts, 'it'll be dark soon and I've got things to do.' He winks reassuringly at him and walks back down the aisle, leaving his brother to slump back into the throne.

Paniko comes out of the kitchen; he has finished cleaning for the afternoon. 'Ena café?' he asks Richard, and Richard nods. Paniko disappears into the kitchen again and appears a few minutes later with two coffees and a fresh bowl of crushed green olives and a plate of *koubes*. Paniko puts them on the table, takes off his apron and tosses it onto the back of another chair. Richard takes a cigarette from the packet on the table, strikes a match, lights it, waits for the smoke to engulf him and lifts the steaming coffee. He smells it first, then sips the golden *kaimaki*, the bitter froth that gives it that golden-brown colour. Paniko looks at him. The coffee beneath is smooth and thick and sweet. Richard puts the cup back into the saucer, drags hard on his cigarette, flicks the ash into the ashtray onto a picture of Cyprus and takes an olive from the bowl. Outside, the drizzle has turned into a heavy rain. Above an off-licence, a red light flashes expectantly, but the streets are quieter now, only an old Englishman stands at the bus stop opposite beneath a black umbrella.

'So you liked Marianna,' Paniko says, pointing at the plate of *koubes* on the table indicating for his friend to eat, but Richard raises his hand, gesturing no. They sit like this for a while as Paniko squeezes lemon juice into the mincemeat filling of his *koubes*, eating and drinking coffee almost simultaneously. He finishes his coffee and slumps into his chair with his arms crossed.

Richard leans over towards Paniko's side of the table and touches his coffee cup. Paniko is not sure what Richard is doing but watches intently as Richard lifts it, takes the saucer and places it, overturned, onto the top of the cup. Holding both tightly together, Richard with one fluid movement, overturns them and places them neatly back on the table. 'What are you doing?' says Paniko, disbelievingly. Richard ignores him, rotates the cup three times and stares out of the window. They sit like this for a few minutes and Richard lifts up Paniko's cup. The sound of the saucer breaks the silence when it unglues from the rim, making Paniko jump by its mesmerising and familiar sound. Richard brings it closer to his face and peers in. Paniko smiles bemusedly. 'Since you been back you have been the driest man I ever meet.'

Richard looks seriously at Paniko, but Paniko forces a smile again and bites another chunk of a *kouba*. Richard ignores his reaction and continues, 'Tasseography has been practised for centuries, not just by the Greeks.'

'Eh, who did you learn from?' says Paniko, in an arrogant voice.

'A Greek,' says Richard, frustrated that his answer has given Paniko a smug smile. Richard is not going to let Greek megalomania ruin what he has been trying to say. 'I couldn't stop thinking about Marianna. Her spirit, beauty and passion had captured me beyond comprehension.

'One night she was gone. She totally disappeared. I was so desperate to find her. I don't know what I was expecting. I didn't care, I just had to see her. I'd walk around day and night, anywhere where I thought she might be, but nothing. I even asked your grandmother and she told me that she had not seen her or her mother. So I went to see Kyria Amalia, a fortune teller that I had met at the festival,' continues Richard, as Paniko raises his eyebrows. 'Don't patronise me. I don't even know why I went. It smelt of chickens and coffee and she led me through her living room into the back garden where we sat beneath the lemon tree. She left me there while she went inside to make the coffee and a few minutes later I watched her walking slowly to me with the coffee trembling in her hand. She placed it in front of me, sat down and watched me intently while I drank it. We sat in silence for a while.' Paniko shakes his head slightly, but Richard takes no notice. 'And a little bit of something else, a bit of the sea had entered my blood. Every aspect of it, including its madness, or magic, or whatever you like to call it.'

Paniko takes a cigarette from the box and lights it. Richard's eyes look heavy now, full of unshed memories. Richard pauses, contemplates and sips his coffee. 'When I finished the coffee, Amalia ordered, with the flick of her hand, for me to turn the cup upside-down and spin it three times, clockwise, in the saucer.' At this, Richard throws back the rest of his coffee and then performs the action with his own cup and saucer. 'And then she watched me in silence for what seemed like a very long time and when she was ready, and no moment sooner, Amalia read my life in this cup.' Richard stops there, and Paniko represses a frown, stubbing his cigarette into the ash-tray and resting his chin on his hand. Richard rubs his own hands as if he is washing them slowly and looks momentarily out of the window. The rain is now heavier and a grey loom falls into the café like a shadow. 'She looked into the cup then into my eyes and back into the cup. She tipped the cup into various angles, pointing into it and muttering to herself. She then told me that I was to meet a beautiful woman with dark hair and that I would live in the shadow of a big clock, and that I was a soldier. Even though I wasn't wearing my uniform that day I had heard enough, this old bag wasn't going to insult my intel-ligence. I stood up, reaching into my pocket to leave her an undeserved tip. But then she stretched out that bony hand of hers and . . .' Richard paused again. When he continued, his voice had a heavier tone as though he were reciting an old poem. 'She told me, like the witches in *Macbeth* or the ghost that visited Ebenezer Scrooge, to wait for three events. One would be a wedding. Not mine. The second, a baby with hair of fire. The third, a visit from an unexpected stranger.' Richard looks down at his hands, then ashamedly up at Paniko. He has not spoken this much for ten years and now he sounds like a Dickens' character.

'I can't believe you went to a fortune teller . . . you!' Paniko says mockingly.

'I know what you're thinking,' Richard continues, 'but the first two things happened just like she said. Listen. I left her house that day, walked back to my bedsit and then fell asleep.

'The following night I was invited to your grand-mother's house, I remember it well: you were roasting peanuts on the barbecue and your dad was drinking whisky with a few friends. One of them was Marianna's father, and he announced that Marianna had gone to meet the man she was going to marry – a man called Mihalis from Limassol. She had travelled with her mum and they were going to stay at a relative's together for a fortnight so that they could meet his family. Everyone was so happy. They kissed and slapped him on the back. I could not move, I just stared at them, every emotion completely ripped out of my body. No one even noticed. I don't think he would have wanted an Englishman congratulating him anyway.'

'And . . .' says Paniko, 'people got married all the time . . . so she guess a wedding . . . I hope you no pay her too much. You are so stupid to believe a crazy woman! What did you expect, you were going to marry Marianna and have lots of children? You are lucky she even looked at you. And luckier no one else saw her looking at you!' Paniko says in a harsh voice. 'If this the root of your depression then I should jump off the top of Mbik Mben with the amount of women I see, fall in love with and not have.'

Richard cannot bring himself to tell Paniko about that night of the feast or even more the night after the festival when they made love.

'Look, I've been trying to talk all day and all you do is either interrupt me or mock me,' Richard snaps, and Paniko is taken aback. Richard has never spoken to Paniko this way, and he sits back, folds his arms once again and listens.

'I can't explain right now, I just . . .' Richard trails off. Paniko holds back the urge to speak and just listens.

'What could I do but wait? For those two weeks I watched every minute tick by, waiting for Marianna to come back so that I could see her, talk to her. I just needed to see her. So I went back to Amalia. I just needed a distraction, or perhaps my utter impatience led me to search for answers anywhere I could. I remember there were lots of cats and one of them even looked like . . . the rat . . . doesn't matter.' Richard shakes his head and then rotates Paniko's coffee cup around in one hand while looking inside.

'When I returned to her I felt obliged to take her a gift, just as I'd seen other people doing. Cyprus had really dug its claws into me.' Richard looks scathingly at Paniko, who is now wiping his lips with a white handkerchief. 'So I turned up at the old woman's house with the only thing I had to offer: a can of baked beans. They were Heinz as well. The old lady inspected the can, walked into the kitchen, opened it, and stuffed a spoonful into her mouth. I watched her patiently, half-expecting her to throw them in my face. She chewed slowly, narrowed her eyes, swallowed, closed her eyes completely, remained seriously still and suddenly smiled broadly with raised eyebrows. "Fasolia!" she declared. She slapped my back, laughed heartily and shook her head. "Fasolia, fasolia, fasolia. Rrready food!" she laughed again. "And all this time I slave at the stove. So, you really *are* hero. It is true what they say!" Then her face changed and she looked down at the beans. "What you want?" she asked suspiciously, squinting her eyes. "British never bring gifts. Gypsies, yes. Turks, yes, shepherds, yes. Sometimes even the Egyptians, although they bring strange gifts. But British, never." She looked at me as if she were about to take my brains out and eat them. I stepped back. This was clearly the wrong thing to do and seemed immediately to intensify her suspicions. She grabbed a wooden spoon from the counter and held it threateningly up to my face. And honestly I thought this was how I'm going to die: killed by a crazed old lady with a wooden spoon! Somehow she'll find a way to kill me with it. They'll find me on the floor. I pointed at the cup on the counter. I told her I wanted her to teach me, trying to sound as sincere as I could. The spoon lowered. I told her I wanted to learn how to read coffee cups, the future, the past, the present. She lowered the spoon even more, her face softened, and once again her mood changed like the wind. She giggled, strangely like a young girl, whacked my shoulder, laughed louder and led me out into the garden, nodding her head.

'She pulled a chair from beneath the little white table and signalled for me to sit down as if I were now an important guest. She then stood behind me and pushed me in, straightened my shoulders and checked my legs. After all these peculiar actions, she stood opposite and stared at me, beaming. Honestly, I didn't know how to get out of it. So I just sat there, like a lemon, pale-faced, probably, and waited to see what was going to happen. I tell you, I regretted taking those beans.

'"Now," she said, "if you going to learn, we do properly. You must here once every day." I tried to protest, but she squinted her eyes and I nodded obediently. When she was satisfied she disappeared into the kitchen and returned, a while later, this time with *two* cups of coffee.

'Sitting beneath that lemon tree, we both sipped the coffee slowly, avoiding each other's gaze. When we were done she turned the coffees over and her teaching began. At first I listened reluctantly, peeking glances at my watch as the time ticked away. I had learnt already that it was Greek nature to be anxious about the future; you loved frightening or reassuring yourselves with exaggerated predictions about your lives and the state of affairs. But my feeble attempt to hold onto that last thread of the imperialist ideal, to stand up high and look at the sun shining down on Cyprus, a great testament to a great empire, had been shattered. As much as I tried to hold onto that elevated state and belief that the Cypriots were evolutionarily stunted, as much as I wanted to be that British cynic that my grandfather had encouraged me to be for fear that the great British Empire would die completely, as much as I tried to remain arrogantly detached, my convictions of grandeur, if they even existed in my own mind at all, had become so elusive that somehow the island and Marianna had touched that hidden part of me that still wanted to dream and overreact.

'It was the smell of the sickly lemon blossoms and the way they fell like snow in that heat and the prolific, heavy manner in which Amalia spoke, the twisted knuckles of her hand and the knotted bark of that old tree. It distorted my mind. You and the slow coffee-drinking and the fumes of ouzo and the inflated lack of social etiquette and the embellished hospitality, it was too much for a superior, haughty, insignificant man such as I. It engulfed me, and every day I found myself sitting at this little white table and with a daily dose of caffeine; I was immersed in a world of grand symbols and little problems. How the lion meant strength for the old and weak, and the seahorse was good news for the wishful dreamer, and the Devil a sign to relax for the tense and anxious. She would insist that the eyes told as much as the cup.

'She believed that each person's soul affects the shapes that are formed by the grains, and over these few weeks I witnessed people from round the corner and from down the road, all seeking answers in the residue of their coffee. And it was there, right there, that I saw what all colonialists, holding onto a concept of grandness and superiority, miss: I saw what was within the water-coloured houses on the hills, I saw the worms before the silk and the ones that writhed in figs, I saw the grey stones in the grey lentils, the flint inside pockets and between toes, I saw the ants beneath the stones, the darkness beneath a priest's robe, the shadows a mosquito makes. Every time I would look into the cup, I would see images that would remind me of Marianna. Amalia would tell me not to be looking for what I wanted to see, but acknowledge what I didn't want to see; but every day my mind would be engulfed with the images and memories of her.'

Richard pauses and looks at Paniko as though he has only just become acutely aware of his presence, and Paniko looks at Richard as though he has just seen a ghost. Paniko breaks the silence by coughing loudly into his handkerchief. 'When words are scarce, hide it with a cough.' Richard recites an old Greek proverb, but this seems to make Paniko's face turn paler. He stares at his fingers now. There is a look of shame in the way his lips are pursed tightly, a look of nostalgia in his eyes and the twitch of fear and anxiety in his fingers. Richard looks into Paniko's cup. 'There is definitely a devil in yours,' says Richard, and this time it is his turn to laugh.

'Does it have the face of my wife?' asks Paniko disparagingly.

Richard smiles sympathetically and takes the last *kouba* from the table. His shoulders have softened slightly, but his eyes blaze with memories; they are somewhat blind to his present surroundings.

'And what was I seeking from the symbols that lingered in corners and beneath mattresses of other people's homes? What was I looking for in those black grains? Something of my fiery, lively mother who had died when I was young and left me with a column-like patriotic colonel for a father? Did I seek to find her in the mysterious creases of the island or was this just a sob story? Was I holding onto something else? I searched unceasingly for that indifferent man that had sat having a lunchbreak by the magenta flowers, before your grandmother and the goats and Marianna had rocked the foundations of my world. I clung onto the apathetic lump I thought my heart was, but it was no use. The little red-soiled island and the beautiful woman with black hair had won my heart and I was nothing but a sad lonely man looking through the window of what could have been his life.

'Two weeks had passed: I woke up in the morning and there was a knock at my door. Marianna stood there awkwardly, and I tried to pat down my hair as inconspicuously as I could. She would not have noticed anyway. Her disposition was uneasy. Her shoulders were tense, her eyes fixed anxiously onto mine, and she rubbed her middle fingers compulsively. I moved closer to her, as I wanted to kiss her, but she took a step back. "I pregnant," she said.

'I backed away, moving to the veranda. She followed me.

'We stood there for a long time looking at the hills while she rubbed her fingers. It was a hot day, full of flies and mosquitoes and dust. She neurotically scratched her arm and then her leg. I turned away and brought her a glass of water, which she drank immediately. Handing me the empty glass, she continued to look at the hills and rub and scratch. At this point I dared to look at her, and I leant forward and put my hand on her shoulder. This infuriated her and she turned away from me and looked over the balcony. I decided to give her some time, so I went inside and busied myself by the bed. She stayed there alone for some time while I dressed. I put on my uniform slowly and purposefully, straightened the collar, combed my hair and stood there, even in all that heat, with a reverential air.

'Finally she came in, stood beside the bed and looked at me. "I love you," I said, and she took a step closer to me, she had been crying and there was something in her eyes as she looked at me, a sadness, as though, perhaps, she looked out at a life she could never have. "Marry me," I said. She leant in, kissed me and looked searchingly into my eyes, and then she stepped back and straightened her dress as if trying to compose herself.

'"I am married next week. Name Mihalis. You leave alone. Always. It must be so." Her eyes were fiery and frantic, they shivered and her lip quivered.

'"No, Marianna, I can't do that." I came closer to her, but she stepped back again and the look in her eyes scared me; I had never seen her look so afraid.

'"If you love me you must go, get out of this town." I didn't say a word. She wanted me out of her life completely. "Please," she said, "please, if you stay my life will be ruined."

'And at those words I nodded in agreement. It wasn't easy for me; she clutched her fingers tightly and I noticed the thin, gold engagement band on her fourth finger. "You have my word," I said, and she frowned and tapped her foot nervously on the floor. She took a deep breath, turned her back on me, sighed and then walked reluctantly to the door. I, on the contrary, followed her resolutely and opened the door in a gentlemanly manner. How stupid I was. I let her go and I would never speak to her again.'

Paniko opens his mouth in shock, but does not say a word.

'I have a daughter,' says Richard. His delicate English accent pirouettes quietly amongst this intermittent silence. The words have finally escaped the prison of his mouth where they had been locked all this time. Paniko moves his lips, but again says nothing. 'An Englishman with a Greek daughter.' Paniko looks down at the table. He brings his hands up to his cheeks, looks up at the ceiling, holds his head and looks back at Richard. He clasps his hand across his mouth, he closes his eyes and nods and then he nods again. He looks at Richard as though he no longer sees a friend, but just an Englishman who doesn't belong.

Richard does not say a word, gets up from the table and paces up and down, round the tables, looking sometimes at the ceiling and sometimes at the floor. Time passes in this way and the room darkens as the rain falls more heavily outside. Buses pass, people walk by, the red light flickers. Richard paces as though he were walking the streets of time. His eyes dart this way and that. The world of the past unfolds in front of him, the faces, the smiles, the gestures, the words, the seasons . . . he walks as the rain outside subsides and umbrellas close and a streak of sunlight shines on the shop, filling it with a golden light. Raindrops slide down the window.

Richard sits once again and stares at Paniko. Outside a rainbow forms in purple clouds. Richard's hands shake.

'I couldn't tell anyone, I couldn't bring myself to tell you because the truth is, when it comes down to it, I am English . . . but I loved her, Paniko.' Richard closes his eyes for a moment and allows the past to open up in front of him. He looks down at his fingers. Paniko's eyes close slightly and shimmer, watery in the grey light from the window. Richard stops and looks at his old friend. Paniko suddenly seems much older. The laughter lines round his mouth, that so characterise him, have sunken into his chin, a thin layer of blue stubble and the cigarette smoke fogs his washed-out face. His eyes are weary and float like shattered boats on grey shadows.

Paniko involuntarily looks up at Richard's grey hair. Richard is tired now. He pats down his hair with his right hand and then looks down at the cup and saucer. The door opens and the sound of London bursts through the door with a cold breeze. An old man enters, brushing rain off his shoulders with his palm and saluting Paniko. He sits on the table nearest to the counter. Paniko stands up, throws his apron on over his head, greets the man warmly and takes his order. The man stands up again, takes off his jacket, shakes the rain off, hangs it on his chair and sits down again, flicking worry beads beneath the table.

As the day dies the room darkens and cools, and the ladies breathe and sigh, rock and cry. There is nothing to dream of any more, nothing to plan, nothing to hope for. The photographs on the mantelpiece, though of strangers, tell the story of a different time; now each woman sits in silence, with her flowery dress, as a headstone of a dead family, and together, as a painting of a destroyed community, separated from those structures of their life that once made the world what it was. Their fingers twitch for the food they would have made and the tapestries they would have sewn; for the joy of a brimming table; and their mouths move involuntarily for the words they would have said on a normal day. The quiet in the room is deep and disturbing and the crickets cannot reply with human voices to desperate demands to come and eat or have a bath. Their spirits move in a different place, insistent on carrying out their normal tasks.

Maroulla sits by the door, with the book open in

her palms. She is looking out at the brambles on the ground. She is the only one left with a dream. She notices the gold thorns and the way the branches dip in and out of one another like tiny paths. She looks far ahead and wonders where it reaches; she imagines following it, tracing it at first with her finger until it opens out into a wide road and then climbs singularly to the top of a hill where that rose grows sparkly and red. She imagines holding it in her hands and gaining her long-awaited prize.

After a while she looks back into the room. Koki is still on the chair, looking at the floor. Litsa is rocking on the edge of the bed. Maria is on the floor, muttering beneath her breath. Costandina has moved as far away from Koki as she can without leaving the room. Sophia stares ahead, her eyes wide and glazed. Outside, just by the door, the dog is still whimpering and scratching the cage with its paws. Maroulla stands up. Some of the women look at her. She walks out of the back door and stands by the cage for a moment while the women stiffen and stare. A noise is heard behind the trees, and Koki stands up. 'Maroulla,' she says, but Maroulla does not seem to notice any of this; she lifts the latch of the cage, opens the door and takes a step back, waiting for the dog to exit. At first it sniffs the air, lifts its brown ears slightly and stretches its emaciated legs, and then walks out and looks at the women in the living room. Its tail suddenly rises and it runs inside towards the old lady on the floor, licking the front of her face. Maria splutters and curses. 'Vermin! Vermin! Away!' she calls, wiping her mouth with her sleeve and kicking the dog as much as she possibly can with her arthritic legs, but her cries produce the counter-effect. The old lady's screaming is probably taken by the dog to be excitement, so it rests its front paws on her shoulders and licks her face. Fourteen-year-old Sophia suddenly laughs out loud and the rest of the women follow. Soon the women are holding their stomachs while the old lady flashes her knickers and stockings in a futile attempt to be rid of the big rat. Soon the dog is bored with her and prances round the room, pleased with itself, while the women and girls stroke it as it passes.

Maroulla walks to the centre of the room, takes the piece of bread that the old lady has left and gives it to the dog. It laps it up quickly and then rests on a rug with its head on its paws. Maroulla and Sophia sit on the floor beside it, and the other women are silent now, but differently this time, for somehow this dog has knocked down the walls between them, and now there are looks of recognition and some sit closer to each other rather than completely alone. Although Maria is now even more intent on sitting on her own and grunts lightly every so often.

The night deepens now and the only light comes from orange lamp flames burning like fireflies at the back of the garden. Outside, crickets chant and bombs fall. 'It is a dark night,' says Olympia, 'there are no stars.' Nobody replies, but a few of the women nod. From the distance a soldier approaches, holding a lamp in one hand and what appears to be a bucket in the other. He holds the lamp high so that only his face is illuminated and in that immense darkness it hovers towards them like a face in a dream. When he enters the living room some women stare at him like desperate children and others look at the floor. Maroulla continues to stroke the dog. The soldier shoots a look at her and grunts, then places the bucket on the floor. He stands for a moment and looks around, eyeing the women intently. Koki looks at his army boots, encrusted with mud, and then up at his badges lined meticulously along his breast, and realises that he must be the soldier in command. His feet shuffle. The lamp on his right reveals a drop of sweat on his forehead. He walks round the room slowly looking at each of the women one by one. In the silence, the dust beneath his feet crunches with each footstep. He seems dissatisfied until he reaches the mother with the child. Elenitsa looks up at him and smothers the baby with her embrace. Her cheeks are red and perfectly round. The rip in her dress reveals the slight curve of her breast. He bends down, puts the lamp on the floor and opens his arms towards her child. Elenitsa pulls the baby closer. Her eyes are wide now and full of unshed tears. He says something in Turkish. 'No!' she replies and her protest makes his face redden and his eyes widen. He brings his arm back for a moment, removes his gun from his belt and then swings it onto her face.

She cries out in pain. Her head drops backwards and her eyes roll inwards and at that point the officer takes the baby from her arms. Blood drips from her face.

The baby's shrill cries fill the night, louder than the crickets and the bombs. Elenitsa has dropped to the floor on her knees and is crying with her arms outstretched. The officer ignores this. He holds the little boy in his arms and rocks him gently from side to side until the baby's crying turns to a whimper and he sleeps once more, soundly, in his antagonist's arms. The officer looks down at the boy strangely. In the shadows the sharp corners of his eyes and mouth appear to have softened somehow, he then lifts his free arm and touches the boy's fingers. And there, as he stands and rocks and sighs, for a moment, is no more perfect a picture of a broken world than this. And there can be no greater reflection of that than this portrait that the women glare upon with so much confusion. 'Virgin Mary, bring down your hand and save this child,' whispers Olympia as the soldier turns to look at her.

He walks towards her. Stops for a heartbeat and holds the baby out for her to take. Olympia pauses doubtfully, looks at the other women, hesitantly opens up her arms and the officer hands the baby to her carefully. Olympia brings the baby protectively to her chest. Elenitsa collapses on the floor in tears, and the room is filled with quiet sighs of relief.

The soldier smiles. He walks towards the crying mother, cleaves her from the ground and pulls her out of the house and into the darkness and fireflies and soldiers, beyond.

Everyone remains still for a moment until Sophia

stands and rushes to the door. 'Where have they taken her?' She looks back at petrified faces. 'What will they do to her?' She erupts into sobs and her crying swells in the room, blazing, and spreading a sense of terror, like a fire. They are all ensnared by it, confined by these flames that seethe around the furniture, touching their limbs and their faces, illuminating the fear in their eyes. With Elenitsa's baby in her arms, Olympia stands up and touches Sophia's shoulder. 'Come and sit down,' she says, masking her own terror with her sympathetic but firm classroom voice, 'sit down with me and she will be back soon.' Everybody watches as Sophia's tears subside and she looks around with uncertainty, searching the others' faces. Maria looks down; in her old age she has seen far too much pain to have such faith. Everyone else watches Sophia as she finally follows Olympia and sits beside her and holds her hand. The baby is asleep and his soft breathing is soothing. Koki wonders what this little boy dreams amongst this chaos, what he will grow up to become; like a god of Ancient Greece he has been nurtured with both milk and fire. Perhaps he will develop wings and save them, or he will grow strong and take them in a golden chariot to the sky. The baby gurgles and his eyes open ever so slightly, and then he is asleep again. Sophia touches his fingers.

They remain like this for a while; each of them in their own world, listening to the sound of the crickets. Suddenly, from beyond the garden, there is a loud scream, and the women lower their faces to the ground, unable to look at one another. Maroulla is now lying on the floor with her head on Koki's lap; she lifts her head and looks fearfully towards the door. The baby wriggles in Olympia's arms and whimpers, twisting from left to right; there is a look of anguish on his face. From the distance another scream can be heard: the piercing and unforgettable sound of agony and torment. It slices through the darkness like a spear and stabs each of them with terrifying thoughts. There is another scream. Olympia rocks the baby and sings a lullaby that her mother used to sing to her:

'Nani, nani, my child.
Come, sleep, make it sleep
And sweetly lull it.
Come sleep from the vineyards,
Take my child from my hands.'

In the background another scream is heard, but Olympia attempts to continue singing, 'Take it to the sheepcote'. Her voice trembles slightly, and, noticing this, Costandina joins in, helping her along, followed shortly by Koki, Maria, Sophia and Maroulla. Together their voices are strong enough to rise above the screams; a sugary, sweet melody wells up inside this room.

'To sleep like a little lamb,
To sleep like a little lamb,
And to wake up like a little goat.
Nani, nani my child.
Come, sleep, make it sleep
And sweetly lull it.'

The baby gurgles, rests his head on Olympia's breast and falls asleep. No one says a word, and the sound of the crickets pounds in the air. There is the sound of rustling and footsteps and they all look towards the back of the garden, holding their breath. Elenitsa emerges, hardly standing, stumbling, falling, pushing off the ground with her arms. Everyone stands suddenly and rushes to her aid; Costandina and Koki hold her beneath the arms, and Sophia runs into the house with Olympia to get water and fetch a blanket.

Tucked into the pavements and shivering lights of Soho, the café windows steam with coffees, and now and then customers stream onto the puddly streets and walk away, leaving behind them, like snails, a trail of nostalgia. Richard has been waiting for Paniko all evening. He has not moved from the little white table where he has been sitting since the morning, and the two cups are still overturned. The rest of the tables are full of men playing cards. The man in the brown suit from that morning, seated at the adjacent table, with his back to Richard, leans on his chair, with a cigarette hanging from his mouth; the ash hangs, long and grey, as he stares thoughtfully at the ten cards in his hands. Richard does not have to try to look over his shoulder. Three consecutive hearts. A six of clubs. Three nines and three queens. Almost a full hand. Richard is pleased with himself at having remembered ten-card rummy, or *kounka*, as the old men of the town used to call it. The man taps his foot lightly on the floor as the other three players take their turn. The old man opposite him takes his time; he looks at his cards purposefully and then at the other players. He pulls his moustache contemplatively, and then touches the top of a card. He changes his mind and leaves his fingers hovering over the top of another card.

'Come on, Yiakovos! Pingo's seeds will be full-grown children by the time you play your hand,' says the man in the brown suit.

'Shut up, Nikos!' says Yiakovos. 'I need time.'

Nikos becomes impatient and taps his foot faster. Yiakovos takes no notice. He looks down at his cards with a serious face. His fingers hover now over the top of another card. He frowns slightly and then resignedly takes the first card and tosses it onto the table. '*Assiktir,*' Yiakovos proclaims, and his shoulders slump like a disappointed child.

It is finally Nikos' turn. He remains still for a moment, then, taking the cigarette from his mouth, he looks each man in the eyes, leans slowly over to the pile of cards in the centre of the table and picks up the queen of diamonds that Yiakovos just threw down. '*Kounka!*' he declares, placing his sets down neatly on the chequered tablecloth. The three other men lean forward and look at his cards.

'The donkey!' shouts Yiakovos. 'All you touch turns to gold!'

Nikos stands now proudly with his hands in his pockets. Yiakovos smashes a fist on the table. Nikos smiles. 'A lucky person plants pebbles and harvests potatoes,' he says, looking down at his cards.

'Paa!' exclaims Yiakovos. 'You planted pebbles and harvested a factory, a wife, a mistress and plenty of the queen's heads!' He bashes his fist on the table again. 'While I plant my own bollocks and out pop peanuts!'

Yiakovos takes his coffee and slumps into his shoulders. 'I should just refuse my wages from now on. What's the point in pocketing them if I am going to just give them back to you?' The man next to him, who has not spoken yet, nods agreeably. Yiakovos shakes his head in resignation; he is the eldest at the table and looks as though time has scratched and battered him, and torn out his hair, leaving him with only a few mocking strands. His skin hangs loose on him like an oversized hand-me-down and the skin beneath his neck wobbles.

'Another game, boys?' Nikos says.

The men nod and Nikos raises his hand to Paniko. 'Bring these men a glass of ouzo on me, to drown their sorrows.'

The other men groan and Nikos deals the cards.

Watching these men play evokes a memory for Richard: of sitting in the café at the harbour, looking at the boats coming in and out and at the men on the table beside him playing cards. At first he had felt like an outsider. He remembers this feeling now, sitting in Paniko's café, watching Nikos and Yiakovos arguing.

Soon Paniko returns with the drinks and slices of melon. Richard, sitting nearby, raises his hand and indicates to Paniko that he would like the same. Paniko nods and disappears again into the kitchen. A few men in the far corner, near the window, argue loudly about war and speak of death and atrocity.

A man sitting on a table nearest the counter slides his chair backwards and reaches over to where a radio is located on the shelf behind him. He turns up the volume and orders everyone to be quiet, holding up his palm. The news starts and finishes, but there is no mention of Cyprus. The men all sit perched on their seats, frozen still with cards in their hands and cups at their lips. There are many groans and sighs, and arguments begin from every corner of the room about solutions and outcomes. 'Danger can only be overcome with more danger,' calls the man near the radio. Many nod and continue to sip their coffee or ouzo. 'Grivas is to blame for all this, damn it! Overthrowing the government, starting a coup, provoking the Turks!' calls a very young-looking man in a business suit.

'You are merely twenty,' calls the thin man near Richard's table. 'What do you know about war and peace?'

'I know that peace never comes from war,' the young man replies.

'He lives in cuckoo land,' shouts the other old man, 'a cat in gloves never catches the mice! We do not need romantics, we need fighters. What has happened to the young generation? They have become lambs. The wolves will tear their smooth skin to shreds and leave their guts for the flies. They will make shreds of their fluffy white paperwork that they hide behind.'

Paniko appears now with a tray in his hand. 'Enough, otherwise you'll all be sent to your wives.' A few of the men sit down resentfully, and Paniko stares threateningly at the ones still standing. Eventually they give up and return to their drinks. The young man does not resume the game at his own table, but takes his jacket and coffee, looks around and then hesitantly decides to join Richard. These Greeks never ask, Richard thinks, remembering Paniko's poor manners.

They assume all is for the taking. He watches the young man sit down and peek curious looks at Richard over his coffee cup.

'I guess you're not in the rag trade then,' the young man enquires in a cockney accent that falls almost ridiculously out of his strong, Mediterranean, mythical jaw.

'I couldn't be,' replies Richard, 'I'm one of *them*.' The young man nods and sips his coffee again. Richard's Englishness forming a barrier between them already.

After a while the young man takes his jacket and leaves, and soon the other men follow his lead and stumble onto the pavements, steaming up the cold streets with the warm smell of aniseed and tobacco. As they speak they blow white puffs of the past into the black night. Richard watches them as they disappear along Old Compton Street, all except the man in the brown suit, who waits beneath the canopy of the grocer, looks right, then left, makes sure the streets are empty and then knocks on the door beneath the flashing red light. The door cracks open and he is quickly ushered in.

For a while Richard sits quietly while Paniko rattles cups in the kitchen. After some time Paniko appears with a plate of *koubes* in one hand, wearily lifting the apron over his head with the other, dashing it onto the counter and sinking into the chair opposite Richard. He puts the *koubes* into the centre of the table next to the overturned coffee cups. The rain outside has stopped and a somnolent wind blows beneath the door. Paniko's lids hang heavy over his eyes, but he heaves himself to sit straight, bite into a *kouba* and look thoughtfully at his old friend. 'See,' he starts the conversation with a full mouth, 'our lives aren't that different. You eat and shit alone and today I done neither.'

Richard smiles. He lights a cigarette and passes one to Paniko.

'So, that's why you left,' says Paniko, nodding slowly.

'What other choice did I have? I didn't want to cause her pain and I couldn't stand to be there while she married another man. I asked to be transferred to Akrotiri on the south coast of the island, an area which the British air force used. I had to get as far away as I could, for my own sanity. I had to get away from Marianna.

'I lived there for eight years and in those years I changed. I was consumed with sadness and isolated myself completely. I preferred to be alone and think about Marianna and the child I had never met. I felt as though I had been left out of my own life. I lost my love of food and conversation and I hid away, working solidly and returning to my room alone each night. During those eight years my hair turned grey and my cheeks became sallow and gaunt. I could see it when I looked in the mirror each day; I hardly recognised myself. The loneliness, the sleepless nights, where I lay awake, hour upon hour, thinking, had stolen my youth.

'In 1952 I received a letter from you, saying that you were moving to London, times were bad and you told me to come with you, we could have feasts again and parties and talk about the days when we drank and danced. You told me you had, finally, found a wife and were planning to make a new life out there, perhaps in the rag trade, or the catering business, and that now you would always have clean shirts. You said there was nothing left for you here, the taxes were even higher and the agricultural industry was economically unstable. You said that you would make a good life for yourself. I wrote back to you, if you remember, and told you that I had to stay, there were still a few things

I needed to do. But the truth is I was lost and a prisoner of my own devices.

'Then one day in 1955 I was transferred back to Kyrenia. Time had passed and much had changed in those short years. I arrived in May, just a month after the bombing of Government House. The EOKA riots had started: the Greek nationalists were determined to get the British out and attain enosis with Greece. There were riots in the streets and curfews; Cyprus was not the place it used to be. I was quite isolated in Akrotiri, so when I returned to Kyrenia I was not really expecting what I found. The streets were seething with rage that marked the walls in the form of red graffiti. I remember the day I arrived, walking by the strip of cafés in my uniform, with my suitcase in my hand. People looked up with narrow eyes as I passed. Animosity breathed in the silence, in the way their chins lowered and their backs stiffened. Nobody knew who I was. I was a different man and their hearts had changed. I was the enemy now. I was the obstacle to independence. Even children looked down when I passed and if I happened to catch a glimpse of their eyes I could see, somehow, the fire burning within their minds. And as I walked I realised that this flame was alight everywhere: behind every window, in each flick of the rosary beads, in every candle, in every hymn, in every bell that tolled across the town; every man, woman and child carried the flame of Ancient Greece as though with every step they took they were ready to fight like Alexander the Great. I walked along the port as though I was an intruder and as I looked at those familiar boats and longed to put my feet in the water again, I knew for sure that life would never be the same.

'I remember on my first day I was invited to Mr Kitchen's, an elderly officer, for an afternoon drink; his house a whitewashed meringue just off the sloping foothill west of the Kyrenia range, overlooking the sea line that swept elegantly to the right. All was pristine: the marble interior and marble conversations, the tailored gardens and tailored attire, the delicate finger food and delicate mannerisms. I remember Mr Kitchen leaning proudly on the balcony, a soft breeze in his toupee, conversing with Mr Smith, Mr Blackburn over a glass of wine. The women by the palm tree, dressed in hazy florals, complained about their peasant housekeepers and compared regional origins for suit-ability. "I have one that comes from Man-dres, I find them somewhat man-ly," said Mrs Kitchen.

'"Yes, and the ones from Limassol are far too cosmopolitan for my liking," replied Mrs Smith. They would not talk about the fear and the uncertainty and the hatred that jumped out at them round every bend. They never mentioned the campaign, led by General Grivas, or "the one who could not be taken" as the Greeks called him, this fight for freedom or power that would glow by torchlight and never slept; and, just then, in the daylight, as I peered down onto the expanse of land I could see that the battle had left sections of land blackened, like the footsteps of small gods or large generals. At that moment a breeze brought with it the smell of desiccated sewers, wafting over wild flowers. All simultaneously ignored it and sipped their wine.

'When I left I realised that I had not spoken a word, except to say that the finger food was delectable, though it was not. I strolled along the foothills for a while and looked down at the carob trees that webbed across the town below and then descended and walked amongst them until that smell of semen which emanated from them got too much. I realized then how much I missed the life that I had had, so I continued walking, spiralling through the neighbourhoods like an unwanted snake, listening to the conversations on the verandas.

It was late afternoon and people were venturing out after their siestas. Nobody called to me, nobody welcomed me into their home as they used to do, they only looked at me sideways and then resumed their snacks or their conversations. One child even threw a stone at me.

'I remembered how the Turks and the Greeks and the British had once lived together, like the trees on the hills. Apart from the divided cafés, they actually lived peacefully; their mosques and their churches side by side; their priests and imams walking along the same foothills. Greek- and Turkish-Cypriot workers even took part in universal trade union struggles. It was only since the Greeks demanded union with Greece and freedom from colonial rule that their lives had become divided. I tried to repress a feeling of shame. The Turkish Cypriots were the object of incessant endeavours at manipulation. Our aim was to use them as an instrument against the Greeks. The British lured Turkey into its dispute with the Greeks in an attempt to dilute the threat: it was much easier to maintain power if the dispute was more complicated. Everyone was at war! The Turks wanted division; they thought that this was the only way they could secure the rights to the island.

They believed that *enosis* with Greece would be an impingement for them. The long path towards the invasion had begun.

'I looked at the path ahead and the houses that tingled with laughter and knew that the walls behind the blossoming gardens were blemished, and that somewhere, even inside the houses, stewed the dichotomy of intolerance; and that here, amongst the olive trees that lined the street, the cicadas muttered the true story.

'I continued towards the harbour, walking past the carob warehouses, the cafés and the supermarket as the fishermen drew in their nets. People were busy about their business here and did not seem to notice me. I couldn't help looking through the crowd for Marianna; I thought I might catch a glimpse of her walking. I remember seeing a dark-haired woman, facing away from me, talking to an elderly lady, and my heart came into my mouth. When she turned around I saw that it was not her and suddenly I could see her everywhere: I thought she was the woman standing by the café, or the one sitting by the harbour, or the one holding a small boy by the hand. I had only been in Kyrenia a short while and already Marianna had managed to crawl into my mind and take it over. That old familiar sense of longing came back to me and captured me.

'People walked with baskets of fruit or carts of wheat, women sold doilies and beautiful tapestries, children ran around with catapults or skidded down the slopes on bicycles. Boys chased lizards and three girls skipped past with rag dolls made from old tea towels. I looked across at the castle and its beautiful towers that marked the entrance of the harbour. For a moment I felt elated, I caught a glimpse of the old life, the Cyprus I had known and loved so well, and for a while I walked contentedly, feeling the last rays of the afternoon sun on my face. I lit a cigarette and walked through the crowd of people, taking in the smells and the colours and the musical sound of their words. And just then, I saw something that I was not expecting. Walking through the crowd with a loaf of bread in her hands was a girl with hair of fire.

'She walked alone and skipped on every other step. I dodged through the crowd to keep sight of her as she passed the other children quietly and made her way beyond the port. When she came to a clearing I stayed further back so that she would not see me. I followed her past the cornfield and up a crooked path that led to a taverna in the foothills. I watched from afar as she ran through the gate and handed the bread to a man and then skipped towards a lemon tree, where she sat down and took some marbles out of her pocket.

'I left before I could be seen and made my way briskly to Amalia's house by the church. It had been eight years and I had no idea if the old woman was still alive. My nerves were aflame, I walked fast across the town and took a short cut through the cotton-field, so by the time I got there I was red and flustered and out of breath. I tried to compose myself and knocked on the door. I heard some movement inside and waited for what felt like five minutes before the door opened. Amalia looked straight up at me and didn't say a word; she held a walking stick and had become so badly hunched that her neck dipped down then up, like a vulture's. "Who is it?" she screeched in Greek, and when I looked into her eyes I realised that she could not see me; the brown of her eyes had now become a misty blue.

"It's Richard," I said quickly. She took a step forward and a look of recognition swept across her face. She suddenly became very animated, her eyes lit up and she lifted her free arm to touch me.

"Richard, oh, Richard," she exclaimed. And I stepped forward so that she could touch me. She passed her hand over my chest and onto my face. "Hah! Richard! Richard!" and she chuckled. But there was something else in her voice, sadness? Regret? Nostalgia? I was right to have picked up on it as her following words were, "Where have you been, my son? The light has gone from my eyes and this town!" and then she cried. The tears came from deep within her, and she reached out and grabbed my arm. "Come, come in!" she said, turning away from me now. I followed her to the kitchen, where she made me a coffee; she knew by heart where everything was, and then she told me to carry the cups outside to the table beneath the tree. "You will have to read your own cup," she chuckled.

"'Amalia, who is the girl with red hair?" I asked, holding my breath, waiting for the answer. And she laughed again.

"'You know who is already," she said. "She your daughter!"

'I put my face in my hands and sat there for a while, finally building up the courage to ask the next question. "Marianna?" and then Amalia's face dropped, and she shook her head.

'"She dead, Richard, she poison by snake." At this my heart came into my throat. The name Marianna seemed to echo around me. I felt as though the darkness of the evening had mounted in on me, I began to sweat and loosened my collar and tried desperately to compose myself.

'"Dear God," I said, and reached out instinctively and held onto Amalia's hand. She must have felt my pain for she held it just as my own mother once had when I was a little boy. She held it tightly and then reached over with her other hand and placed it on top so that my hand was nestled between the soft skin of her palms. I did not move, I allowed my shoulders to relax and, in the safety of her hands, my life flashed before my eyes. Her hands were warm and enveloped my sadness. The more the years of loneliness seared through my veins, the warmer her hands seemed to become. And she allowed me to sit there like that while the evening fell upon the town and my life.

'The next day I went back to the taverna and took a seat at one of the tables that overlooked the hills. I noticed a few men on other tables looking up from their newspapers or conversations; one man even threw some change on the table and left the taverna.

The man behind the bar watched him leave and came to me with his pad. He smiled at me, which I was not expecting, and spoke to me warmly. "Anger make people react in many way," he said, and then welcomed me and told me that his name was Mihalis and that he was the owner of the taverna and that he welcomed all guests. I thanked him for his kindness and ordered a drink, at which point I must have looked over at where the girl sat beneath the tree. He followed my gaze, and I looked back at him and told him quickly that I wanted a warm Zivania and a bowl of nuts.'

The rain starts again and another red bus rumbles past. Richard looks out of the window; across the street the man in the brown suit has just stepped out onto the pavement, he sneaks a look around, walks with his head bent past two shopfronts, then shakes his shoulders, takes the self-aggrandising stance of a successful businessman and walks off.

'His wife thinks he works late every night,' says Paniko. 'My wife thinks I don't.' Richard takes the box of cigarettes from the table and offers one to Paniko. Paniko shakes his head.

Adem lies on his back on the floor of a deserted house. He is not on night attack tonight. This is the first time he has lain down in four days. The priest's shoes are by his side. He can smell the leather. When he closes his eyes he sees Engin's grey face and open eyes. He cannot sleep. There are other soldiers in the house, all sleeping soundly. The dissonance of snoring and deep breathing and the crickets is unbearable. He stares out of the open window at the sky. The night is thick. There are no stars tonight. Adem holds the little red Bible in his left hand that is straight by his side. He fingers the leather and the embossed letters on the front. He feels the edge and tries to imagine what lies within these thin pages. He brings the book up and rests it on his chest. The smell of dusty corners and candlewax drifts to his nose. It feels as though he is holding the Qu'ran.

All he wants is a chance to continue his search, but the small house is brimming with sleeping soldiers. If he moves someone could wake up. Just then there is a noise from the room on the left. A soldier emerges like a shadow in the night. From the type of soft noise, Adem imagines that his arm is raised and that he is rubbing his eyes. Possibly a nostalgic image of peaceful nights in another place. The soldier steps lightly, barefoot on the white flagstones, and reaches the kitchen. He fumbles around and uses the grey square of light from the window as a dim guide. Adem hears water poured and drunk, and then the soldier makes his way back. A few other soldiers move a little, and one soldier suddenly jumps mechanically and shouts 'Stop or I'll shoot!' Most of the snoring stops abruptly. One soldier laughs, and the walking soldier, who has now stopped in his tracks, says, 'It's just me, Asad, go back to sleep.' There is some shuffling and mumbling, but no one says anything, and a few moments later the snoring resumes and Adem is left to look at the square of charcoal sky.

He imagines her again as she was then. First he sees white fingers and a round shoulder. Then, that red hair in flames about her collarbone. Then, those invisible lashes and mirror-like eyes that always reflected the world in a peculiar blue haze, distorted by what lay within. Then he hears that locked-away laugh, and words and thoughts that were hidden from the rest. He remembers the ridicule and the name-calling and that stone body they had created. The dry eyes and stiff walk.

One of the soldiers to his right mumbles something about eggs in his sleep. Adem feels irritated. He feels trapped. He looks again at the square of sky and decides that his next step will be to search the houses of prisoners. He knows there are definitely three, all guarded by soldiers. He will be on guard tomorrow night. He will find her. And just then, with the smell of dust and candles and leather and the coal-like darkness and the never-ending chattering of the crickets and the snoring, he drifts off to sleep, to the world of darkness and fireflies and soldiers, beyond.

Day 3: 22 July 1974

It is early afternoon, the next day, and Koki and Maroulla sit side by side on two chairs in the garden of the prisoners' house with trays on their laps; they are picking small stones out of some lentils that Olympia found in the larder. Suddenly moving across the garden is a chicken followed briskly by Maria. She has decided that today they will eat their own food; they will not touch the scum that the soldiers bring. The chicken flaps hysterically as Maria rocks from one foot to the other and moves, if one were to remember her arthritis, at an unnaturally high speed. But she has strong lungs and a strong heart and better still, a strong will, which she will insist are all on account of the olive oil and lentils and black-eyed beans and raw onions and good chunks of white bread. She has the shoulders of a bull and certainly the bloody-mindedness, as her husband would have said. In her old age Maria had actually become even more bull-like, as the neighbours agreed. Her shoulders had broadened, her moustache had deepened, and as the children of the town insisted, the hairs on her chin had lengthened. It was true. She could kill animals with her bare hands, and not just chickens or rabbits, which was common amongst some of the older women, but rams and cows and pigs and even snakes. She owned a gun, for the most challenging animals. Maria lifts her dress and her knees higher and stomps around the garden. Maroulla giggles at how funny this old lady looks, and Koki nudges her gently.

In a few seconds Maria captures the chicken so that it flaps manically in her tight grip and she walks to the front end of the garden where she has already laid out, on a garden table, a tray, a towel and a knife. 'Well, you're a chunky one, aren't you?' she speaks to the chicken. 'They must have fed you well. Now you'll feed us well.' She cracks a smile, bends down, breaks the chicken's neck and then rips off its head. Then she releases it and allows it to flap in a frantic frenzy until it finally subsides to the ground and twitches slightly. Blood has splattered on her arms and she wipes them with the towel from the table.

Sophia is on a small stool collecting lemons from the tree at the front of the garden. The dog watches her with its head on its paws. Once Sophia's apron is full, she secures it under her arm and climbs down from the stool and goes into the house. The dog follows lugubriously. The house is cool and grey compared to the garden that glows yellow with sunlight. Elenitsa can no longer hold her child. She lies in the bed, on her back, with her eyes half shut. Olympia sits beside her, with the little boy in her left arm and a damp cloth in her right hand, which she uses to dab Elenitsa's forehead. The room is consumed with a pungent smell of sharp alcohol. There is a bottle of pure spirit on the floor which Olympia has used to clean cuts and gashes on Elenitsa's face and arms and some on the delicate skin on the inside of her thigh. Elenitsa has endured the pain without crying and has not spoken a word since stumbling back through the garden late the previous night. Now the room is quiet; only a cockroach scuttles in from the heat and stops by the chair where Sophia sits peeling the figs. From the porch doors the song of the cicadas bursts in with the immense light. The bed is on the other side of the room, embalmed in silvery shade. Olympia bends a little to her right and dips the cloth into a bucket of water by her side. The excess water drips back into the bucket and the sound trickles gently round the room like a cool river. 'Thank God and the saints that we have this,' says Olympia, looking up at the ceiling, as though she expects to see them there. They are lucky to have a well at the bottom of the garden, which Maria had discovered last night. 'This we can have!' she had said. 'It is a gift from God.'

Maria comes in from the garden holding the dead chicken by the feet. She finds a large bowl in one of the kitchen cupboards and sits on the table to pluck it. She instructs Sophia and Maroulla to collect branches and old twigs. Sophia leads Maroulla out and they walk about within the confines of the garden, filling their aprons with twigs and their arms with larger branches. When they have collected enough they put them all in two large piles where Maria lights two fires. Maroulla and Sophia then sit on the floor and play with marbles, while the dog lies beside them, watching, and, every so often, looking towards the back of the garden, sniffing the air.

Having searched Elenitsa's bag, Costandina heats up two large pans of water and, before doing anything else, she sterilises the baby's bottle in one and then mixes the powder with some water to make the milk. She takes the bottle to Olympia, who feeds the baby, and then returns to the fire and puts the chicken in one pan and the lentils in the other. On the floor, with her knees bent to the side, Maria sits protectively next to the chicken, flicking the firewood with a long stick. Costandina mixes the lentils. As the day dies, the prisoners become engrossed in preparing the meal and they perform each task with the soft touch of familiarity; they mix the lentils, find vegetables in the garden, add lemon and rosemary to the chicken and with trays on their laps and knives in their hands, they chop and dice, cut and slice. They sit on chairs around the garden, doing the things they have always done; and perhaps it is at this time, these moments when the world spins back to a near-normality, that the emptiness appears in its truest form.

Soon the only light comes from those crackling flames, and into the house drifts the smell of wood and smoke and home-cooked food. Elenitsa has fallen asleep, and the baby is now tucked safely in a bundle of quilts in a wicker basket that was probably used to collect fruit.

When the meal is ready Olympia takes the basket with the baby and reluctantly leaves Elenitsa sleeping on the bed as everybody gathers round the fire. They sit in a circle and pass around their plates. Maria distributes the chicken evenly and whispers a prayer before they eat. They all bend their heads and thank God for the food they have before them. Suddenly a hot breeze blows and the fire crackles and rises. Orange light moves across their faces. Koki's headscarf is unable to contain her curls any longer, and as another red wind blows it flies off before she can lift her hand to secure it. Her hair explodes into the dark night, surging luminously about her. Costandina stares at her fearfully. 'God is telling us that red devils do not deserve to be fed,' she says, hardly audible against the wind. The others look up. Koki feels their eyes burning on her face; that menacing look of hatred she had become so accustomed to, a look so full of ignorance and fear. Koki's anger flows in her veins with her blood, but this time she does not reach up to hold down her hair, she simply sits there staring at the fire ahead. She is expressionless with her porcelain-doll-like face, but in her glassy eyes, there is a glint of something wild. The others stare upon her, transfixed, frozen, stone-like, as though they have set their eyes on the face of Medusa. Maroulla looks around, and then jumps up and walks about the garden. She finds the headscarf flapping on a bush. She returns it to Koki. Koki looks up at the little girl's warm eyes and takes the scarf.

'The food is getting cold,' Koki says in a cool voice, and the others immediately pick up their knives and forks and begin to eat without looking up again.

Once they have eaten, the women clear up and sit inside watching the fire that still flickers outside. Now that the expectation of the meal is over they are even more aware of the soldiers' blinking lanterns at the back of the long garden.

'They haven't brought us bread tonight,' says Litsa.

'They probably smelt the chicken,' replies Olympia.

'The barbarians would kill us just to get the chicken from inside our gut,' says Maria, passionately, removing a piece of chicken from her back tooth and wiping it on her skirt. Sophia's eyes widen with fear and for a moment she stops stroking the dog.

'Is the dog Greek or Turkish?' she asks.

'Well, it—' begins Koki.

'Turkish,' interrupts Olympia quickly. 'All dogs are Turkish and all cats are Greek. Dogs eat cats,' she concludes, and immediately Sophia stops stroking the dog.

'What do they teach you at school?' Olympia stares at Sophia, and Sophia timidly shrugs her shoulders and then says the word 'enosis'. In the far corner, Litsa sighs irritably, but covers it with a cough. Olympia raises her eyebrows approvingly. 'And Koutalianos, the Captain of Saint George, and Dighenis the hero and the EOKA leaflets, and Gregoris Afxentiou, who sacrificed his life like Jesus . . . and Kolokotronis who fought for the Greek war of independence against the Ottoman Empire,' Sophia adds with an air of certainty, boasting her knowledge with a stretched neck and straight back as though she were in class. Sophia waits for the schoolmistress's approval. Olympia nods. She is pleased.

'Our heritage is Hellenic,' Olympia adds. Costandina, who is sitting beside her, nods incessantly. Olympia looks specifically now at Sophia and then at Maroulla. She instinctively avoids Koki. She continues, 'A child belongs in its mother's arms.' She looks momentarily at the sleeping baby and then at Elenitsa. 'Safe from intruders and danger and false love.' The other women, even in the dark, instinctively follow her gaze. There is another long silence, when the dog whimpers slightly and rubs its head on Sophia's knee, but the girl pushes it with her elbow.

'When I was a teenager,' continued Olympia, 'I learnt that we had two enemies. The British colonialists, who would not give us independence,' she pauses, while Maria nods her head agreeably and grunts, 'and the Turks, who wanted to divide our fragile island, who wanted, from then, to cut us in two.'

Koki shifts uncomfortably in her chair. This time, some of them look at her. She feels compelled to remain silent. Litsa, who is plaiting her own hair into pigtails, suddenly leaves one undone and stands up. She paces around the room, and then stops by Olympia.

'Why?' she asks. Olympia looks up at her in the darkness with a confused look. 'Why did they demand partition?' persists Litsa, and looks down at Olympia. There is a long silence. Olympia cannot answer; the breadth of her knowledge is restricted. There is something about the question which makes the humidity in the room seem thicker.

'It is not a question of why,' says Olympia, this time with a change of tone; a slight tremor in her cricket song. A miss-beat in the heart of her convictions.

'Of course, it doesn't matter,' mutters Litsa. Olympia nods, but she is pressing her body uncomfortably into the back of the chair so that she is as far away from Litsa as physically possible without having to shift the chair or stand up.

Koki looks at the gold cross between Olympia's fingertips, reflecting the firelight. It glows as though it is burning. Koki puts her hand to her chest. She begins to feel the anger again. That scalding, disconcerted, variable anger. Who could she hate? What side of the line was she on? She feels split; caught on barbed wire. Unwhole. For falling in love with the enemy and giving birth to a hybrid, as the neighbours would have said. She thinks about her life since; the abuse and violence and hatred from her own people. She is the Whore of Babylon, adorned in purple and red, with a gold cup in her hand filled to the brim with the filth of her ways. She is the mother of the abominations of the earth. She gave birth to the Antichrist. Suddenly her complexes force her to tie the headscarf tighter round her head. She reaches behind for the knot, unties it and fumbles nervously to fix it. Her hair slithers through. Pokes out for some air. Strangely, like snakes' tongues. Silent though. And desperate.

Maroulla notices, runs towards her, stands behind her, takes the two purple ends in her own fingers, ties them safely and pushes the stray hairs into the sides. Maroulla sits beside her. Koki looks at the little girl, feels the warmth of her thigh near her own, but cannot reach out to touch her for fear that she may be cold. Unreal. There were too many years of hatred to believe in anything.

From the distance, a trembling light moves closer to the living room. The women remain still. Nobody speaks. A soldier approaches and, as he enters the house and his army boots crunch on the ground, it is clear that he is not holding a basket of bread. He has a lantern and a gun and has obviously come for a different purpose. His badges glint in the light of the lantern. It is the commanding officer. He looks at the faces of the prisoners, one by one, with his head held high. His right foot moves forward, towards Olympia. Every small sound is amplified in that silent room and the prisoners hang their heads and peek at him fearfully from the corners of their eyes. He looks down at the floor where the baby sleeps in the basket. He walks forward, crouches down, looks into the basket and whispers words in Turkish. The prisoners sit rigid and tense, fear swelling inside them. Olympia raises her arm towards the basket, but the commander grabs it with one swift move and twists it so that her body bends and coils. He looks into her eyes threateningly and then releases her arm with a violent push. She holds her arm, but her mouth is straight, her face unreadable.

The commander looks into the basket one more time, then he gently lifts it and, trying not to wake the baby, walks out of the room.

Adem offers to take the bread to the prisoners. In the distance, and close by, bombs stamp about the island. He stands beside a lamp that is hanging from a tree and looks across a garden into a house where a group of women are held captive. Apart from the fruit on the trees, the bread would be all they have to eat, there are no chickens in this garden and he is sure that the soldiers have cleared out the cupboards. Two other soldiers guard the back of the house and he knows that there is one at the front. The soldier standing beside him hands him the tray expectantly. Adem takes it and hesitates. Kyriaki is either already dead, a prisoner in one of these houses or else she has somehow managed to escape. Adem looks across the expanse of garden.

He unhooks the lamp from the tree and walks along the edge of the garden that is skirted by orange and carob trees. He holds the lamp low so that his face cannot be seen.

The garden falls downwards into the house like a dry river into a waterless sea. It is not a humid night and there is no air. He wonders if he should have insisted on bringing a jug of water as there does not seem to be a well in these grounds. As he approaches a familiar stench fills the air. Nauseating and heavy. He remembers at once Engin's face and those dark eyes. Those dark, open eyes. He stops when he reaches the open doorway of the house and holds up the lamp. He becomes aware of a set of eyes staring at him, shielded behind a shawl, and shifts his own face so that his features sink beneath the shadow of his cap.

The smell is overpowering now, and there seems to be a heap on the floor, covered neatly with a blanket. He moves the light over it and sees the contours of a body beneath the white lamplit sheet. He moves away from the body and places the basket of bread on the floor. None of the women move. Their eyes remain still and white in the darkness, like stars. Not too far away a bomb explodes and the floor trembles, then three other bombs explode in succession, further away, probably towards Nicosia.

Adem walks around the room, using the lamp to search the women's faces. The first woman, sitting near the body, hugging her knees, has hair darker than the night. The second, who lies behind the first with her ear to the ground, is not much older than seventeen. Next to her a young girl buries her face in her mother's lap. Next to them is an old lady, twisted and gnarled like an ancient olive tree. Adem lifts the lamp higher: black hair, in plaits or ringlets or matted over shoulders, fills the room, like the heat. He takes a deep breath, lifting his chest heavily. The bombs beat like his heart. 'Kyriaki,' he says, but nobody answers. He holds the lamp higher, and his hand shakes. The light filling the room from his lantern strobes over the faces of the women, from face to face, never touching the same one twice. He grips the iron handle tighter, but the light now wavers and everything before him seems to be shrouded in a layer of sea. The air becomes thicker. He struggles to take a deep breath. The bombs beat again . . . or is that the crickets? Time is loud. It stamps amongst those living with the feet of the dead. Adem uses his free hand to wipe the sweat from his forehead.

He then presses his temples together and brings his palm down over his eyes, nose and mouth as if trying to wipe off his features.

He breathes in, but his chest is tight. 'Is there a lady here called Kyriaki?' Adem says in Greek. His voice breaks the incessant beating of bombs and hearts and crickets. A few of the women look up at him, but say nothing. 'You may know her as Koki.' A woman on a chair coughs, and this is followed by the muttering of the crickets and another explosion. His shoulders slump and his chin drops slightly.

He moves with the lamplight through three other rooms, all filled with darkness and that inimitable smell of death. He is amazed by their silence. The women do not speak or cry in his presence, even the children seem to comply. He notices how the women force themselves to sit a little straighter as he passes. The immense dryness in the air is engulfing, like a sandstorm, and the women's limbs intertwined in those small rooms are like the dust roads; those almost-there paths in the seams of Kyrenia that would appear to lead one to a different place each time. Like the elusive string of a memory.

A bomb falls nearby. The crickets pound. The air is

stagnant. He takes another deep breath and proceeds to follow the path of limbs to the door, but stops when he reaches the body beneath the sheet. 'What are the chances?' he thinks, but he cannot leave until he knows for sure. He pauses for a beat. He bends down and holds the lamp over the thin sheet so that the colours of flesh and clothes wash through it. He reaches over to the edge near the face, holds his breath and lifts the sheet. The eyes are closed, the lips parted, the skin drawn and old. White hair rests on the white sheet. Adem breathes out. He covers the face with the sheet and stands up. His hand shakes uncontrollably now, and the light rocks on waves of darkness. He turns to face the garden and walks back beneath the orange and carob trees, feeling the outside air on his face, cool now compared to the dense smells and heat of that house.

As he reaches the back of the garden he notices two silhouettes; one tall and straight, the other smaller and hunched. As he moves closer he sees that it is Serkan and the soldier from the church with the long arm. They are talking passionately. He can hear them muttering amongst the trees like the crickets. Adem nods at them and hangs the lamp back on the tree.

'You didn't bring a woman out for us,' calls Serkan after him, disguising his question as a comment. Adem does not answer. The man beside Serkan laughs. 'I remember young Serkan, of twelve or thirteen, forcing me to take the sesame fingers from the tray while Mrs Theodoulou slept on a chair beneath a tree. With a naked pot belly poking over his shorts and a mud grin on his face, Serkan would say, "C'mon, idiot, I'm hungry, drag your bent self over there and bring some back for us. She's sleeping, she'll never know."' The man laughs again and slaps Serkan on his back. Strangely, Serkan does not respond. Instead he looks down at a basket on the floor.

Day 4: 23 July 1974

In the early hours of the morning, in that short slice of time where everything is completely silent, Serkan sits beneath a tree at the base with a baby in his arms. He picks up the bottle that he had taken and attempts to feed the baby, but the baby turns his face the other way. It is at that very moment, between darkness and light, when the sun is but a golden outline across the landscape, that the whole island is still. It stops for a moment, as brief as the gap between heartbeats or the pause between the ticking of a clock. For this short time even the crickets seem to sleep and the sea breathes in, away from the shore, slow and heavy and languid. It is 23 July and it is the beginning of a ceasefire. By the end of the day yesterday, a bridgehead had been created between Kyrenia and Geunyeli. It was now fully controlled by Lieutenant General Nurettin Ersin.

Today Turkish forces had initiated their attack on Nicosia International Airport. Serkan had sent two M47 tanks into the attack with the Turkish armoured force, moving through roads along the Kyrenia–Agyrta–Nicosia bridgehead. Now they had been ordered to stop fighting. How long could that last? He never liked waiting. Never could stand intervals. He wanted things to be done there and then.

Serkan sits, somewhat restless without the bombs. He remembers a particular time as a boy when he would wake in the middle of the night, tiptoe past his parents' room and round the edge of the field, avoiding the sheep that hovered like clouds in the darkness. He would sit on a tree stump in his make-believe home, a circle of sticks and stones, and wait for that moment of silence when, for a brief moment, the flapping wings of time would embrace him and hold him in the night. Nobody knew of his secret nocturnal escapades until the morning his father had woken to find three of his sheep dead. They had been poisoned, he was sure. Who was the perpetrator? The Greeks, surely! That day Mohammed had paced up and down, sneaking looks into Mrs Theodoulou's home. At that time, years before they left for Turkey, they were unfor-

tunate enough to live in Lapathos, Famagusta, in a
Greek-Cypriot neighbourhood. His father insisted that
times were not as they used to be and that now the
damned Greeks would do anything to get them out.
He watched her every free hour of the day: while Mrs
Theodoulou hung the clothes on the line to dry, while
she sat in the shade and cleaned grain in a large tray,
while she chopped onions and dried her eyes, while
she wiped her hands on her apron and sat down for a
little siesta. He watched even while her husband came
home for lunch with his spectacles on his head and
new leather shoes in his hand. Pavlos Theodoulou had
made all kinds of things out of leather: from shoes, to
purses, to bags, he had even made Serkan a catapult
once, which he had kept hidden from his father for years.
'I'll rip the skin off his back and make myself some nice
boots,' Mohammed had said before sitting down to lunch
that day. 'If I catch who did this, I will—'

'Sshh,' his wife said, offering him a tray of bread.

Mohammed stood up, raising a hand to her face.
'Keep your mouth shut. I am the shepherd of the house.
Without me, you would not have this bread to put in
your mouth. Never shush me!' His mother had flinched
and withered and hunched deep into her shoulders.

Then they ate in silence. This was a different type of hush, though, full of tension and expectation and fear. It was not like the silence of dawn, where there was nothing to fear but the beating of the world again.

That night, while Serkan tiptoed past the sheep as usual, someone grabbed his wrist viciously from the shadows and brought the boy close to his face. Serkan could feel warm breath on his cheek as nails dug into his hand. 'So it is *you*!' his father's voice bellowed in the night, breaking the buzzing of the crickets. 'You are the perpetrator!' he whispered vehemently, with clenched teeth, bringing Serkan closer to him, his arms strong, his body firm. Serkan tried to protest, but his father pushed him to the ground, into the thorn bushes and jutting stones. His father's foot crunched by his side as he stepped nearer to him. 'All this time I was looking for an enemy outside of my own home and all this time it was you!' He spat onto Serkan's face, kicked him in the head and left him there, with the crickets pounding in his ears.

Serkan could not move. He stayed there until he finally fell asleep, and when he woke again it was morning and the August sun had burnt the side of his face. Or was it a bruise that now throbbed? He scrambled up and dragged his feet into the house. His mother said nothing about the incident, she simply said that she was pregnant, and that he would have another brother or sister, and Serkan had somehow felt sad about this. Since that day he never woke in the middle of the night again.

Serkan looks down at the baby in his arms. He sleeps peacefully. The sun has risen now, the crickets beat the air and bombs fall in the distance. There is a tear in Serkan's eye, but nobody will ever know this. He blinks so that it falls onto the blue quilt in which the baby is wrapped.

'Have you been here all night?' a voice says from behind him. 'I've divided them into units and sent them out with the new ammo,' says Hasad, looking down now at the baby in Serkan's arms. Serkan does not reply. 'The mother?' asks Hasad.

'Dead,' Serkan finally replies. Hasad nods.

In the prisoners' house, Olympia is crying soundlessly. She is kneeling on the floor as still as the air and is muttering words to God. She has an icon in her hands, which she holds close to her heart. Her hair is in a grey bun that is no longer neat and spills out at the sides. And her head drops over her chest. The tears from her eyes fall to her lap.

The other women in the room are quiet. Elenitsa is slowly turning blue, like the sea when the sun rises. She has not moved for hours. Her baby has gone. The sun is rising, and slowly the shadows extend in the room and the picture of these women, in this old abandoned house, hangs frozen in the silence like an old photograph. Sophia complains about being hungry while the dog whimpers by her side. She still will not touch it. Some of the women look up now from their solid positions, irritated by Sophia's childish demands, and take this opportunity to look again disgustedly in the direction of Koki. Koki shifts uncomfortably in her chair, and Maroulla stands up instinctively, walks towards Koki and perches on her lap. Koki puts her arm round the little girl's waist and Maroulla leans back onto Koki's chest. She likes the sound of her heart.

Maria, who is of course sitting on the floor, grabs onto the leg of a nearby chair and heaves herself up. She pauses for a moment, perhaps to regain her balance, and then walks towards the bed where Elenitsa lies lifeless. Olympia is still motionless by her side, but is now holding the dead girl's hand. She grips it close to her chest. The icon is on the floor beside her. 'You must let her spirit go,' Maria says, but Olympia does not move. The other women look in their direction. 'You are keeping her from God,' Maria insists and then moves closer, leans over Olympia and peels her hands away from the young mother's. Elenitsa's hand hangs limp. Olympia pauses for a moment, as if contemplating for the first time the true horror of the scene before her, and removes a handkerchief from her skirt pocket and looks down at it dejectedly. Then her body judders, her firm exterior shatters, her hands shake uncontrollably and she begins to wail. A deep, pounding sobbing that pumps dark sadness into the room. Her chest thrusts and her breath rips out in shreds. She cries into the silk handkerchief that her grandmother had given her when she was a little girl. She cries for Elenitsa, because she is no longer a mother and no longer a wife. She cries for the life this young woman could have had and for the boy who has no mother and no father to love.

The crying transiently mutes the crickets and the silence. The women sit still. Maria puts her arm on Olympia's shoulder and Olympia's storm eases into a drizzle of tears. The heat is heavy and full of unspoken words. The women's sadness hangs in the air like a brimming cloud. Maria moves away from Olympia, disappears into the bedroom and returns about five minutes later with a Bible and a ceramic incense burner. Although it is becoming lighter outside, she finds the matches, brings a lamp from the garden and lights it, throwing the room into a golden glow. She gives the lamp to Olympia, instructing her to hold it up, and then lights another match and brings the flickering flame to the olive leaves in the incense burner. She blows into it gently, and soon a plume of sweet smoke rises and Maria circles it anticlockwise over Elenitsa's body, creating a grey halo. The smoke fills the room. Maria puts the incense burner down and picks up the Bible. She opens it, licks her middle finger and leafs through the pages. Then she signals for all the women to stand. They all rise and bend their heads and close their eyes. Maria clears her throat and starts reading the Prayer for the Dead. 'Christ, our eternal King and God, You have destroyed death and the Devil by Your Cross and have restored man to life by Your Resurrection; give rest, Lord, to the soul of Your servant Eleni, who has fallen asleep, in Your Kingdom, where there is no pain, sorrow or suffering. In Your goodness and love for all men, pardon all the sins she has committed in thought, word or deed, for there is no man or woman who lives and sins not. You only are without sin. For You are the Resurrection, the Life, and Repose of Your servant Eleni, departed this life, O Christ our God; and to You do we send up glory with Your Eternal Father and Your All-holy, Good and Life-creating Spirit; both now and for ever and to the ages of ages. Amen.' Her words resonate around the room as clear as a bell. The women repeat 'Amen,' and cross themselves, and Maria circles Elenitsa's body once more with the burning olive leaves. She then leans forward and puts her hand onto Elenitsa's chest. 'To stop breathing is to free the breath from its restless tides,' she says softly, reciting the words of a Lebanese prophet. And then she straightens her back, clenches her fist, scrunches her face and, spitting viciously, says, 'If I could feed their brains to the dog I would cut their heads open myself.' And there is not a woman in that room that does not believe her. She then bends down and lifts the lamp.

'Devils,' she proclaims, stamping her foot. 'The Devil. The Devil. The Devil.' The light of the lamp sways over the faces of the women. Most of them look now at the floor, not knowing what else to do. The dog is sitting as close to Sophia as it can get to her without her shuffling away. Litsa has been unusually quiet for a while and sits now with her elbows on her knees and her fingers covering her eyes. Costandina is, once again, staring at Koki, but this time her eyes glow with anger.

'Devils,' continues Maria, 'the Devil. The Devil. The Devil.' She stamps her foot and the lamplight rocks in the darkness. 'The Devil. The Devil. The Devil!' She stamps her foot and the crickets pound in the darkness. 'The Devil. The Devil. The Devil!' She stamps her foot and cockroaches scuttle in the shadows. The heat clings to their skin. Costandina scratches her arms manically. The dog whines. The cicadas pound and pound and pound, like blood in one's ears. It is all of these things that burn Costandina's nerves, that scorch her itchy skin. It is all of these things that cause her to stop scratching, jump from her chair and pounce, head first, at Koki. Costandina grabs Koki's red hair, clenches her teeth and drags Koki off the chair. The lamp is lowered and the room darkens, but nobody moves. Costandina pulls Koki's hair desperately, pulls until blood drips from Koki's forehead. Koki clutches Costandina's wrists in an attempt to loosen her grip. The other women watch. Maroulla stands there with fear in her eyes. She kicks Costandina's leg manically and punches her back with her little fists. Costandina screams as she pulls the other woman's hair harder, and Koki cries now in pain and begs her to stop.

Litsa finally stands up. 'Stop, Costandina,' she pleads over Koki's crying, but Costandina continues. Koki's eyes and skin are now stretched and covered in blood. Costandina's hands are red. Costandina sobs now and stops pulling, but she does not let go. 'Stop, Costandina,' implores Litsa again and pulls at Costandina's shoulders, attempting to draw her up. Costandina drops Koki's head and moves back. She looks down at the mass of sticky orange hair in her hands. Koki whimpers, on the floor, and Maroulla takes her hand and holds it in hers. The lamp is on the floor and the night is bruised with shadows. Maria removes the dead body, and with her own bare hands digs a shallow hole in the garden. A few of the women lift Elenitsa's body into it, and all, apart from Koki, help to cover her with soil and blossoms from the trees.

Later, Sophia and Maroulla collect more twigs,

though this time they meander dolefully round the garden, avoiding the grave. After lighting another fire, Maria sits in the garden cooking a chicken. Koki has managed to sit up, and Litsa is patting her forehead with a wet cloth, gently wiping off the blood. Koki winces from the pain, and Maroulla sits beside her. Soon the chicken is served and the women eat in silence. Koki pushes hers aside and leaves it on the floor. The women then huddle in the garden on their knees, just as they once would have done, on a normal night, and clean the dishes using the water from the well. When all is done they sit in the house with blankets on their legs, for there is a cold breeze tonight. Koki sits without a blanket, self-consciously patting down her hair. She looks around for her headscarf, hopelessly, and then rips another purple strip from the bottom of her dress. She raises her arms to tie it round her head, but then lowers them and drops them in her lap. She looks down at her torn dress and at the blood under her fingernails. She sighs deeply, sinks as she thinks of her son and then gazes up at the ceiling. She clutches her fingers, contemplates them and then looks ahead at the women.

'I've been hiding all my life,' declares Koki suddenly.

The women turn to look at her, some suspiciously, others ashamedly. Costandina looks at the wall. 'You pull my hair, ostracise me, beat me, call me names and then you turn your faces to the wall!' Koki twists the headscarf in her fingers, tugging, clenching, coiling and pulling at it with fury. 'You talk about the Turks and the British and what they have done to you. What about what you have done to me? . . . What about me?!' Koki's voice rises and resonates around the room; years of anger blazing from within. Everyone is now staring at her. She looks intently at each and every one of them and pauses longer when she gets to Costandina. 'You have put me in a prison and left me there alone. You are just as bad as the people you detest!' She looks around again at those wide, expectant eyes; she sighs and her eyes shimmer in the lamplight. As her mind wells up with memories, her shoulders soften. She lets go of the headscarf, looks down and then up again at the others. 'I have been a target of everybody's anger. You have stripped me of everything! Even my name has been taken from me! Even my beautiful name! I have nothing left that is mine. Nothing!' Koki looks again at the women. 'I have been the enemy, the scape-goat, the Devil, Medusa, the English whore, the fiend with red hair, the motherless child! None of you have ever heard my real story . . .' Koki's voice softens and her red hair and white skin glow in the lamplight. She takes a deep breath and as the light flickers on her face pictures of the past seem to move across the blue of her eyes.

'My name means "red arse",' she says. '"*Koki*" comes from "*kokinokolos*": as you well know, a word used in the village to describe English people. I was never meant to be called Koki; I was christened Kyriaki because I was born on Sunday. My father didn't like his mother's name and my mother didn't like her mother, and both grandfathers had fallen to the coincidental misfortune of the name "Bambo": a most unsuitable name for a girl, especially one of my kind.' Koki pauses and looks around at the faces of the women, half glowing in the lamplight and half shrouded in darkness.

'All this forced my parents to be the first in the town to disregard the tradition of naming the children after the in-laws and upset them to the point of heated Sunday discussions over glasses of ouzo, accompanied by grand hand gestures, followed by some fainting and a considerable amount of referring to each other as donkeys.'

Koki stops there and points at Litsa. 'Your older brother Andreas was the first to call me *kokinokolos*!' Litsa looks down, and Koki continues obstinately, 'I was six at the time and Pappa and I had been invited by your family for Sunday *souvlakia*. While the women were preparing coffee in the kitchen for the men an army jeep rolled up outside the farm's entrance, and a beaming captain waved at Pappa and, lifting his hat, revealed a mass of bronze curls that protruded out-wards, like the red-polished Horned God I had once seen in a book about the Bronze Age. Andreas was instantly amused by the resemblance between me and this captain and pointed at both of us, shouting between explosions of laughter, "*Kokinokoli*! Mama, look, both of them are *kokinokoli*!"

'In spring, the hills were wounded with poppies and the neighbours said that my hair was made of those blood-coloured petals. Or, in the summer, when at midday these same hills were pale, scorched English-men's flesh, the neighbours said that my skin was made of that same flowerless plain. It was also certain that my hair was made of fire retrieved from hell on the wick of a candle. The Devil! Or, perhaps, my mother, God rest her soul, had been poked by an Englishman;

this belief was so great that "*Engleza*! *Engleza*!" would be screamed out from behind the lemon groves.

'I was the only daughter of Mihalis Koufos, the owner of the hillside taverna and renowned storyteller, who was believed to be the ear of the earth; although originally our surname, which means "deaf", was my great-grandfather's nickname, who acquired it as a result of his selective hearing, especially in the presence of my great-grandmother, and other Cypriot women.

'As I waited on the guests I listened intently to Pappa's endless facts and hoped, with the conviction of youth, that stories of war lingered in the ripples of the furthest wave.

'On velvet-blue nights I'd carry the small coffee cup, brimming with Greek coffee, to the table where my father sat; usually running a thumb over his chin and staring at the slopes covered with olive trees that dropped down to the sea. I remember how, one night, when I rested the cup on the white tablecloth, spilling more than half the contents into the saucer, he chuckled quietly, lowered his hand on to mine, and said, "It's money! One day we'll have a dowry big enough to make a great housewife of you, just like your mother, God rest her soul." But he did not, this time, purse his fingers and cross himself, but said instead, "The good housewife makes the house laugh." Poor man,' she says, nodding her head. 'Poor man, how could he have known.' Koki pauses for a few moments. The women are silent. Only their breathing can be heard.

'Some nights I'd serve ouzo and cucumber to the guests who argued continually, but the aniseed fumes unfortunately never helped with their worries; as the men conversed, with loud voices and giant gestures, their anger drifted over the hills. Pappa's taverna became more of a café than a restaurant, where men gathered on long nights and Sunday afternoons to discuss the fate of this troubled island.'

In the shadows Koki's body changes. It moulds into the silhouettes of the past, into the movements of the people of whom she spoke.

'"Backgammon, Dimitri?" Pappa, as usual, did not wait for an answer and had already started opening the lacquered board, separating the black pieces from the white. The taverna was empty apart from a familiar Englishman, who sat alone at the furthest table beneath a lemon tree, overlooking the hills; his usual seat. He was there so often that I hardly noticed him any more; he would sit slumped in the chair, looking so sad. As he coiled over a newspaper, his face was so grey, as though it reflected the print.

'"What I love about this game is that it's not necessarily he who has annexed his opponent who wins. One must use the luck of the dice to one's advantage." Pappa's face creased as he smiled. But Dimitri turned away. Alone beneath the lemon tree, the Englishman ruffled his paper.

'Pappa, noticing Dimitri's oddly angry expression, bombarded him with what seemed like an absurd series of insults. "What is it now, Dimitri? Is it the rumour about your wife and the tailor? Don't worry the neighbours are stirrers, she loves you with her life, the mad woman." Pappa laughed, Dimitri remained silent. "Or your Litsa?" Pappa continued. "She is not still interested in that delinquent, Marcos' son? He does nothing but smoke and visit those awful clubs for the *Englezi*!" Pappa's feigned fatuity was ignored. "Or has that donkey son of yours not starting cultivating the crops yet?" A strange way, it may appear to some, to brighten his old friend's mood, but Pappa and Dimitri, for as long as I could remember, had calmed many worries with the often humorous trivialities of their everyday lives; funnily enough, the very same trivialities which, according to Dimitri, knocked the women to their hands and knees in despair.' Koki pauses again and stares at Litsa, who is now looking at her sternly. 'Do you have something to add?' Koki looks Litsa straight in the eye and Litsa does not reply, but looks down, avoiding the eyes of the others.

'I'll continue then.' Koki coughs and looks again at the others. 'Dimitri opened his hand and looked down at it; I remember it was so covered with lines it looked as though he had never stopped toiling. Then, from the backgammon board, he snatched a white piece and flung it over the veranda: it glistened as it spun and then faded as it fell too far for us to see. Pappa flung shut the backgammon board, as if issuing a punishment to a disobedient child. "What's wrong with you, Dimitri?"

'Dimitri sat straight in an attempt to gain power at this table and pulled at his moustache. Then he burst out, "Let's wait for the right black numbers, they will never come!"

'Pappa breathed out and shot a sideways glace at the Englishman, who was still fixated on the paper, even though there was little chance an Englishman would understand Greek. Pappa's face darkened as he lifted the glass of ouzo to his lips, drank it impatiently, rested it back on the table and leant towards Dimitri, towering over his much-smaller frame heavily and resolutely whispering, "We have given a hundred and three rounds to this subject."

"'Anathema!" Dimitri protested, flicking his hand like the wing of a captive bird. "Maria saw my Litsa talking to a Turk by the well, she was laughing and" – Dimitri paused and drew a breath – "showing her thigh."'

At this Litsa interjects, protesting her innocence. She stands up and looks around at everyone in the room, with sweat on her brow. 'This is ridiculous! What does any of this have to do with me? My family have done nothing to you!'

Koki looks up at Litsa. 'Sit down, Litsa. It's my turn now,' she says in a soft voice, unaffected by Litsa's anger. She glances around again and the others gaze at Litsa expectantly. Nobody speaks. Litsa sits down slowly, and Koki takes a breath, looks around and continues. 'Pappa struggled to keep a straight face. "Well, it is certain then! Will we christen or crucify the baby?"

'Dimitri looked angry. "Passing from mouth to mouth it was learnt by a thousand, and by the time it came to be heard by the king he learnt of how a cow laid an egg!" said Pappa, chuckling.

'But Dimitri's mind was fixed. "The Turkish KATAK is giving the *Englezi* a reason to continue! The Turks are in our way! They are the one's stopping the union with Greece! They have no right to be here, they are fucking us and my daughter is fucking them! I will spit on her!"'

At this Litsa adjusted her position and tried hard not to look at the other women. Koki continued without stopping, 'Dimitri spat over the veranda and then looked at his hands in calculation or resignation. "Did you know," he began, tapping the edge of the table with index and middle finger, the shape of which resembled a young boy's imitation of a gun, "when Britain took Cyprus from the Ottomans, Article 117 stated that Turks were either to return to the main- land or lose their nationality?" He said this as if he were reading the Bible or saying a prayer. "These English are playing us against each other. To them we are the pieces; we are a strategic necessity. We are not a home to the English; we are not the olives or the grapevines, the chickens or the donkeys, the bleeding in the fields! We are Air Quarter Middle East and glasses of wine! We serve our masters' masters. We are twice slaves." He paused and looked for a fleeting moment at the man on the other table and exclaimed in English, "Freendom is never wan withowt bloodshed!"

'An unexpected wind gushed from across the sea. It seemed to have a calming quality on Dimitri's nerves, as he reclined far into his chair. He paused again, pulling the left side of his moustache. "The English are parasites!" But after this comment he sighed and something seemed to change from within him. "Enosis and only enosis," he said in a deflated tone, opening the board. "We had nothing when we were young, despite my dad's hard work. Our life was controlled by high taxes! I remember I used to go with my poor father to protests. We still suffered. There is only one solution."

'The Englishman stood up, closed his newspaper, left some money on the table by his coffee cup and walked towards the wooden gate that would lead him to the falling path.

'"Yiasou, my friend!" Pappa called after him, and the grey man nodded gently, then proceeded; but as he did so I noticed a slight hesitation, as brief as the pause of wings in flight, as he passed the table where

I sat. For a few moments Pappa waited and looked towards the path as if to make sure that the Englishman was far away enough. "In Ancient Greek '*parasitos*' means a guest at a meal." Pappa exhaled deeply through his nostrils, which flared and shrunk, but soon realised that it was no use.

"'Koki!" Dimitri called; his voice was full of malice and hatred. "One coffee! Metrio." But as I stood to obey his command, I stopped, as he looked at me up and down. "It's a shame you have no other children, Mihalis, this one's lacking. Her skin is too white, her eyes colourless, her hair like the red of the Turkish flag and her legs bend like those of a donkey's. I know she is still young, but how will she ever marry?"

'I never really became immune to such comments from the neighbours; the words hurt and shattered my confidence. I am not trying to excuse my sins, but it explains the incidents to come. I shuffled off to the kitchen not waiting to hear my father's reply.

'But, this time, when I returned, Dimitri's coffee tipsy in my hand, Pappa was sitting alone, staring towards the right of the hills where the whitewashed walls of St Hilarion's Castle were just visible through the lemon groves and carob trees. This was not the first time Pappa had asked Dimitri to leave. Taking the coffee from my hand, my poor father, staring at me as though he were responsible for my torment, sat me on his lap and told me the story of Aurora. With hair the colour of the froth of the sea beneath an orange sunset, and skin so white, one would have thought she was made entirely from the snow on the Taurus Mountains. Sleeping Beauty slept for many years without waking in the dark turret of St Hilarion's Castle due to a spell cast by a witch and was rescued by a prince who was swept away by her beauty. It would have been a magical story, had the witch not been Vassoulla and the prince Mustafa the fishmonger; but it was difficult then for Pappa, and for everyone, to envision life beyond the Cypriots.

'In the breeze stories reached us like the light of an ancient star. As the night darkened and the ouzo emptied in the bottle, Pappa's stories and tone changed; the sound of the forgotten trample of many colonisations beat either in the distance or in our imaginations. The white Taurean wind, beating through the branches of the olive trees, brought the footsteps of the early settlers: the Assyrians, the Egyptians, the Persians, the Macedonians, the Romans, the Byzantines, the Phoenicians, the Lusignans, the Genoese, the Venetians, the Ottomans, the British, the sails beat wildly in their port, the sea to the shore, the lemons to the floor. And still in the distance echoed more.

'Pappa's face was smooth against the wind, as if under the protection of a god, and once more rubbed his thumb over his chin. "Cyprus is a great watchtower, and he who stands at the top has the advantage of a god that can see at once Europe, Asia and Africa." At this, his forehead folded and eyes creased as he sipped Dimitri's cold coffee and placed it back in the saucer. "It is an intermediary between three worlds. It reaches high above and goes deep below the ground with its rubble of hatred and war; where people fought to be gods. But they can only expect to reach Paradise when they drop it from the sky, and once it falls . . . well . . ."

'Remembering a story he had told me in the past, I replied, feeling proud that I was able to reiterate a few words from one of my father's tales, "But we have horns to fight them with!"

'My father laughed. "Yes, yes, promontories that thrust into the sea, but the island can't fight its own battle."

'Whether he expected me to understand his allusions

to war and colonisation, or whether he knew that for me these stories lived with the fairytales in the shadows on the hill, I will never know.' Koki stops and looks round at the women in that half darkness.

They are all still, with the blankets pulled up now to their chins. A cool breeze blows across the garden and with it comes a floating lantern. Soon the commanding officer is standing amongst the shadows. Koki looks at his army boots encrusted with mud. He lifts his lamp and looks at the faces of the women. The crickets pound behind him. Olympia moves to stand up, but Costandina pulls her back down. The commanding officer spins round to face her and holds the lamp so close to her face that it can be seen reflected in her eyes. 'Speak!' he demands in Turkish. Olympia understands and drops her head, staring intently at his foot. 'Speak!' he demands again. Olympia shakes her head slightly. He slaps her with the back of his hand. She holds her face and hunches her shoulders. 'The baby,' she whispers into her chest, and then she repeats these words a little louder in Turkish.

The officer laughs. He laughs from his chest and his body shakes. He then stops, moves a little closer, bends down and laughs again so that she can feel his breath in her face. 'The baby,' he says, chuckling, 'I'll show you the baby.' He grabs her throat, forcing her to stand. Olympia cries now and struggles to breathe. 'Don't cry,' he whispers in her ear, 'it won't last long.' At this, he propels her by the neck to the back of the garden.

Adem sits on a rock by the church of Saint Evlavios with his head in his hands and the photograph hanging from his fingers. Soldiers pass by, attending to their tasks, but Adem takes no notice. He straightens his back, tucks the photograph into his palm and stares at it. His eyes loom over Kyriaki's glassy eyes and with his finger he touches her hair. He then brings it closer and looks at the darker boy by her side. He sighs deeply, looks up at the sky and indignantly tucks the photograph into his top pocket. Ahead, some soldiers stand on the dust plain and throw stones at cans. They cheer triumphantly. Far below, the sea at Pente Mile shimmers with crimson ripples, and opposite a red fire rages in the mountains. Although the shelling has stopped, the island is not calm: in fact, as the dust settles in the cracks of broken roads and homes and bones the crevices become deeper and the island seems to rattle and crack. 'It is only the sound of the crickets,' says one soldier standing close by, who has been looking his way. Adem nods, but does not reply. 'We have lost a lot of soldiers,' continues the soldier and gives Adem a testing, knowing look. This time, Adem looks up at him and notices only a roll of fat beneath his chin, which, from this position, obscures his face. The soldier reaches down and retrieves a box of cigarettes from his pocket. He takes one out and puts it to his mouth. Adem watches longingly. The soldier strikes a match, which glows orange in the darkness, and then looks at Adem thoughtfully. He steps closer and sits on the wall beside him, looking across the falling slopes. The soldier takes out a cigarette and offers it to Adem. Adem reaches out his hand to accept it, but the soldier draws it back again. 'Something which, once made, can never be destroyed, once destroyed, can never be repaired. What is it?' The soldier looks eagerly at Adem.

'Serkan,' Adem mutters dejectedly, and the man chuckles shortly, then looks fearfully over his shoulder. He then looks back at Adem and draws the cigarette further away, as though he were tempting a stray dog with a treat.

Adem sits quietly. He imagines Engin's body in the basement of the church and Serkan's face and Hasad's distorted words and disjointed body and the body of another young boy; something which he has not allowed himself to remember until now. He shakes his head and presses his fingers into his eyes. He thinks of the bottle of ouzo and wishes to have it in his hand just to ease the cracking and the smell of rotting corpses.

Adem waves his hand, indicating both his refusal to work out the riddle or to win the cigarette. The soldier nods apologetically. 'Everyone's lost their humanity,' says Adem. 'We have all become monsters,' he continues slowly, and the man looks at him side-ways. Something has been bothering Adem, eating at his heart and intestines. Something he has done which he can never change. He looks at the man sitting beside him and suddenly feels the urge to tell someone, to confess.

'I killed a child,' he says, and the other man scrunches his nose against the sun. 'It was early morning, the first day of the invasion. Serkan had captured some men and had them kneeling in a row ready for assassination, and I remember one of the men suddenly jumped up and started running. Before Serkan could respond the man was already obscured by the trees in the lemon grove. Serkan ordered me to kill him so I went after him. When

I entered the orchard all was still and I stood there looking around. I thought of firing my gun so that Serkan would think I killed him, but just then I saw him move; he dashed from one tree to another and had a rifle in his hand. I thought my life was in danger; because of that something shifted within me. It was as swift and easy as changing a shirt. I suddenly saw the face of a killer before me, a monstrous enemy; the poison of the war had got into me and I pursued him like a warrior. I could hear the crunching of his footsteps and followed him to the other side of the grove to a clearing just beyond the town, and when I got the first glimpse of him I fired. I pulled the trigger and the man froze for a second, then he fell, face down, to the ground. I had shot him right through the heart. I ran over to where he lay and turned him around and when I looked at his face I realised that he was just a child. He hadn't even developed a beard yet. He had his whole life in front of him and I killed him because I am Turkish and he was Greek. But when I looked at his face, as he looked up at me blindly, I couldn't see what separated us.' Adem stops there and clasps his hands together in silence for a few moments. The other soldier does not speak.

'I held him for a moment and closed his eyes. I felt

so awful that I found a rose and placed it on his chest. And then I left. I left him lying there while my life continued.' Adem looks over at the man now. The man lowers his head and doesn't say a word, he stares at the ground. After a while he stands up and leaves. In his place he has left a cigarette and a match. Adem looks up to thank him, but he has gone. He strikes the match on the wall, lights the cigarette, inhales the smoke deeply, exhales and watches the men playing through a shield of smoke. His head pounds, his nerves crack, his heart rattles. His fingers holding the cigarette tremble. He thinks of his life in Istanbul in his parents' empty house with that old typewriter and that torn armchair and those matted dreams. He should have stayed in Cyprus. What a coward he was. How he left. How he turned his back on her when she wanted him to stay. They would have killed him. He remembers that grey look in her eyes, glinting like metal, hardened over the years, even at her young age. He remembers that red hair consuming her and poisoning her thoughts. He cannot leave without her again.

Adem stands up, looks at the soldiers playing and throws his cigarette on the floor. He looks over his shoulder and begins to go towards the road that leads from the mountain into the town and promises to himself that he will find her. In fact he will never leave this place without her.

Day 5: 24 July 1974

In the prisoners' house, it is a bright morning. The
rooster at the back of the garden rises to attention and
salutes the sun with a hearty cry, showing its victory
over the night. Maroulla has stepped out into the garden
and is holding the green book in her hands; she looks
ahead, imagining the rose on the hillside sparkling red.
Most of the women stir now and Maria stands up and
joins Maroulla on the veranda. She takes a deep breath
and lifts her chest as though she is about to cry out
like the rooster. The cry pierces the silence again. 'The
solar emblem of the Greeks,' says Maria, squinting ahead
at the rooster, 'a sacred sign to Apollo, Zeus, Persephone
and Attis. He sings for us and we will be victorious.'
The little girl looks up at her, closes the book, tucks
it into her apron and enters the house.

The sound of the rooster is replaced by another

sound. A screeching howl riding the waves of sunshine. The desperate shrill of an abandoned baby. Most of the women look down in desolation as the shadows quail from the sun. The baby cries and cries, but nobody answers. There is no end to its tears, no respite to its feelings of emptiness and unfulfilled needs. Nobody comes, nobody answers, nobody soothes. The baby howls endlessly from beyond the garden. One woman bites her lip, another digs her nails into her palm, and another cries; for they know they cannot reach the baby. They think of the blackness of its world. They know that if he lives he will never recover from such desolation. The empty world will be etched on his brain like ancient pictures in a cave.

Soon the baby stops crying and once again the cicadas can be heard rattling as a hot wind blows and the broken bones of old flowers are swept across red soil. It is at this time that Olympia appears, walking from the back of the garden. She adjusts her grey bun, straightens her collar and walks as straight as she can. She enters the house with her head held high and sits on a chair. The dog shuffles over and sits straight and alert by her side. Olympia crosses one leg over another. She is a schoolmistress ready for her morning class, except that she sits with an unconvincing authoritative air, her presence uncommanding, her fingers trembling on her knee. And though her features are firm and her eyes dry, there is a necklace of bruises clasped round her neck. Like a gift of bad intent. When the women stare she lifts her hand and touches the necklace, like a lady of glamour, elegantly, as though it were encrusted with amethyst or topaz. She lowers her hand gracefully to her knee, encompassing it protectively as one would an egg. She is a grey, sculptured statuette, the goddess Artemis on the hunt with her dog by her side, a figurine of days gone by, an effigy of grace and strength, though in this case, it is feigned.

The women stare and do not speak. Olympia holds her stance loyally. The air is thick with dust from the wind. Litsa stands, takes a blanket and places it onto Olympia's knees. Olympia accepts the gesture and adjusts her stance, placing her hands on top of the woven blanket. The dog sighs and rests its head on its paws. It is clear that the women know neither what to say nor where to look. Their eyes dash about the room and Maria crunches on her nails. Litsa contemplates for a moment, then sits beside Koki. 'Why don't you continue your story?' she asks encouragingly, and the women's eyes dart in their direction with sudden interest. Koki looks around at the eager faces and is soothed by the sudden change of atmosphere. She nods and adjusts her posture. Maroulla runs from near the doorway and sits down next to her. Koki coughs lightly and looks again at the women; they wait expectantly.

'It was a few years after Cyprus gained independence,' she begins. 'Yes. After Makarios had been resurrected like Christ. After the EOKA leaflets stopped flapping like birds over the fields and the Turks and Greeks had a hope of living side by side. It was the year when it all went wrong, the year that fighting broke out around the island and the communities split into two. It was also the year that the shoemaker died. The year of 1963, when my life began and ended.

'Every Saturday Pappa gave me jobs to do. On this particular day I was to go to Vangeli's *kafenion* to post a letter to Pappa's brother, Theio Nikos, who had moved to Archway, London, to try and make some money, as he too, like Dimitri, had been a struggling farmer; and this letter was to congratulate him on the birth of his new baby boy and his promotion in the clothes factory where he worked. A double celebration. I was also instructed to take Pappa's shoes to

Mario the shoemaker as the soles had been flapping like dogs' tongues for about a month. Mario would not fix them sooner as he had to mend the farmer's boots first. My last job was to take a basketful of eggs to a woman in our neighbourhood who would dye them red for the Easter feast.

'Of course, the real post office had closed down long before I was born, during the end of Ottoman rule when hospitals, schools and printing presses were scarce, so we were forced to make do with the poor efforts of Vangeli, the café owner, instead of travelling for three-quarters of an hour to the only real post office, on the other side of Kyrenia, which had been rebuilt since the British occupied the island.

'It was the beginning of March, and the people had not yet been lured to the cool shower of shade. In his black cassock the priest stood beneath the frowning arches of the church, talking with an old widow, who was also dressed in black. She had contorted her face and was complaining about the detrimental effect fasting had on her health, and I could not help watching them as I passed: two shadows of religion, one straight, one curved, she talking with her hands, he nodding his head, impassioned in discussion beneath this fallen smile. If you looked closely enough, you could see the world changing.

'"Good morning, Koki!" Pater Yiousif waved dutifully, but the old lady felt no need for such an obligation and did not even grunt. I lowered my face to the ground, arms full of eggs, feeling very aware of the way I was walking, and kept my eyes on my feet until I could hear the faint plucking of the bouzouki trickling gently up the hill as soft as rain, as grey as rain.

'Old Bambaji the Turk sat on his veranda playing and singing in Greek the same macabre ballad that I had heard him sing every day.' Bamabaji was not really a Turk, she explained to the younger girls, his name had come from '*linobambaji*', what they called the Greeks who converted to Islam in the hope of an easier life during the Ottoman Empire. 'But not even he could bring himself to wave. He stopped for a moment to look at me as I passed, and then the music sank down the hill and the words faded.

'I followed the path through a basket of white, terraced houses tipping either slightly upwards or slumping downwards. The street had no name then, as the English road name had been painted black. I walked until I could smell the armpits of the sailors and until

I reached Vangeli's café: the crumbling hut with blue shutters, built to face the shadows and not the sun; where four men sat outside on a table, beneath the red Coca-Cola plaque, smoking rolled-up tobacco over their morning coffee.

'"What's this, Vangeli, no *kaimaki*? What kind of coffee do you make?" said Hadgipetros, with his dark, leather-like skin. He held his coffee out in protest and the other three men, looking down at their own, nodded in agreement; but Vangeli did not stir and remained indoors, leaning on the counter over a newspaper.

'At the point when Hadgipetros' eyes narrowed and reclined into reddening cheeks, Kyrios Chrysanthos, the eldest man, sitting opposite Mehmet, noticed me standing by the entrance of the café. "Koki! How is our little English flower?" The rest of the men followed his gaze and looked my way, where I stood probably as red as a single English rose, on those grey, uneven pebbles, and as misplaced as that same rose would have been sitting in a delicate glass vase in the centre of the Cypriot man's table; and I remembered then that the ancient Greeks knew the rose only as a white flower until the grieving Aphrodite, mourning over Adonis' death, picked a rose from the ground and pricked herself on its thorn, causing her blood to drip like dew onto the petals and stain it forever red.

'"Well actually," I replied, "I am definitely not English and I can't possibly be a flower." The men remained still for a moment and then exploded with laughter, and I noticed Kyrios Chrysanthos' coffee spilling onto his trousers as his body shook.

'I ran into the coffee shop and approached Vangeli, who was still leaning over the counter with his back to me, sweating profusely; I coughed slightly but as he didn't turn I peered over his shoulder, stealing a glance at *Eleftheria*, which contained a photograph of Archbishop Makarios. Suddenly noticing me, he pulled the paper nearer to his wet clothes and smacked my ear with his large hand so that it burnt and warbled. "What do stupid little girls need to know about politics? Eh, women, you are the problem with the world, trust me there is a woman behind all wars." He raised a large fist into the air and then stuck out his thumb, followed by his forefinger. "Eleni of Troy, Samson and Delilah, Aphrodite who sparked the Trojan War by offering Paris the Queen of Sparta! They stir the world with their spoons, and the men do mad things or the really stupid ones fight *for* them. Either way it is all women!" At this he stubbed a finger onto the newspaper. "See! All women. Their fault!" And at this he grabbed a handful of nuts from a tray and threw them into his mouth. "Well?" he said, and I put the letter onto the desktop and waited as he retrieved a stamp from behind the counter, licked it with his peanut tongue and smacked it onto the envelope, where I could see one side had not stuck properly, due to the residue from his mouth. "Leave it with me," he said and resumed his position over the newspaper.

'I slipped out of the café as silently as I could and proceeded to follow the path to the sea, trying to avoid the group of youngsters that leant on a white wall, for if they had seen me they would have thrown stones at me, or, worse, dead snakes. They were still angry with the English, so they hated me. I was one of them because I looked like them. As always, I was a target. Sometimes they even threw dead rats. That was worse than the snakes for they stank of decay and sewers.

'I ran to the shoemaker's and when I arrived Mario was not there, someone else had taken over. That's where I met him. The person that would be the height of my happiness and the pit of my pain. The one who would give me hope and yet be the cause of my utter desolation. The one who would be my companion and yet be the reason for my lifelong loneliness. The one who would start my life and end it. He was everything I had ever wanted; he gave me the little things in life that everybody else has and takes for granted. He talked with me, walked with me and laughed with me. When I was with him I felt like a normal human being rather than a devil or an object of hatred. Apart from my father, he was the only person in the world who accepted me. But it wasn't just that, I loved his mind and the stories he told and his moodiness and even the way he hid from life and looked upon me for sup-port, for motivation. Through his eyes I became some-body else.

'When I walked in he was standing at the counter, rubbing the brown leather of a shoe with a shoebrush. He did not look up immediately, so I put the eggs down on the floor and placed Pappa's shoes onto the open newspaper on the counter. His clothes were brown and black so that he blended with the earthy leather-ness around him in that dusty, sticky room of shoes and polish and newspaper print. He put the shoebrush down and picked up the rubber glue-brush, dotting it gently onto a scratch on the leather, then he ran his finger delicately along the seam of the sole. I pushed the shoes closer to him and coughed. He looked up suddenly as if he had just realised that I was there. He was young, maybe a few years older than me; his skin was dark and his eyes a honey-hazel that caught the streaks of light from the doorway and window opposite. He smiled and I signalled to the shoes with my eyes. He put the brown shoe down, reached to his left and took Pappa's, all without removing his eyes from my face. He then shook his head, very slightly, and rubbed his right eye, smearing brown shoe polish over his face. I tried not to laugh and pursed my lips tightly, but he saw my beaming face and thought I was smiling at him, so he smiled back again. And that was the problem. He smiled. Nobody but Pappa ever smiled at me; no one except the other kids at school, or the girls that drank lemonade beneath the lemon tree, or Dimitri's son Andreas, but that always preceded mocking laughter or snide giggling.

'I lowered my head, shuffled my feet and attempted to move inconspicuously to the left so that I would not be facing him directly, but this smile threw me into a gawky frenzy and, as elegant as I tried to be, I ended up lumbering clumsily into the eggs. My foot crunched through the shells and I ended up standing in a pool of raw egg. He heaved himself onto the counter and looked down at my feet, tutting and shaking his head. He jumped back down, grabbed a stool, placed it right next to me and signalled for me to sit down. I lifted my foot out of the egg and broken shells and sat down on the stool. He laughed to himself as he disappeared into the back of the shop and appeared again with a bucket of water, a cloth and a newspaper. I didn't know where to put my face; I was so embarrassed I could have died on the spot. He knelt before me, gently removed my shoes and wiped the egg off with some newspaper, then dipped the cloth into the soapy water and cleaned my foot. At the touch of his fingers on my skin, my face reddened and my heart fluttered. He scrubbed the sides of my foot with circular motions, then the sole with long sweeping movements, then he held the two ends of the towel, alternately pulling on each end so that he polished the top of my foot. He scrubbed and rubbed and washed as though my foot were a shoe. Then he looked at my shoes, which were tattered enough even before being covered with egg and had been cramping my toes so much that you could see the shape of them moulded into the leather. He measured my foot using his thumb and forefinger, scrunched his eyes and tossed the shoes into the bin. My eyes opened wide, but he ignored me and disappeared into the back again, this time returning with a pair of sparkling new black leather shoes in his hand. The toes were rounded and pretty. He held them up to my face. They were so shiny that I could see the reflection of the window in them. He put them on the floor, knelt down and slipped my polished feet into them then masterfully threaded the laces through the holes with the speed of a professional shoemaker. He looked up at me, tied them and then placed my feet together.

'I was beside myself. I was engulfed by the smell of leather and polish. I was so enthralled that my heart pounded and my breathing deepened and I silently longed for him to touch me again. My lips parted slightly, but I could not speak. He rose and looked down at me while I sat motionless on that stool.' Koki stops suddenly and looks around; the women stare, rapt at the story. She is comforted by their interest in her, reassured by their attentiveness, warmed by their silence. Just then the baby's crying begins and the women's shoulders suddenly tense. All look out beyond the garden and shift their positions disconcertedly. The crying propels them into the present and shatters the picture of the past.

In the far distance Adem hears a baby crying. The wail drifts like a dark shadow over remnants: the residues of life, the remains of rotting food, the ruins of churches and cold cadavers now dissected by birds and cats and rats. He passes the tree of hearts and the well and the port and the café where the old men used to sit flicking worry beads and sipping coffee. Walking in that morning heat, he imagines the ouzo, cold and clear. Hunched at the shoulders he follows his shadow west into the heart of the town. The heat is worse today, oppressive and red, carrying with it that lost dust from the African deserts. Adem looks up at the red sky and across at the Pentathaktylo Mountains that are now barely visible. Dust is never allowed to settle when diamonds twinkle beneath it, he thinks. Like Africa, Cyprus will always bear the waste of the outsider's greed.

Once the island had sparkled copper and bronze, prospering in the hands of the Mycenaeans and

Phoenicians, but later became the prey of many conquerors, shaken by avaricious fingers and stamped on by covetous feet. All now lay in the dust, those that clutched from the east: Darius the Great, Ptolemy, Haroun al-Rashid, and those that clutched, from the west: Alexander the Great, Augustus Denarius, Richard the Lionheart. They held onto the ends as though it were a Persian rug; at first they laid their thumbs on the edge of the carpet to tell the threads in a thumb's breadth, for the more there are, the dearer the work is, and, deciding its worth, they pulled and shook and tugged to make it theirs. And though these men of power seized the island at different times, the ghost of their clasp still dented the shores, and the dust still hung in the sky over the cathedrals and mosques they had left behind.

King Evagoras of Salamis was the first to try to unify the Greeks on the island, long before Christ, when the Persians invaded. Adem thinks of the teachings of Isocrates, and Alexander's campaign to unite all Greeks. Would EOKA be the last? Adem looks at the sky; it is woven with the colour of the earth, like the carpets that travelled over Europe and the East, that were touched by all and ridden on by many on those high commercial waves of the world. The dust falls gently, like rain. Except the comparison could not be further from reality. Rain seems as unreal now as the untouched sparkle of that first copper.

When the reservoirs are dry and cracked, even the priests pray for rain, but now most are probably dead, he thinks. Adem remembers that long drought, long ago. What was the year? 1963? No. 1964? The year of all the fighting. He is not sure, there were many.

He looks down at his shoes, now veiled with dust. The road is dry. A goat crosses his path, probably searching for water, its skin white and withered. There is no other movement now, only the trembling heat in the far distance, blurring the edges of the land.

The screaming is insistent, turning into a mechanical, motor-like sound: from helpless baby to machine. The persistent sound is more unrelenting than the cicadas. Its motive resolute. He wishes he could mute it. In fact, he wishes he could mute the world for it is sounds that disturb him the most: the crickets, the cicadas, the shelling, the crying. But not just that, also the ellipsis of sounds, removed like words from the story of the town: the laughter, the muttering, the gossiping, the cacophony of drama, even the birds. He looks at the sky again, and then stops and looks ahead. He has searched the houses already; the next logical place to look would be in the remaining hostage camp of the town. It would not be too far from the first, as Serkan would have needed to commute between the two easily.

Adem continues to walk with his head down. The soldier's riddle pops into his head. 'Once made, can never be destroyed, once destroyed, can never be repaired.' He tries to focus his mind, but it is full of heat and the baby's screaming. He hunches his shoulders further, takes off his hat and throws it on the ground.

From the far distance, a vehicle appears in the quivering heat. An army truck. It approaches almost statically, as if it were the fuzzy backdrop of one of those bad films in Istanbul. Adem looks around him and runs beneath some trees and into a garden full of open-mouthed clay ovens. He ducks behind one and watches the truck as it approaches. One soldier calls out and the truck comes to a halt about a hundred yards away. Two soldiers jump out with guns and look around. It is Hasad, with another soldier. The latter picks up the cap from the ground and they both look at it. 'One more soldier down,' he says, as though it were the punchline of a nursery rhyme. Hasad is not listening to him, though; he steps away and looks around, first into the road ahead, and then into the trees and gardens.

Adem holds his breath. A bead of sweat slides into his eye. He can hear the crunch of the soldiers' boots. 'Just think,' says the soldier, looking philosophically at the cap in his hand, 'this could be all that's left of us in the end. I wonder why they always lose their caps. Doesn't that always seem to be the case?' Hasad doesn't answer, but he continues, 'The whole island will be dotted with caps in the end. Green caps on the hills instead of red poppies.' Hasad glares at him suddenly with a look of extreme irritation. Even though his body leans to the left, folding itself into his longer arm, he stands resolutely in that heat. 'Back in the truck!' he demands and the soldier obeys and climbs in. Hasad takes one last look around and heaves himself up into the front, and the truck continues and subsides into the background. Adem breathes out and relaxes, allowing his body to lean completely on the clay oven. He notices that the screaming has stopped and now, in the earthy shade of the trees, he is immersed in the rattling of the cicadas.

He takes a few deep breaths, rubs his temples and stands up. He wishes there was a drop of water somewhere. He must continue; there is no time to waste. He passes the tailor's old house and sees the same old lampshade in the window, and the baker's house with the wooden armchair in the doorway and the butcher's house with the copper basin in the garden. Not much has changed since he left, except things have withered, or corroded or become tarnished with rust, and people speckled with liver spots and silver hair. He remembers the fishmonger's body and shudders.

He approaches the first prisoners' camp and decides to walk round it in case there are soldiers passing. He passes the area safely and easily enough and reaches an opening, where a few houses face each other to make a small square. Adem touches his jacket pocket where the Bible is and takes a deep breath. Just then he hears the rumbling of wheels. He freezes suddenly. An army truck just behind the houses. He sees the flash of green in between walls. He darts into the front garden of the houses and looks around for the best place to hide. There isn't much time. The rumbling increases as the truck approaches. In the garden is an olive tree whose trunk is too thin. The wall lining the garden would not be high enough to hide him properly. He decides to try the door, and to his relief it is open. He slips inside and jams it behind him. If they found him now, surely they would kill him. All soldiers should be contained within their regiments. What would he be doing, wandering the streets of Kyrenia on his own? What business did he have in these areas when he has not been commanded to be here?

Adem hears the truck approaching and reaching a halt. He moves through the still shadows of the house into the front room, props himself up on the floor and looks out of the window. Three men step out into the heat. There seems to be no one else in the truck. They do not enter the house from the front, but wander round to the back and disappear amongst the bushes and lemon trees. There is a sudden dissonance of clucking and flapping wings. In a short while there is silence, then the men return, holding a young girl by the arms. They stuff her into the belly of the truck, jump in and head off again. He is sure that they will bring her back shortly. It is safer to wait.

★

Richard wakes up in his brown studio flat with the sun shining on his face. A pigeon cries on the windowsill and the rush-hour train lumbers heavily below. This time he has woken in his bed. It has been years since he has slept in his bed and stared at the cracks on the ceiling from this position. He notices how the crack that once reached the midpoint of the room has now crawled almost to the other end. There is a sinking feeling in his stomach as he realises how much time has passed.

There is much noise in the block this morning. People coming and going, doors opening and closing, a girl laughing, the clunk of pram wheels on the steps, a dog sniffing at his door as it passes, the flap of sandals on the floor. And the sounds from outside carry a similar chord of jolliness: people's voices sound happier, music thumps from cars and open windows. Richard wonders if it is a national holiday he has forgotten about. The sun is hot on his face. Ah ha! Of course! The damn curse of five minutes' sun! We leave our damp holes like blind moles and squint along the street until the rain begins again. He turns away from the light. A phone rings in the distance and a cockney voice far below boasts about Jamaican tomatoes, Spanish bananas and Serbian lemons. Stupid man.

Richard heaves himself up and brings his feet out of the bed. He looks down. His slippers are there. He had remembered to place them there last night, just as he used to; in the days when he still had hope. Hope and slippers come hand in hand. When there is no hope one does not care about wearing slippers, the cold slabs are good enough; there is no real desire for warmth. Is there hope now? None whatsoever, he decides. Not from now on, anyway. But maybe for walking in his former footsteps. The sickly hope of nostalgia; a walk along old avenues, the feeling one gets when watching a slide-show of the past.

He puts his feet into his slippers, stands up and meanders to the sink basin. Looking at himself in the mirror, he pats the sides of his hair with the palms of his hands and picks up his toothbrush. After brushing his teeth he moves to his wardrobe, takes out his brown jumper and grey trousers and dresses himself, slowly, carefully. He has already decided that he will go back to the café. It is the only place he can be now that the small island is being ripped apart. He imagines it desolate and shelled and his beautiful little girl . . . she would be a woman now . . . tall and fiery, with sad, watery eyes. Just like him. And that little island was exactly where his carefully tied laces got caught in the dried thorns and his thoughts became trapped in the heavy net of vines and the barb of carob trees. 'But that is what islands are for,' he says in a voice that he imagines would have resembled Lawrence Durrell's, 'places where destinies can meet and intersect in that full isolation of time.' But his feelings cannot be so detached. Although both he and Durrell had stepped, during the same decade, onto the same port of Limassol, into a dense haze of morning sunshine, Durrell had managed to keep his feet steady along the curling, cobbled streets. Richard had failed to follow this very simple, unspoken path bestowed on the traveller and soldier alike; somewhere, he had stopped walking, forgotten his journey and planted himself in the soil of somebody else's field. Don't sprout where you haven't been planted, Richard thinks, remembering an old Greek proverb.

The man far below boasts about Syrian melons now, and a couple of dogs bark at each other from across the vast landscape of fences and washing lines. He rummages under his bed and looks for Durrell's *Bitter Lemons of Cyprus*, which was his loyal guide and companion after he had bought it at a fair in 1958, just as *A Lady's Impressions of Cyprus* had been for Durrell himself. Back then, he could not help but feel an excessive affiliation with the man; he had clung onto the book with some hope that he might be able to rekindle a little of that romantic fictionalisation of the Englishman in his crown colony, experiencing the smell of almonds and peach blossom, enjoying salty cheese and sweet wine, basking in the shade of the vines while making mental time-lines of the various conquerors. He finds the book in a box with other trinkets, such as his mother's locket and his grandfather's old coins and stamps and a rusty pocket knife and a recipe on a torn piece of paper. The book is just as he had left it, with the dog-eared cover and certain pages folded neatly. He turns a few pages, flicking past publishing and printing notes to where the story begins, and there, beneath desiccated drops of coffee, are the beloved and familiar words, 'Journeys, like artists, are born and not made.' He contemplates for a moment, tucks the book beneath his arm and exits his flat, passing the man with the Russian coconuts and walks, once more, across St James's Park, up through Piccadilly and right into Soho towards Old Compton Street.

However, this time, he does not enter the café immediately, but stops by the secondhand bookshop, where a pickled-looking lady sits frugally on a stool behind a counter, reading a book. She takes off her spectacles as the bell above the door rings and looks at Richard as if he had just entered her home uninvited. 'Yes?' she says, in a tone that reinforces her irritable disposition. Richard looks at the book in her hand – *Everything You Wanted to Know about Sex (But Were Afraid to Ask)* – walks towards her and places *Bitter Lemons* on the counter. 'That'll be fifty pence,' she says, her skin creasing extravagantly as she smiles and a lavish yellow illuminating her teeth. Richard steps back. Her breath smells of used cigarette ends.

'I just brought this in,' he replies. 'I'm handing it in,' he reiterates, stressing each word clearly.

'Oh, well, you win some, you lose some,' the lady responds, looks at the book, tosses it onto a pile and looks down again, intently, at the open book on the counter.

Richard exits the bookshop and continues along Old Compton Street to Amohosto Café. Due to the temperate weather, Paniko has put a small white table outside the shop, where an old man sits with a coffee, flicking worry beads contemplatively. His foot taps on the tarmac. He nods at Richard as he enters the café. The shop is filled with the usual breakfasters, preparing for a long day in the factories. Richard notices that the man in the brown suit is not here today. But the fat man is in the same seat by the window, sucking audibly on a mint. Richard avoids him and finds a table on the other side of the room, near the counter.

Richard sits down and keeps his eye on the kitchen door, waiting for Paniko to appear. Instead Elli, Paniko's wife, sprints out with two trays in her hands. Richard met her only a few times when he first returned to England, but since then they have had many phone conversations, when she has called looking for her husband. Like a fly, now she whizzes round the room depositing coffees and cakes on various tables, every so often removing a pencil from behind her ear and taking a new order. As usual, she wears all grey, with that large gold crucifix round her neck. She passes Richard's table, stops, removes the pencil from behind her ear and rests it on the pad, ready to write. She looks up impatiently and then smiles sadistically. 'So, it's you at last! The one who holds onto my husband's bullocks so tightly.' At this she clenches the fingers of her left hand into the shape of a claw as if she is squeezing something. Her features distort. 'How about some *lokoumades* today? They still sizzling in the pan.' Richard creases his brow, seeking further clarification. 'Donald balls,' she says. Richard creases his brow further. 'Donald balls,' she repeats impatiently. 'Donald balls!' she stresses, but at the look on Richard's face she pushes an open palm toward him, saying 'Na', to indicate her resignation at his stupidity and walks away, shaking her head.

A few moments later she returns to his table with a coffee and a plate of *lokoumades*. 'Doughnut balls,' says Richard.

'That is what I said. You English know nothing. Do you think we came over on a donkey?' she says, passionately pressing forefinger, middle finger and thumb together, waving at the sky. She looks down at his clothes and then into his eyes. 'So Paniko has never managed to drag you out of that hole of yours. Is good for me really. I surprised actually to hear that you no kill yourself yet. But anyhow, this is, how you say? Strange and uncharacteristic. What you want?' She places the coffee on the table next to the *lokoumades* and stares at him right in the eyes. When Richard does not reply she says something angrily in Greek and walks away towards a new customer with the pencil in her hand.

Richard uses the tiny, three-spiked fork to pick up a doughnut ball, which drips with syrup, and polishes all five off in a matter of seconds. Greeks may drink slowly, but they eat fast, he thinks to himself. Then, overwhelmed by the sugar, he takes a sip of the bitter coffee and leans back into his chair.

The rest of the day passes bearably. Paniko does not show himself from the kitchen and Elli confirms that he will be busy scrubbing and frying until one outdoes the other. Richard waits patiently until late afternoon, when Elli leaves to make dinner and invites Richard to join them, but reminds him that it is not a kind invitation on her behalf, rather that she has been left with no choice. If she wants to see her husband she will have to make do with Richard as well.

That night Paniko closes the café at nine, throwing out groaning, unsatisfied punters, and they walk across the street and wait at the bus stop along Old Compton Street for the bus to Archway. The red bus pulls in, chuffs to a halt and the two men enter, pay their fare and sit on the two seats nearest the door, in front of a sleeping drunk man with a carrier bag full of beer. They remain silent for the journey and do not speak even as they walk along Archway Road.

Paniko takes a single silver key from his pocket and unlocks the door. They enter, engulfed by the smell of mothballs, into an unreasonably narrow but elaborately decorated corridor, with a red patterned carpet and crystal wall lamps hanging outlandishly over a long console table packed full of vases, gold picture frames, sparkling animal ornaments and pot-pourri. Paniko takes his shoes off on the mat and places them next to myriad other tiny shoes and hangs his coat on a mahogany stand. Richard does the same. An oversized crystal chandelier hangs too low for them to pass comfortably, and Paniko indicates to him to duck. They walk towards a closed white door at the end of the corridor, which Paniko pushes open, throws his arms up in the air and calls, 'O Pappas! O Pappas!' A young boy and a girl run into his arms, and two more, slightly older, scramble towards him from behind. There is a toddler on a highchair tossing food at the floor. The children, in their excitement, step into the food, and Elli, turning suddenly from the stove to witness the probably familiar frenzy, whips all of them, including

Paniko, with a towel and orders them to sit down sensibly, either with their work or with their friend. This last comment, she makes looking at Paniko.

The children disperse, reluctantly resuming their previous tasks, and Paniko offers Richard a chair, but of course, not at the head of the table, as this is reserved for himself.

Elli brings Richard a glass of red wine in a crystal goblet, and shortly after she sets the table with sesame bread, olives, dips, feta cheese sprinkled with coriander, salad, artichokes and in the centre a large casserole of rabbit and onion stew, or *stifatho*, as the Greeks of the town used to call it. Richard remembers the name, as this happens to be one of his favourites. He had even had Amalia teach him how to make it once, after their usual coffee-cup reading, and Richard had written the recipe in a little journal he used to keep. But of course, that was a long time ago now, and there was never an occasion that required such elaborate cooking.

Richard looks guiltily at the table. 'You should not have gone to so much trouble for—'

'Oh, you poor disillusioned Englishman,' she interrupts. 'You think this for you benefit?' she asks, placing silverware and decorated china plates round the table and then digging a large silver spoon into the stew. She calls something in Greek and the children come running to the table, kicking each other, or screaming, or singing.

'Bravo Paniko!' says Elli to the little boy with no front teeth. 'He has learnt the Greek national anthem off by heart,' she says, beaming. 'He will be either a fighter or diplomat one day, I am sure.' Paniko Junior continues to repeat the song while Elli slaps stew into everybody's plate and the family dig into the dips and olives and salad. Paniko Junior only stops when there is too much food in his mouth to be able to continue, but he doesn't cease humming the song until the end of the meal, when the children clear the table, run away to play and Elli serves Greek coffee to the men. 'I take little one to bed,' she says, pulling the oversized toddler out of the highchair. 'Now watch yourselves,' she says warningly.

'You are not talking to the children now,' Paniko reminds her.

At this Elli laughs. 'Old men are twice children,' she says, looking at Richard's hair. 'Grey hair is only a sign of age, not wisdom.' She laughs, satisfied with her own observations, heaves the toddler higher on her chest and exits the kitchen, leaving the door open a crack behind her.

Paniko's posture relaxes and he sinks into his large shoulders, taking his coffee and bringing it to his lips. He follows Richard's eyes, who is staring at the china ornaments that gaze at him from the top of the kitchen cabinets. 'I tell you, my friend,' begins Paniko, 'you good in that little box on your own with your TV.'

Richard smiles and picks up his coffee.

'You've been bugging me for years to move out of that box, as you call it, and now you say that I am lucky?' Richard says and sips his coffee. Paniko nods.

'Is true, a miser is ever in want,' says Paniko. 'Come on, old friend, why you no find some place better? You have money. You no buy anything.'

'I don't live in that . . . box . . . because I'm stingy. I have my reasons,' replies Richard scathingly. Paniko raises his eyebrows. Richard takes a deep breath, feeling Paniko's anticipation for an explanation. 'Back then,' he begins, 'before the independence of Cyprus, after I had followed Kyriaki and met Mihalis, I visited the taverna regularly. I never spoke to anyone and Mihalis never really said much to me again. I always sat at the same table, beneath a lemon tree, overlooking the rolling hills. I drank coffee, and observed the drying of the land as each summer approached and secretly watched my little girl as she grew. I watched her as she learnt to ride a bike, as she grazed her knees, as she cried alone beneath the olive trees, I watched her as she learnt to read and as she sang songs over the balcony. I watched her hair grow and her body change and her fingers lengthen, so that she made beautiful delicate tapestries, which Mihalis would hang proudly on the walls. He loved her. How that man loved her. Sometimes I would catch him looking at me but he never said anything and I was never too sure whether somewhere deep down he knew . . .' Richard pauses there, sips his coffee again and resumes. 'Her eyes were exactly the colour of the shallow part of the sea, the part that laps the shores. And they always moved, they were curious eyes, full of questions and tales and turmoil; her life was not easy. With the way she looked and the chaos of those troubled times, she became an easy target, a scapegoat. People treated her as though she were an alien.' Richard stops there, squints his eyes shut and rubs the sides of his temples with his palms, bringing them down the sides of his face and round to his neck as though he is trying to relieve some tension. He then stands slightly and reaches into his pocket for a box of cigarettes.

'Outside,' says Paniko. 'She can't hear.'

Richard nods, and they move into the garden, where they both blow cigarette smoke into the balmy night. A siren is heard in the distance.

'Although I never spoke to her, I knew her. I knew what made her cry and what made her laugh. I knew her loneliness. I knew that she had a mole on her left shoulder and a small scar on her forehead, from when she had fallen off her bike when she was nine. I knew her favourite dress and that she hated lemonade and that she loved to walk barefoot, which Mihalis always insisted was exactly like her mother. And as she grew, during those five years, I knew that she longed for something, from the way she tapped her foot on the floor, just like her mother, and from the way she paced around the olive trees.' Another siren is heard, the toddler cries and Elli shouts something at the children.

'I never spoke to her until the day I was to leave Cyprus in the autumn of 1960. She was thirteen, but looked like a woman as her eyes, by then, looked much older, as if her thoughts had aged her. I grabbed her arm as she walked past me and held a letter out for her to take. I looked her hard in the eyes and told her that if her father ever found out what was in this letter it would destroy him. I told her not to open it until she was ready for her life to change. She looked into my eyes, and then down at my fingers that gripped her arm desperately. She took the letter, I let go of her arm, and she stood and stared at me for a while. She leant forwards and touched my fingers, which were gripping my knees. That was the last time I ever saw her.

'When independence was on the cards I rang you and asked you to get a bedsit ready for me so that I would have somewhere to stay when I got here. You sent me the address, which I put the details of in the letter for Kyriaki. In that letter I told her the truth about who she really was. I've been waiting all these years. That is why I never moved. I have been holding onto some hope that one day she might come and find me.'

Paniko nods reassuringly and puts his hand on Richard's shoulder. 'You sad little man,' he says, and laughs. 'Why now?' he asks.

Richard ignores his tone. 'Because this damn war ignited my pain, and my fear that I may never see her again. Now it seems impossible and my torment is too much for me to keep. Now she may even be—'

'Don't think these things!' interrupts Paniko. 'I did for only one day and nearly went mad! If they are all dead we cannot change anything with worry. We will wait and see; it is all that we can do.'

Richard nods this time and throws his cigarette on the ground. Paniko bends down, picks it up and throws it into the next-door-neighbour's garden along with his own.

'Fear your wife more than your neighbours, for to them you can close the door,' says Paniko, and Richard forces a laugh.

Serkan looks up into the dome of the church. The Virgin Mary stares down at him and he remembers then the face of his mother, so still, so unchanging, sitting at the kitchen table, holding Hasad in her arms. Serkan walks through the church towards the icon of mother and child by the altar. He leans forward and touches her hair, then he puts his hand in his pocket and paces up and down the aisle. The bloodstained walls scream red, and the cicadas and the sunlight pound beneath the wooden door. From above, light streams in through the stained-glass window. Serkan presses his knuckles, then adjusts his shirt to make sure that it is tucked perfectly into his trousers. The door bursts open and the pounding island enters the church. Hasad stands at the door, his longer arm dangling close to his knee. 'We will not progress forward,' Serkan says aloud, and his voice bounces within the high dome of the church. Hasad nods and walks in further. He looks down, noticing the girl that he had brought in a little while ago is half-conscious on the floor; her eyelids flicker. She has a bruise around her eye and blood on her arm. 'They are animals,' says Serkan. Hasad puts his hand in his pocket and retrieves the pocket watch, which sparkles in the sunlight; he holds it in his palm and looks at the time. 'Take her back!' Serkan demands.

'The baby's crying can be heard over the hills,' says Hasad.

Stepping out of the church, Serkan hears the baby crying. Its howl pierces the air like a siren. Serkan shuts his eyes tightly to block out the sharp light and adjusts the gun to his trousers. He charges down the hill, past the port and the well, towards the houses of prisoners, and with each step the baby's shrill crying becomes increasingly loud. He turns right into the orchard and towards the basket where the baby lies screaming, red-faced, with its little arms reaching for the air. Serkan bends down and touches his fingers, and the crying misses a beat and becomes irregular. 'Little man,' he says, putting his large palm on the baby's head. He then leans over, lifts the baby up and brings it close to his chest.

Serkan walks for a while round the orchard while the baby hiccups in his arms, and he hums a song his mother used to sing. He stops suddenly and looks up at the blue of the sky through the trees and feels a surge of pain at the base of his spine. He winces and inclines his head affectionately towards the baby's. The little boy is as quiet as the breeze now and his eyelids heavy in the cool shade of the leaves. He yawns.

Sophia is tossed into a bush of skin-coloured thorns. Her flesh is ripped and blood drips from her forehead. Maroulla walks out and looks down at the girl's golden limbs intertwined with the twigs and imagines that she is not there. She envisions the twigs as a path that would lead her to the rose. Her mother said so . . . her mother said so . . . she will not dare, though, take a step beyond the garden trees. Her heart flutters with fear at this thought. She looks down at the flesh and thorns as Sophia opens her eyes and the women come running from within. They lift her body and it droops lifeless in their arms as they carry her into the shadows of the room. 'Don't die, young girl. Don't die,' says Maria, while Litsa watches with wide eyes. Olympia sits rigid on the chair, still with her face to the wall. Costandina cries. The dog whimpers and follows the women that carry Sophia to the bed, where Elenitsa once lay, and cover her with a blanket. Maria fetches some water, holding the flask up to her lips, but Sophia will not drink. The dog licks her arm and face, but Sophia does not flinch. Maria wipes the blood from her face and arm, gently, with a wet cloth.

'Let her be,' says Olympia suddenly. 'Just let her sleep.' Maria holds the wet cloth up to Sophia's face and looks at her lifeless eyes and cracked lips. She pauses, pulls the cloth away and rests it resignedly on the bed, sighing deeply. She positions a chair next to the bed so that she can be nearby if needed. She touches Sophia's forehead with the palm of her hand and hums gently. Sophia closes her eyes. Soon her breathing deepens and Maria removes her hand and places it on her lap. The other women sit awkwardly around the room, all full of fear and expectation. At any one moment there is always one pair of eyes looking towards the back of the garden. A green uniform can still be seen flickering amongst the trees.

'We cannot be like this,' says Litsa, standing up. 'This way they will not have to kill us, we will simply die of fear.' She lifts her chin higher as she talks, and the women look up at her from the floor or from various chairs scattered about the room. 'There is always something to live for,' she continues, 'the past is always alive in the present, it is never behind us.' At this she looks at Koki, and the rest of the women follow her gaze. Maroulla is sitting by Koki's feet with her arms wrapped around Koki's leg. She too looks up at Koki. 'I think I can speak for everyone when I say we would like to know what happened with the shoemaker,' says Litsa. Sophia breathes heavily now in her sleep, and the dog sighs by her side. Koki smiles and the women look at her eagerly.

'OK,' she begins; she leans back into the chair and looks at the floor. Her eyes become distant and full of shadows from the falling sun. Her red curls slumber onto her shoulders and others tumble onto her purple dress. The headscarf is on the floor. She sighs and her eyelashes cast shadows on her face, and she looks, for a moment, like a china doll, lost in time. The women stare at her as if she is a recovered toy, found at the bottom of some long-forgotten trunk, igniting again the mislaid dreams of childhood. Koki moves her fingers. 'In the church, on the night of the Resurrection,' she begins. The women shift their positions and Maria leans over and looks closely at Sophia before fixing her gaze on Koki. '. . . On the night of the Resurrection, darkness rose. It rose from the black robes of the widows. It rose from the place where palms held the wax of unlit candles. The Christians waited eagerly for midnight when the bishop would chant "Christ is risen", and holy light would be passed from candle to candle and the good Christians would at last be able to go home and feast on already prepared platters of meat and egg-lemon soup after forty days of excruciating fasting. The men stood at the front of the church, normally quiet, and praying for the prosperity of their own businesses; while the women stood at the back passing news of the town from mouth to mouth. Standing at the back of the church with Vassoulla, Litsa's mum, I listened to the conversations of the women. "Antonia just told me that there is a new shoemaker

in town," the seamstress leant over and said to Vassoulla
in what was much louder than a whisper.

"'It's about time, Dimitri's farming boots are as useless as a donkey's tail. Mario was hopeless, God rest
his soul." Vassoulla said this, looking at the ceiling of
the church, and crossed herself, which, unbeknown
to her, led to a succession of crossing as the women
near them mindlessly followed the gesture, bowing
their heads to the front with exaggerated looks of
martyrdom, thinking that the priest had constituted
the motion.

"'He is a *levendi*!" the seamstress interjected.
"Beautiful face . . ."

"'Pppaa," Vassoulla spat. "He is a Turk! From the
mainland! They are an ugly race."

'The seamstress nodded in agreement and both
crossed themselves and bowed their heads as they
noticed the people around them doing so.

"'There's news that he will marry Bambaji's granddaughter, he is eighteen and coming of age," continued
the seamstress. Bamabaji's granddaughter was sixteen
at the time, a year older than me, and was considered
the most beautiful Turkish girl that Kyrenia had ever
known. God had put the colour red in the right places:

on her lips and her cheeks, and her skin was the colour of baked bread.

'"It is time you sorted out your Litsa, Vassoulla," said the seamstress. "It is a problem for a girl of fifteen to be gallivanting around without a husband. It looks bad for our community. We will be ridiculed by the Turks."

'Vassoulla's face tightened into a smile. "Oh, there is a doctor's son who is interested. From Larnaca," she added quickly. The other lady's eyebrows folded as she opened her mouth to speak, but Vassoulla looked away from her to where I was standing and pinched my arm – "Stand up straight in the house of God or you will be punished severely." I pulled back my shoulders and heard the other lady whisper, "She is not normal, the poor girl has been burdened by the sins of her ancestors."

'"She is a bastard," whispered another woman nearby.

'"We must pray for her, it is our duty," said Vassoulla with a false tone of sympathy in her voice. Again, another two women, standing nearby, nodded in agreement and bowed their heads.

'The first bead of light merged with the darkness at the front where the bishop stood; and then the light moved through the church as each member of the congregation lit their candle from their neighbour's, passing the holy light from hand to hand. As the light approached, the women's faces became reflections of the light of Christ; as it rose and stole portions of darkness some faces appeared even darker in those shadows than they had in the former obscurity.

'Soon Vassoulla passed the light to me from her own candle, being careful not to look my way in case that holy light might just be supernatural enough to lift the veil which she wore, or else that this gesture might have revealed a flicker of genuine shame and a shadow of the face beneath the mask.

'And then a chant rose, like the light, but murkier and heavier, though not dimmer; breaking the gossip as the light the darkness. And the collective voice of the good Christians of Kyrenia town rose and fell as they joined in the singing, and for a brief moment, for they truly believed it, they glowed like the light, in a simultaneous blaze of denial. Then the crowd dispersed and went on their separate paths.

'"Christ is risen, Koki." The seamstress leant over me and kissed each of my cheeks.

'"Truly He is risen," I replied.

'"And don't worry, God will notice you too one

day, just like he did my Avyi." She opened one of her arms to welcome a very pregnant daughter, whom she kissed on both cheeks, wishing her a good rising of Christ, to which her daughter replied, "You too, Mama," and then continued through the crowd of people, proudly stomach first, hugging and kissing on her way.

'I looked around for my dad, but instead saw Kyrios Christos' wife, who was a very good cook; the tailor's daughter, Aphrodite, who was ugly despite her name, but a very good girl; and a widow, Andiyoni, whose sister's husband's brother had lost all his money in a game of *kounka* three years ago, and that was *not* a good family. Dimitri was standing at the front of the church, as usual, in an attempt to proclaim his patriotism, or "faith", to use his preferred choice of word. He was kissing the hand of the priest as I approached, and, as he saw me, raised his arms. "Christ is risen, my Koki," he shouted, kissing me on both cheeks, but this time I did not repeat the expected phrase.

'"Where is Pappa?"

'"Koki, you will be punished by God!" he said, astonished.

'"Truly He is risen," I said finally.

'I worked my way through the crowd in the church and the crowd beneath the arches and when I stepped into the clearing, and could finally feel the breeze on my face, I remembered the shoemaker's touch. I felt his fingers on my skin and I longed for him in a way that I had longed for nothing else. So, with hot cheeks and a fluttering heart I ran through the town, beyond the port and the café and the well, beneath the olive trees and vines, round the golden field of wheat, all the way to the shoemaker's hut. When I got there I rested my hands on my knees to take a breath and noticed a flickering light in the window. Was he still at work? I composed myself, walked over and knocked gently on the door. There was no answer so I sat right there on the doorstep and listened to the singing of the crickets and watched the fireflies in the trees beyond.

'It was a few minutes later that the door finally opened and the shoemaker stood in the doorway with a shoe in his hand and looked down at where I sat. We said nothing to each other; he smiled, left the door open and resumed his work, while I sat silently on the step and watched him. This same thing happened night after night, night after night, for many, many months.

I would sit and watch him until the town had silenced and the crickets' song had become so deep that you could not tell it from the darkness.

'One night, however, in September, after a particularly cloudy day, it started to rain as I sat on the steps. I didn't move, and he looked up from his work and watched me as the rain drenched my hair and my dress. He laughed, walked towards me and signalled for me to come in. I looked at the floor. "You *have* to, *now*," he said, ducking his head through the door frame to look outside. So, I stood up and stepped into the dry room, shedding droplets of rain onto the floor like a stray dog. He stood there in the flickering candlelight and watched me. "I've been waiting for it to rain for six months," he said, and I stood, as wet as a blanket, dripping, as thunder sounded overhead.

'"It's good for the crops," I replied, and he laughed, then fetched a towel from the back. I wiped my face and rubbed my hair and he went into the back again and returned this time, a few minutes later, with two cups of steaming coffee. I sat on a stool on the counter and sipped my coffee while he continued to work in the candlelight and amid wisps of coffee mist.

'From that day on, and for weeks to come, I would

sit on the stool, indoors, whether it was raining or not, and watch the shoemaker while he worked into the night. Every so often he would make, especially for me, a new pair of shoes, and present them to me as I entered. One pair, if I recall, was black patent with laces, another, brown with a little buckle; another, red, embossed with flowers; another emerald-green with a small heel. All of them I wore with pride, even as the neighbours stared and muttered beneath their breath. Of course, the neighbours talked. They talked endlessly like the crickets. Always something to say about somebody else; always a story to tell. They muttered and whispered and murmured and moaned and all proclaimed to know the truth, about everything and everyone and all the large affairs of the world and all the little sordid affairs of our town. You all know that life in the town is empty without the stories. The stories bubble in the pan of beans, rise in the steam of coffee, splatter from the washing, are woven into the tapestries of silk.' Koki stops and looks at the faces of the women. Their eyes are wide and the shadows rise from the corners of the room. Although the doors open up into the garden, the air is still and the room is humid and the women's faces shine in the half light.

'I confessed my sins to the priest. At first, Pappa, God rest his soul, never said a word. Never let the gossip bother him, and never questioned me about what he had heard. He was not a man of pride; he believed, only, that we must all bear our destinies, whatever they may be. He never asked me where I went at night and why on certain nights I came home with new shoes. He knew. Of course, he knew. There were many things Pappa knew, but never spoke of, I am sure of it . . . Any other father whose daughter was seen with a Turk would have beaten her and locked her away. But Pappa was different, he let me live the way I wanted to. It was unheard of for a father to do such a thing, but he would always say that he could see my mother's passion glowing in my soul and who but God should guide the flight of a bird.

'All the other girls in the town were getting married. Avyi had been introduced to her husband over an evening meal; they were married a fortnight later, once the dowry had been agreed. Her family were very well off, so the groom had the benefit of receiving three acres of land. The farmer's daughter married in the same way. The tailor's daughter married a man she hadn't even met.

'Eventually, as time passed, Pappa changed. The whispers of the town had somehow entered his veins, their convictions had taken hold of his mind, he became fretful and worried, wondering in his moments alone whether he had made the wrong choices. I could tell by the way he flicked his rosary beads and rubbed his forehead again and again as though the answers that he wanted were hard to find. One day he looked at me anxiously and said, "I must do what a father is meant to do."

'He started writing letters to the families of prospective grooms. Late every night, after he had cleaned up the restaurant, he would sit on the veranda and by the light of a candle he would write letters to the families of young men from other towns. He would first contemplate for a while, looking out across the hills, and then he would glance at me with a look of sadness on his face. Although he tried to hide it I could see how he felt sorry for me, how he thought I was destined always to be alone. However, while I sat beneath the tree and kneaded dough or made pastries for the next day, he would scribble away, then very neatly fold the letter and seal it in an envelope. The following day he would give me the letter and instruct me to take it to Vangeli's café. Of course I thought about burning the letters or throwing them into the sea, but I knew that Pappa would be waiting for a reply. So I did as he wished, but I secretly hoped that all the families would decline his offer.

'Not long after, the replies started arriving. I remember one night I brought three letters out with Pappa's ouzo, and he nodded, smiled at me and put them on the table. He tapped them a few times with his middle finger as though he were making a wish, straightened them so that the corners of all three letters were together, and sat back. He left them there unopened while he drank one ouzo, then two and then asked me to bring him a walnut sweet. I went into the kitchen and put a walnut sweet into a glass of water with a fork. My hands were shaking with nerves; I took it to him with the fork rattling against the glass and as he took it from my hand he looked up at me. He looked as though he wanted to say something, but he didn't. Once he opened that letter he knew that my life would be in his hands. Perhaps he knew that for the first time in my life I was happy and he didn't want to be the one to take that away from me.

'He ate his sweet, waited longer still, had another

ouzo and finally, as though he was exhausted by thinking, slammed his hand on the table, sat up straighter and opened the first letter. He had made his decision. He read it slowly. He did the same with the second and the third, then he sat with his chin in his hand, sliding quick glances in my direction, while I rolled *koubebia* for the next day, trying to look as aloof as possible. He then called me over and told me that two men had asked to meet me: one was a doctor and the other a farmer. He looked at me right in the eyes and then leant across the table and touched my hand. "This is the way of the Greeks," he said, "it's the way things must be." I didn't say a word, returning to my task.

'The meeting was arranged and a few weeks later the doctor from Paphos came for dinner with his parents. Pappa welcomed them at the entrance of the taverna while I peeked out through the crack of the door. I could see them shaking hands and Pappa opening his palm and gesturing for them to enter. They looked around haughtily, right and left, up and down, as though Pappa's taverna was not good enough for their educated son. "Koki," Pappa called, and I ventured out with my head down, looking up only when I finally reached the middle of the restaurant, where they were now standing. Immediately the doctor's eyes widened and a look of disgust spread across his face. "Oh, *you're* the one that everybody . . ." he blurted out, without thinking, and I saw his mum nudge him. His dad coughed loudly and then asked Pappa how business was doing. We ate in silence and when they finally left Pappa asked me to sit with him while he drank ouzo and ate his walnut sweet. He did not talk for a while and I watched him as he dipped his sweet in and out of the water again and again. He did not eat it, though; he allowed the sweet to drop to the bottom of the glass and rested the fork on the side; by this time the water had taken on the sickly-brown of the sweet. "Education comes from within," he said suddenly. "A doctor can read all the books in the world and know how to tie up a wound or heal a broken leg, but if they don't know about social etiquette and how to speak to people then they know nothing!" I smiled, and seeing the look on my face Pappa felt satisfied, and finally ate his sweet.

'A similar thing happened with the farmer and in the end Pappa did not write any more letters. A good Greek girl should have an arranged marriage with a good Greek boy. I was not a good Greek girl. In fact most people doubted my Greekness altogether. As more stories bubbled round the town, anger brewed around me. I was already the misfit, and now I had completely violated the rules. I had defied my religion and culture. I had mortified the face of our town. How dare I show up our neighbourhood in such a way? What kind of social education had I had? At first they blamed Pappa for having a restaurant open to all, but after much deliberation it was unanimous that Mihalis was a good man. Consequently, the next question to arise was how such a great member of the community could produce such an oddball; the answer to this was: "From a thorn a rose emerges and from a rose a thorn." One cannot predict what one's offspring will become in life; an honest, respected man's daughter may turn out to be a whore. Then, they would remember poor Mama and say that in fact, I could have taken after her and that I might have some other man's genes. At the end of the day, it was decided, over washing lines and cups of coffee, that that was the most likely explanation.

'Anyway, one particular night, in November, high on the hill with Pappa, when the customers had all dispersed, I brought him a little cup of coffee and placed it on the table where he sat. He did not smile and thank me as usual, but instead continued to look down at the flickers of light from the neighbouring homes. His face looked stern and gaunt and that golden colour of his skin now looked pale. His broad shoulders slouched over his stomach and his foot shook beneath the table. He looked at me, momentarily, with red-rimmed eyes, then cast the back of his hand on my face, so hard that my head spun, and I dropped to my knees and sobbed, and when he did not move or comfort me I stood up and ran out of the gate, tumbling in the darkness down the hill.

'When I returned, Pappa said only that the neighbours had tongues like snakes. He put his hand on my shoulder and his eyes shimmered with sadness. It was not spoken of again. But other things happened, and much worse. One other night, on the way to the hut, I was attacked by a group of youngsters. They called me a whore and pulled my hair until they saw blood. They threw small rocks at me, knocked me to the ground and stole my shoes, the black patent ones with the laces. Then they ran off and left me on the floor. At first, I was ashamed to go to the hut, so I walked around, barefoot. Finally, a few hours later, I swallowed my pride and made my way along the port.

'When I got to the hut, the door was closed and I sat on the step, with the candle flickering in the window above. About half an hour must have passed when he opened the door, probably looking for me, and found me sitting on that step. He leant over and touched my arm and I stood up as he looked at the bruises on my arms and my bare feet and the red of my eyes. The shadows moved across his face as he stood still and watched me. There was a strange look in his eyes, maybe of anger or sadness, and he looked away from me and out towards the setting sun. Then, he took a step closer so that his face was next to mine, leant in awkwardly and kissed me on the lips.

'The more our love developed and grew the less he ventured out of the shoemaker's hut. Not even for a midnight walk along the sleeping streets. He simply said that the shoes he made were for other people's journeys. He would not let me question him about this, and over time his skin became pale and his eyes shrunk and he touched only residues of the world from the soles of others' shoes: granules of sand from the beach or small grey pebbles from the mountains and sometimes strange-coloured soil from other regions or other lands. Often he would hold the dirt in his fingers and smell it as if he were inhaling the scent of a wild and foreign herb.

'Sitting in the safety of his hut, he loved to tell me stories. He spoke as he worked and I often lay on the floor, with my head resting on my hands, and listened to the sound of his voice. He told me that Cyprus was the most beautiful place in the world because on its shores one could find the footprints of many conquerors who shaped the island into what it is today: a place so intricate and strange and full of fear. He said that everyone that came brought both something dire and something new.

'He told me about the Roman rulers, Cato and Julius Caesar, that occupied Cyprus when the rule of Ptolemy came to an end. He made the shoes that Cato had worn just so that I could see them; the military sandals, called "*caligae*", which had so many layers of sole with nailed edges. He made other Roman shoes with straps and grid patterns, or triangles or circles. He explained that before that the Greeks walked barefoot or wore very simple shoes. He even made me a women's pair; they were delicate, with patterns of ovals and squares.

'He loved to tell stories of Caliph Haroun al-Rashid of Arabia, who was an intellectual man of poetry and music. He described the type of shoes he would have worn when he occupied Cyprus. Then one night, I went to the hut and found the door was wide open and a candle flickered on the worktop. I walked in and called his name, but he did not answer. Then, I noticed, illuminated by the candlelight on a piece of red silk, the most exquisite shoes I have ever seen in my life. They were embroidered with gemstones and glittered majestically as I picked them up and turned them over in my hand. I took my shoes off and slipped them on.

'He appeared from the back of the hut. "They are the same style worn by Sitt Zubayda, Haroun al-Rashid's wife, she set the trends!" he said, and I told him I loved them. Then he took my hand, drew me close to him and we danced. At first I stumbled and laughed and stepped on his feet, but he put my fingers on his palm and led me with his hand and with his feet and soon I felt as though I was being moved by something within me, my body relaxed, and with my face close to his neck and my eyes closed we danced to our own music, we moved to the sound of the crickets and the sea and the wind. "Perhaps one day you can wear them out and we'll dance." He said these words quickly, with a slightly wistful tone, as though he knew that it would never happen.

'Time passed in this way and I imagined that it always would; that one day I would live with him in his little dark hut of soil and dreams. But one cuckoo does not bring the spring. Soon the hut was full of graffiti, red words which warned of death and massacre and dripped, conveniently, like blood. Soon all the windows were smashed, and as the winter breeze whistled through the shards he would sit at the counter, with distant eyes and listen to the changes of the wind. I should have believed the tone in his voice rather than his words; I never wore those shoes again.

'At that time my breasts swelled and my monthly bleeding stopped, and I remembered that these matched the changes that Vassoulla had once described about her body one day when she was reminiscing about being pregnant with Litsa. At first I told no one and I prayed to God and begged him to take it away. But soon my fears came to life and a small bump started appearing, which I hid beneath layers of clothes. The bump was not getting any smaller. I had to tell him; I was afraid, but he had to know.

'It was a particularly cold night and the neighbours were all indoors and they peeked though their shutters as I walked by. I strolled down the hill, past the church and the port and the cafés. The younger ones opened the shutters and called words like "traitor" or "whore" and even as I passed the silent fields, I could still hear their voices ringing in my ears.

'As I approached the hut, it started to rain heavily. The red soil bubbled and small rivers of puddles streamed down the hills. I arrived wet at the hut, as on that first night, but realised that the candle was not flickering in the window. All seemed dark within. I rushed to the door and knocked hard, but there was no answer. I turned the handle. Locked. I felt a surge of panic and looked around, but the streets were empty and still. I looked in through the broken window, but there was no movement within. I sat on the step and waited till the rain stopped and my dress and hair dried. I waited until the cockerel sang and the sun came up and bleached the houses white. I imagined that he was called away or taken on some emergency and that soon he would return.

'As the days and weeks passed and he was nowhere to be seen, I continued to hope that he would turn up. During this time Pappa started to look at me suspiciously; he would often say that I looked different and that something had changed about me, but that he couldn't quite figure out what it was. I was terrified. I knew the day would come when he would realise that I was pregnant. Soon the bump was big enough to show through my dresses, and it was at this time that Pappa called me to the little table where he sat, late one night.

'I perched down on the chair opposite him and looked at the ground; I knew what was coming. He stared at me for a very long time and then said, "Can you tell me that you are not pregnant?"

I looked straight into his eyes and said, "No, Pappa, I cannot." He deserved to know the truth. Then I waited for him to say more, to reach over and touch my arm, even to look at me as though he felt sorry for me; but he did neither. His face was severe and expressionless as he looked out across the hills. He did not look at me as he spoke this time.

'"You have brought shame on me, Koki." His voice trembled slightly as he spoke, but he made sure that he held his chin high and kept his face away from me. "Go to bed," he said, and as I walked away he spoke again. "You see," he exclaimed, "you have brought too much shame this time. Too much!" He shook his head from side to side and looked at the floor. I ran to my bedroom. With those words he had shattered my heart. I was devastated and I fell asleep that night crying. I had lost everything.

'The next day Pappa told me that he had arranged for me to move into a derelict hut on the outskirts of the town. He said I would be far away enough there. When I asked him what he meant by that he simply said that the neighbours would not bother me as much. He said that he would fix the hut for me himself and that it would be good enough for me to raise a baby in. I asked him if I could stay there with him, but he did not answer and from that day on few words passed between my father and me.

'But he loved me still; he never stopped loving me. I could tell by the way he hammered away at the walls of the hut, how he rebuilt the fireplace so that I wouldn't be cold in the winter, how he planted lemon trees and fig trees for me. But all the while I felt as though he was building me a prison and I dreaded the day that it would be finished. Luckily, it took some weeks, as he could only work when the restaurant was closed, which was either at midday or very late at night. I would go with him; with the midday sun on our shoulders we would walk together down the hill and across the town. He would hold a sun umbrella for me, and when we arrived he would put a chair for me beneath the shade and wait for me to sit down, and fetch water or peel some figs that he had picked along the way. He put them on a plate, sliced them and brought them to me where I sat. It was at these times that I felt his love, just like I had when I was a little girl, and sometimes as I ate the fruit I would catch him looking at me, staring with a faraway look in his eyes as though it was not really me he saw sitting before him, but that little girl who had once sat on his lap and listened to his stories.

'As I sat on that chair and watched him work I saw him gradually become older; his hair turned white and he seemed to shrink and shrivel. I loved Pappa so much; so many times I wanted to run to him and put my arms around him and tell him I was sorry for what I had done; but I was too ashamed, too embarrassed even to apologise, and I was terrified that he would tell me that he could never forgive me.

'Soon enough the hut was ready. I was eight months

pregnant by this time, and I moved in, frightened and alone. During this whole time I never stopped going to the shoemaker's hut. Every night I made the usual journey to his hut. I did this until my shoes had worn thin and the neighbours sniggered and the bump of my stomach had grown so big that I could barely walk down the hill. But he never again returned. No, he never returned.'

There are tears now in Koki's eyes. The women's eyes shimmer in the darkness as the air pounds with Koki's last words and the sound of the crickets. Sophia stirs in the bed, and the dog lifts its ears and sits up. Maria straightens her posture and strokes Sophia's hair. Sophia sighs, tosses from side to side and protests at something, swinging her arms in the air. 'Her eyes are closed. She is asleep,' says Maria, and the women remain silent.

Adem stands patiently at the window overlooking a garden of rosy pomegranates. A cockroach scuttles by his feet. The house is dark, and cloudy with fleas. Adem looks down at the priest's shoes and taps the right one on the floor, then the left. He stands very still and looks again out of the window. Although Hasad brought the girl back a while ago, he has still not left. First Hasad hovered around the house for a long while, passing up and down, smoking cigarettes, then he sat down on a wooden chair and has been there ever since. Adem must not be seen. He feels his nerves knotting up: his fingers tingle and his breath is shallow. If she is not here, he will lose all hope of ever finding her.

Hasad finally stands up and paces up and down the street again, with his longer arm on his chin as if deep in thought. He walks unrhythmically, with a limp, and his head lifts up, then drops down. Another half an hour or so passes and Hasad now looks up at the sky.

Adem takes a deep breath and stands straight. He knows that this is his last chance to find her. If she has not escaped or died there is every possibility that she may be in this last house. He looks at his shoes. He is torn between wishing that she has already fled and wishing that she is here, a prisoner, Serkan's captive, just so that he can see her again. He thinks about all those years, all those wasted years, and retrieves the photograph from his pocket. He remembers that red hair, dripping wet on that doorstep, so many years ago, and the way her skin smelt of the outside world, of the sea and lemon blossoms, and the way she always left traces of sand from where she had been walking along the beach. Whenever he looked out of his window he would imagine that she existed wherever fire flickered: in the hovering flames of candles, in the sun's rays that streaked through windows and in that invisible heat that rose endlessly. He remembers her eyes, so distant, so detached from this town. Where is she now?

He wipes the sweat from his forehead and suddenly feels a sinking feeling in his heart. The past! he thinks suddenly. The answer to the riddle is: the past! The past can never be destroyed and never be repaired! Somehow, in the confinement of this riddle, the two opposing words have come to hold the same meaning. No matter what, the past cannot be altered, whether to be broken or fixed. What's done is done. Adem cries into his fist. He cries for everything lost and bends down and takes off the priest's shoes. He finds a cloth, spits on it and rubs the dried-on soil, scrubbing hard until the shoes shine slightly in the light.

Richard leaves Paniko's house late and walks to the bus stop. He is not in the mood to walk tonight and it is now raining. The bus arrives promptly and Richard climbs to the top and looks down at the multicoloured umbrellas bopping along Queen Victoria Street, passing the Palladian structure of the Mansion House, hanging like a painting of an ancient Greek temple in the rain; despite its grandiose pagan mannerisms, it fits neatly into the landscape, just as the foreign banana trees once did on the hills of Kyrenia.

The Victorian buildings dotted along the street sit on the pavements frugally, stiff-lipped, reticent and beautifully grey in that grey rain, a picture of a forgotten people; just like the baggy-trousered patriarchs that once lined the streets of Cyprus. The old men there became landmarks for the British colonialists trying to find their way through the winding streets. 'To get to Bella-pais, turn left at the corner where the old man sits; you'll know it's him by his black pants and his white eyebrows. You'll know you're going the right way when you see a goat.' Richard smiles nostalgically.

Arriving shortly at his bedsit, Richard stands in the kitchen in the corner and stirs a coffee on the stove. He watches it intently as the top layer becomes sand-coloured, and then lifts the pan off the stove just as the bubbles bloom around the rim. He pours it into a little cup and walks over to the television, turns it on, sees the familiar image and hears the monotonous tone that means the day's programmes are over. He leaves it on and walks across to the open window that overlooks Queen Victoria Street, and looks out. Somewhere amongst the stout Victorian buildings the sounds of Black Sabbath rise disobediently; how times have changed from the world his grandfather had told stories about. Now, in the eyes of his grandfather, every Brit's step would be defiant. 'The insubordinate world is a subordinate world.' That was his motto. What would he think now of the contraceptive pill and the hippies that held spring flowers in the winter? What would he think of the disco sounds and the all-nighters who strolled to work with the echo of Bee Gees still beating the rhythm of their steps? And the no-fault divorce law and women with lives of their own? This would be a travesty! When the churchgoing and pipe-smoking are a dying race, this will be an omen of the imminent breakdown of society! Richard smiles. He looks down at passers-by, even at this late hour, with their array of business suits and colourful clothes.

Richard brings the coffee up to his lips. Maybe, he doesn't have to be here? His talk with Paniko has changed something within him, shifted the barriers that he had created in his mind. It was all out now. No more secrets. No more hope. How could he still be hoping that she would turn up? So many years had passed. Now that it is all out in the open Richard realises how fragile his dream was. Perhaps he could start his life again? He dispels the thought quickly as he thinks of the little girl with red hair and porcelain skin. He sighs deeply, puts the coffee on the windowsill and takes his pyjamas out of the drawer. He stands in front of the basin mirror, pats down his grey hair and brushes his teeth. The man downstairs boasts now about British watermelons. Does he never sleep? Richard raises his eyebrows and proceeds to undress himself. He remembers his coffee, walks back to the window and looks at the familiar net of clouding sky that hangs heavy over grey buildings and grey pigeons and those English splashes of red, like roses. He watches that graceful sweep of rain into the river. Someone calls something in a foreign tongue and a dog barks. For a moment a hole appears in the clouds and the rain is illuminated by the moon. A lady with hair dripping to her shoulders runs across the street with a pram in one arm and a crying child in the other. All noises are muffled and merge into one: the wailing, the distant sirens, the rain, the rumble of traffic, the mixture of tongues. Richard looks down at the displaced cherry tree, leaning uncomfortably over a bus stop. The woman stops beneath the tree and leans the pram against the bus stop. The bus pulls up and she is gone. The rain eases slightly and the tree drips onto the pavement below. The sound from the television drones on incessantly.

Richard feels suddenly alone. Although all these years he has had no one, he had somehow become accustomed to it; learnt that that was his life. But now something stirs within him, a different feeling; the realisation of where and who he really is. He sees himself as if from afar: a sad old man looking out of the window. They will find him here one day, dead in the armchair. Like William at Number 27. Richard turns around and looks at the worn furniture of this room: the brown armchair, the bed with the peeling frame, the crumbling tiles in the kitchen, the cardboard box. If his life doesn't change, they will find him here one day.

The prisoners watch fearfully as a man enters from the side of the garden. He is not holding a lantern and stumbles in the dark. The thorns crunch beneath his feet as he ducks under the net of the carob tree. In the clearing, in the moonlight, his face is illuminated and the little girl beams. She recognises him by his hazel eyes, like crescent moons. She closes the book, tucks it into her apron and runs to greet the man in green.

She curtsies and holds out her hand and tells him that she has been waiting for his return. He looks down at her outstretched hand, unmoving, then turns his face away. 'When will our journey begin?' she asks, lowering her arm. His eyes dart into the room ahead. He looks quickly over his shoulder. His thoughts are his own.

He says nothing and looks down at her red shoes. She runs inside and leans on the chair where Koki sits, amongst the other women, next to the orange light of a candle flickering on the table beside her. Koki puts her hand on the little girl's shoulder and continues to look at the floor in the half light. There are footsteps in the garden and the women hunch their shoulders at the expectation of another soldier. Sophia is still asleep, but stirs restlessly. Maria sighs deeply. The other women look fearfully at Sophia and wonder if they will be next. The soldier approaches without a lantern and without a gun. He walks slowly and pauses between every other step. His hesitation makes the women tense and they all attempt to hide their faces in the shadows. Olympia, though, sits a little straighter and adjusts the collar of her shirt before wrapping the crucifix in her palm. Her lips as straight as the horizon. Litsa digs her nails into her palm. Koki keeps her eyes on the floor.

The soldier enters. He brings with him the smell of burning fields. Koki looks at his feet. He is not wearing army boots. The front of the shoes glimmer in the candle light. They have been polished and the laces fall neatly beneath the rim of his army trousers. There is not a crust of mud upon them. Koki swallows a ball of nostalgia that builds in her throat. She remembers the shoemaker's hut so many years ago and the shoes that glimmered in the moonlight. She dispels the thought. The toes of the shoes scan the room; they shuffle on the flagstones, then stop, pointing in Koki's direction. They take a confident step towards her. Koki looks at the reflection of the candle flame within them. The women wait for her to be taken away. Koki keeps her eyes on his shoes. She is as still as a picture, as still as an airless night. The dog whimpers slightly by Sophia's side and then is silent once more. The soles of the shoes crunch on the flagstones. Koki breathes quietly and grips the sides of the chair. The heat, thick, shivers with fear. The night, opaque, shimmers with light.

The shoes move closer.

'I'm . . .' he whispers, and his voice is lost like a wisp of smoke as he hovers above her in the dark. She can hear his breathing, the sound of his heart beating. He leans in towards her and the glimmer of his shoes is cast in darkness.

'I've come to bring you in from the rain . . . I . . .' His voice trails off as if he is using the last breath of air in his lungs. Koki's eyes dart up to his face. He is shrouded in darkness. She looks at his silhouette. He leans forward into the glow of the candlelight and his face is illuminated. His eyes, unexpectedly, as familiar and strange as a drop of rain in the heat. Like new moons in the shadows, a cloudy, lost time suddenly sweeps across them. She remembers sitting on that step all those nights. She looks at his face, disbelieving; she looks at the lines round his mouth, deeper yet unchanged, and the colour of his skin and the way his forehead is creased in anticipation, bringing his eyebrows, dark, over his eyes.

'I've been waiting on your step all these years,' she says, exhaling as deeply as though she has been holding her breath all this time. And just then, from beyond . . . a baby wails.

The baby cries on the passenger seat of the army jeep as a fighter jet sears through the sky; the flash of its lights dart above them like a falling star. Serkan looks quickly at the crying baby, stirring on its back, then out at the dusty road. He follows the path past the black field, skimming the orchards, and towards the house of captives.

A flock of jets rips through the black sky. The baby shrieks and Serkan looks down at his red face. The shrieking slashes the air, and Serkan winces and desperately begins to sing, but his voice can hardly be heard. The car bumps up and down on the road. The heat in the car is oppressive; the open windows seem to bear no purpose, except to bring in the smell of charred fields. Serkan's face drips with sweat, his collar is tight around his neck and he becomes all the more aware of the searing pain at the base of his spine.

The planes fade away in the distance, leaving him with this insistent shrieking, interspersed with the sound of the engine and the crickets and the distant bombs. Around the town, sporadic clashes continue. Serkan turns the knob on the radio and puts the volume up as high as it can go. First, he can make out some discussion about the coup on 15 July against Archbishop Makarios, when a large force of troops and tanks attacked the Archbishopric in Nicosia and the EOKA guerrilla, Nikos Sampson was placed in power. 'Yesterday,' the radio host announces, 'after support for his regime collapsed, Nikos Sampson resigned.' Although the rest of the words are muted by the crying, Serkan smiles. This last fact is extremely pleasing; the safety of the Turkish-Cypriot community has always been his main goal. And to think that Nikos Sampson was meant to have been assassinated in 1957 but was freed in 1960 when Cyprus gained independence from Britain. This militant nationalist had lived to steer the coup and provoke the Turks! Good riddance to him, thinks Serkan. He looks down at the crying baby; his eyes are wide and full of anguish, the skin of his face distorted. Serkan then looks out at the black road ahead. In the far distance a hill can be made out by the fire that flames upon it. The rest blends with the sky.

In a very short while he arrives outside the second

prisoners' house. He stops the jeep, turns off the engine and the headlights and looks to his left at the crying baby. Its screeching fills the night like a war siren: full of warning and panic and that imminent, all-consuming terror. Serkan touches the baby's tiny fingers, then leans across and brings him onto his lap. 'Little man. Little man,' he says softly, and the baby's crying suddenly subsides and turns to a hiccup. Serkan smiles. He looks into the baby's eyes and sees a part of himself in them; something of the way they look out at the world reminds Serkan of a feeling long-forgotten; a feeling that stabs him in the heart and rips his insides, a feeling that creeps up on him and is as unbearable as thirst.

The baby feels warmth near Serkan; he feels a fatherly touch and thinks that the world is safe. Serkan remembers his father again and those vicious eyes and his hands that came down on him like hammers, knocking him into shape, into the man he has become. A war is no place for a baby. Why should he be the one to steal his childhood? He holds the baby as though he is holding a part of himself. He brings the baby up to his chest and the baby rests his head on his shoulder.

'Into the garden the calves did stray.
Gardener, quickly, turn them away,
They'll eat the cabbages without delay,
Eh-e, ninni, ninni, ninni,
Eh-e, ninni, ninni, eh!
Eh-e, ninni.'

Serkan whispers the song tenderly into the baby's ear. The baby yawns. He sings the song three times until he is sure that the baby is asleep and then looks towards the house, where the windows flicker with candlelight. 'It's time to go home,' he whispers to the baby and stands up carefully, trying not to wake him. He uses his free hand to grab his rifle and the bottle from the back seat, then, leaving the keys in the jeep and the door slightly ajar, he carries the baby round to the back of the house and into the garden. At first he is sure he can hear movement and some muttering, but as he approaches all is silent.

From within, the stench of death and old *zivania* spills out, hot and humid, hitting the back of his throat, as pungent as bleach. He winces and steps through the open doors into the living room, where the women sit still amongst the light of a candle. All have their faces to the floor. They are shrouded in shadows, and headscarves lie discarded about the place. He scans the room, looking for the stern-looking lady in the white shirt and suddenly spots her on a chair in the corner; the only woman with her eyes fixed on his face. He walks towards her assuredly, but suddenly hesitates with a jerk, as though involuntarily, his foot hovering just above the ground, like a puppet on a string. He lowers his foot and stands there rigidly with his face to the nearest wall; unmoving, in the stillness of the house. Towering over her, with the baby still sleeping in his arms, Serkan stands there as the crickets beat and the bombs fall; rigid in the darkness, sculpted in the shadows, like a statue lost in time. He has no thoughts now, just a feeling of sadness, so immense that it has no shape. He tilts his head down and smells the top of the baby's head. Burnt fields. 'Stone baby, I have enveloped you, With cradle straps supported you, By day and night protected you, Mevlsm, send you a soul, Stone baby, stone baby,' Serkan sings in a sibilant whisper.

A breeze blows through the door and touches the sweat on his forehead. The room fills with the smell of fire and lemon blossoms. He looks back at the lady.

She does not seem to have moved her eyes; he can see her stiff expression in the flickering light. He takes a step closer and, leaning slightly, with the baby spread across his palms, he offers him to her, as though he has brought a gift, a ritual offering to a deity: a platter of dates or figs or pomegranates or carrots or turnips or poppies or herbs or edible flowers . . . Serkan looks at the baby. He wriggles slightly on his palms. His little hands outstretched, he whimpers. The lady sits still and looks at him with a look of disbelief. He steps closer, slowly and carefully, and offers her the baby by lowering his stance further, keeping his eyes fixed on hers. The lady breaks his gaze, and as though she has just awakened from a dream, releases the crucifix from her palm, then jolts her arms up with such sudden force that it takes Serkan by surprise. With desperation she reaches for the baby and snatches him from his arms, as if there were a chance that he might change his mind. She brings him quickly to her chest and exhales with a long groan full of agony and relief. She shoots Serkan a look of piercing hatred and fear, and then, dropping her face to the baby, she searches his tiny body with her hand.

Serkan turns away from her, straightens his posture,

shifts his collar and looks around the room. The women immediately drop their faces to the floor. He paces round in a circle, hesitating before each one, watching their bodies shiver as he passes as though he were a gust of bitter wind. He looks down at a young woman huddled in the corner, then at the sleeping girl on the bed, passes an old lady and stops for a brief moment at a woman on a chair, nearest the candle, with hair like fire. He looks down and glassy eyes glance up at him. He waits, sighs, then turns to the lady next to her, dark-haired, dark-skinned, staring manically at the floor. Serkan shifts his feet, moves closer, pauses for a beat, then steps away. He stands in the centre of the room, stares at the ceiling, then, spinning round deci-sively, heads towards the door.

Just then he notices a young girl at the doorway, dressed in red. She stands still, wearing an apron and holding a little glass cup in her hand. Has she been there all this time? He looks at her, drenched in moon-light with the little cup in her hand and a look of expectation on her face. Serkan remembers his mother, so many years ago, walking out onto the balcony with that small glass of ouzo in her hand. His father would drink it slowly and watch his sheep long after Serkan

had gone to bed. His mother never touched the stuff;
it was frowned upon for women to drink ouzo. It was
a man's drink, full of muscle and fire.

The little girl stands still with her apron and the cup
in her hand. A cup for spirits. White spirits. Serkan
looks at the liquid inside. Clear. He walks towards her,
leans down, places his rifle on the floor and takes the
cup from her hand. She does not protest and lowers
her arm. He smells the liquid. Ouzo. He smells again.
Definitely ouzo. Crouching there, at her level, he looks
straight into the little girl's eyes. 'Who's the ouzo for?'
he says in Greek, his voice spiked with a sense of
urgency. The smell of charred fields and lemon blossoms drifts over them in a balmy breeze. The little girl
stares back at him blankly. 'Who's this ouzo for, little
girl?' he repeats. This time, his voice sharper, prickly,
uneasy. The girl looks at him with wide, unblinking
eyes.

'It's an offering for our guest,' a gruff voice suddenly
bursts out from behind him. He spins around and sees
the old woman standing up, a look of terror in her
eyes. 'The ouzo is for you—'

'Shut up!' he commands, cutting into her words. He
looks around the room, scrutinising the women's faces

in the darkness and sniffs the air through his nostrils like a hunting hound. He looks back at the girl suspiciously, then at the ouzo in the cup. He places it on the floor, and then takes the little girl's hands into his. The heat presses upon him and the sweat builds on his forehead. A searing pain surges through his spine. The room is silent; only breathing can be heard within. He tightens his grip round the girl's fingers, his palms damp, his collar tight, he moves his face closer to the girl's and squeezes his voice into a rasping, brittle whisper. 'My sweet' – his voice bitter like lemons – 'now, don't be afraid. Tell me who the ouzo is for.' He tenses as the little girl opens her mouth, but a frantic shuffling noise interrupts their thoughts and something from behind him makes the girl freeze and look over his shoulder.

Serkan instinctively reaches for his rifle. Nothing. He looks at the floor and rummages with his hand in the darkness. He spins around. Looming over him, a dark figure. He looks up and realises that standing there, ferociously, with the base of the rifle held high above his head, is the old lady. In black clothes and a black headscarf in the black night she stands above him like the Angel of Death. The moon shines in her eyes;

scrunched-up like fists, only the black of her pupils are visible. Serkan raises his arm in defence, but the old lady brings the rifle down upon him with so much force that the pain and the darkness consume him.

On the living-room floor of the little house is a man. He lies still by Maroulla's feet, red flowers all around him. The petals blossom from his head and make a dewy pool, which trickles, like a river, to join her red shoes. She remembers her mother. The girl looks up at the horror-stricken faces of the women gathered around. Maria holds the rifle in her hand; her body is stiff and frozen, with the rifle still firm in her strong grip. She looks down at the man strangely. There is a moment when all the woman are frozen in this stance, as if time has been paused for a second, if only to give clarity or scope to this moment that will one day flicker in their minds, so that it can be embossed on their memories for ever, along with all the other images of horror. For now, the only movement is the expanding pool of blood. The only sound: the crickets.

Maroulla is the first to move. She bends down and puts her hand into the blood, then looks at it oddly. The women stare. The next to move is the dog, who,

343

tail down, circles the body and the women. Sophia groans from the bed, and the dog returns to her side. Costandina screams. 'Shut up!' Litsa quickly slaps her face. 'We will be caught because of you!' she whispers fearfully.

Litsa then runs forward and takes the man's wrist. She checks his pulse and nods her head. A few women sigh, but there is a sudden and noticeable change in Maria. She softens her stance so that the rifle hangs by her side. Sighing deeply, she looks down at the man, fixes her eyes onto his smooth face and the softness of the skin around his eyes, and the creases around his mouth that could have once been laughter lines, and says, 'Poor, distorted warrior. What the world has made of us.' The women watch her, unmoving. She leans over and, gently, with the tips of her fingers, closes his open eyes. She drops the rifle to the floor and allows herself, with an exhaling breath, to release: her knees bending, her shoulders hunching and, instantly, as though someone has just pushed forwards the hands of time, she melts and withers into old age. Her eyelids sink into the bags beneath her eyes, her jaw loosens and her skin softens, allowing her body to be liberated into its descent. The candlelight wavers over her face, and the women, all at once, see an old lady with deep lines and liver spots and disappearing eyes, standing by a rifle that now seems larger than she is. The old lady allows the rifle to be taken from her hand and stares fixedly at the man she has killed.

'Quick!' Litsa says and runs to call the man hiding in the basement.

Adem enters the living room, looks at the commanding officer dead on the floor and, bewildered, looks up at the women and then at Koki. Nobody says a word. He crouches down beside the body, checks Serkan's neck for a pulse, then looks back at the women hovering above him. Adem smiles, a smile that only the little girl can see. Then he shakes his head. 'They put the wolf to guard the sheep,' he says to himself and moves quickly, searching the officer's pockets. He retrieves a key from the top pocket, holds it tightly in his fist, kisses his fist sharply, smiles again and looks up at Koki, who hovers above him, hair aflame. He then turns and looks at the young girl, who stares at him expectantly.

'Let's go!' he says finally. 'Let's go. This is our only chance.' Suddenly his eyes are wide and full of fear. His fist, still tight around the key, trembles slightly. At first the women do not move; they hover uncertainly. 'Let's go!' he says louder, standing up this time. 'They'll be expecting him back soon. Let's go!' His voice trembles, and all the women, except the old lady, suddenly spin into action, whizzing around the room in a hurry. Adem touches Koki's fingers, looks into her eyes, nods reassuringly and runs out to start the jeep.

Litsa tries to wake Sophia, and the other women snatch a few blankets and some fruit hastily from the trees in the garden and run outside to the jeep. Koki finds five empty bottles from the cupboard and fills them with drinking water. Litsa helps her take them to the jeep. Meanwhile, the old lady walks slowly towards the flickering candle, lifts her petticoat slightly and lowers herself steadily into the chair. She rests her arms on her lap and leans her head back. She closes her eyes and listens to the shuffling of feet, the manic whispering and the distant falling bombs. And somehow, for now, she manages to mute the foreign sounds and listen only to that familiar rattling of the wind in the leaves and the scuttling of the cockroaches. Somehow, she succeeds in dispelling the smell of fire and inhales only the smell of the red soil and the ferns and the lemons. If she focuses well she can even smell the sweet jasmine flowers and beneath that, the whiff of the cesspits. Into her mind flash pictures of long ago: of her childhood, of her brave brother, of her wedding day, of her poor husband. She crosses herself. 'My beloved Vasos,' she says aloud, but does not open her eyes. She does not want to lose the flickering of faces moving across her mind, they will merely dissolve like sugar in water, just as they always do. Her hands shake involuntarily on her lap, and though her knuckles and knees throb with that incessant agony of arthritic pain, her expression remains placid. She thinks for some reason of the olive grove that her husband had planted before he died and how the trees had grown and joined arms, creating a cool, grey roof. She remembers the fresh mint in her garden, drying in the sun. She remembers the nettle field beyond her balcony and the silhouette of Bella-pais against the sun. She remembers the brown armchair in her living room and the colour of her crockery and the bric-a-brac shop on the edge of the port that sold everything from sewing needles to driving licences. She remembers, suddenly, that she has left beans boiling on the stove and bread cooking in the oven. A breeze blows. 'I will never forget,' she whispers, but her voice drifts away unheard.

Adem ushers the women into the back of the jeep, his eyes darting around, searching the night, listening for the sound of an approaching engine or footsteps or a plane overhead. He helps the women jump onto the step of the jeep and then runs back into the house. Litsa has managed to get Sophia standing, but the girl is lumbering heavily in her arms, causing Litsa to struggle and stumble backwards. Adem runs towards them, lifts Sophia into his arms and takes her to the jeep, resting her gently on the floor. Sophia forces her eyes open, tilts her head up and attempts to look around. She is about to speak when suddenly she sees the dog running towards her. She cracks a smile and it jumps in with her, sitting by her side. She lowers her head again and closes her eyes.

Adem looks quickly at the women's faces, glances urgently at Koki and orders them to cover themselves with the blankets.

'Wait,' announces Koki, looking around her and fumbling desperately out of the jeep. 'Maria,' she says, and her voice trails behind her as she rushes towards the house.

Inside, she sees Maria sitting on the chair nearest the candle. She appears at first to be asleep. 'Maria!'

Koki whispers from the doorway, but there is no reply. 'Maria!' she whispers again, moving towards the old lady. 'Maria,' she says again, her voice urgent, puffing into the silence like a foghorn. She leans over the old lady and touches her arm. 'Maria,' she says, her voice cracking, on the brink of shattering completely.

Old Maria opens her eyes and tilts her head up to look at the pleading eyes of the young woman before her. 'Let me be, my child,' she says, but Koki becomes more agitated; she tugs the old lady's arm, then grabs her shoulder, trying desperately to propel her into action. It is no good. The old lady will not budge.

'We have to go,' Koki pleads, now gripping the old lady's hand. 'This is our only chance to live!' The old lady looks at her, leans forward slightly, brings her other arm up and cups it gently over Koki's hand.

'My child, I've had my chance to live.' Her eyes are heavy and sink into her face like ships disappearing off the horizon. Koki opens her mouth to argue, but stops and looks at her shrunken body, sunk in that chair, and notices the coarseness of her palm upon her hand, and sees that the lines on her face are part of the paths of the town and the colour of her skin is the colour of the soil. Maria's eyes are set and unyielding. The old lady nods at her reassuringly. 'Leave me,' she says, 'you must leave me.' Koki observes the old lady and reluctantly lets go of her hand; then, leaning in, she kisses her gently on the cheek.

'Thank you,' she whispers and the old lady smiles and nods again and then looks quickly over Koki's shoulder. 'Go!' she insists. 'Go quickly, you don't have much time!'

And this is true, for as they set off and drive round the bend to the next row of houses, Koki notices, flickering through the trees and buildings, the movement of another jeep pulling up outside the house.

For miles through darkness in the back of the jeep, beneath the blanket, the women's bodies are buried in one another's; they feel as though they are suffocating in the heat. The stench of their bodies is overpowering. The engine drones along the bumpy road and every so often the sound of a passing jeep or tank is heard. Nobody stops them. They rock silently in the darkness. Everyone is awake, apart from the baby, who sleeps peacefully, cradled safely between Olympia and Litsa. The women's hearts beat hard beneath that blanket; their breath and their blood warm. In that cocoon they lie as still as they can manage. Only their chests rise gently. From a small gap between the blanket and the jeep floor moans a strong wind; it whines like an old song of lament. As the jeep rushes through the streets of Kyrenia the wind sings a song and sadness rises within them, darker than the night. And from that very gap Koki watches the world zoom by in all the colours of darkness: the coffee-black of the sky, the grape-black of the edges of flowers and leaves, the luminous white of the houses, the wink of silver wherever the moonlight falls, and all along their journey, gliding behind the olive-black outlines of the town, is that unmistakable, desolate, opaque blackness of the sea. It slithers alongside them like a gigantic snake from a prehistoric, mythical world. It moves at the same speed as them and breathes salt on them whenever the wind blows.

In a few moments, they are stopped by a man speaking Turkish. His voice is heavy and rises with the tone of a question. Adem answers, and although the women do not understand his words, his voice sounds confident; steady and full of conviction. Then they all wait for a reply. The other man groans, and there is the sudden flicker of torchlight, slipping into the gaps of the blanket. The women hold their breath. Each one hopes fearfully that the baby will not wake. Not now . . .

The light moves away, there are footsteps, and the foot soldier mumbles something and laughs. Adem laughs too and the foot soldier bashes the side of the door with his palm as if to send it on its way. The engine rumbles again, the wheels move and the women exhale.

Only a minute passes before Adem stops again. Koki peeps through the gap and, noticing the rows of houses, believes that they are in the centre of Kyrenia, probably not too far from the port. Adem jumps out and rushes away somewhere; his footsteps disappear into the night. The women remain still, they hardly dare to breathe. Minutes seem to pass and they lie there, engulfed in darkness, their ears pressed upon each other with only the beating of their hearts and that monotonous sound of the crickets to be heard. Then there is a noise from beyond and the women hold their breath completely. The baby stirs slightly. Just then a shuffling noise is heard, some muttering, what seem to be heated words, and then the passenger door of the jeep is opened. Whoever it is is instructed by Adem to get down, and the jeep starts once more.

The jeep bumps and swerves through what feels like winding roads: the veins of Kyrenia, the ones that lead to the sea; the red-soiled veins within that white maze. Memories flash in Koki's mind but she cannot distinguish one from the other, they all blend into one; into one walk, one misplaced stroll along the cobwebbed paths. The salt of the sea becomes heavier in the air and she can hear the waves now, shushing, shushing, shushing the night. The wheels of the jeep sink onto soft sand, and the sea rolls closer. Its chest rises, the wings of waves bring the sea air onto the shore, like Hypnos cooling Aphrodite, bringing that dense darkness from beyond. In the distance a bomb whistles. The sea inhales and exhales. It breathes out deeply, then breathes in heavily. It lashes and laps the shore and whispers and whimpers and sighs. It reaches its fingers up to the wheels of the jeep. The jeep stops and the dog lifts its ears. They have arrived, they can feel it! There is a sense of urgency and expectation and fear and elation. Adem lifts the blanket from them, but the darkness is just the same. The women emerge into the starlight like crumpled butterflies. Their clothes creased, their eyes scrunched up against the sea. They emerge, skeletal, celestial lost souls, as though from the grave, as though in a nightmare, and they stand with Kyrenia behind them, squinting at the black abyss beyond.

The salty sea air lifts their hair and blows hard in their ears. As they stand there, they notice the expanse of darkness before them, with the slight reflection of a silver moon on the top of the ripples. Olympia remains seated, with the baby pressed to her chest. Even Sophia stands now, and the dog jumps off the jeep and runs round to smell the person in the passenger seat.

From there emerges an old man. He stands as straight as he can and lifts his face up to the darkness of the sea. He inhales. Portions of his face are highlighted by the moon. His glasses glimmer. White wisps of hair. He looks over at Adem and points at something in the water. The sea swishes in and touches their toes. Ahead, in that black void, the shoreline is invisible and the flickering lights of the warships hover in the darkness to the east of Pente Mile. The sea hisses in and touches their toes. The two men walk into the lapping waves, their feet slogging through water and sand, and they bend over something that glimmers slightly blue in the moonlight. There is much sloshing about and the two men pull something onto the beach. A boat. Big enough to fit five people at the most. The old man climbs in and struggles with the oars, then looks at Adem standing beside him. The black tongue of the sea laps the wood of the boat. 'Psaroboulis, your home will always be with you. You will never be too far from the sea,' Adem whispers.

'If that's the best I can have,' the old man replies. His voice rattles with phlegm. 'I married, had kids, drank more wine than there is water in the sea, drank my life into a haze . . . but thank God for my boat. I would have drowned a long time ago if it wasn't for her.' He bashes the side of the boat with a flat palm, then looks out to the black gulf of sea. 'We will follow the coast west and dip south until we reach Pirgos. It will take us a while.' Adem nods, then turns to face the women. He dribbles out of the water and stands to face them.

'It is time,' he says simply, and the women stare at him, with wind in their hair and salt on their skin.

The women slosh through the lapping water and into the boat. The dog follows and sits next to Sophia. The boat rocks in the shallows of the sea. The sea rolls in and out, endlessly, rattling its liquid bones in the darkness. It whispers something gently: familiar stories, familiar words and its voice travels up and down, to and fro, not unlike the man that walked its shores calling endlessly 'Watermelons, watermelons, watermelons.' And not unlike the man that called the fish from the depths and sang as he pulled his net. And not unlike the bells that chimed from the hill, and the priest that sang words from the Bible.

Koki hesitates at the edge of the water, with Maroulla by her side. The little girl shivers. Koki looks down at her. 'My dad used to say that lost spirits skim the surface of the water. They feel safe here as they can see the reflection of the heavens in the sea. It gives them hope,' Koki whispers to the little girl as the wind blows harder and another bomb whistles in the distance. The sea moans now. Adem walks closer to where they stand and first looks down at Maroulla; he takes her hand and holds it inside his palms. She looks at him straight in the eyes:

'You are the green man.' The little girl smiles. He looks back at her with tears in his eyes and squeezes her hand.

'. . . It is time for your journey to begin.'

The little girl nods. 'Aren't you coming with us?' she asks.

The sea laps their feet. 'It's always harder to let go of someone once you've opened your mouth or opened your heart.' Adem reaches into his jacket pocket, retrieves the Bible and holds it out. He looks at it and touches the leather cover delicately with his fingers. 'I want to give you this to always remember me,' he says. 'Like I'll always remember you . . . the bravest little girl I've ever met.' He places it into Maroulla's hand and she looks down at it with wide eyes, then she walks away and stands close to the old man.

Adem touches Koki's hand with his fingers. He strokes her hair and her face. 'I'm sorry,' he whispers, 'I didn't want to leave you.' His face is close to hers and he leans in and puts his arms around her, he holds her close to him with his arms clasped across her back. 'I'm sorry,' he says again as the tide draws the sea away and the boat clatters about. 'I didn't want to leave.' His voice breaks and he buries his face in her hair. 'There's so much I want to tell you, to explain . . . they gave me no choice, it was the only thing I could do! I was a coward . . .'

Koki pulls back, reaches up and holds his face; her eyes are soft and as she feels his skin against her palms she remembers how much she loved him.

'I have never loved anybody else,' he says, looking

at her in the eyes. He holds both her hands and the wind passes between them. Adem's eyes are full of tears.

'Come with us,' Koki says, but Adem looks down. 'Come with us,' she pleads. 'Why aren't you coming with us?' Her voice is desperate and shrill, but he cannot reply. He kisses Koki on the lips again, a lingering kiss, full of pain.

Koki clutches his hand. 'You have to come with us,' she says, but notices a look in his eyes that is too familiar to her; that look full of longing and sadness and hopelessness.

'I am a Turk,' he says. 'An old enemy can never become a friend. They will kill all of us if they see me with you. I will come and find you, I promise.' Then his eyes lower to the ground. 'Our life could have been much different.' He says these last words more quietly.

'You would have been a great father,' says Koki. Adem looks at her. Koki looks at those familiar eyes and his skin, dusted with time. She takes his hand and feels the lines on his palm and then his fingers. She reaches up to his face and leans in and kisses his lips. The wind blows and a bomb whistles in the distance. He holds her face, her shoulders, her arms; touching her manically, as though, perhaps, he cannot believe that she is real.

Time is running out. He kisses her again, and again; on the lips, on the cheek, on her forehead. He clasps her arms. The wind blows and the darkness spills over them, heavier than before. She looks at him uncertainly, then out at the black void ahead. She has waited a lifetime to get to see him once. What if there is another lifetime between this time and the next?

'We can start again,' she says, as a fighter jet flies overhead and somewhere in the distance is the rumble of wheels. She looks back at him resolutely this time. 'He had your eyes,' she says. He clutches her arms tighter, frown marks crawl across his eyes. 'I named him Adem, after you. But they could not accept it and his name became Agori . . . I came to tell you, that night . . . but . . . you had already . . .' Her voice shatters and is taken by the sea. She swallows the salt of her tears. 'The monsters killed him in the orchard; they shot him in the heart.' Her voice rises higher than the wind, it rips the air, tears at his features so that they are distorted and wild in the moonlight. The sea pulls them and their feet sink into the sand. 'The monster left a rose on his body. A rose on his body. A rose on his body.' Her voice rises further, battling with the wailing of the sea. Her shoulders drop, her eyes close and she cries into the night. Her last words roll with the waves, reverberating again and again and again, a rose on his body, a rose on his body, a rose on his body. The body of the sea rises. Rises, rises, rises and falls. A rose on his body, a rose on his body, a rose . . . a rose . . . a rose . . .

He takes a step back. The look in his eyes, menacing, unnatural. Tears fall and he clasps his hair brutishly. The wind blusters over him. His eyes, ferocious and wild, wide against the wind. The rumbling in the distance is nearer now. Headlights piece the darkness.

'They are skirting the shore!' His voice manic, untamed, trembling senselessly. 'You must go. Now! You must go!' His face is torn with tears. His features twisted, disfigured by the shadows. He takes her hand and pulls her to the boat. Maroulla follows. They climb in and Koki clasps onto his hand. She looks behind her at Maroulla, Sophia and the baby and reluctantly lets go. He winces and turns his face away from her and hits the side of the boat. 'Go,' he says to Psaroboulis, 'go as far into the darkness as you can.' The old man starts rowing, madly, madly, the oars flap like wings over a black sky. They plunge and plunge and plunge into further darkness; into the thickness of eternity. The shore drifts further and further away. Adem stands there, a shrinking silhouette in the darkness until the women see nothing but black. Nothing but black. And then, a flash of headlights, and a few moments later, a gunshot . . .

Koki stands up in the boat and cries from her chest, 'Adem!' She whispers through her tears, 'Adem . . .' She leans over the boat and cries into the sea. 'Have they killed him?' she says frantically, 'have they killed him?' But none of the women answer. Litsa stands up and puts her arms round Koki's shoulders and eases her onto the floor of the boat. And there Koki rests her head and cries into Litsa's arms. She cries as the boat drifts further and further away.

Day 6: 25 July 1974

Richard wakes up to the sound of waves, the foaming of the sea on the rocks, the sound of the crickets and the fishermen whistling and cursing on the shore. The seabirds soar over and screech. A ceaseless screeching. He opens his eyes, and as they adjust to the darkness, he realises that the couple in the flat below have been arguing. 'Bloody hell!' he says out loud, lifts his head and looks out of the window at the blinking lights of Queen Victoria Street. The traffic lights change to red, but there are no cars on the road. Somebody slams a door. Richard groans. 'God damn you!' he says, pushing the covers off his body, heaving himself to sit up and swinging his legs over the bed. His movements are slow, his joints stiff. Big Ben chimes in the distance, the sound of the bells flap overhead like singing birds. Too early even for the damned birds! thinks Richard.

Who the hell would argue before the birds start singing? From as far back as his army years he was not keen, to say the least, on waking up before the crack of dawn. He remembers his regiment officer, in his junior years, bashing a rifle on the floor of his room and ordering him to do laps for disobedience. Nothing ever changed. Some even said that he would have missed the whole of the Second World War and never known the difference. He was a good pilot, though. The best there was. He just believed the birds should sing first. Of course, his opinion didn't really matter, even though he had covered more air miles than a falcon. The sky became his home. That bottomless sky. So full of possibilities and emptiness. His stomach churns.

Richard stands now, scraggy, like an old bird. His legs scrawny, his neck, bony, bending downwards. The clouds drift over and all becomes darker. He dresses himself, combs his hair and makes his way out of the bedsit and takes a long walk to Paniko's café.

He approaches the café and sees a closed sign hanging on the door that he has never seen before. He leans forward and presses his face to the glass. It is dark inside and there is no movement at all. Richard looks at his watch. Six forty-five. Paniko should have definitely opened up by now and been preparing for the breakfast rush hour. Richard leans against the wall and lights a cigarette. Soon Nikos strolls towards the café, nods his head at Richard and, without even looking up, continues straight for the door. There is an almighty thud when he thumps straight into the glass. Slightly dishevelled and still not looking up, he rattles the door handle. Bloody Greeks, thinks Richard, always ignoring the signs, even when they are staring them in the face. Completely bewildered that Paniko has not opened the café, Nikos stands there for a few seconds, staring up at the shop sign almost as if he is checking to make sure he is at the right place. 'Hm,' he says beneath his breath, and then, not knowing what to do with himself, he stumbles away.

No one else comes and Richard is just about to leave when a black taxi pulls up outside the café and Paniko steps out, holding the door open for a young man. The taxi starts up and disappears along the street. Paniko stands, beaming, outside the café. 'Little Cyprus!' he says to the young man, with the enthusiasm of a Labrador, but the young man looks it up and down, as though sizing it up, and then nods once, completely unconvinced.

They walk into the café. 'This is Vakis,' Paniko tells Richard, 'my nephew. He has escaped from Cyprus.' He leads Vakis to a table and indicates for him to sit down. The boy does not move. Paniko speaks to him in Greek, in a volume that would only be acceptable if the boy were standing on the other side of Soho. If that, Richard thinks. He shakes his head. Paniko asks the boy a question and the boy tuts and throws his head back to indicate 'No'.

'Vakis, this *Englezo*. Friend,' he says and Vakis looks at Richard beneath heavy brown lids, scornfully, as though he would have shot him if he had a gun; but strangely, from that look, a yawn emanates, with completely visible tonsils. The boy chews the air a few times and his lids droop lower. He stares at Richard until Paniko speaks again. 'Come. I'll make coffee.'

Paniko takes Vakis' small backpack and puts it behind the counter, then Vakis sits down. At first Vakis' closely shaved head bobs over his chest, but then, for some reason, as though mustering the last bit of energy he has, he lifts his eyebrows and looks around with half interest at the café. Richard notices that he is looking at these new surroundings, not with excitement, but with the air of someone both unimpressed and overwhelmed.

Paniko returns with the coffees and takes his own cup stiffly. His eyes look worried. His hand trembles slightly. He opens his mouth to speak, but closes it again. He sips the coffee. He takes a deep breath. 'Maria?' he says suddenly, and the boy shakes his head dejectedly and continues to bite his nails. Richard sits upright in his chair and feels his nerves moving. Perhaps this boy could be his link to Kyriaki? Perhaps he knows something, has heard something? But then Paniko freezes for a moment with the coffee in his hand and speaks again. 'Andreas?' The boy shakes his head once more. 'Panny?' Paniko asks now, his voice trembling. The boy shrugs this time and looks down.

'What about Kyriaki, from Kyrenia. Do you know anyone called Kyriaki?' Richard says, hearing the desperation in his own voice as though it were someone else speaking. Vakis looks at Richard with a blank look on his face.

Paniko holds his cup in the air and slams it down into the saucer. The black coffee spills onto the tablecloth. His heavy features suddenly scrunch up and he stands there and sobs, with his shoulders jutting up and down. He does not speak. He sobs hard while Richard and Vakis look at the floor, then he stops abruptly and wipes his tears on his apron. He gazes out onto the heaving London street. 'They will be here in only a minute,' he says bluntly and then turns and disappears into the kitchen.

He is right. In just a short while the café is brimming with Greek men of all ages, pulling up chairs and sitting down to steaming coffees and bread fingers. Vakis remains uninterested, only staring at the floor, with eyes like heavy sacks. Soon an old man passes and tells Richard that his face has become as familiar as that misplaced English portrait; pointing up at the wall, where a picture of some unknown, pompous-looking aristocrat sitting on a chair with a hunting dog by his feet hangs over a wicker breadbasket, in a humorous attempt, perhaps, to portray a forced acceptance of the foreigner's vision of British culture. Richard feigns a laugh and sips his cold coffee. He smacks his lips together at the sudden bitterness of it. Bloody Greeks! he thinks. He should drink it all at once before it goes cold. There's a reason why the British do things the way they do!

At midday Paniko instructs Richard to show Vakis 'round'. He says this, twisting his finger into a quick circular motion as though the task would be over just as briskly. Richard grudgingly agrees, and the two men stroll the streets of Soho, then along Piccadilly and up Regent Street in silence. Vakis looks mostly at his feet as he walks, but, every so often, cannot resist and gives in to the grand sights of London. At Trafalgar Square they sit on the low wall and watch the pigeons fighting for portions of bread. Hundreds and thousands of grey pigeons, dropping and rising, fluttering and scuffling as grey as the rain and the clouds and the drizzle, as grey as the pavements and the buildings and the soft mist. For a moment everything shimmers as though in the reflection of a lake, and Vakis sighs. 'Really is beautiful!' he says, without looking at Richard, and Richard nods as a pigeon waddles over to where they sit. It looks up at Vakis and Vakis laughs and reaches out his hand, but the pigeon panics and flutters madly away. Richard wonders what to say. Sorry for your loss is not enough. What this boy has suffered is not a mere loss, but an utter catastrophe. Sorry for your loss is what one would say to someone who has lost a relative to cancer or old age or an undetected heart problem. Sorry for your loss are not the words one utters to someone who has lost everything. Richard decides that it is wiser to remain silent, and they sit for a while and watch the pigeons padding about and, occasionally, swarming over a little boy or girl holding bread in their fingers.

It is late afternoon when they get back to the café. 'My God!' announces Paniko, as they walk through the door. 'What town rounds did you take?' He tells Richard to take Vakis home, his wife should be in now, wait for him to wash and shower and bring him back in a few hours. Richard agrees, and they take the bus to Archway.

Richard knocks on the door, and a moment later Elli opens it, already crying, and throws her arms over Vakis' shoulders. She wails like a siren and pulls the poor boy's arms, mumbling and screeching words in Greek. The boy watches her, seemingly unmoved by this spectacle, and starts to bite his nails again. She lets go of his arms, crouches, holds her knees, sighs, straightens herself, swallows hard, and then, as though that whole exhibition was performed by somebody else, she asks if they are hungry. Richard replies, 'No thank you' and Vakis shrugs. 'Very well!' she says, looking as dishevelled as a rag doll amongst the sparkling ornaments and the grace of the Royal Doulton petite ladies and the translucent china of the

Royal Albert figurines that line the console table and windowsill. Elli takes out a hairpin, opens it with her mouth, readjusts her hair and pins it back neatly. She shows the boy upstairs to the bathroom.

Richard feels like a giant amongst the figurines. He notices that one of them is an unknown warrior of the Second World War, or perhaps the Cold War, a naval officer returning home, dressed in navy-blue and white. Elli walks down the stairs and follows his eyes. He remarks, 'A nostalgia figurine, a proud tribute to the heroes of war. My mother used to collect them.' Elli creases her brow.

'Royal Doulton!' she says. 'The best china.' Richard sighs, and she turns away from him as though he has wasted enough of her time and leads him into the kitchen, where she begins to heat up soup on the stove. Richard sits at the kitchen table.

'The children?' Richard asks.

'At friend's,' she replies and continues to stir the soup. The soup bubbles and the kitchen fills with a lemony steam. Then, with a ladle, she fills two bowls to the brim, squeezes more lemon on to them and sprinkles them with salt and a little pepper. She places one bowl in front of Richard and another in the empty place where Vakis will soon be sitting. 'Egg-lemon soup,' she says to Richard.

'For the one returning home,' he replies, taking his spoon, and Elli suddenly looks at him as though he were a stray cat from the town sewers.

'Home?' she says, spitting. 'You think this is home?' Richard stares at her in fright, unsure whether she actually wants him to reply, and to his relief Vakis walks into the kitchen with a yellow towel round his shoulders. 'Come,' Elli says, pointing to the bowl of soup, and Vakis sits down, takes his spoon and laps the soup manically, like a hungry dog, without lifting his eyes from the bowl. Elli sits right next to him, with her chair positioned diagonally to face him properly and speaks to him endlessly in Greek. The boy nods every so often, and occasionally, when she is not looking, rolls his eyes at Richard. Richard smiles and listens to the lyrical words bouncing around the kitchen; she stops only to fill Vakis' bowl again and then continues as before.

By the time they get back to the café the sun has started to set, but it is not quite dark and the streetlamps are flickering on. Richard notices immediately that Nikos is sitting at the corner table, puffing on a cigar.

The gold of his cufflinks twinkles slightly as he moves. Nikos nods as Richard and Vakis sit down at the table nearest the counter. 'Ah!' Paniko shouts, coming out of the kitchen, 'my wife look after you well!' Paniko lifts the apron over his head, tosses it on a chair and joins them at the table. There is sweat between his nose and his upper lip and the sides of his temples shine beneath the electric lights. He breathes heavily, his olive complexion almost starched. 'She a good woman,' he says, but Vakis does not reply. Paniko's eyes look glazed and he focuses on the ceiling above Vakis' head. He smiles to himself and then wobbles his head right and left, a gesture of good-humoured resignation. 'Po, po, po,' he says, and shakes his head again. 'I remember one day, when I was a little older than you, Vakis, I saw beautiful woman on balcony. She tall, with black hair and skin gold! The most beautiful woman I saw! Like Aphrodite, or Greek god! She marvellous. Her face' – he pauses, purses his fingers together and kisses them – '*Manamou, mananou, manamou!*' he exclaims, shaking his head again. A bit of colour flushes his cheeks now. 'So, I waited and after one week I went back and asked her father for permission to marry his daughter. The father looked me up and down. "You work?" he asked.

'"Sure," I said.

'"You have money?" he asked.

'"Some," I said.

'"Your father?" he asked.

'"Alexandros of Pappa Georgiou," I said.

'"OK," he said and called his daughter from inside. It wasn't her, though. It was the eldest daughter, of course. She short and fat-arsed and dressed all in grey. She looks like should have been a nun. Anyway, no choice now, I ask Father, now must marry. One month later, she my wife.' Paniko forces a laugh and wipes the sweat from his lip with the back of his hand. 'She no beauty,' he says, 'and breaks camel's back or even Atlas' back, who holds whole world on his shoulders.' He looks into Vakis' eyes now. 'She good to me, though, and good mother. There are worst!' Now his features drop, and his eyes become distant again and his skin pale. He breathes heavily.

'So they all gone?' he says abruptly, unable, at first, to look at Vakis. The boy shrugs his shoulders nervously. Paniko shifts in his chair uncomfortably, and then he jolts upright. His face turns red. 'How you no know, boy?'

Vakis looks up at him. 'Pappou make me leave, he

says when God want to destroy an ant, he puts wings on him so it can fly to its own destruction. He no want me to fight. He said, he who has brain will flee. So I fled. I must to go before them, otherwise I will forced to fight, they pack me off and say they follow soon . . .' Vakis' voice trails away now. 'I no look back,' he whispers, as though he is ashamed of his own words. 'I just keep going, just keep going. I join convoy to Dekelia. We stopped few times for National Guard to check that no Turks with us. There one thousand cars and three thousand people. Anyway, I lucky, I have British passport, my family were of Greeks of nineteen fifties, I born here and moved back when I just two years old, so I OK to leave from British base.'

Paniko raises his arms and pulls the sides of his hair. He looks, for a moment, like a man drowning. He then lowers his arms and taps his top pocket, looking for his cigarettes. His hand trembles. Richard feels the panic and utter hopelessness that his friend feels, but he does not say a word, takes his own box out and offers one to Paniko, who takes one, lights it and inhales deeply. The smoke crawls across his features.

It is the end of another hard day's work in the rag factories and the men come in and collapse into the chairs and call out for coffees and whiskies. Paniko dis-appears into the kitchen. There is a time of quiet, when the coffees have gone cold and the ashtrays are filled with olive pips and pistachio shells, and the only noises from outside are the rumbling buses and the singing sirens in the distance.

Nikos stands up and throws a pack of cards onto the table. 'Nikos, I may as well give you my underpants!' says Yiakovos. 'I will never beat you.'

'Everything in its time and mackerel in August,' replies Nikos, and smiles, pushing back his hair so that his gold cufflinks sparkle in the light. Yiakovos shakes his head. 'No, I no give you my money again. I no play!'

'You can't dye eggs with farts!' replies Nikos. 'Wealth is a gamble!'

Yiakovos reluctantly takes the cards out of the pack and starts shuffling.

'There more of us today,' says Nikos, looking around at Richard and Vakis. 'Let's play to forget,' he says, looking over at Vakis. 'New challenges,' he says, this time eyeing Richard.

Day 7: 26 July 1974

There is a boat moving along the ripples of the sea at dawn. Maroulla looks at the horizon and the tip of the sun. Psaroboulis rows steadily and Koki watches the darkness turning purple, then navy-blue, with a tinge of citrus spilling over the scales of the sea. She watches the slow blossoming of black into oranges and golds. In the shimmering ripples of the water she sees her father serving breakfast to the morning guests and Agori running through the garden with a kite. No. She can no longer remember his face as it was. She sees it lifeless and still, as it was the moment he died. Almost unrecognisable, he wore it like a clay mask of himself. It is the spirit that gives the face shape; it is the spirit that heaves within us. Her heart aches and her stomach churns. She remembers Agori's eyes like stones. They will never move again. She touches her chest where the crucifix lies beneath the folds of her dress. In the water she sees Adem, now, mending shoes in a stream of golden light.

The oars break the water and Psaroboulis pulls, breathing out heavily through his mouth. The oars rise up now, splashing, and then plunge in again, followed by the same heavy pull. There is sweat on Psaroboulis' brow and the deep creases on his face are visible in the light. They have stopped many times so he can take a break, and Litsa and Costandina had taken over for a while during the night. Now he has been rowing for hours, but despite the heat and the sharp rays of the morning sun, he has kept going. Inhaling and exhaling with the sea. He has not said a word, but every so often he hums a mournful song, his gruff voice almost muted by the moving of the sea. The women sit huddled together, with torn portions of their dresses tied around their heads to protect them from the sun. There is only a drop of water left, but they will save it for the baby. Koki feels as though her mouth is full of salt and that her pores are clogged with sand, and that her mind is full of darkness and the sound of that gunshot. Was he shot? She imagines the fear in his face and his last moments alone. Why would they have shot him? Had he sacrificed his life for theirs? Did they see him helping them? Or, did he shoot himself? Did he decide there and then that this awful life was too much? Koki weeps silently. She knows in her heart that she will never know the answer and that she will never see him again.

Often, the women move restlessly and feet crunch on the base of the boat. Just then a flock of white sea-gulls fly overhead towards the grey-green haze of the Troodos peaks.

Psaroboulis starts rowing inland and soon, soaked in the colours of the rising dawn, the edge of the land appears, surrounded by the trellised hills of the mountains. As they row nearer they see the nettle fields and green slopes, and, emerging from those fields, the white houses of the occupants, looking straight out into the rising sun like the faces of saints shrouded in white scarves, and, to the left, the white turret of Ayia Irini sparkling in the sun.

There is not a fire in sight. Not a single tank or warship or soldier. The breeze blows and the smell of old Cyprus drifts over them; the comforting whiff of home-cooked meals and sweet red soil; the smell of life as they once knew it. And they look upon their surroundings as one would look at the face of a long-lost loved one, suddenly captured by that essence of longing and familiarity or a time capsule.

Litsa stands up and holds her hand above her eyes. The boat rocks. All the women face the land with wide eyes and straight backs, and Psaroboulis finds, in the sight of this new land, a surge of energy, and pulls manically, excitedly, towards the shore. And soon the water is so shallow that the women can see the rippled rocks beneath and the tiny fish darting to and fro. 'Kato Pyrgos,' says Psaroboulis, speaking for the first time and looks ahead with his hand shadowing his eyes. The women squint. Behind them the sky and sea blend together in a haze of azure. Heat trembles at the tip of every shrub and every building. Psaroboulis wipes the sweat from his brow with the back of his hand. The sea laps the sand.

Psaroboulis climbs out of the boat and into the water that reaches just below his knee. The women follow. He bends down, cups his hands, fills them with water and splashes it onto his face. Maroulla dips her fingers into the water. They all slog together towards the beach and stand motionless, for a few moments, on the land, somehow rocking as though their blood has kept the rhythm of the sea. After a kilometre of flat sand the land juts up, a small but sharp rising into Pyrgos. 'Come on,' says Litsa, 'we must keep going.' And they all bend their heads away from the sun, and with their shadows pointing behind them they make their way into the small town of Kato Pyrgos. They pass a grove of eucalyptus trees and finally reach a thin, winding road: a white ribbon through the nettles and shrubs and dainty peach blossoms that brush at their feet as they trudge and trudge and trudge with what feels like their last breath, their last heartbeat. The young girls moan and cry, their lips cracked with dried blood, and the baby whimpers in Olympia's arms, even the dog walks with its tail between its legs, all the while following Sophia's footsteps. Every so often, when Sophia lags behind, the dog turns and waits until she catches up again. 'Keep going,' says Litsa, 'just keep going, it won't be long now.' And somehow her voice gives them a surge of energy, if only for a few seconds, to straighten their backs a little and take an extra step.

Maroulla suddenly points at something in a pool of shade beneath an olive tree. She remains transfixed, with her hand still outstretched. They all follow her gaze, and there, sleeping soundly, is a litter of kittens, huddled together, their paws criss-crossed in all directions. The dog growls slightly, but obeys Sophia's command to sit. She taps its head. But the litter of kittens does not seem to be what Maroulla is staring at, open-mouthed. Behind the litter, in a hollow part of the tree, is a cat, probably the mother, licking its paws and devouring one of the kittens. She has blood on her whiskers. Sophia puts her hand to her mouth.

'Sometimes cats eat cats,' says Olympia, nodding, as though she is shocked by this realisation herself. But her voice is tired and her words not much louder than a whisper.

'We must keep on,' says Litsa. It is not too long before they see a donkey, as grey as the olive tree where it stands, and in the field beyond, a middle-aged man, crouched down, pulling turnips from the soil. He throws one into a basket and continues, cursing the sun and the heat. He does not turn around to see what the noise behind him is and simply raises his hand in salute when Psaroboulis calls, 'My friend!'

'We have come from the mouth of death,' says Psaroboulis as they walk nearer; their limbs at the point of collapse, their feet dragging behind them. At this, the man turns around and looks at their blackened faces, their lost eyes, their bodies that hang above him like the limbs of trees, their features and bones sharp in the sunlight. He jumps up now and looks at them, his face twisted as though he has just seen what others have only spoken of. He opens his arms and hunches, in a strange position, as though he were preparing to catch them. 'My God,' he says. 'My God!' He looks horrified at the faces of the women. 'Come,' he says, 'come,' gesturing towards the donkey. He lifts Olympia up with the baby and puts Sophia behind them. He takes the donkey's rope and they head off, along another dust path into the town.

'We have travelled two days by boat from Kyrenia, just west off Pente Mile,' says Psaroboulis. The man nods. Koki looks at his hand holding the rope and notices that his skin has the twisted look of a tree, and though he is not too old his back is slightly hunched at the top of his spine. 'I am Petros,' the man says. 'I live in Pano Pyrgos,' he says, pointing towards the hills. Soon they reach a clearing, which opens into a nettle field with the carcass of an old bus in the middle. This narrows further into another dust road, dotted with bikes and houses and dusty irrigation tanks. First, they pass an old lady, dressed in black, sitting beneath the shade of the vines, picking stones out of lentils. When she sees them she stops and stands, a look of horror on her face, balancing herself on the arm of her chair. They pass a group of young women sitting in a circle in the shade of their house, snapping beans; they too rise from their seats. The farmer freezes with his spade just above the soil. The women, who walk in a multi-coloured trail towards the fields, freeze with their baskets beneath their arms. Another old woman, standing on a chair, reaching for figs, stops with her fingers outstretched. The seamstress freezes with her hand in the air; her needle sparkles in the sun. As they pass, everyone looks.

Petros does not salute anyone and does not stop. He continues instead, up the little ribbon of road to the limestone walls of St Irini. The bells chime as they ascend the last part of the hill and stand, drunk from the heat, beneath the frowning arches of the church. Petros puts down the donkey's lead and runs into the church. A few moments later he comes out again, this time with a priest, three nuns and a tall candle-lighter. There is a brief moment when all five people pause, horror-stricken, before they run again towards them with open arms. Olympia and Costandina burst into tears as soon as they feel the safe touch of the nuns' fingers upon their shoulders and Costandina's knees give way as though there is no need to attempt to keep herself standing any more. The priest instructs the dog to wait outside, Psaroboulis lifts Sophia from the donkey and the nuns lead them all into the cool shade of the church, assuring them that there are no Turks here and that even the Turks that once lived amongst them have been taken away to the north. The nuns usher them to the benches, take the baby from Olympia and bring glasses of water and wet towels. 'The island is being cut in two,' says the young priest, pulling at his black beard as if he has been carrying the weight of the world on his shoulders. The candle-lighter, towering above him, nods and pulls nervously at his long fingers. 'The Turks are finally achieving *taksim*,' the priest continues, then pauses. 'None of us can imagine what you've been through,' he says, darting worried looks at the nuns. Litsa opens her mouth to speak, but is interrupted by the priest. 'There is no need for words now,' he says softly. 'We will take you to rest; there is a house that was previously owned by the Mehmet family. You can stay there for the time being. And you,' he gestures to Psaroboulis, 'can stay here in the room upstairs.'

On the way to the house, in the back of an open farmer's van, the priest looks over at Koki and asks the women if they are happy to stay together. Litsa, understanding what is meant, straightens and purses her lips. 'Why wouldn't we be?' she asks, and the priest shrugs and looks out at the passing fields.

The house has green shutters and a jasmine tree that climbs the walls so that there is a carpet of white flowers at the entrance. Inside, there is a large room with four beds, a kitchen and another room with two beds. There are cobwebs in the corners and the smell of old oil seeps from the kitchen. There are no pictures on the walls. The priest stands importantly in the centre of the room. He looks around at them as one of the nuns enters with a bucket of clean water. She fills some glasses and passes them around. 'The toilet and well are at the back of the garden and the basin on the veranda,' says the priest. 'Unfortunately, they have taken all their clothes so we will bring you some from the town,' he says confidently. He pulls at his beard again, but this time with a different air; he has the look of one who is pleased with himself. 'Once you are settled and bathed I will send a few to bring some food and later I will send the doctor.' He says this looking concernedly at Sophia. Nobody replies. 'You will be comfortable here.' He looks at the women, pleased that he could help and that they had come to him, and waits eagerly for a response.

'You cannot imagine what it was like to—' starts Litsa, but once again, the priest interrupts her.

'Relax, my child,' he says with a smooth smile and skin pale from the shadows of the church. 'There will be time for this later. It will do you no good.' He touches Litsa's shoulder and looks reassuringly at the other women. He is disappointed that the women stand motionless, as though hanging from the air, like old linen. The young priest looks at the women, and just then another divide is created: the divide between those with a story and those who will never understand it, those with a tale and those who cannot hear it. The priest darts another inconspicuous look of disgust at Koki and then turns on his heel, exits the house and the rumble of the engine is heard as the farmer drives him away. The women stand still, dejected. They stand like vessels filled to the brim with horror, like bombs filled with anger, like books filled with a scramble of words. And just then, they swallow their stories, as one would swallow one's tears.

Olympia sits on the bed and looks at the concrete floor. Litsa collapses into an armchair and Costandina ventures onto the other bed with Sophia; the dog sits on the floor beside them. And, just then, they all shrivel and fold their wings, full of fire, into themselves, and submerge, with tired eyes, into their cocoons. Koki looks down at the little girl standing beside her. 'Come,' she says, and Maroulla follows her out onto the veranda, where they both sit on a wooden bench. Ahead, white wisps from the cottonfield rise as a breeze blows. The heat ripples above it and the church bell tolls again. A young man passing with a carriage of veined figs stares at them, but he does not salute as is the custom of the Cypriots. Inside, the women sleep and Koki and Maroulla sit on that bench beneath the speckled shade of the vines, until the sun softens in the west and the neighbours venture out and stroll into the house with arms full of dresses or blankets or bread. Others carry bowls of salad or pans of stew or beans. 'There is enough here to feed a whole town!' says one woman as she exits. All avoid conversation with the refugees, and as they walk away Koki and Maroulla can hear their words tumbling back to them. 'They are dirty!' says one, looking over her shoulder. 'Some say they have all been raped,' says another. 'Their life has ended!' agree all three. Koki and Maroulla listen to these words as though they are the truth carried by the breeze, the real meaning behind the whistles of the wind.

Koki touches her chest. First she takes out the carved crucifix and touches the sharp end with her fingers, then she takes the small silver tin from her apron. She opens it up. This is all she has left in the world. She touches the contents of the tin with her fingertips; small, sentimental items resting on top of some money that lines the bottom of the tin. First, a delicate gold cross and chain, once owned by her mother. Her father had given it to her when she was nine years old and had told her always to look after it. Koki had run to her secret hiding place beneath her bed and put it in this silver tin. She knew her memories and her secrets were safe in here. Beneath that is a photograph of her mother holding Koki in her arms. She looks at her mother's face and her dark hair and her beautiful smile. There is a lock of her son's baby hair, a gold coin given to her by her grandfather and her dad's wedding band. She picks up the wedding band and puts it in her palm. It glints in the sunlight and she closes her fingers round it, so tightly that her nails dig into her palm. 'Pappa, Pappa, Pappa,' she whispers, with such a pain inside her that her shoulders fall and her head drops slightly. Maroulla looks up and places her hand on Koki's knee.

Koki looks down at all her belongings. Everything she has left in the world. She then pulls out the money from the bottom and counts it. She sighs. There is enough to get by for a short while. As she attempts to put the money back she notices that the bottom of the tin is lined with white. Suddenly, something flashes into her mind and leaves her fingers shaking and her body unable to move. She stares down at the tin; she remembers herself at twelve years old, fearfully opening the tin, folding a white envelope and pressing it down into the bottom. She remembers how she sat on the floor by her bed for a long while, breathing as though she had run five miles, terrified that her father would find it. Now another memory: a grey man sits before her, lonely, sad, beneath the lemon tree. He grabs her arm and hands her a letter. Koki's heart flutters. Her mouth is dry. She closes the tin and looks down at her distorted reflection in the crooked silver top. She remembers his eyes, clear like the shallow part of the sea, and the way they were brimming with tears. She had never known why, but there was something in his eyes which had compelled her to reach out and touch this stranger's fingers. She remembers his words, how he had told her not to open the letter until she was prepared for her life to change and how its contents would destroy her father. From that day on she had lived in utter fear. The letter, although tucked into her secret tin, had hung over her like a dark cloud. It followed her wherever she went; its potentially disastrous and devastating contents became her greatest source of fear. She did not dare to touch it, let alone open it, and, each night, she felt as though it was slithering around beneath her bed, like a snake. She had imagined it biting her; filling her with poison, making her hair turn redder and her eyes more clear, so that she looked like a monster. Koki shudders as she remembers her childhood fears. She recalls how as she grew older she covered the bottom with a pound note or two and eventually forgot about the letter in the tin. So many things had happened in her life that the letter had become a distant memory, as one would remember a childhood phobia. Koki looks down at the white envelope. A surge of that distant but familiar fright fills her heart. The past always finds a way to bite you in the end; brushing things under the carpet never makes them go away.

Koki rests the tin on her knees and rubs her eyes and her face. She looks out at the town ahead, at the dry cornfield, at the unfamiliar dips and grooves of the road ahead. The heat clings to her. There is nothing left to lose, she thinks. Nobody left to hurt. Nothing left to prove. Nothing left to fear. She looks again at the tin, opens it and quickly pulls out the envelope. But her hastened movements slow down as the panic rises inside her again. She looks at the frayed edges and how it has yellowed over time and the flowery letters at the front, with her full name in English letters: 'Kyriaki'. She glances quickly at Maroulla and opens the envelope, pulling out the letter, and she reads it with trembling fingers and a pounding heart; her life suddenly dissolving, distorting and re-forming before her eyes.

For a while, her lips move, whispering inaudible words, and her eyes blink too fast and then too slowly, until she finally closes them completely and her eyeballs move across them as though she were asleep. She takes a deep breath, purses her lips, opens her eyes and looks down at Maroulla, who stares at her expectantly.

Koki stands up, composes herself for a moment only, takes the girl's hand and walks purposefully into the house. She looks around at all the gifts from the visitors, piled up high: mountains of soft white towels smelling of the jasmine-scented air that passes through them as they dry in the morning breeze. Bars of soap and bowls of soft grey ash from the ovens, used as hair conditioner. Piles of multicoloured dresses, perhaps previously worn by the women and children working in the fields. Headscarves of silk, tossed across a small table, shoes of all sizes and colours lined up along the wall, like flowers. Pots and pans still sizzling and bubbling with smells of garlic and sweet onions and tomatoes. Pastry parcels dusted with sugar, jars of honey sweets dripping with syrup, bread fingers still soft from the oven, baskets of lemons and figs picked from the trees, a watermelon already sliced in a tray, olives in pots of oil and lemon, yoghurt, jars of fresh milk, halloumi, pink *lounza*, *zaladina* in glass bowls, carob fruits and pumpkins, turnips and golden shoe-figs. And herbs too: dried mint and coriander, daphne and aniseed. 'All that's missing is the cow,' Koki says, and the little girl laughs for the first time. It is a strange laugh that flutters beautifully, but briefly, and falls like the white wings of those silk butterflies.

Everything rests. The others sleep and their breathing is heavy, making the house rise and fall, rise and fall, slowly, as though over the ripples of a waking sea. The shadows are still and mosquitoes move through them. Koki breathes in and sighs. In the distance is the sound of a passing car and from the other side a man calling his sheep and a dog barking. She pauses for a moment as though she is deep in thought and then rummages through the dresses. After a few moments she pulls one out and holds it up to Maroulla, tilting her head slightly. It is brown, thin cotton, with little red roses embroidered on the collar and red buttons trailing along the front. She hands the dress to Maroulla and proceeds to find one for herself. Amongst the pile, she finally pulls out a dress she seems happy with. It is that dusty, uncertain colour of the distant mountain haze, or the leaves of olive trees, or the misty hues where the sea and the sky join. Koki holds it up against her and looks at Maroulla. The little girl looks up, nods, and tells her it is the same colour as her eyes. Koki smiles.

She takes the crucifix and the tin and puts them on a console table next to a hairbrush full of dark, matted hair. Maroulla looks up at her and reaches into her apron pocket and pulls out the scissors and the little green book and places them neatly next to Koki's belongings. Koki looks at them uncertainly and then at the girl. She smiles faintly and pulls her torn purple dress over her head. The girl unties her own apron by pulling the strings at the back and takes off her red dress and kicks off her shoes. Koki takes two towels from the pile on one of the beds, wraps one round Maroulla, one around herself, takes two jugs from the kitchen cabinet, two bars of soap and a bowl of ash and walks off outside towards the well.

Koki and Maroulla walk back and forth from the well at the back of the garden to the copper basin, filling it with cool water. They stand in the basin, lather themselves thoroughly with soap and rinse themselves with water. It shimmers gold and silver in the after-noon light. A soft breeze blows and the smells of the evening rise up to meet them; the fragrant nightflower and the whiff of evening meals heating on the stoves in kitchens and the sweet red soil releasing the heat from the day. A cockroach scuttles close by and some-thing slithers in the bushes, perhaps a snake or a lizard. Koki fills her palm with ash, massages it into the girl's hair and rinses it with water. The water runs off, grey, and as soft as sand. She then rinses her own hair and the girl stands on a golden patch of grass and watches her with the towel wrapped around her shoulders. She passes the other towel to Koki as she climbs out of the basin.

They enter the house, splash their skin with rosewater and pull on their dresses. Maroulla runs her finger along the red buttons and realises they are made of silk. Koki takes the hairbrush, rips out the old hair and, sitting on one of the beds, brushes the young girl's hair. She takes her time doing this, pulling the brush from the top of her temple down to where the tip reaches the girl's waist, with such precision and care, running over each section so that the hair is as smooth and sleek and straight as it can be. It shimmers black, like tar. Koki lowers the brush, runs her palm along Maroulla's hair and feels a heavy feeling in her heart. She then picks up the brush and does her own hair, quickly this time, her eyes darting to and fro in thought, as the room fills with shadows and the humidity of the coming moon and forlorn jasmine flowers brought in by the breeze. Sophia stirs slightly and Costandina mutters something, but nobody wakes.

Koki moves over to the kitchen, finds a knife, cuts

some tomatoes, and peeks into each pan. She fills two bowls with rabbit stew and grabs two forks. They sit together at the table, savouring the warm, familiar taste of soft sweet onions and cinnamon and wine, and then dip into the honey sweets in one of the jars. This one, a preserved walnut, soaked in deep red syrup. They top this off with a glass of milk, and lean back, for a moment, in their chairs. But Koki cannot be still for long; she finds a wicker bag, rummages again through the gifts, and throws into it some underwear, some bread fingers, a jar of sweets, a towel and a bar of soap.

After this, she walks barefoot across the room, to the row of shoes. She walks up and down slowly, looking at each pair carefully. She walks to the left, stops, looks down and continues. Passing brown ones with laces, red ones with two buckles or one, black and camel-coloured sandals. She is not satisfied. She walks back again, sizing up each pair, with her hand on her chin and her eyes almost closed, so that she looks upon them through shadows of lashes as though she cannot face them head on. Finally, in the furthest corner, nearest the door, she stops, bends down and resolutely picks up a pair and holds them up to her face. Black patent with a buckle, slightly frayed and worn beneath, but their rounded toes sparkle in the half light. Round and smooth. Like eggs. Koki smiles. She slips them on, they are slightly small and cramp her toes, but they will do. She picks out a pair for Maroulla, the only pair small enough. Black, with laces, and small embroidered hearts. The girl slips her shoes on and Koki stuffs some tissue into the back where they are too big. She then grabs the wicker bag and they both stand in the doorway with their feet straight, pointing at the path ahead.

Stepping out into the rising dusk, they pass the white cottonfield and the white field of bleating sheep and walk beneath a tunnel of eucalyptus trees until they reach the café where the Greek men sit. An old man looks contemplatively at the floor while rolling his walking stick between his palms, another flicks rosary beads, another sips coffee. All three stop and look up as they enter the café. One whispers something to the other and the other grunts. Inside, a younger man sits beneath a spinning fan and tosses cards onto the table. He has sweat on his forehead and along the front of his white vest, where a mass of curly black hair juts out from the top and sides, reaching his armpits. He holds a card in his hand and looks up. He does not sit any straighter, he is still slumped back in the plastic chair with his stomach spilling out of his clothes, but his eyes widen in acknowledgement of their presence, about all the energy he can muster.

'Good evening,' says Koki, and the man nods ever so slightly, throws down the card and moves his large hand across the table and picks up a toothpick. He puts it in his mouth. 'We need a taxi,' Koki continues and the man nods again and heaves himself out of the chair, chewing on his toothpick. They follow him out of the café to a house across the street where the man bashes a fist onto its white shutters, probably around seven times, all the while chewing on his toothpick, as though this were the normal procedure, until a man with a thick grey moustache and a black waistcoat opens the windows, looking hot and irritated.

'Taxi,' the café man says bluntly. 'Those two,' he says simply, pointing a stubby finger in their direction, and the other man stretches his body out of the window so that he can look at them better. He looks confused, thinks for a moment, contemplates seriously, purses his lips and then nods. 'OK, OK,' he says, closes the window, disappears inside for a while and then emerges again, from the front door this time, holding a box of cigarettes in his hand. He nods at them briskly and then takes his keys from his pocket and signals to a white, battered saloon, parked half in his garden with its boot jutting out into the road. He opens the doors, rolls the windows down, and they climb in and are immediately engulfed by heat and the smell of cigarettes and strong cologne. A wooden crucifix hangs from the rearview mirror and swings as the car starts and reverses into the road behind. The driver puts his hand onto the back of the passenger seat and looks back. 'Where to?' he says.

'Limassol Port,' replies Koki, and they set off, past the street lined with houses, along a dust road and onto a smoother road, running south, parallel to the sea. They drive in silence as they pass the pebbled shores of Lachi and the rocky cliffs of Paphos and the Baths of Aphrodite on the Akamas Peninsula where the goddess used to take her beauty baths in the pool of the grotto, beneath the shade of the fig trees. And soon, as the sun disappears for another night behind the slithering body of the sea, they rumble past the industrial-looking plains of Limassol and towards the port. There, large vessels filled with plastic containers creak, and west, along a small gulley, little fishing boats, and beside them, shelters for the coastguards. Lights flicker and cigarettes glow from beyond, as men load a ship with cargo. The driver stops the car half on a rise of pavement, and swings open the door. He releases a gasp of air, straightens his shoulders and inhales deeply. They are met by the salty air of the sea. Then Koki reaches into her bag and retrieves some money. The man refuses to take it and smiles at them. 'Good luck,' he says sadly. Koki thanks him and steps out onto the harbour with Maroulla. The driver also steps out of the car and walks towards a guard who is leaning on some cargo at the edge of the harbour. They mutter a few words to each other. The driver then gets back into his car and rumbles away, and the guard walks towards them and ushers them both to the east side of the harbour, where, from the darkness, emerge the forlorn faces and torn garments of hundreds and hundreds of refugees.

Maroulla gasps and they both freeze for a moment and look at the people, blossoming from the floor of the harbour, swaying slightly, as silent as roses. By their feet an old lady rocks and from somewhere in the middle an old, gruff voice, full of phlegm and full of tears, sings,

'And I was born a shepherd,
Born amongst the flock in the barn,
And my poor body
There will die.
Goodbye, pine and oak,
Myrtle, we envy that you don't know death,
Or the white of old age,
And when I die,
Put my body in the flock's spring,
Where beside it grows the tall and beautiful
cypress.
But my poor body there will not die . . .
But my poor body there will not die.'

His voice rises out of the darkness and drifts out to sea and the crowd remains silent.

Evening in London, and Richard sits in the armchair, staring at a flickering television. It is an episode of *It Ain't Half Hot, Mum*, a favourite of Richard's. Another example of Britain's fading imperial status. Far from home British soldiers would rather dance and sing than fight. Richard thinks for a moment about his grandfather's impossible longing for the old British Empire.

Richard's lips are dry and the taste of acid suddenly fills his mouth. He swallows hard. The room is full of orange light from the streetlamps, and there are still drops of rain on the window from an earlier drizzle. The audience laughs in the background. Richard remembers his grandfather's coin collection and how he used to line up the coins on the table and wipe them with a white handkerchief whilst talking about values and traditions and the privileges and duties of the British Empire. Richard stands up, meanders to the window, pulls up the rusty latch and opens it halfway. A soft breeze blows in bringing that smell of buses and tarmac. A sort of grey smell, like the smell of a ten-pound note, or the Underground, or what one would imagine the pavement to smell like. It doesn't matter where you are in London, it always smells the same; Harold Wilson at Downing Street would be greeted by the same smell, as would the street vendor and the woman that sleeps in a bag at the corner of Queen Victoria Street. He moves his toes inside his slippers.

He looks over at the cardboard box, at his cold cup of tea and looks then at the neat little pile of money in the gold money-clip. You know you've beaten the table when you've won the money-clip. Nikos would have had no choice but to go straight home. Richard smiles a little. The other men had sang and clapped and stamped their feet on the ground. 'A new winner now!', 'Someone has defeated Nikos the Great!', 'A British man has won a Greek man's game.' Panikos had opened a new bottle of ouzo and they had drunk till the crack of dawn. Now, there is only a bitter taste left in his mouth. 'I have Granny Smith's!' the man downstairs calls. 'Fresh, crunchy Granny Smith's.'

Richard stands up, walks over to the sink basin, splashes his face with water and pulls his eyelid up, noticing the slight yellow of his eyeballs and the greyness of his skin. Fresh air is what he needs. Maybe he'll move away, up north somewhere in the country and live out his days facing the hills or those purple moors the Yorkshiremen always speak of. Or, on second thoughts, maybe he could just throw out that cardboard box and buy a coffee table. No, he needs to change his life. She must have read the letter by now; he just has to face the fact that Kyriaki is not coming. He splashes some more water on his face, wipes it with the towel, throws off his slippers and sits on the armchair to put on his shoes. He then grabs his umbrella and raincoat and leaves the bedsit. He waits for the bus, climbs on, pays his fare, takes a seat and watches the lights of London flicker by as he approaches Soho. He stands up as they reach St Anne's Church and decides to jump off one stop sooner. A little walk will do him good. He looks up at the beautifully bleak church, part of the diocese of London, and glances at parts of its churchyard around the tower. And attached to it, like a peacock's tail on a stallion, Shaftesbury Avenue, brimming with colours and the curious eyes of travellers, and the indifferent eyes of the Londoners, and the hopeless glare of the old tramps. Richard decides to take this route and crosses the street with a pair of pink-haired punks holding a stereo between them.

Apart from some drying puddles on the pavements, it is a warm, dry night and the same old man sits on a little table outside the café, flicking rosary beads and watching the passing traffic. The man nods as Richard enters. Vakis, who is sitting, rather dejectedly, by the counter, beams brightly and stands up to greet Richard, 'My friend!' he says. 'My hero!'

Suddenly, Yiakovos, who is sitting by the window, smashes a fist onto the table. 'You should taken his underwear too!' He chuckles hard with a mouth full of bread. 'We no see him now for two weeks, like time Angelo come from Derby and won his car! Has any one ever seen a chip-shop owner with Royals Royce?' Yiakovos finds his own words hilarious and laughs hysterically whilst trying to chew the bread, and stamps his feet in sheer excitement on the floor. Vakis and Richard cannot help but laugh too. Just then Paniko emerges from the kitchen with two coffees and greets Richard with a broad smile.

Yiakovos' prediction proves to be true. The night passes and Nikos is nowhere to be seen. Richard sits with Vakis, picking at juicy portions of melon and salty halloumi as they listen to bursts from the radio, as the customers, from time to time, attempt to get a signal. There are muffled words about the oil crises and news about President Nixon. This is shortly followed by information on talks in Geneva, between Constantine Karamanlis of Greece, Bulent Ecevit of Turkey and James Callaghan of the UK. The men in the café prick their ears and sit up; there is mention of a peace deal and something about Cypriot refugees reaching British soil. 'Damn it, Panikos!' calls Yiakovos. 'Get Richard to buy you a new radio with Nikos' money!' Despite his frustration at not having heard the news announcement properly, he finds his own words hilarious and stamps his feet on the floor again.

Richard smiles, takes a cigarette from his box and shakes his head. 'I have something else in mind. I will put Nikos' money to proper use.'

'That a first!' laughs Yiakovos. 'Is only ever been used for two things,' he says, holding up two fingers. 'Sex and gambling!' But while Yiakovos is laughing Paniko glances over at Richard, and Richard looks back at him and nods as though he is answering Paniko's thoughts.

A ship is rising and falling in the darkness. Faces, red with anger and tears, sway on the deck. The girl imagines a ship full of roses. Red roses with the shimmery dew of night. In the distance Cyprus is now but a flicker of fireflies, or stars, or fairies. Its lights shrink, dissolve into the darkness as the ship rolls, rolls, rolls away. The refugees look upon their home for the last time with eyes full of tears and hearts full of fear and minds full of memories and horror. A woman sobs, a child cries, a voice mumbles 'No, no, no', a withered old man on the deck forces himself to stand. His limbs shake, his legs no thicker than a branch; he pulls himself up onto the rail and reaches out his hand. He sobs like a child who has lost his mother. He sobs as his home is plunged into darkness for ever more. 'Goodbye, my sweet Alasia!' he calls, and his voice is carried over the sea, louder than the waves, louder than the wind, as loud as the myths and the stories and the memories that live amongst them. 'Goodbye, my sweet Alasia,' he calls once more, and his voice flies high, first like a dove, then an eagle; the shadow of the refugees' souls merging with the night. 'Goodbye, my sweet Alasia,' he says for the last time, and for the last time he feels the air of his home on his face. Abundant in those black waves. In that dark sea. Deep as light. The ship rises and falls. Rises up as heavy as heat and falls as light as rain so that the mind and the stomach cannot help but do the same. In this turmoil, this is the place where the soul can get lost, where one is a fool enough, or human enough to think that it is in fact the waves that are rising and falling. On the deck, in that immense darkness, the old man sings,

'Within, my dear, within a rose-petal
blanket.
Within a rose-petal blanket is the way

> you should slumber.
> A star, my dear, a star fights with
>   another star.
> A star fights with another star, the sun
>   fights with the moon too.'

His voice drifts over the red faces like a cool breeze as the ship rises. The women bring their blankets tighter over their shoulders. The ship falls. The old man is silent. The white of the moon catches the sails and his hair. It is silent for longer than anyone can bear, silent until the children weep and the women cough and the old men puff on their cigarettes.

Day 8: 27 July 1974

Another grey morning and the bedsit is drab with the colour of rain and that grey tint of money. Richard has separated his winnings into piles on the cardboard box. The money-clip is on the windowsill. A taxi rolls by on Queen Victoria Street, past the memorial, and a flock of seagulls flies high above the Thames and dives left, towards Trafalgar Square, to pick up the first crumbs of the day.

On the cardboard box, resting on a small saucer, is a cup of Greek coffee. Cold now. But Richard is still drinking it. He reaches forward, takes the cup in his fingers and takes the last sip, tasting the bitterness of the dark residue at the bottom. He looks into the cup and turns it over in the saucer, spinning it three times. Then he leans back in his chair and waits. What for? He wonders. He never knew what for. But those damn

Greeks always like to wait. Always waiting. Mostly in cafés and beneath trees. Waiting for the sun to set and bring relief from the heat. Or else, for it to rise. Or for the rain, which never comes. Or for the crops, which will grow only when the sun is fair and the rain comes. Always waiting for the wine to ferment or the mint to dry or the silk butterflies to fly and die. Always waiting. Always waiting. Just like him. Richard looks down at the little cup. He sits up abruptly and picks it up indignantly. He looks inside at those sullen marks, at those snakes and ladders. There is always bound to be a snake and a ladder, he thinks. He remembers Amalia passing her finger up, over the ladder, and down, into the mouth of the snake. She would smile about the ladder and then shake her head in rebuke. 'One cuckoo doesn't bring the spring,' she would say.

'Don't worry,' he would reply, 'I don't even have one cuckoo, let alone the spring!' and she would call him a gloomy Englishman and laugh heartily with the lungs of a cockerel.

Richard looks into his cup. A cigar. Prosperity. An air balloon. Drifting to new places. A cup. Be thankful for what you have. A fence. Of course! What contradictions! thinks Richard. He clatters the cup back onto the saucer and leans deep into the armchair. His foot taps on the floor. He pushes himself up and walks towards the bed, crouching down and reaching beneath it to retrieve the box of trinkets. He looks down at the brass, embossed figure of a frog, resting on a rock. He opens the box and looks again at his mother's gold locket and his grandfather's old coins and then at that array of British Central Africa stamps, dull purple and olive-green, grey and carmine, blue and mint. And the rusty pocket knife, and beneath all, the recipe. A recipe from Amalia, now torn at the edges. He remembers the day she gave it to him. She had looked at him seriously and said, 'Your cup shows a bowl of soup, you will be welcoming visitors. I must show you how! Too many beans is no good for the situation, if you know what I mean!' and she had smiled broadly and plodded off to the kitchen, expecting him to follow.

Richard looks down at the roughly written recipe: 'Egg-lemon soup.' He smiles. 'First we need eggs and chicken and lemons,' she had said, grabbing two baskets and a large knife. The Co-op meant nothing to her. 'I no give money for something I make better myself,' she had said. Although she always accepted the beans. Richard had continued to take her cans, even after he returned, and she had always accepted them begrudgingly, giving them a look of disgust, but then tucking them into her cupboard. At eighty years old, the woman could have survived anywhere, she even made her own olive oil, and her own blankets from cotton that she had picked from the fields. Richard remembers now the sweet, dried-syrup fruits she used to make and serve to him on a little fork balancing in a glass of freezing cold water, and how he would eat the sweet and then down the sugared water. He suddenly tastes the bitterness in his mouth again. He looks down at the recipe, folds it neatly and stands up. He takes off his slippers, puts on his shoes, looks out of the window and decides he will not need an umbrella today.

Outside, a soft breeze blows, carrying white puffs of clouds across London. Richard walks for twelve minutes to the east, towards the tall pillars of the Royal Exchange building, between the converging streets of Threadneedle and Cornhill. He then follows the road to where the Baltic Coffee House once stood, a rendezvous for merchants and brokers for hundreds of years. Many deals had been made over coffee. Richard smiles now and remembers walking hand in hand with

his grandfather, all those years ago, as he told him stories about each street and explained to him how the
history of the nation was carved in every stone and
how even the chronicle of trade drifts with the aroma
of every coffee grain. 'Much can happen over coffee,'
his grandfather used to say. Richard thinks about his
conversations with Paniko these last few days, and suddenly his grandfather's words take on a whole new
meaning. Without thinking twice, he spins on his heel
and walks briskly towards the first travel agent's he can
find, and without hesitation walks towards a woman
at her desk, waits for her to get off the phone and
books himself a holiday to Paris, leaving tomorrow. A
short flight and a great hotel by the Eiffel Tower; as
easy as that! What had he been afraid of all these years?
Terrified to make a move, to get on a plane, to make
a decision, to live his life. Things have to change and
this is the first step! In Paris he'll eat and walk and
relax and make decisions about his new life.

Now Richard inhales deeply and drifts, like a balloon, around London, past Buckingham Palace and
Westminster Abbey and St Paul's, and Westminster
Bridge and the Houses of Parliament, in every direction, he flows aimlessly with the rhythm of the traffic

and the footsteps of the Londoners, following the steam of coffee from every corner, until dusk falls and everything is soaked in that silvery light and everything suddenly takes on that grey haze of unfamiliarity, like when you look at your face in the mirror for too long or stare too hard at the lines on the back of your hand.

He stops on the footpath of Westminster Bridge and looks at the smoky reflection of the Houses of Parliament in the water's surface. As the sun sets the reflection turns to a shadow and the evening traffic mounts. From beneath, a boat's horn, and from the road, a siren. People rush past him faster than the cars. He looks down into the river. A wind blows. Cool and crisp. Richard reaches into his pocket and takes out the recipe. 'Egg-lemon soup,' he reads again and shakes his head and laughs. He stuffs the piece of paper back into his pocket and heads home to pack. But first to the Co-op!

It is late by the time he starts making the soup as he wanted to pack first. In his bedsit Richard boils the chicken on the hob, with the recipe on the counter by his side. He runs his finger down to the next instruction and nods, as though somewhere inside he is listening to Amalia's voice. He takes three eggs and cracks them into a bowl. He squeezes two lemons and puts the juice into the eggs and whisks. Then he lights a cigarette and moves over to the window and looks down at the lights and people and cars until the chicken boils. The steam and the smoke roll out of the window.

When the chicken is done, he takes it out of the water and puts it on a plate. He then fills his palm with rice. 'One palm full for each person,' Amalia had said, 'but always make double. It is the Greek way!'

'What the heck!' Richard says, and pours two palms full of rice into the pan of chicken broth. He waits for the rice to soften and expand, and then, with a ladle, he scoops some of the chicken broth and pours it slowly into the egg-lemon mixture. 'This part is the most important,' Amalia had said. 'You must introduce the hot water slowly to the eggs, otherwise they will be in shock and break.' Richard fills up the ladle with a second helping of broth and pours it slowly into the mixture. He inspects it closely, holding it up to the light and smiles to himself. He looks down again at the recipe. He nods and pours the mixture into the rice and broth. He mixes it with a spoon and watches as the broth turns creamy-yellow. The kitchen fills with lemony steam. Richard inhales deeply. He adds salt and sprinkles it with pepper. He fills up a bowl with the soup, cuts some chicken into it, grabs a spoon and a piece of bread, and sits in the armchair. With his slippers on and a soft evening breeze flowing through the window and the television flickering gently, he finishes the bowl and falls asleep for the night with the taste of Cyprus in his mouth.

On the last page of the little green book is her mother's blood. Not a rose. Not a rose that sparkles with sugary dew. Not a rose, whose stem is a hundred miles long. Not a rose. Not a prize. Nor immortality. Just her mother's blood. Her mother's blood spread upon the page. Nothing more. Nothing less. Maroulla flicks through the pages. White. She flicks again. Nothing. All white and bare like the snow on the Troodos Mountains. The girl sighs as the bright lights of the airport shine on the pages.

She closes the book and Koki leads her through a spinning door into a dark street full of people and cars. They are bombarded with cool air, like that of the winter, and enveloped by the smell of fumes, and sounds, almost as loud as the war. Koki looks up at the lights of a departing plane. 'Can you believe we were just on one of those things?' she says, and Maroulla looks up, bewildered. She does not answer.

A taxi pulls up in front of them. The driver looks at them expectantly. He has his elbow out of the window and his hand on his chin. His features are hard and heavy. 'Taxi?' he says, and Koki nods. They climb into the back of the car and Koki pulls the letter out of her bag and shows him the address. The driver nods and the car starts and edges through miles of traffic along wide roads. Koki notices a Bible on his dash-board at the front. Maroulla notices how the houses are joined together, 'Like people ready to dance the *kalamatiano*,' she says, and Koki laughs at this comment and then the two remain silent as the traffic clears and the car cruises through unfamiliar streets and beneath unfamiliar trees. The air sweeping in through the window is dry and smells of ash.

For the whole journey the driver picks at some fish and chips, half wrapped in a newspaper on his lap. The smell is nauseating and the tang of vinegar hangs in the air. After a while the streets become dense and the buildings grand, and the people scuttle here and there manically. It is strange; unlike Cyprus, there are no stars in the sky. They pass buildings with pillars and arches, churches with tall towers, parks and cafés, barbers and Co-ops; some are already closed and others have metal shutters pulled halfway down over the door. Soon the car signals and stops at the first convenient place. The driver turns around and, with a disinterested air, stares at Koki. 'That'll be one pound,' he says mechanically as Koki takes the money from her bag and inspects it in her palm. Having changed the money at the airport, Koki looks down at it, confused. The driver points to the one-pound note in her hand and Koki passes it to him. Then she reaches into her bag and retrieves the address. She looks at it, and then at the road sign, and then at the buildings. The driver points ahead at the block of flats they need to go to. Koki turns to face Maroulla, opens the door and they step out onto the pavement. They walk past a few shut market stalls; on one a woman packs away her boxes. But as they approach the last stall, a short man in a leather jacket calls out to them, 'Watermelons! Watermelons! Juicy and red, like the heart of the Mediterranean! They are authentically Russian!' The two look towards him, and there, on a stool brimming with lemons and apples and pears and strawberries and cherries and grapes, are a dozen green watermelons.

Koki takes Maroulla's hand and they walk towards the entrance of Williamson Court and enter swiftly as an old lady exits. They stand in a concrete corridor that smells slightly of urine and has a closed umbrella propped up against one of the walls and muddy shoes against another. There are voices and the sound of a television or a radio emanates from above. Koki hesitates for a moment, swallows hard and looks down at Maroulla. 'Number nine,' she says to Maroulla, and they head up the staircase.

As they climb the steps, following the numbers, a familiar smell drifts down towards them. There, in the middle of London, within these grey walls, is that comforting and very distinct smell of egg-lemon soup. Koki cannot believe it. She cannot understand how on this cold evening, in this strange place, hugging her with warmth, is the scent of home. It becomes stronger as they reach the third floor; the smell of Cyprus seeping towards them, teasing them, luring them into its arms. Koki stops and waits outside the door. She looks down at her shoes, then at Maroulla and finally builds up the courage to knock on the door. They wait a couple of moments. There is a loud cough and then slow footsteps. The door opens.

There, standing before them, with a perplexed look on his face, is a middle-aged man with grey hair, holding a spoon in his hand. He looks from Koki to Maroulla and back up to Koki. Koki stands awkwardly in the doorway while the lines of his creased brow unfold, and suddenly his face lights up, he gasps and a stream of tears run down his face. He drops the spoon. Within the slits of his grey eyes unravels before Koki a picture from long ago; of a man beneath a tree, a world yet to be broken. His eyes are eyes that she knows; a glassy, grey reflection of her own.

Maroulla looks up at this strange man and watches as he raises his hand gently to Koki's face and touches her red hair, with the tips of his fingers, as though he were touching a flame. The man slowly shakes his head, pauses for a moment and then embraces her. He holds her tightly and cries as Koki returns his embrace. 'Kyriaki,' he says. 'My daughter.'

The little girl peeks into the bedsit and heads towards the smell of egg-lemon soup.

Acknowledgements

I am indebted to all the people who opened their hearts and told the story of the past, painful as it was to remember. Reliving the memories of good and bad has been an emotional journey I will never forget. With special thanks to my uncle Chris for the journey we made to the north of Cyprus. Thanks to Katina Evangelou, Tasoulla Hadjipetrou, Elli and Christakis Blissi, Georgina Loizou, Eva and Agathi Spanou, Helen and John Christodoulides and many others for answering questions and sharing the details of your lives. A special thanks to my dear grandmother, Katina Evangelou, and my grandfather, Kyriacos Lefteri, for the hours they spent telling me stories.

I would also like to thank my good friend Claire Bord for making this happen and for always being there. Thank you also to Dr Rose Atfield for being an inspiration, a mentor and a friend from the very beginning. A big thanks to Celia Brayfield for your time and advice, and thanks to Brunel University's Creative Writing Programme that has guided me along this path.

I am grateful to my lovely agent, Marianne Gunn O'Connor, for everything you have done and for making magic happen. Many thanks also to Vicki Satlow. A humungous thank you to Jon Riley at Quercus and especially my editor Charlotte Clerk for all your time and wisdom.

Thank you to my dad for his constant support and to my brothers, Kyri and Mario, for reading it and for endless and wonderful conversations.

Thank you to my husband, Michael. He touched this book with his imagination and his heart. He knows every word and every page inside out, back to front and mixed up in a Greek salad! Thank you for all your help.

Finally, to my mum, whose encouragement and unconditional support gave me the strength to write this book. Thank you for the stories at bedtime, for holding my hand, for opening doors, for being my friend. I miss you x